THE SPIRIT OF THE ARENA

BY

Koel Alexander

Raven & Fire Series

Print ISBN: 978-1-66788-388-5
eBook ISBN: 978-1-66788-389-2

Printed by Bookbaby,

7905 N. Crescent Blvd. Pennsauken, NJ 08110

Raven & Fire Series

TABLE OF CONTENTS

DEDICATED TO

My wife Carolyn for continuing to push me and reassure me that I can do anything I put my mind to.

I dedicate this to the life I have lived that has allowed me to discover my imagination and bring it to the audience.

To my book club for sticking with me through round 2. Rough drafts, day-long debates about characters, and exchanging ideas.

To every single person that purchased a copy of The Axe & The Spear.

I appreciate all the love

Thank you!

K.A

1 – Interview With A Vampire — Gio

What can I say, over the years I may have developed a love for the theatrics. If there's one thing us Romans love, it's putting on a show. I could smell the stench of my past on them whenever they were in my presence, the aura of the gods was all over them.

The memories pained me constantly, taking me back to a state I haven't felt in centuries... *"vulnerability"*. At this point, Kole and I have yet to break from our staring competition. If he were smart, he would be spreading the news to his friends, but none of that mattered now we needed each other. I mentally scoffed at the thought of my needing anyone, yet here I was at the mercy of some young Viking still faithful to the ever scheming gods. The gods had lured them into the snares of their twisted games, and I unfortunately knew about being in that predicament all too well.

"Let's raise our glasses to our newfound alliance. You may want to make yourselves comfortable as I have a tale to share with you." It was now or never to tell my story, the abridged version anyway. "I know I don't look it friends, but I am over 150 years old. Like you Octavia, I was once a Roman living in this world way before your people called your home Gracia. The gods ran free, and the people lived under their torture. The ones above always deal in puzzles and mystery, but in my time, it was glaringly barbaric. Any day could alter your entire life."

"I think we can relate to that obviously," Kole interrupted.

"What do you know of your history, my dear?" I shifted my focus to Octavia.

"I know that everything I have been told is a lie. I know that the gods have been pulling strings to clean up the massive mess that they made, so if there is anything else you would like to reveal to me while my identity is being carved into a million pieces now would be the time," she said sarcastically.

"My dear we are just at the tip of the spear… you have no idea how far this rabbit hole goes, but I can be the one to show you the way down."

"Before we listen to anything else you have to say Gio, you need to explain to me what you are and why you are drinking blood," Kole slammed down his cup and waited intently for me to respond.

He must have been the only one to see because the rest of his group was looking at me now more bewildered than before.

"What do you mean drinking blood?" Octavia questioned.

"I mean he drained blood from a woman's wrist and poured it in that giant goblet he is holding while all of you were enjoying yourselves," Kole stated rather dryly.

"What the fuck, you drink human blood? Is that like for fun or is there something I'm missing?" Rollo joined.

I barely suppressed the urge to roll my eyes. "I would be more than happy to tell you what I am, but for you to understand what I am you must hear the tale of how I came to be."

I was definitely going to need this drink to go over this again. Something with more bite to it would be amazing but nothing took the edge off like the blood straight from the source.

"I was an adventurer, sailing and exploring anywhere I could reach. I was a cloth for knowledge, eager to soak up any information I could get. I had a dream to explore new lands beyond the mere understanding of men. I prayed and sought guidance from the gods, for I knew they had thousands of secrets that we could uncover. I stumbled upon this land, as I said, years before your people called it Gracia. Question, poor girl, do you know why they call us Romans?" I asked.

"I have no idea and this story seems like a long one, so I won't hold you up," Octavia responded sarcastically.

"This land was first conquered by a man named Romulus who eventually settled his followers in the eternal city; hence the word was shortened to call all his people Romans. Rumor has it the gods were so pleased with the conqueror that they walked among his people. Now back then it seemed like the greatest blessing as people would do unspeakable things to walk amongst the gods, but in hindsight, all of us in this room can see that such thinking was foolish."

"Did the gods come for you immediately for searching for their secrets?" Rollo asked.

"No, my young Rollo. Allow my tale to unfold, and please eat and drink as this story is a lengthy one. In the legend of Romulus, it is foretold that the only reason he came to conquer this land was with the help of an all-powerful oracle who told him what he needed to do to succeed. So, in the name of fulfilling my destiny, I dedicated my life to uncovering the mystery of the Oracle and imploring her to show me how I could find what I was seeking."

"What were you looking for?" Kole asked.

"At the time I didn't know yet. All I knew is that I needed to find her, and after years of searching and finding nothing but dead ends, I finally got my hands on a map that led me to the Delphi Caves," I smiled.

The four of them took a minute and then it finally registered in their heads. I have forgotten how long it takes their young brains to put together the puzzle. Though I would never admit it, though I haven't relived this story in some time, the trauma and pain although ancient history were still fresh.

"I ventured into the caves following the map. I was not sure what I was expecting to gain but the gods made sure I never had a chance in the first place. The spirit of Delphi was inhabited in a decomposing body that awakened the moment I stepped closer to the pedestal."

"What did you say?" Rollo interrupted.

As much as I was starting to become fond of these children I really hated to be interrupted; it was only going to make my story longer.

"I didn't get to say anything, young king. A green mist swirled all around the cave as Delphi dealt me my fate."

"The curse upheld, the moon as distant as your love, blood and death is your lifeline."

The three of them looked toward each other trying to figure out how this pertains to me. Humans are fascinating but they can be unbelievably dense. I was one of them at one point, but those feelings are long gone. I glanced over to the girl Kole said was his sister. She was the only one fully engaged in my story, like she was living every word. The more I assessed her, the more intriguing I found her. She was a beautiful girl, far too untouched for this type of life. I snapped out of my trance to finish my story.

"The body went limp after the message was delivered, and the cave became dark, empty and lifeless. I dedicated everything to find that cave but walked out feeling completely underwhelmed and uninspired, until I saw her."

"Okay now this story is getting good, who is this mystery woman?" Rollo smiled.

"She was the most beautiful woman I had ever seen, seeming all the more alluring as she serenely began planting and tending to flowers outside of the cave. Her platinum hair sat perfectly down her back and traced down her linen gown. She turned when she heard me come out of the cave as the light glimmered over her, almost as if it could not help but be drawn to her beauty. Her light brown eyes sparkled as she brandished a perfect smile. I felt like my knees would give out under the weight of her presence."

The cave was silent as I recalled my story, and it crossed my mind that maybe all my children haven't heard how we have come to exist. I motioned for more blood as the difficult part of my story was approaching and I was not a fan of all this undivided and unwanted attention.

"I'll save you some of the tedious details but eventually she shared her name with me... *Selene*. Every day I returned to converse with her as if I were obsessed. I couldn't understand how someone so beautiful could give me the time of day."

"Octavia has told me plenty of Roman stories and they always end in tragedy. I assume this one is no different," Kole said.

"You are correct, young king. Selene was no ordinary woman but a goddess living amongst mere mortals. She was being followed by a god that was seeking her love, but she had no interest in being courted and spent all of her time with me spurning his efforts. If only rejecting a god's attentions could result in no consequences." I scoffed. "As the prophecy foretold, he laid a curse upon me out of jealousy, one that would never allow the sunlight to touch my skin ever again. Selene and I attempted to make it work but a life of living in shadows was not fair to her, so I sought the services of another god. I was mortal and would eventually die, but the very thought of being without her was so crippling that I convinced Selene to take me to Hades to bargain for immortality."

"Wait a minute," Octavia interjected, "you made a deal with the god of the underworld and thought it was a good idea?"

"People do crazy things for love, and I know for a fact you can attest to that," I looked at Kole. He stared back with a haunted look in his eyes. Yes, indeed, he knew exactly what I meant.

"Hades took my soul and allowed my body to remain on earth. All I had to do was steal the silver bow from the huntress Goddess Diana." The roman girl put her face in her hands reminding me of all the bad decisions I have made. "My amazing charm worked, and Diana allowed me to join her group of hunters but when I tried to steal her bow, I was caught. In order to avoid her wrath, I needed to prove my remorse and loyalty, so I pledged myself to her."

"This is literally one of the best stories I've ever heard, it just keeps getting better and better… no offense," Rollo said.

"Well, if you would allow me to finish sometime this century, you may come to learn that this fascinating story is shrouded in tragedy, as your fellow comrade has surmised. Of course, I could always stop here…" I suggested, hoping my words would give the younglings pause before they interrupted me again. Rollo put his hands up in defeat.

"As much as it pained me, I pledged to be a hunter of Artemis, which means that you have to give up all hopes of love and marriage. In return, she blessed me with strength, speed, healing, these beautiful fangs containing my venom, and the ability to shift my physical form into anything I please." All of their eyes went wide with amazement, but before they could interrupt further, I clarified "Before you ask, no I will not show you, as it is quite messy and painful." The excitement was drained from their faces. "I became one of the best hunters she ever had, and after some time I proved my loyalty. Diana freed me from her vow and gave me the bow to bring to Hades so that he would grant me immortality. The thought of being allowed to be with Selene again was the only motivation I needed. I could not wait to see her after all the time that had passed and all I had done to secure our future. The gods assured me I was free to love again and being immortal, all I had to do was find her and we would be together forever."

I took a long sip from my cup; the blood was warm and delicious, the only pleasantry I would have for the rest of this story.

"What I found was a tragedy. Even though I left Selene, she never stopped searching for me. The god that coveted her grew even more jealous that she wouldn't give up on me, so he stripped her immortality as a punishment for all the time she wasted looking for me. The years of being alive were crashing in on her all at once and she was dying. When I found her sick, brittle, and barely able to keep her eyes open, I was frozen in place. Out of everything that I had been through, the weight was crumbling me, so I did what fools in love do. I crawled back to the monsters that set me on this path. I yelled for any of the gods to help and none responded except my mentor, the huntress Diana. She told me there is no way for her to physically survive, meaning we would never be together, but her spirit could live on."

I don't remember what it is like to cry but the pain feels the same, that pulsating ache in my chest reminding me about everything that I have lost.

“Diana showed me how to administer the bite, then I drained Selene’s body of blood. The ritual restored her soul but, even with my ability to create hunters, her body was breaking down and would eventually give out. Diana took her soul and carried her to the moon, and till this day she watches over me and our children. I vowed I would never love another.” I buried my face in the goblet knowing that the blood was the only comfort to me now. “I returned to this cave, killed Delphi and promised the Romans they would feel my wrath and one day suffer my vengeance.”

“Why would they have to suffer for what the gods have done?” Octavia asked.

“Because of their blind devotion to the gods that value their lives no more than I do this cup,” the goblet gave way to my strength. I had to wave over a servant to bring me another.

2 – Setting The Board — Kole

I had no need to question Gio's motivation; he was used by the ones he worshipped, as well. He did everything for love, and, out of everyone, I could relate. The events of the holmgang still haunt me when I don't keep my mind busy.

The images of my father giving me the blessing to remove him from this world were plastered everywhere when I close my eyes, the pain never truly settling. I was used and it changed the course of my journey, making me question who I am, all so that I could gain control of the kingdom. I didn't know whom to blame. Well, actually I did but I couldn't kill a god, so my enemies will have to do.

Gio was punished all because a god could not accept something not going his way, could not handle the loss of control stemming from Selene's rejection. The rules seemed very subjective when it came to them interfering in human affairs. I was starting to believe it is less a rule but more of a preference. Gio was the perfect instrument of revenge, but I wanted to make sure he understood that all Romans shouldn't be in the path of his vengeance. We all sat attentively while he finished his story, though I made sure to take notes on all the questions I had. An immortal who is forced to live apart from the love of his life, needs blood to survive, has incredible strength and speed, and is also nearly impossible to kill.

"If the Romans were keeping track of all your movements, how have you been able to make more of your kind?" Octavia beat me to the question.

"I retreated to the caves where it all started, and I have killed anyone dumb enough to find their way here," he said coldly. "Humans yearn for power, and you fear death more than anything, so I had no shortage of volunteers," he signaled for more blood in his goblet. "I was unable to find this place without the map so I figured others couldn't either."

I looked over to Kare finally understanding what she meant when she mentioned recognizing someone she saw in the cave. It's the reason some of the others looked so familiar, as well. That would explain all the disappearances; these people ventured into the predator's lair completely unaware.

"And what do these volunteers gain from becoming one of you? I have a few ideas myself, but I would rather not guess," I asked.

"As I told you from my story, my kind is cursed, our skin never to touch the sun or silver again; but our gifts are immortality, heightened endurance and agility, and being nearly indestructible... we are very hard to kill," he smiled. "Forgive me if I prefer to leave that part out, although I will say human blood sustains us, without which we are weak, so take comfort in the fact that as much as I would love to kill every Roman I cannot or I would be burning my own food source."

He did have a point; wiping us out would ensure his own extinction, so at least I could trust him up until that point.

"This shit just keeps getting better and better," Rollo replied sarcastically and grabbed his cup, as if needing the distraction. "As soon as we think we know everything, someone drops even more surprises on us."

"I think that closes the chapter on Ambrogio, my friend," he smiled and drank from his goblet again, almost as if it was a compulsion.

"And what exactly is your kind called? Blood-drinking, cursed monster seems like a mouthful," Rollo joked. I can tell that Gio and everyone else did not find it funny; Rollo was going to get us in trouble with his loud and careless mouth as usual.

"I have been called many things… hunter, cursed, abomination, monster but vampire is the preferred term," he said.

Now I see why Halfdan would reach out to him to be allies. He could have unleashed Gio on the Romans with no remorse. Nothing would have stopped him from killing anyone he considered faithful to the gods, and I'm almost sure he would have turned on us next. Gio wanted to be recognized amongst the kings, but Halfdan would have never honored that request as he wanted the entire kingdom to himself.

I was stuck between a tyrant and a psychopath, but what choice did I have? His unique situation and his disdain for the Romans made him perfect. All we had to do was steer him toward Marcus. Before that, I must establish a plan and determine where we stand as far as an alliance goes.

"Tell me what's your master plan?" I asked.

Rollo and Octavia stared at Gio after everything that we have learned, yet I knew the two of them were on edge. I had some ideas of my own, but I still did not trust him, so I needed to keep him talking. It wasn't likely he would give up information. He was smarter than he led on; hundreds of years of life experience will help you put some things into perspective. Either way, I wouldn't call a single soldier from Najora until we had a plan of attack.

"My young king, are you always so pushy? I've shared more with you than I have with any human in decades," his tone started to become more rigid. "I've shown you hospitality in my caves and you give me an interrogation. No moves will be made tonight so I suggest you eat, drink, and get comfortable. And after you are full and buzzed get some sleep because once we head down this path there is no turning back."

"Don't take my haste for disrespect, friend, but we have been through a lot to get to this point. The finish line is nearly in our grasp."

"Fools rush to their deaths, kings set the board and execute," he leaned back into his throne.

"Kole, let's table this discussion for the night in honor of our new alliance and Gio's hospitality. We can pick this up in the morning," Rollo said.

A smile stretched across Gio's face, and I decided Rollo was right. I've come this far, what was one more night? In a moment of temporary defeat, I raised my glass toward the throne and gave him a slight bow. It would soothe everyone for the moment, but even he knew this conversation was far from over.

Ω

I couldn't tell you when I woke up, it's hard to tell what time of day it is when you are inside a cave. Octavia was snuggled up next to me, so close I could feel the relaxed rhythm of her breathing. I could stare at her for an eternity. She brightened up my world every moment she was in it. But at some point, we were going to have to make a move. Gio was right in that I should have treated him differently considering his hospitality. I should probably apologize at some point. I tried to slide out of the makeshift bed without waking Octavia; she deserved some rest, but I needed to get some air.

I walked out back into the main throne room. I expected to see tons of people like last night, but only a few people lingered cleaning up from last night's feast. Blood stained the floors mixed with food and wine looking like a bull came through here and knocked everything out of place. All but the tacky throne that sat in the center. Gio was nowhere to be found. I walked over to try to get some information from one of the women sweeping

"Good morning, friend," I wanted to greet her properly, but I had no idea what her name was

"Good morning, your majesty," she gave a slight bow as she addressed me.

I almost corrected her and then I realized that I was a king now.

"Where is your master? I wanted to thank him for the feast," I asked

"Sorry, your majesty, he is resting for the next few hours," she continued to sweep.

"Does he always sleep long after he throws an amazing party? Maybe he overdid it with the blood." I gave her a curious look, hoping that it wasn't clear I was sniffing for information.

"The master usually sleeps throughout the day as you know the sun has betrayed him. He rather not stay awake and be tortured by things he can never have," she spoke with her head down refusing to take her eyes off her task.

"Your friends are outside if you are looking for them."

"Thank you. If you happen to see your master, let him know I wanted to share my thanks." I headed up the cave yearning for some fresh air. Even if it was a dead forest, anything was better than the cave. We spent all night drinking and exchanging pleasantries and I still feel like we didn't have a solid plan. Gio was being extremely careful about how much he was willing to tell, especially that part about his weaknesses. I could hear voices just outside the cave, it sounded like someone was yelling commands and instructions.

"Keep your elbow tight when you shoot," Rollo yelled.

"I can't bring my elbows in anymore, it's going to affect my shot," Kare shouted back.

"When you miss your target, you're going to wish you listened to me," Rollo said.

My sister was standing on the far side of the cave entrance shooting toward multiple targets. She has been working on her skills with the bow for some time and she's getting better by the day, even I couldn't deny it.

"Good morning, dear sister. You're getting better every day... at some point we might actually have to consider you dangerous," I greeted them with a smirk on my face as I made my way out of the cave.

"Good morning, brother. It's about time you recognize that I am not little anymore," she flashed her own smirk out the side of her mouth.

"Kole, whenever you're done being a distraction we can get back to our lesson," Rollo said.

I raised my hands in defeat relenting control and let them get back to it. Ever since Kare decided to join us on this adventure, which I was never happy about it, we dedicated time to her training; if she was going to be with us, she needed to know how to defend herself.

"Go!" Rollo yelled.

Seven targets all around the forest sprung up at once and Kare sprang into action. She pulled three arrows out of her quiver, adjusted them all on the bow and let them fly. She hit three targets dead center with one shot before moving on to the next. To say I was impressed was an understatement. She spun around and dropped to one knee to improve her accuracy. The next arrow had so much force it pierced straight through the target. She was moving with deadly precision, every movement calculated and delivered with purpose. It was hard to believe this young woman is my baby sister. She drew another arrow back aiming at a target almost fifty yards away. She kept her eye on the trees to get a feel for the wind, adjusted the bow, and released the arrow at an angle to compensate for the elements. The arrow effortlessly struck the target.

Kare's smile stretched across her face, she had one target left probably the easiest shot of them all. She took a deep breath and aimed for the last target, but right as she was about to let the arrow go a bolt of lightning shattered through a tree behind us. It startled us both and the arrow missed the target badly.

"What the hell was that Rollo? You ruined my shot!" Kare screamed.

"You think the battle will be perfect? In the heat of the moment, chaos will be ringing off in every direction. You need to be able to keep your cool," Rollo said calmly. He was holding his hammer in his right hand as the lightning still danced on its surface.

"You did that because you knew I wasn't going to miss," Kare retorted

"No, I did that to show you that shooting at targets in peace and quiet is a lot easier than what real battle is like," Rollo answered.

"It doesn't matter how much you teach her because my sister isn't fighting in any battles," I told them both.

I walked over and stood in between them and grabbed Kare's bow.

"Unfortunately, we have no idea what will happen when we get to Alexandria. I would rather her be prepared than naïve," Rollo countered.

"Can both of you stop talking about me like I'm not here? It's insulting," she snatched her bow back out of my hands. "I just wanted to practice and you two managed to turn my practice into a lecture. I'm going back inside to get something to eat. Let me know when you two are done being stupid." She walked back into the cave without looking back at us.

“I can’t lie, I was impressed, but if I tell her that she’s going to want a front-row seat when the fighting starts.” I looked at my best friend, knowing that now we are both kings every decision has to be thought out. No more impulsive decisions as we didn’t speak for ourselves anymore, an entire country depended on us.

“I know you worry about her, but you know I would never let anything happen to her. You both are family, and I would give my life before I let someone hurt either of you.” Rollo hooked his hammer to his belt, and we made our way back inside.

3 - The Next Level— Octavia

The whole waking up alone thing was starting to get really old; Kole and I would have to discuss that at some point. I was new to the whole fiancé thing, even saying it out loud made it seem unreal. We also had to talk about where we would hold the ceremony. Would it be a Norse or Roman celebration, and where would we live?

All of it was nerve-racking, it was almost enough to make me forget that I woke up in a cave after breaking bread with an immortal who drinks blood to live and could not wait to tear my country into pieces to atone for the sins of the past. In the meantime, all I could do was eat some breakfast and deal with the full scope of the mess we found ourselves in later; the ability to compartmentalize was like a superpower in and of itself.

I walked out into the main throne room finding everything from the night before was gone. It was decorated differently, though I was unsure what warranted the change. The servants from last night were sweeping and bringing fruit, bread, and drinks to the table.

"Where is Gio?" I asked the girl setting the food down on the table.

"My master is asleep, he will join you later this evening. While you wait, you may come and go as you please and help yourself to some food" she explained as she pulled a chair out for me. I didn't push the issue as I didn't want to spend more time around Gio than I had to after the whole blood-drinking fiasco. Just thinking about it had me on edge all over again. I shuddered imagining what it would be like to live amongst such predators and be drained for their consumption. Gods forbid.

I would catch up with the others in a bit, the food looked so delicious my stomach was growling. My head was heavy, most likely from all the wine we drank last night. I scooped some bread and fruit on my plate as Kare stormed in and plopped down in the chair next to me. I know she had something she wanted to say so I was just going to sit back and wait. She's never been one to hold her tongue and before I could take a bite of my bread, she started to let it all out.

"If my brother thinks he can keep me away from all of this, I would really love to save him the trouble," she snatched a piece of bread with such force I was sure it would crumble in her hands.

"I'm sorry Kare, can you catch me up on what going on? I just woke up."

"I was outside working with my bow just trying to practice for anything that is coming. I know he won't admit it but I'm getting really good, and yet he wants to keep me on the sidelines," she practically growled. I could tell she was frustrated, and I couldn't blame her knowing I would feel the same in her position.

"Maybe he is just trying to protect you, Kare. We have all lost so much already and we have no idea what we are walking into." I wanted to reassure her, but the sting of Tiberius would never go away and each passing day without him or Floria made it rough.

"I know deep down that we are all family, and we would do anything to save each other, but at some point, I need to be able to grow into my own person," her eyes strained to hold back such immense emotion. "We were not raised to be protected. It's frustrating because no one knows me more than my brother, so his insistence on me being sidelined as if I'm incapable of handling myself is the biggest insult he can give me." I could try to convince her of Kole's good intentions, but I know what she meant. Protecting her was one thing but treating her like a piece of glass that could be so easily broken would feel stifling.

"How about I talk to him for you? He usually listens to me, and if he doesn't, we can keep it between us," I winked at her.

"Thanks, Tav," she smiled. We had to make the best of the situation; it's not every day you have a gorgeous breakfast deep inside a cave carved in the side of a mountain. The boys walked in a couple of minutes later, finishing up whatever conversation they were having before they got to the table.

"I know at this point this isn't important, but does anyone wonder how he gets all this food down here in this cave surrounded by a dead forest?" Rollo asked, curiosity getting the better of him. We all looked at each other because he had a great point, especially considering we haven't seen anything edible for miles. I shrugged, thinking we better just go with the flow at this point.

"How about we just let it slide for now? If he wanted something to happen to us, he could have done it while we were asleep," Kole said.

"I don't know how many nights I can spend in this cave, so I hope we are coming up with some type of plan. I can't help starting to feel like the walls are closing in," I said.

"In a couple of hours, when Gio is done with his beauty sleep, we are going over our next move," Kole grabbed more fruit from the center of the table.

We had to come up with a way to get close enough to Alexandria without alarming anyone close to Marcus. As far as anyone knows, I should be dead. We had to find a way to sneak into the city without being spotted, which is going to be nearly impossible already with Kole and Rollo looking and acting as they do. We had to tread carefully; Gracia was not nearly as lenient as their home country.

"I have an idea to get us into Alexandria without looking suspicious. I propose that we travel to the outpost my father used to tell me about called Perseus," I suggested to the table as I saw Rollo and Kole look at each other. Rollo had a smile that stretched his entire face, but Kole looked nervous. "We could stay off the main roads and make our way to Alexandria with Marcus' spies being none the wiser." I waited for them to respond but it looked like they were going over everything that could go wrong.

"What about the armies? We need to get most of them in by boat, and that many Norse traveling by sea or land will get noticed," Kole said. He was right, getting thousands of warriors in would be tough. We had to draw Marcus out and divert his attention so we could at least be within striking range.

"I have an idea I'm almost certain you won't like, but it should work." The entire table looked his way. Rollo never had a plan, he usually just likes to run in and smash things. None of us expected him to be serious, but the day was short and he could always revert to his old ways. He must have been able to tell what we were thinking because he seemed kind of insulted by our reaction.

"Don't look so surprised, I've come up with plans before," he huffed. We all laughed at the same time. I kind of felt guilty for a moment, but the anticipation was killing me. "We will need Gio on board, so maybe we should wait for him so I can explain it all at once; I really think this will work."

Apparently, this guy was going to sleep till nightfall, but I couldn't blame him. Being cursed by the touch of the sun, I would probably sleep the day away myself.

"We won't be seeing him until nightfall, so what shall we do while we wait?" I asked. Kole shot me a devilish look across the table, and I didn't have to read his mind to figure out what he was insinuating, but this cave wasn't exactly putting me in the mood no matter how gorgeous that smirk was.

"I have some ideas I wanted to run by you when it comes to our powers," Kole said.

"Not this again," I put my face in my hands, "Do you not remember the last time we tested our powers? Rollo almost killed you."

“Trust me no one remembers more than me,” he glanced at Rollo, “but I have some ideas that we don’t need to test on each other. If I’m right, it would be cool as hell,” he laughed.

“We don’t have anything else to do so why not? While we are exploring the possibilities, I want to see what Kare can do,” I looked over at her and she silently mouthed a thank you.

“She wasn’t chosen like us in Midselium, but she is still royal blood we need to include her in what we do.” The smirk that was on Kole’s face disappeared immediately. I knew he wouldn’t be happy, but I would not be a part of his plan to keep her on the sidelines. She was a person, not a prize to be protected.

We finished up breakfast and made our way back outside of the cave. I still had my reservations about this, Kole almost dying freaked me out enough, but all I could remember is what I did to Kyut when I lost my temper.

That chanting in my head was calling for blood and I had no idea if I could control it. Maybe it was better to leave it under the surface, so I couldn’t hurt anyone. A little practice can’t hurt as long as I keep my temper in check.

The air was so thin near the mountain I shivered. I think the boys were used to this terrain, but it would take me some time to adjust. The sun was high and that helped keep me warm, but without it I knew I would probably freeze. The trees remained the same, dead and hopeless. Maybe the curse placed on Gio was also affecting the cave and the surrounding area.

“Let’s head away from the entrance, I wouldn’t want to disturb his majesty,” Kole jested. We hiked up the mountain until we found another clearing, the land flat with enough space for us to move around without being on top of each other. Kole stood across from the three of us with his arms crossed over his chest.

"So, I have been thinking about what we would need to have a chance when we get to Alexandria," he started to pace back and forth. "After the Holmgang with my father, I had time to think about how lucky I am to be alive. If my father had time to prepare for my abilities, he could have killed me easily."

I could tell he was still tormented by what Odin forced him to do when he was reunited with his father, something you can easily see anytime he brought up the holmgang.

"My father was one of the best warriors in the world. Rollo we know the stories about him in the war, and he had years to test his limits."

I hope he was going to make a point soon because all I could remember was him breaking down on our shoulders the night before the fight.

"My point is, if my dad was that strong, what do you think will happen if we run into Marcus? I don't want any of us to barely survive. We need to be prepared," he stressed as he stopped walking and looked at us. His eyes were pitch black, a forever reminder of the one who molded his fate. I wanted to do anything I could to just make sure he knew how much I loved him, and that I would be here for him whenever he needed it.

"You're right, so what did you have in mind? And please tell me we can do it without killing each other," I replied with a tremor of anxiety in my voice I hoped wasn't obvious.

"Of course, we can. Remember what the gods told us when we were in Midselium after they amped up our gifts? They said we have access to them all, and it's up to us how we use them." We all looked at each other, then back to him because he said a lot of words but there was no explanation to be found.

"Go on," Rollo broke the silence.

"I believe we can manipulate the powers to give us other strengths; for example, I opened a portal for myself the first time but eventually I could bring others," he recalled as he continued pacing back and forth like the idea was running around his brain faster than he could speak. "What if I manipulate that same gift and use it differently?" I loved this man but if he didn't tell me something that we could use I was going to punch him in the face.

"Kole, please get to the point. You are rambling a mile a minute, but you aren't telling or showing us what you mean," I started to walk toward him in an attempt to ease him into his point. He was clearly frustrated.

"Okay, so let me simplify this. Octavia, when you tap into your powers, your hands glow. And when you reach deeper, they are covered in flames," he walked over and grabbed my hands. "When you fought my brother, the flames healed your hands, and you were able to spread them onto the spear," he gestured to the hint that we all still refused to grasp.

"Kole, I was there, I remember what happened. I really need you to get to the point," I smiled straining to keep my frustration from leaking through.

"You guys need to open your minds! The fire is the gift, the flame of Roman pride, and you are the one that can control it, like Rollo and the lightning," he explained as he grabbed my hands and drew them up to his face to kiss them tenderly. "I want you to tap into your powers and, when the flames take over, I want you to let them go towards a target. Manifest the gift into a different type of weapon." He had the biggest smile on his face like he solved a puzzle from the gods.

"That sounds like a great idea," Rollo interrupted. "When do I get to try because I've been dying to figure out what else I can do."

"I got a different plan for you, brother. I already know you can project the lightning; I want Octavia to try this out first."

Ω

Kole promised me no one would get hurt, so I figured I could give it a try. All I had to do was tap into that well of power in the pit of my stomach and let it go. He made it sound so easy, as easy as breathing. I couldn't forget how things went down in Lundr; I was so angry I honestly didn't care what happened, I just had a burning hunger for revenge.

Was that a one-time thing or is that a common threat every time I sink myself into this gift? The feeling was terrifying, and for the first time I didn't feel completely in control. I've seen the consequences of fighting within yourself. Kole almost teleported everyone in the longhouse into oblivion when he lost control.

"Octavia, you okay?" Kole yelled from behind me. I completely forgot they were behind me waiting for me to try.

"I'm okay, just trying to figure out how I can do this," I answered with no confidence at all.

I closed my eyes, located the flame, and pulled it out firing it to life in an instant. My hands started to glow, I could feel the energy vibrating my hands. The heat was pulsating against my skin making it feel like my hand was too close to a fire. It was a constant presence, a feeling that scared me but gave me a legendary rush. My vision darkened to a red glow, yet I could still see different colors albeit with a dark red undertone.

I'm not sure if I ever noticed the change in my vision before today. I looked back to the group expecting to get a reaction out of them, but they stood still waiting for me to do something. Kole smiled at me which was all the reassurance I needed. It still amazes me how he always calms me down without words, how we are connected so much deeper than mere words could describe. I closed my eyes again and funneled the power to my hands until they ignited in flames. Now I just needed to direct it toward a target... but how was I supposed to do that?

"Rollo, how do you make the lightning go where you want?" I screamed.

"You just visualize where you want it to go and force it to that spot," he answered. I barely restrained the desire to pummel his face for giving such an unhelpful directive, but lucky for him my fear of losing control saved him from my fiery fists. The whole problem was I didn't know how to force it out; I felt so stupid just standing here, holding my hands out.

"Focus on a target, no matter what it is, and just let it go. You're not going to hurt anyone, don't worry," Kole tried reassuring me, but it still didn't tell me how I was supposed to do it. I walked over to one of the dead trees and placed my hands on it, closed my eyes, and tried to transfer that radiant burn to the trunk of the tree. I felt the heat drawing from my stomach flowing through my arms to the palms of my hands. When I opened my eyes, I could see the tree trunk starting to discolor and my hands were sinking into the wood.

"Holy shit its working, Kole, it's working!" I yelled excitedly. I could hear them laughing and cheering behind me. I felt so good, the power just felt familiar and comforting, but as soon as I started to feel triumphant, the chanting was creeping up my spine. The sounds of battle, the smell of the blood, and the intoxicating feeling of the freedom of battle manifested as images that flashed right before my eyes and sounds that filled my ears.

I tore my hands off the tree, and frantically looked at myself, seeing not only were my hands covered in flames, but it was stretching all the way up my arms and down my legs. I was completely covered in flames, and the drums in my head were deafening. All I could see was flames, and all I could smell was blood.

I fell to my knees, trying to block out the voices as my hands were burning the dirt under me. The panic was building but the lust to burn everything down was stealing any logic I had. I was losing myself all over again, free-falling down the rabbit hole the gods made for me. I felt an arm on my shoulder, it scared me so much that I jumped.

"Just let it go, Octavia. Don't listen to the voices, they don't control you," Kole practically whispered in an attempt to soothe and guide me. I was shocked I could hear him through the many sounds fighting for dominance in my mind.

"I can't they are too loud, I can't take it," the voices slammed into every part of my head leaving no stone unturned.

"No, you're the strongest person I know. You won't hurt anyone, I promise; just let it go and embrace it," I felt his hands on my shoulders.

"Get back, I don't know what I'm going to do Kole! I can't control it!" I screamed

"No matter what," I looked up at him and realized he wasn't afraid. He didn't look at me like I was broken or a problem to be solved; he respected me and loved me. I closed my eyes, grabbed the flame, and released all the fear, the pressure. The voices all but disappeared and shot back down into my body. It was like a mountain-sized boulder was lifted off my back; the voices weren't gone but they were muffled which made them much easier to manage.

I expected to feel tired, I expected the power to show me how much of a toll it could take on my body if I refused to conform to it, but I felt good. I grabbed Kole by the collar and pulled him down to kiss him.

"No matter what," I smiled at him.

"I don't want to ruin your pretty moment, but I think we can all agree that this experiment was a failure," Rollo and Kare were laughing together.

"Fuck you, Rollo," I smiled at Kole and the two of us walked back.

4 - You Get The Point – Kole

"Okay, so maybe that wasn't the best experiment, but my point is proven," I claimed to the group trying to spread positivity, knowing Octavia was internally freaking out. Octavia still had some residual feelings after everything that happen with Kyut back home, I could understand her hesitance to dive right back into it. It will take some time to come to terms with what we have become, but time is something we had in short supply. I needed everyone to be on board with my theory because I knew this would work.

"Outside of the flames covering your body, you were able to burn the tree trunk, so it's possible for you to manipulate the flames. Technically I was correct." I could tell that everyone had some doubts, but I had another idea. Rollo has way more control over his powers; if I could get him to manipulate the lightning then everyone would believe me.

"Listen, humor me for a couple more minutes. I guarantee it will be worth it," I pleaded.

"Fine. You're lucky the weirdo in the cave sleeps all day or I would be sitting down enjoying some wine by now," Rollo said.

"You know how to control the lightning, you can force it out of your hands and call it down from the sky, but I think you can take that a step further if you had a little more imagination."

"No one imagines things more than Rollo," Kare interrupted. I couldn't help but laugh even though I was trying to be serious.

"Rollo, listen, instead of calling the lightning down to a spot, you should be able to harness it within and force it out of any part of your body… like maybe your feet." He looked at me like I had three heads until suddenly his expression changed, the biggest smile replacing his confusion. I think he finally understood what I was trying to say.

"Thor's beard Kole, are you saying what I think you're saying?"

"What exactly do you think I'm saying because I'm trying not to ruin this moment?"

"What the hell are you two talking about?" Kare questioned sounding exasperated.

"Are you telling me that if I shoot the lightning out my feet that I can fucking fly!?" He could barely hold in his excitement.

"Yes, Rollo, if my theory is right, I think you can among other things but it's a start. The powers are ours, we decide how we use them, so why don't you give it a try." Before I could get out of the way, Rollo was laughing and covered in the element, a loud rumble came from the clouds as the sky parted open and the bright streaking light came down engulfing him.

I was impressed, but I started to get worried because he would not stop laughing as the power possessed him. He has come so far, quicker than any of us, and that is because since day one he has never questioned what he could do. He was proud of what he was and proud of what he had become. He turned towards us, and his eyes were replaced by streaking light firing in all directions.

"Are you ready?" he yelled. He didn't wait for an answer. He closed his eyes, shifted the power down to his legs, and then pushed off the ground as hard as he could. The ground split open under the force as Rollo shot directly into the air, screaming in triumph as he continued to ascend to the clouds.

He managed to jump way above the trees, suspended in the sky like the god of thunder himself, and then suddenly, he started to plummet back down toward us. Panic struck me quickly, because I had no plan to make sure that he could get back down safely.

"He's not stopping Kole!" Octavia was yelling.

Rollo was starting to flail his arms and legs, trying to produce the same force, but whatever he was thinking on his way down was causing a lack of focus that wouldn't allow him to call on the element.

"Do something Kole, he's going to break every bone in his body!" Kare yelled. I should have thought about this before I had him try this, I needed to come up with something quickly or Octavia was going to kill me. She was the one that suggested we don't test out our powers anymore, and of course, I decided to do it anyway.

"I got an idea, stand back," I told them both. All I had to do was wait until the perfect time. I hoped to the gods this worked. Rollo was still falling, his screams getting louder as he got closer to the ground, but I still couldn't completely see him since the trees kept obstructing my view. I had to get this right because even if I was off a little bit he could be hurt.

Finally, he fell into my view about a full tree length above the ground. I closed my eyes and pulled the power out of me to open a portal directly under him. All I had to do was hold it in place long enough for him to fall in, which was harder than I imagined it would be.

Rollo fell into the portal in midair, and I stretched out my left hand towards the ground in front of us. Rollo popped out of the portal and slid face-first into the dirt. It took so much energy from me that I had to take a knee.

All I could hear was the pounding of my heart in my chest. Apparently, I was pushing towards my limits, something I had never done before. Rollo picked himself up out of the dirt. I looked over to him expecting him to be angry, but he was still laughing.

"That was fucking awesome! I still don't know if I can fly but that was amazing! Let's go again." He was pulling the dirt out of his hair with a crazed look in his eyes.

"I think we are done for the day," I decided as I took a seat on the ground trying to catch my breath and slow down my racing heart. Rollo walked over and told us exactly how it felt to shoot up in the sky and almost fly. He also noted in detail what it felt like to almost fall to your death.

Octavia gave me the side-eye during the entire story reinforcing that her advice was probably correct. I tried not to give her that satisfaction because, regardless of what happened, we made a step forward. Every time we learn something new about ourselves, it will help us in our upcoming conflict.

“Let’s go inside and get cleaned up. The sun is going down, our new friend Gio should be joining us very soon, and Rollo, I want to hear about this plan,” I said.

“I will be right behind you guys, I want to stay out in the fresh air a little longer,” Octavia said. I grabbed her hand and kissed her. Rollo, Kare, and I walked back down the trail to the cave.

5 - MEETING WITH THE WARLORD – OCTAVIA

I was not ready to go back into that stuffy cave; the soft breeze sweeping off the mountain was refreshing, especially after I almost set everything on fire. The murderous voice in my head and my temper were going to eventually hurt me or someone that I care about. I need to get this under control before I confront Marcus, we needed to be cool-headed and clever to win this war.

Kole lectured us every single day. We need to come to terms with and embrace what has been given to us. How he became an expert so quickly on what we needed to do was as irritating as it was astonishing. It wasn't that long ago that he almost had a breakdown and portaled his entire home into oblivion. He was taking this way better than I expected considering everything that has happened, but the advice was not wrong.

I need to face it head-on, but I could only do that if I got some peace and quiet. I loved my friends, but it was incredibly difficult to focus when everyone was around, not to mention I still had Floria's precarious situation ever present in the recesses of my mind. There was very little time to actually reflect on all that has come to pass, as well as all that has yet to transpire.

I had moments where it made me guilty about moving on and forming this new life. I hadn't forgotten about Tiberius, but I never truly mourned him, and the thought of it weighed heavily on me. I could never for a second forget Floria was stuck with that evil family, forced to marry that worm, Titus. The death I was going to give him would be glorious, but not before he told me everything he knows about his father's plan.

This was going to be the only time I was going to get some privacy. As soon as Gio got up, I assumed it was going to get a little heavy in the cave. I closed my eyes to focus on the flame inside of me. I didn't know what I was planning to do but I needed to get some clarity on what Mars has done to me. I walked closer to the flames and listened to the distant chanting. My instincts told me to back away, but I was done running.

The voices got louder, and the familiar drums of battle started to vibrate through my body. I couldn't be afraid of myself. How was I going to do what I needed to do if I ran away from this? I reached out to grab the flame, not knowing what the result would be, but before I could get a hold of it, an ember jumped out of the fire and landed on my arm.

My natural reaction was to pull away so the ember wouldn't burn me, but when it landed, I didn't feel any heat. For the moment, I was calm until I looked back down at my arm. I couldn't feel the ember, but it began to grow and spread all over my body faster than I could put it out. I backed away from the flame swatting my arms and legs but it was not helping. I dropped to the ground to roll but nothing was working.

All around me the air was getting thin. I couldn't breathe, the flames and smoke grew more intense, burning my eyes. My cough was raking the back of my throat, and I fell to the ground as the world turned black.

Ω

The sky was red and dark like the world was on fire. The sting of the wind and the dirt forced me awake. I was surrounded by broken swords, helmets, and shields. Remnants of fallen soldiers.

It didn't take me long to realize where I was, I'd been having the same dream every night before the attack on Alexandria. This is the place that started the whirlwind that is my life today. While I gained some amazing people and a fiancé, I lost so much in the process. There was no need to drag this out, so I got off the ground and rubbed the dirt off my face and clothes.

"Mars! I know you brought me here so let's not prolong this. Tell me what you want," I yelled into the distance.

All I could see was destruction as the stench of sweat from battle permeated the air. The aroma was stuck in my nose; I was starting to grow tired of it.

"Come on, I would really like to get back to the life that you and your friends screwed up. I mean in hindsight this is all your fault."

A giant spear came falling out of the sky and pierced the ground right in front of me. The explosion knocked me off my feet sending me flying in the other direction. My ears were ringing, and although the pain wasn't too bad, I was definitely going to feel that later.

The smoke cleared and a man about eight feet tall appeared, his familiar golden helmet donned on his head was shaped like a lion's head to match his breastplate and the skulls hanging from his belt. Flames replaced his eyes, and his face was still and hard as stone. He reached down and ripped the spear out of the ground before storing it in a sheath on his back.

Mars stood angrily before me, looking at me as if I am the source of all his ire. The last time I saw him maybe he was happy to see me, but this time I can see that there was no compassion between us. I hope my mouth didn't land me in trouble once again, so I did what I assume anyone would do if they offended a god. I fell to my knees and kept my head down.

"If that was the greeting you gave when you first arrived, I wouldn't have had to almost kill you with my spear," he spoke, his voice present in every direction sending a chill through my entire body.

"I meant no disrespect Mars, I am just anxious about returning home."

"I see you have been very busy, and very stupid, my child." Smoke from the fire was pouring out of his eyes, as he sat back in a chair that was not there when I looked before. A bench appeared behind me, so I got off my knees and took a seat.

"Stupid?" I asked likely sounding as confused as I looked. He was the one that put us on this path. What could I

have possibly done wrong? "I'm doing exactly what you wanted me to do, I am making sure I have the strength to take back Gracia."

"I wanted you to take back our land, but I never told you to seek out that parasite, Ambrogio. He is cursed among the gods, and his return to our lands is not something that we can tolerate," he stated sternly.

"It sounds like the gods have a problem with him, but if I can be honest, he is a creation of your choices," I braced myself to pay for my sarcasm.

"Careful, princess. While we have made mistakes, immortality is something that your mind cannot grasp. Ambrogio may have been a misstep by us, but what he has become now is an abomination allowed by the huntress, and you should proceed with caution," his voice was stern, clearly holding a warning. "I assume that Odin waited until I left Midselium to tell you of Ambrogio's existence, and I assume he negotiated quite a steep deal in order to give up that type of information." I just put my head down and he took my silence as a confirmation of his suspicions.

"Kole and I have done some things that neither of us are proud of, things we will have to live with forever, but we have come to terms with our decisions," I said to him confidently.

"I hardly believe that. Humans eventually crack under the weight of the world, I've seen it happen a million times. You aren't the first and you will not be the last."

"What do you care as long as we carry out what you expect of us?" I asked.

"I have come here to add one missing piece to the tale Ambrogio told you," he explained as he leaned up in his chair.

I knew Gio was leaving something out, someone as old as him was not so different from the gods. He was most likely a master of divulging just enough information to reel us in while leaving some of it out.

"The tale he told is mostly true, but he believes that he killed the spirit of Delphi to spite the gods. What he does not know is that the spirit cannot be killed, it passes from one host to another. She has been congregating with the gods... and I don't think I need to explain that she is very angry." He had an evil smile on his face, drawing out the last part of that statement for as long as possible.

Gio thought he killed the spirit that led him down this road, but if it simply passed on that means it could be used against him at any time.

"So, you mean to tell me that an oracle spirit that usually leads heroes to their death is alive and feeling scorned?" I asked as I attempted to sort out the mess in my head.

"I'm telling you that you should be careful whom you team up with. We are on Roman lands now. While the spirits hold no stronghold in Najora, they are very much empowered here. Do what you must but keep Ambrogio at arm's length or you will be wrapped up in the wrath that he has coming his way. In the end, nature demands balance... remember that."

I couldn't tell if my vision was starting to blur or if Mars was disappearing. That question was answered when I woke up in the clearing back in the forest with another piece of the unsolvable puzzle of the gods.

“Fuck.”

I got up and walked back down to join the others.

6 - Thinking of a Master Plan - Rollo

We made our way back into the cave. I was still filthy from my little incident with the dirt outside, but I was too excited to be upset about it. I mean yeah, I almost died but I didn't. Kole had my back as usual, even if it wasn't a part of the plan. I haven't felt this alive in years, and I know my father would be proud if he were here today. His drunk, impulsive son was now a king, and he was going to save not one but two countries. Not to mention I was so close to learning how to fly. I could barely contain the excitement I feel thinking about mastering that God-given talent.

On top of that, I was going to get to present my plan to everyone, even that psychopath Gio. He wouldn't be my first choice as an ally, but I had a way to use him perfectly. But first, I needed to take a bath and wash off the day. This cave did not lend a ton of privacy, but I had nothing to hide. I pulled the thin fabric across the doorway of this tiny room, stripped out of my clothes, poured the cold water over my head, and started scrubbing. This was going to take a while.

When I came back into the throne room it was full of life, nothing like it was earlier. Plenty of familiar faces were lounging on the couches, talking amongst themselves. I didn't notice everyone holding these dark goblets before, but now that I know what they all are I could not unsee it. It also explains why they look at us like starving dogs, waiting for someone to drop a piece of food on the floor. Even after a couple of nights here, I felt like we were one sharp movement away from setting them off.

The others were sitting at a table that was strategically placed almost directly in front of the throne. Kole was holding a piece of parchment, reading it aloud to everyone at the table. I took a seat next to Kare. I was surprised anyone noticed that I sat down.

"What's going on?" I asked.

"Shh, it's a letter from home one of the servants delivered to us when we sat down," Kare said. I had to move closer to hear him, it was so loud in the cave. I asked Kole to start over. I wanted to make sure I didn't miss any details.

Ω

I hope this letter finds you well, son. I hope the raven you sent to us finds its way back to you. It would have been easier to send a messenger, but I understand your whereabouts need to remain a secret right now. I hope you and Kare are well, life in Lundr is not as bright without my children here. I miss you both dearly. I regret letting her leave with you, but I know she would be miserable if I tried to force her to stay. I guess the birds have to leave the nest and learn at some point. I hope all is well with Octavia, I really wish you would have waited till after your engagement to run off and save the world. I can feel you rolling your eyes right now, so let me get to the point of this letter. Lundr is settled; it seems that leaving me in charge for the beginning of your reign was a great idea.

Some of your father's loyalists weren't happy about the series of events, but they will keep an open mind about their new king out of respect for me. I have received steady reports from Ivar and Kyut from the north. The kingdom is running fine, and the first payment of taxes have been received, as you commanded. I know now is not a great time, but I really would like you to rethink his punishment. He is your brother and I know you love each other. It will take some time, but I know you both will find your way back to each other. Please consider bringing him back for me. Tell Rollo that his mother and sister are doing well. The people have always loved his family, they are both in amazing hands. They come back and visit to check on me from time to time; the whole ordeal has brought us a lot closer. I pray to the gods that this letter eases any worry you had about leaving home. The armies are waiting for your signal, and they will start marching wherever and whenever you tell them to. May the Odin be with you all.

Love always Astrid.

Ω

A weight fell off all our hearts when Kole finished that letter. None of us would admit but I know personally I was worried about leaving my family. They had to pick up all the pieces of my father's death and it wasn't fair, but what choice did I have? This may have started with Kole and Octavia, but it was clear that my name would be a part of this saga, as well. The servants set the table as they did every night. There was enough food to feed a village. I would never understand where he was getting this food from.

"I know I asked before, but seriously is anyone going to question how this guy has so much food even though he lives in a cave?" I spoke in general to the table hoping someone would answer me.

"Something tells me it's better just not to ask, I don't know how much truth I can take at this point," Octavia said.

"We could be eating anything. I'm not complaining, but after finding out that everyone here survives off blood, it's made me think a little bit," I shrugged and leaned back in my chair.

"I understand, but beggars can't be choosers. We have to deal with what we have whether we like it or not," Kole said. He was right, and I must be honest, it was annoying that he always knew what to say.

The commotion in the throne room dropped down to a silent chatter. Out from his chambers dressed in a black robe, his hair hanging loosely over his shoulders and his fangs on full display, Gio emerged stretching and smiling that devilish grin.

He rubbed us all the wrong way. We agreed that he was a necessary evil, but I could not figure out his end game. He was immortal so maybe this was another way of biding his time, but he was ancient and powerful. If he decided to cross us it would be a problem. We needed to find out what his weaknesses are, which is why my plan was perfect.

"I see that you have received the letter, Kole. I was told a raven arrived with news from your home," he said.

"You read it before I did... that isn't very respectful Gio," Kole responded, his voice laced with venom.

"My servants read your letter and reported it back to me when I woke up. You can understand why I require this level of scrutiny. I can't have you telling anyone where I lay my head," he waved his hand, and his servant brought his goblet to him.

"This place just gets better and better," I rolled my eyes as I picked up a chicken leg off the table, immediately wondering if it was actually a chicken leg. "If we are going to make this work, we need to trust each other completely," I looked at both Gio and Kole. They nodded to me and then to each other.

"Rollo has a plan of attack that he wanted to share with the group. I have not heard the details yet, he found it best to tell us both at the same time," Kole said. He looked over to me encouraging me to begin.

"Good evening, your majesty. Thank you for allowing me to address the room," I tried to project my voice.

"Rollo please cut the pleasantries; I just woke up, don't lull me back to sleep," Gio interrupted drolly.

I guess I was going to have to get right down to business. The plan sounded great in my head, but now that I had to say it in front of everyone, I was already getting nervous. My eyes scanned the room. Everyone was looking at me, and then I saw a dark-haired woman smile at me, the grey in her eyes almost froze me in place. It was quick, but it was enough to calm my nerves. I rubbed my eyes and looked again, and she was gone. The details of this plan were going to upset someone, or maybe everyone, but to me, it seemed like our best chance. I wasn't sure where I should begin, so I just took a deep breath and let it all out.

"First of all, we have no idea what we are dealing with when it comes to Marcus's army. We need some eyes on the inside, at the very least so we can see how many warriors he has.

Even if it's just a surface number, we need to have an idea of what we are walking into."

I was looking around the room. Everyone still had their eyes on me, still looking engaged, so I hadn't said anything stupid yet, thank the gods.

"You may not want to hear it, Octavia, but I do not see how it is possible for you to sneak anywhere near the city without someone noticing you. Sneaking in will not work, but the problem is only you know where we need to go." They were still listening to me, so now seemed like a good time to drop the first bomb.

"So, you need me there to show you around, but you don't think I'll be able to move around unrecognized. But back in Lundr, Kole was able to get into the longhouse unrecognized and he was next in line for the throne," she said.

"If I may answer your question, Octavia, you were one of the jewels of Alexandria, and men always notice beautiful women. You will most definitely be seen," Gio interrupted before returning back to his drink. He gestured for me to continue.

"Continue, Rollo. I can't wait to see where I come into this master plan."

"We all are going to go to the outpost, Perseus," Kole's eyes flew to mine clearly surprised that I would suggest that place of all places.

I know he didn't want to tell Octavia about Persephone's, but we had no choice.

"From there, I want you and Kole to go to Alexandria willingly and request to parlay with Marcus." If the first suggestion didn't make him angry, this one surely did.

"Rollo, are you out of your mind? You want me to go and look that man in the face after what he has done to all of us and try to come to a bargain?" Octavia didn't need to say anything, the death stare was screaming all the words she had running through her mind.

"Listen, Kole… hear me out. You are the new King of Lundr, and with Octavia by your side you present a united front. We need to know what he is up to, or we won't be able to make an advantageous move."

"What is going to stop him from killing us on the spot?" Octavia asked.

"Because I believe that he would want to know the same thing. If he is going to wage war on the rest of the country, he needs to know who he stands against. If I'm right about him, he will want to probe your strength, which will act as a distraction for the other parts of my plan," Kole and I glanced at each other for a moment. Like many other times, we were sharing a silent moment where we clearly had an understanding, knowing one of us were in the right, even though the other didn't want to admit it.

"I'll keep an open mind until after I hear the rest of the plan," he said.

"While you two are in Alexandria, Kare and I will remain in Perseus waiting for our armies to arrive before we start to move towards the city," I said.

"How will you manage to get to Alexandria without being spotted by someone else? I'm sure Marcus has spies all over," Octavia asked.

"That is where our new friend comes in to play," I turned to Gio. He must have been waiting to be included because now he was sitting up on his throne, very attentive.

"Finally. Tell me how I can help, and please tell me it includes killing Romans." I looked toward Octavia, knowing hearing him talk this way could not be easy. These were still her people, regardless of her engagement to Kole.

"Before Kare and I travel to the city, you and your children will scout the roads ahead every night, any forces you come across should be small. You should be able to take them out no problem, this way no information gets back to Marcus, and by the time he realizes we are coming, it will be too late." I turned to the crowd so I could wait for everyone to tell me how good the plan was. I thought this was easily the best way to make this happen, but it was so completely silent, you could hear a pin drop. This was certainly not the reaction I was expecting. This cave was not big enough for all this tension.

"So, you want to let Gio run wild through my country killing any Roman that he comes across? Some of those soldiers are just following orders, how do we know that they even agree with Marcus?" Octavia stood up abruptly. I could see that she was angry, and I knew that she would be, but this was truly the only way. "Did we kill every warrior in Lundr when we found out they were working for Halfdan?" she asked.

"No, but a little birdie told me you killed a handful of them to get to Kole's family, so what is the difference?" I responded.

"The difference was those men made their allegiance known. I was not the aggressor in that situation. My question for you is, do you think that Gio will do the same? Because I can almost guarantee he will kill anyone that crosses his path," she snapped.

I didn't have anything that I could say to that; war was messy, and if we planned to win, we would all have to play in the mud occasionally. I looked down at Kole as he remained silent, but I could tell that he agreed with her. This plan would never work if the two of them weren't on board.

"I can see that we have hit an impasse, so how about I help move this process along. My child, I promise that I will not take any Roman lives that don't deserve to be taken," Gio exclaimed calmly, clearly aiming to ease Octavia's tension and concern.

"And who gets to determine what is deserved?" Octavia answered.

"Well, you have met the Gods. Are you going to sit here and tell me that they should decide who deserves what?" he asked, but he didn't wait for an answer. He continued with his point, "Did your family deserve what happened to them when the gods decided to play with your fates like puppet masters? Did I deserve to never lay my eyes on the sun again and have my Selene taken from me? All I can tell you is that I won't harm anyone that doesn't deserve it, take it or leave it." He licked the blood off his lips and sat back on his throne before crossing his legs.

"Think about it this way, Octavia. We can cut off the scouts, supplies, and weapons before they even get to Alexandria, and the battle can be less bloody. Neither side loses warriors and Marcus is the one who pays," I walked over to the table and took a knee beside her. I wanted her to understand that I was on her side, but this was necessary. "We have both lost so much, and I have no desire to harm your people, but I need this to end. My mother and sister need me, and we all know Marcus is not going to stop. We need to stop him," I pleaded with her.

"Fine," she said but then she looked right up at Gio. "If you hurt anyone that is innocent, I promise you I will find a way to put you down." Gio smiled as he took another sip from his goblet. Octavia got up from the table, storming out in the direction of her room.

She grabbed a cask of wine on the way out but made sure she stopped and pointed to the throne.

"Oh, by the way, Ambrogio... a giant god-sized birdie told me that Delphi is still alive, and she is not happy with you, so I would be careful while you're on Roman soil." I didn't think it was possible, but Gio's face turned a shade whiter than it already was as the smile was yanked right off his face.

I didn't know what to say after that. If she was trying to make a statement with that exit, she succeeded. I was just hoping that the disrespect wouldn't get us all killed because Gio was livid. I also sensed that for the first time he was afraid.

Everyone in the cave could sense that something upset their master, like his emotions were somehow connected to all the others. This all started with Delphi, and now Gio had to endure being immortal, living with the same pain every minute of every day. If he was so afraid, how was he going to be able face her again?

"So, I know some touchy things were said, but can we get back to the plan? Because I think it's our best chance," Kole punched me in the arm, I got the hint.

“Listen Gio, she didn’t mean any disrespect. She is just stressed out about going home, that’s all,” Kole said.

“Don’t waste your apologies on me, young king, my skin is thicker than you think. Without that outburst, I wouldn’t have been able to hear the most important information. Though the news of Delphi doesn’t change things, it makes things much more complicated,” he rolled his eyes. I understood the sentiment. I was just about done with this entire fiasco hand-delivered to us by the gods. What I wouldn’t give for a normal day back in my own kingdom, with a woman on my knee and a drink in hand. Though I suppose I would have fewer of those days ahead of me now that I’m a king.

“How does it complicate things? What does Delphi have over you?” Kole asked.

“If she is talking to the other gods, then what would stop one of them from making an appearance to Marcus and warning him?” he surmised. Something about his response was too simple. I haven’t known him long, but it was hard to believe that a warning was all he was worried about.

“How about you tell us what you’re really worried about?” Kole asked him. “A warning wouldn’t mean anything to you, there has to be something more.” Gio got up out of his throne and made his way down towards us, carrying all the tense energy with him. That tension hadn’t eased since Octavia told him about Delphi, but I could tell he was hiding something, and we needed to find out what.

"You going to tell us what has you so spooked, or are you just going to keep pacing?" Kole said. He was starting to lose his patience; I could feel the power trembling all around him.

"If Delphi is alive, she obviously wants to punish me, even though this immortal torment should be enough. Let's be clear, I am not spooked, but as I said this can complicate things," he repeated.

"Yeah, we got that part, but stop playing games, Gio." Kole was face-to-face with him now. "Fucking talk, I've put up with the riddles long enough." Gio's demeanor didn't change, but there was a low growl in his voice.

"She is the only one outside of the huntress that knows how to kill me, so you see how that can get complicated, but know this... I will bathe the country with blood and use it for a swimming hole before that bitch gets the upper hand on me." His fangs rested on the sides of his mouth. I reached down to my belt to grab my hammer, just in case.

"Are you guys done?" Kare spoke. I had forgotten she was even at the table.

Kole and Gio turned to her, finally breaking the staring contest they were having, the intensity in the room was slowly dissipating.

"Delphi is alive, what does it matter? I think the plan should remain the same. What about you, brother?" I was impressed. She would always boss us around in Lundr, but this was the real deal as words could have had serious consequences. I lowered my hand off my belt and Kole relaxed his shoulders.

"I agree, sister; write letters and send ravens back to mom. In a few days, we leave for Perseus. Don't forget your promise, Gio."

“I also agree, my little flower, the plan remains the same and my promise upheld,” they shared another long glance before Kole made his way out of the room.

“That was very impressive, Kare. I figured it was about time to break out my jokes, but your way was much better,” I laughed.

“I know men, gods, and vampires are all the same, Rollo, swinging your egos around the room instead of focusing on what’s important,” she shook her head and walked away.

She was right. This didn’t go down the way I envisioned it, but there was one thing that was certain: the plan was a good one and it was going to work, if everyone played their part.

7 - WHY NOW?! - KOLE

I wanted to chase after Octavia as soon as she stormed out, but there was no way I was going to let Gio off the hook without explaining his reaction. Killing Delphi never solved his problems, and to be honest, I doubt it even made him feel better. Her being alive seemed to lay a whole new list of problems at his doorstep.

He refused to tell us his weakness, but now there was someone that knew exactly how to kill him. Even though it did create some complications, this revelation could be a good thing for us. I would have to put that to the side because I had no idea what kind of mood Octavia would be in when I got back to the room.

She was sitting on the edge of the makeshift bed, still holding the cask of wine. I was hoping there was some left inside. Whatever conversation I was walking into was not going to be a pleasant one. The bed was just fur laying on top of some hay, doing nothing to stop the solid floor of the cave from killing your back. This was not a place I would recommend anyone to stay in. It was a miracle anyone got any sleep here.

"Are you okay, my love?" I sat down next to her. She let her hair hang free directly over her face, covering the tears she thinks I can't see. "I know none of this is what you wanted, and you know I'll do everything in my power to keep that monster on track." I reached out to grab her hand, but she pulled back before I could touch her. I didn't know what else to do, so I sat next to her keeping quiet. I decided to wait until she was ready to talk.

After a couple of minutes, she passed me the wine, still not speaking, but I wouldn't complain about progress. I had to put myself in her shoes. It couldn't have been an easy choice, but my mom told me before the holmgang that kings make difficult choices that they believe are right more often than not. If we were going to rule together this would not be the first time nor the last that we have a difference in opinion, but together nothing could stop us. I was prepared to sit here in silence, but she finally cracked her shell.

"Why am I the one that always has to sacrifice?" she asked as she had tears rolling down her cheeks. "Have I not lost enough already?"

I really didn't know what to say. I couldn't explain why she had to sacrifice so much. I wish my mom was here, she would have some profound advice that would make all of us feel better.

"I know it's not easy, love, but what did we promise each other when we left Lundr?" I wiped the tears from her face.

"No matter what," she said.

"You left the room before you could see the damage you did to Gio. Although he won't admit it, he is afraid of Delphi, and for the first time he seemed unsure and nervous," I was hoping this would lift her spirits a little bit. It wasn't an amazing victory, but any small win was worth it.

"Why would he be nervous about Delphi being alive?" she questioned.

"Because now there is someone besides the huntress that knows how to kill him, and if she is alive and on the loose, she could tell anyone his secret." She looked up at me and I swear she was trying to hide a smirk.

"So, you're thinking that if we can find Delphi first, we can find out how to kill him, just in case he gets out of line?" she chuckled as she so easily read my mind.

"Exactly, but only after we defeat Marcus. We need to use him for as long as possible to make sure we save your sister and restore your home."

"Be careful Kole, your Odin is showing," she laughed.

"Yeah, yeah, yeah," I grabbed the wine from her and laid back against the wall. Octavia laid her head on my chest. Her small victory was my small victory, because even if it was for just a moment, I can tell she felt better. Her beautiful eyes looked up toward me and, judging by her smile, she seemed content for the time being. I ran my hands through her long hair taking in this precious time that we never wanted to let go of.

She turned around to lay on my chest, moving closer so there was no room in between us. I could feel her warmth as she was pressed against me. My hands made their way down her back and grabbed her thighs to pull her closer. She let out a tiny gasp before she smiled and kissed me. It felt like we haven't been this close in ages. I didn't realize how much I needed it until her lips crashed on mine. Her lips were warm and soft, and I could taste the wine on her tongue. It was salty at first, but then you could taste the sweet flavors of the fruit.

Octavia was playing a dangerous game if she keeps kissing me this way. I don't know if I have the strength to contain myself right now. She pressed against me harder, and I know she could feel me growing against her. She broke away from the kiss and smiled before she reached down my pants and wrapped her hands around my shaft. The shock in my nerves caused me to throw my head back and groan in pleasure.

"You like that?" she leaned down and whispered in my ear before she kissed my neck.

"I'm not really sure if I can answer at the moment," I smiled. She started to move her hands back and forth, faster and with more intent.

"Is something funny?" she asked with a smile.

I decided to let this play out, so I just shook my head and relaxed knowing I was going to enjoy the result. This woman had so much power over me. I didn't think it was possible, but she made me feel unstoppable. In the same sense, she showed me that it's okay to be vulnerable with her. It was okay to let her take control; it didn't make me any less of a man and I loved her for it.

I put my hands under her chin and brought her lips back to mine, it had been long enough since I felt her lips. I reached my hands towards the bottom of her tunic and moved it up. I didn't have to say anything else as she shifted her body up and, with her other hand, guided me inside of her.

There wasn't a lot of privacy but neither of us cared at the moment. We tried to muffle the moans, but we were lost in each other. Octavia moved her weight back and forth on top of me and I matched her rhythm in unison. Her nails were digging into my chest and mine were gripping both of her thighs.

We forgot all about the cave, we forgot that the only thing that separated us from everyone else was a thin curtain covering the entry of the room, we forgot all about our worries that awaited us when this moment ended. Nothing else mattered but what we were both feeling right now, and we wanted it to last forever even while knowing in this life nothing does.

I was locked in her eyes, completely sunken into my desire. The same desire that has eluded me for way too long, until we both heard an ear-wrenching scream coming from the throne room.

The noise scared us both. We stopped moving to make sure we weren't hearing things until after the silence, we heard the scream again.

"You have got to be kidding me. Out of all the nights, it has to be right now," she complained. I had no words. All I know is whatever is going on better be serious because I could kill someone for interrupting this. I grabbed my axe and followed Octavia out of the room.

Ω

"What the hell is going on?" I asked angrily, still not able to shake off the need to pummel someone for interrupting my time with Octavia.

The throne room was in a frenzy, people were running in and out but none of them were screaming. Gio was sitting on the throne unamused while the rest of the room was in chaos. His servants, children, or whatever he called them, were staring at the cave entrance, snarling with their fangs exposed.

"You plan on telling me what is happening?" I asked Gio.

"You will know soon enough, Kole. Please sit and enjoy the show," he made himself comfortable.

The screams were coming from the cave entrance, and it was getting closer. Gio's men were carrying in two women. They threw them down in the middle of the room. I guess that answers my question about where the screams were coming from. After that, three more men were carried in, all of them dressed like Romans.

"What is going on here, Gio? Why are these people here?" Octavia asked warily.

"These unfortunate souls discovered my hideout. I can't just allow them to walk free," he said. I didn't want to know what was going to happen next because there is no way this would end well.

"Maybe they just got lost on the path, why not just send them on their way?" I asked.

"How do you think I managed to remain here undetected for so long?" Gio asked. "I have to protect my home. These people could have been sent here, no one can be trusted." I wanted to argue with him but, even though I didn't agree, I could understand the strategy.

We have no idea where these people came from, and there was no way to prove that if he lets them go they will keep their mouths shut about what they have seen. Octavia was fuming but she didn't say anything. Unfortunately, this was only going to take her hatred for Gio to another level. I knew he was going to kill them. What other option did he have?

"What are you going to do with them?" Octavia turned to Gio, the flames dancing inside her pupils.

"In the interest of our alliance, I want to offer you a gesture of my mercy, as an olive branch towards you and your future husband," Gio stood up off his throne.

"Please spare me the fancy words and tell me what you are going to do to them," Octavia was losing her patience.

"Usually if I have intruders, they wouldn't even make it into my cave. I have my children kill them on-site. It was the only way to ensure that we remained a secret, but now I will give these intruders a choice," he said calmly. "I will pass along the gift of immortality to those who are strong enough to earn it, the others will die."

"What kind of fucking choice is that?" she was storming toward Gio before Rollo grabbed her.

"Let me go, Rollo!" she screamed.

"I can't. I don't want anyone to get hurt, promise me you won't do anything that is going to put us all at risk," he said.

"Octavia, we are in his home. We can't tell him how to resolve his conflicts, I am not king here," I pleaded with her.

“Are you fucking kidding me? Are you really going to condone this? Either they become a monster like him, or they die, how is that fair? How do you know they weren’t just lost?” She was screaming so much her voice was starting to go hoarse.

“The problem is that we don’t know. I've done my best to show you I’m on your side, princess, but I am what I am and I do not ask for permission,” his fangs were exposed and his eyes absent of any feeling. He continued, “the bite chooses whom it wants, I have no control. You either survive or you don’t, this is my decision whether you approve or not.”

I looked back at her, not saying a word. Something was telling me that this decision would be the first thing to fracture us. The way her eyes pierced mine was like she shoved one of her daggers straight through my heart. It was the first time she seemed disappointed in me. So far being king was miserable. No matter what I chose to do someone was going to be hurt by my choices.

“Let me go, Rollo. I won’t do anything I promise,” she said calmly. She was too calm. I didn’t need to press any further to know that she was not happy.

“I know you’re upset,” I spoke softly.

“No shit,” she interrupted.

“I understand how you feel, but if we let them go and they talk we lose our element of surprise. If Marcus knows we are coming, he may hurt your sister purposefully.” I tried to walk over and comfort her, but she pulled away from my touch, a gesture that I pushed to the side the first time but this time it sent a ripple through my chest. The first seed of doubt was being planted.

“I understand, Kole. I’m not a child, but it doesn’t mean it’s right and it doesn’t mean that I need to be happy about it. I have been forced to accept it, so let the monster do what he pleases since these lives mean nothing to any of you,” she never looked at me when she spoke.

How was I supposed to respond to that? It was as cold as she has ever been towards me. She didn’t even hate me this much when I found her in that carriage in the middle of the woods, and I didn’t have the slightest idea how to fix it, but the idea of her hating me was like a festering wound that wouldn’t heal.

“Are you sure there is no other way to make sure these people keep your secret?” I asked Gio.

“Sorry, my young king. They leave dead or in my control, those are the options. At least I am giving them a chance.”

He walked back to his throne, and with one wave of his hands, the servants were moving the tables and placing all the intruders in the center of the room so that he could relay their fate.

“For whatever reason, you have ventured into a forbidden area, and while I would love to let you all go, I have a family to look after. Therefore, you have a choice,” he got back out of his seat and stood before them, “you accept my bite and, if the gods will it, you will be reborn as one of us. You will live among us as a family, a hunter capable of more than you have ever dreamed of. If you refuse, you will die and be food for my family.”

The room was silent, but I wasn't surprised. How were you supposed to answer a question like that on the spot? One of the men stood up and, based on his body language, he was not going to be one to bow down to Gio.

"Let us go! We have nothing to do with whatever blasphemy you have going on here. We just want to be on our way," the man tried to show authority while he spoke.

"Now why do I not believe you? The dishonesty in your heartbeat gives you away. Although it's of no matter, make your decision or I will make it for you, Roman," Gio said coldly.

The man refused to back down and I understood his decision, sometimes dying for what you believe in was better than being a slave.

"I'll never join your demented family, the gods have cursed you and they will have their revenge." All our faces turned towards the man in disbelief, and at that moment, he knew he had said too much. Gio knew it too.

"How do you know of my curse, human, and why would the gods want revenge on me?" Gio stalked out of his throne. Something in his demeanor had changed.

The man looked down at the others, fear sweeping across them all. He knew he said more than he was supposed to.

"I don't know what you're talking about, I'm nervous. I must have been rambling. I just want to get out of here," the man tried desperately to clean up the mess he just made.

"No, no, my friend. You spoke of a curse and revenge. If you and your friends were just traveling here by accident, how would you know about such things?" Gio was circling the man like a hungry shark waiting for an answer.

The man remained silent, and now I had a feeling this was going to turn into a waiting game. But that was never going to be a game a mere mortal would win over an immortal who had all the time in the world.

Gio turned his back to the man to walk up to his throne, which made it seem like the man had gotten off easy. He clearly knew more than he was letting on, so why was Gio just walking away without pressing for more information? It didn't make any sense. As soon as the man thought he had a chance, he pulled a piece of wood whittled down to a sharp edge from his clothes and lunged to stab Gio. Before any of us could react, Octavia caught the man's arm.

The king turned around slowly like the assassination attempt was not surprising to him. Gio had a smirk on his face as if he was amused at the attempt. He nodded a thank you to Octavia and kept walking to his seat.

8 - Compassion Strikes Again - Octavia

I should have been smarter than to give people the benefit of the doubt, but here I am. After everything that I have been through, you would think I would have learned not to blindly trust anyone. Now I would have to do something that I never wanted to do. I'm going to have to actually defend this monster. I was still holding the man's arm in place because I haven't decided if I want to let him go or break it myself.

"I spoke up for you, I believed that you were telling the truth about just finding this cave by accident, but you were looking for it and now you need to tell me why," I let go of his arm and kicked the back of his leg, so he fell to his knees.

"I'm not going to tell you shit, traitor," he snapped at Octavia.

"Traitor?" I said surprisingly.

"Yes traitor, here you are sitting with him and breaking bread instead of siding with your people. He is an abomination and should be removed from this world," he spit toward Gio.

"Well, the only thing standing in between you and that abomination is me so if you are in a hurry to meet your end just say the word because I am tired of Romans lying to me," I told him.

The man was looking past me barely acknowledging my existence. A green smoke was swirling through his eyes. It was faint at first, but if you looked hard enough it was there.

"Ambrogio!"

Gio was completely caught off guard by the mention of his real name.

"How do you know that name, human?"

"We were visited by the spirit Delphi. She promised us riches beyond our wildest dreams if we managed to spy on you. Killing you wasn't a part of the plan, but I figured she wouldn't mind," he smiled.

"The old dusty bitch made her first move and she missed. I'm offended by this weak attempt, but then again the gods always use humans to do the things they are too scared to do," his lips curled over his fangs. Clearly these men had struck a nerve.

"Oh, she has so much planned for you Ambrogio. As soon as she finds out where you are she's going to make sure that you pay," the man said.

The spirit led more desperate people down an impossible path to fix something that it broke. Why am I not surprised? The world was confusing enough and slowly my trust was being swept away with every encounter. Even though I was still unhappy about the fact that he was going to sacrifice these people, considering how this is playing out, I may have lost my hill to stand on.

"This has been entertaining but I'm growing bored. Do you have any last words before you die?" Gio said it almost cheerfully.

"Just a message from Delphi, you monster."

"Go ahead, spit it out. I don't have all day."

"You are an imbalance of nature, and it will be corrected."

As soon as the man finished the last line of the message, Gio swung and separated that man's head from his body in one quick strike. Blood sprayed all over the floor as his body crumbled to the ground while his head tumbled along the cave floor.

"Okayyyy... outside of him just killing that guy, did anyone else think that message sounded like a love letter?" Rollo joked.

"Odin's beard, shut up Rollo," Kole said. None of us knew what to do, but I couldn't take my eyes off the man's body.

The sight of blood didn't frighten me. It was the carnal growl that vibrated the cave. Gio's children were surrounding the intruders who were covered in blood, hunched low and snarling like starving animals. Saliva was dripping from their fangs, nothing but rage and hunger lived in their eyes, and in less than a second, the intruders were being ripped apart right in front of us all.

The screams were horrifying, but not as much as watching the flesh being peeled off their bodies as Gio's pets' tore into their necks. I wanted to look away, but the gore paralyzed me. For whatever reason, I couldn't take my eyes off this massacre. If I was going to force myself to watch, I would make sure I never ever forget what these monsters are capable of. Kole grabbed my shoulder and pulled me away. There was nothing that needed to be said, but I knew neither of us would ever forget this night.

We went back to the room and held each other in silence. I wonder if he was second-guessing the alliance with Gio as much as I was. I hated to admit it, but the warning Odin delivered in Midselium always had a way of creeping back to the forefront.

The guilt washed over me, but it was something I could not ignore. Was Kole doing this all for power? Was he willing to let Gio hurt anyone just so we could get my home back? Was there a subconscious part of him that will always seek out the path to obtain more strength? And the question that would literally keep me up at night, could he really shapeshift? A smile spread across my face.

"What has you smiling all of a sudden?" Kole asked.

"Nothing, just wondering when you are going to grow wings and fly me out of this mess," I put my head on his chest and closed my eyes.

"Soon, my love, very soon," he said. We laid there not sure if sleep would come after the events of this night.

Ω

Over the next couple of days, we made preparations to sail to Perseus. The ride wouldn't be long, but none of us knew when we would be comfortable again.

Our lives consisted of traveling, hunting our own food, and sleeping on the ground. The conditions didn't make me feel like a queen-to-be. The only caveat was that I was getting closer and closer to my goal day by day.

It felt good to think about going back home. I've spent so much time amongst the Norse, if Gio didn't remind me every five seconds I would have forgotten I was a Roman myself. The idea of a parlay with Marcus was a slap to the face, but I would do anything to keep him from hurting Floria. Even if we didn't manage to win the war, I had to save my sister. The ravens from Lundr informed us that the armies were on their way, so the time was now.

At nightfall, Rollo and Kare with the help of some of the servants carried our belongings to the boat. I wanted to help instead of playing nice with Gio, but Kole convinced me it was polite to acknowledge our host before you leave. And leaving without a thank you would not be a great way to start the alliance. It made me sick to walk up to this tacky ass throne; the sooner it was out of my sight, the better.

"*Make yourself presentable, Octavia,*" I could hear my mother's voice in my head almost bringing tears back to my eyes.

"Thank you for your hospitality. It was nothing less than eventful," Kole gave him a slight bow.

"You're right, it was eventful, wasn't it? Until that bitch crashed my party, but at least the food was included," he laughed. I wanted to slap that smile right off his face.

"If you two are done with the chit-chat, we should get going. We can expect you to follow the plan once you get the signal from Rollo, correct?" I asked.

"Of course, we are in this together, my friends. The King of Lundr, the future Queen of Alexandria, and little old me. It's the only way I can get a seat at the table." Kole and I looked at each other clearly tired of the theatrics.

"Spare me the speech, just be there, okay?"

"Lightning boy signals and I'll be there," he nodded his head exaggerating the gesture.

"Awesome, now we will see to our leave. Next time we meet hopefully this long nightmare will be over." I didn't bother to say goodbye, I just turned and walked out hoping I never had to see this hole in the mountain ever again.

Ω

After a short hike down the mountain, we made it back to our boat. It was gigantic, and I would never get used to it. Covered in the best wood you could find, the gold and black runes danced across the surface. I couldn't read them, but Kole assured me they were runes of protection on the hull and the raven sigil on all the sails.

Anyone could see us coming from a mile away, especially Marcus, but that was the plan. I've had some time to think about the idea of going to him willingly, and Rollo really did have an amazing plan. Marcus was arrogant enough to believe that he would have us in a corner.

Kole and I made ourselves comfortable on the backside of the boat. Rollo and Kare sat across from us. The company raised the sails, grabbed their hoars, and pushed away from the coast. I can't believe I was going home, and I suddenly felt so nervous.

"Are we going to talk about what we are going to do when we attempt to parlay with that tyrant?" I asked.

No one was quick to answer which only made me more nervous. I was under the assumption that we had a game plan with this.

"The more I think about it, the less comfortable I am with you going into the city. How do you know he won't kill you both as soon as you get there?" Kare asked.

She was right. Marcus tried to take me out once already, but his crew ruined that plan. Now that I was aware of what he was doing, he would need a different tactic. The assassination didn't work, but I know he was too clever to not have a backup plan.

"We have that to our advantage. All of Gracia thinks that the oldest princess of Alexandria is dead. Once we show them that you are alive, he would lose the love of the people. If he killed us in the villa," Kole said.

"All you have to do is keep him talking and give us enough time to get into position," Rollo said.

While I agreed that Marcus wouldn't benefit from killing us on sight, he could do other things to make this uncomfortable. The real question was: how long could I hold keep my temper in check?

"How are we supposed to get any intel back to you guys once we get inside? He isn't going to let us just roam the city freely," I asked.

Rollo started rubbing his hands in his beard, pondering the question, which gave me no confidence.

"Are you telling me that you did not plan for that at all, Rollo?" I asked nervously, trying not to freak out.

"I assumed you had a way of getting a message out, there has to be someone you can trust," he said jokingly.

"I haven't been back there since they kidnapped me and killed my family. I'm pretty far removed, don't you think?" I snapped.

Rollo put his head down, and I knew he didn't know how to respond. I know he was just trying to help, and I shouldn't have snapped at him that way, but if we were trapped in the villa on some pretend mission for parlay, we needed to have a way to get a message to our allies on the outside.

"I have an idea," Kare interrupted. We were going in circles so anyone that had a suggestion was welcome to share it. "I can pose as Octavia's handmaiden. Since you are going to be married to my brother, me being Norse won't be suspicious. I should be able to move around as I please, seeing as I will need to retrieve anything you will need," she explained.

I looked at Kole to try to gauge what his response was going to be. I know he didn't mind walking into this danger but putting his little sister in the lion's den was not a part of the original plan. I was sure that he was going to refuse.

"That plan is actually good," Kole said. I turned to him so fast that my head almost flew off my shoulders, I can't believe he was going to agree with this.

"You need to do everything Octavia says, this is a dangerous land. There is a lot we do not know about the enemy, you need to be on your toes," Kole said.

“I will, brother. This plan will work and, while you two play royalty, I’ll slip a raven out to Rollo and pass along any information we can get,” Kare said.

We spent the rest of the day going over some of the tiny specifics but this plan was coming together great. This was our best chance at doing this without a ton of bloodshed. We have all lost enough up to this point, I don’t think anyone was ready to lose any more so soon.

Ω

The sun began to set, and the crew was raising the sail; it let us drift through the night so they could rest. We should be in Perseus in a day or two. I suppose I should be excited to be back, but everything that has happened left a gruesome stain on the idea of a homecoming. I had no idea who I could trust. I had no idea who else was involved in overthrowing my family, and how long they harbored those ill feelings against us. I know Marcus and Halfdan were the orchestrators, but they didn’t do it alone, that much is clear. I should thank Mars they didn’t because I would most likely be dead. Whoever botched the plan to kidnap me was a blessing in disguise.

It was a bright evening with no clouds in the sky and the moon was full, illuminating the river. It looked like it was so close that you could grab it right out of the sky, but you could never hold something so powerful.

If we were to believe Ambrogio, the moon belonged to him. His long-lost love Selene is watching over the world every night. Kole’s chest was rising and falling underneath my head and the water was so quiet that I could hear his low breathing.

We had to enjoy these small moments of peace whenever they come.

"I can feel you running laps in your mind," Kole startled me. He was talking with his eyes closed.

"I thought you were sleeping," I told him.

"I was sleeping, but I could hear you overthinking all the way in my subconscious. You're really anxious, I can feel it," he said calmly.

"Sorry, but I have so many different feelings about going back. I have so much to fight for, but I built a life with you in Lundr, and while I want my old life back, I feel conflicted about risking my new one," I admitted.

"I know that I will never have all of you if we do not see this through. You will live in regret wondering if you made the right choice staying with me after I found you," he said.

I knew he was right. Most of my family was gone, but Floria was still alive, and I knew she needed me. Even if I had to spend the next decade apologizing for taking so long to come back to her, I would do it just to be with her again. The things she must have endured gripped my heart; my only hope was that there was something left of her beautiful soul.

"There is something that we need to talk about... because if Marcus is the type of man I think he is, we need to make sure we are on the same page," he rubbed his fingers up and down my arm.

"What do you mean?" I asked curiously.

"From what we know and what we have seen, it's clear that Marcus is full of himself. He believes he is a god, and while we will arrive as united as a couple, he will do everything he can to separate us," he spoke softly and gently rubbed the strands of my hair.

"It doesn't matter what he says, he could never come between us," I turned so he could see how serious I am. He just started to smile.

"I don't mean he will come between us, but as a man that's looking to assert his dominance, he will seek to test me. How, I don't know, but you have to promise me you won't lose your temper," he was still smiling clearly amused.

"I'm more than capable of keeping my cool, Kole, no need to worry," I rolled my eyes and laid my head on his chest.

"Of course, you can," he was speaking sarcastically, "in all seriousness, he is going to try to get a rise out of us by testing me as a man and specifically a king. Law dictates no guest should be harmed when granted hospitality under a parlay so we can't give him any reason to try to sway the rules."

"I will be fine, Kole, don't worry. I won't kill him until it's time to kill him."

"That's my girl," he kissed my forehead, "now get some sleep." I let the calm current of the river rock me to sleep. Marcus was a nightmare, but I was not going to lose sleep over him any longer. His days were numbered.

9 - WHO THE HELL ARE YOU? - OCTAVIA

"Wake up Tav!" Kare was shaking me, but my body was fighting for just a few more minutes. Sleeping on this boat was a step up from the stone floor in that cave but not by much. It would be an amazing step up when I get back to a bed. I may not leave that type of comfort for a year.

"We are about to dock in Perseus, this place is beautiful," Kare was hanging over the edge of the boat.

I wiped my eyes and tried to situate the knots in my hair, but that was going to require way more attention. I could smell the air and knew I was home, the nervous feeling I had leading up to this washing away.

The sky was a dark red tone that swept over the skyline, I'm not sure I would have noticed it if I didn't spend so much time in Lundr. The sun was high, and the heat was stifling, but it was familiar to me. It was the reason most citizens wore linen robes instead of the tunics the Norse wear. The closer we got to the port, I could smell fresh fish being cut in the market, the fruity sting in your nose from grapes being crushed, and the black smoke from the blacksmith forge. I hated myself for even considering not coming back here, being this close to my home.

I felt more powerful the minute we sailed into this space, a feeling that was faint in Lundr. The flame felt like it was blossoming from that tiny ember to a steady fire.

The boat was positioned to dock, and I could tell Rollo and Kole were on edge. Being foreigners here, their eyes were skimming back and forth every second checking for anything that could cause a problem for us.

The energy here was off but nothing that seemed out of the ordinary, though they were right to be cautious with Delphi on the loose. We had no idea when she would make a move again. She doesn't know about our alliance, so we should be in the clear, but better safe than sorry.

I wonder how far Gio has traveled since we left; he needed to be in Perseus by the time Rollo was ready to leave. A demon on the loose would never sit right with me, especially since I couldn't see what he was doing. No need to stress about that right now. We needed to navigate carefully. Word would reach Marcus about our arrival soon enough and I intended to go to the busiest tavern and make sure that the people see me.

The alleged kidnapped princess is alive and well. Someone would bring this rumor back to Marcus, and by the time I get to the gates of Alexandria, he won't be able to turn me away without losing the fragile support of the people. The company took our things off the boat and loaded them onto a cart while the four of us walked ahead.

"So, where are we going to stay?" Kare asked.

"My father used to tell me about a tavern in the town that welcomes both Norse and Romans. We should be able to blend in no problem," I answered. Kole and Rollo looked at each other again like they knew something that I didn't.

"What's wrong with you two?" I asked.

"Nothing, it just feels weird to be back here, that's all. This is where Kole and I stopped before we headed up to Midselium," Rollo was stumbling over his words.

"This is where I found your daggers. I assume Titus sold them to the blacksmith before meeting with Ivar to give him the map," Kole said.

"Great. Well since you two have been here, let's stay in the same place you did." They just stared at me in silence, and I was starting to get annoyed.

"What are you not telling me because you two have been acting weird ever since we got here?"

"Nothing, that place just isn't very ladylike that's all, no place for a queen and a princess," Rollo said.

"I'll be the judge of that. Let's go, I'm tired of standing on this dock," I let them take the lead.

Ω

Like every Roman town, it was full of traders and travelers. Fresh meats and bread were displayed on all the carts, women hassled us as we walked by trying to get us to purchase jewelry and perfumes. I don't remember the last time I wore either, except for the arm ring Kole gave me before we left Lundr. I made sure that I walked through the outpost with my hood down. I wanted to make sure I was visible to everyone.

Anyone here could start a rumor about the prodigal daughter that has come back from the dead. We made a left past a statue of Perseus, the roman hero that this town was named after. He was the bastard son of Jupiter or Zeus, whatever name you decided to use. Why this town was named after him I do not know. We headed towards the edge of the town as the giant building came into view. It was taller than any of the other buildings here, I'm surprised we couldn't see it when we arrived. There was a sign wrapped in vines out front.

"Persephone's Garden?" I said out loud. "This is where you stayed?"

"Yup, this is where we stayed. Perfect place for a couple of warriors to relax before a journey that was probably going to end with us being dead," Rollo laughed.

There was something familiar about the name Persephone. It kept replaying in my head, but I could not remember why. We walked through the front door, the inside was decorated from the ceiling to the floor. The tables lined up were full of travelers, warriors, and patrons all mingling together. It was something I have never seen with my eyes, only through the words of my father's stories. The tables were painted with bright vibrant colors. Vines and flowers followed the trim around the room, it was a beautiful setup.

The candles were burning dim and servants were carrying wine, bread, and cheese. My stomach started to growl. I didn't realize how hungry I was.

As soon as I walked in the door, it felt like all my problems and stresses just washed away. All I wanted to do was grab a seat and have a drink. Luckily, a table was wide open against the back wall with plenty of room for us.

The four of us made our way to the table. Kole and I sat on one side and Rollo and Kare on the other, and we waited to be served. Kole's eyes kept scanning the room like he was waiting for something to happen. Ever since we got here, he was unable to relax.

“Are you okay?” I asked him. Before he could answer, a woman walked up to the table, smiling like we had made her day.

“Welcome to Persephone’s, can I interest you in some food or wine?” Before we could answer, her eyes landed on Rollo.

“Look who came back to visit us. How are you, pretty eyes?” Kare and I turned and waited for his answer and, as soon as she was gone, an explanation.

“I’m great, feels good to be back. We will have some food and wine, please.” He turned back to us trying to hide the awkwardness.

“Wow, you must have left an impression while you were here, Rollo,” Kare laughed.

“Nothing crazy, she is just showing great hospitality,” Rollo tried to laugh it off.

“What did you show her to receive such great hospitality?” I couldn’t hold in my laughter.

“I’m a man of the people, okay Octavia. These pretty eyes will be the death of me,” he said.

“There are so many other things that will kill you first,” Kole said.

The woman returned with the food and the wine and placed everything on the table in the back.

"If you need anything, just call me over. If you decide to stay, talk to the girl next to the steps, she can provide you lodgings," the woman gave a slight bow and returned to the crowd.

"Thank you," I said to the girl as she skipped her way back through the crowd.

Ω

Without delay, we filled our plates with bread and cheese and all our cups with wine. There was no disrespect to Najora and the Norse, but there was nothing like food made here. The bread was baked crispy on the outside, yet soft on the inside, lightly topped with various spices that are harvested right here in our fields. The wine was perfect. It had a fruity aftertaste, and it was kept at the perfect temperature. I know I had a job to do but why couldn't I just stay here forever?

The others were enjoying themselves, pouring more and more wine. It was never-ending, I couldn't even remember why we were here. All I wanted to do was let loose and be free and this felt like the place to do it. I looked over towards Kole. He was finally relaxed, sharing a laugh with his sister. I could stare at his smile for hours, everything about him was perfect.

I could get lost in his presence. My eyes started to sweep over him. He wore his light vest to hold his weapons and nothing else under it. His arms were covered in tattoos, the Norse staff and the ravens that trailed all the way to his shoulders.

I don't know why all of this was hitting me at once, but I didn't care. All I could think about is him, so I reached over to him and pulled his lips down to mine. He tasted like wine, the sweet fruit lingered on his tongue as he returned the kiss instantly. Rollo and Kare sat across from us looking on with wide eyes when we broke away from the kiss. Thank the gods they were there because who knows how far I would have gone if they weren't.

"I'm sorry, I don't know what came over me," I explained. I have no idea why I did that in front of them. Something about this place was messing with me, and I couldn't figure out why.

"It's okay, maybe a heads-up next time. I'm not in the business of watching my brother do his thing," Kare laughed.

How long have we been sitting here? The time, the laughs, the food, and even the drinks seemed endless. I had no concept of how long we have been stuck in this spot. My mind was full of fog and ignorant bliss. I didn't want to know the answers to the questions, all I wanted to do was enjoy my future husband and show them how amazing my home is.

"But this is not your home, your home was taken from you," the voice pierced my ears from every direction.

"Did you hear that?" I asked everyone at the table.

"No, we were talking about your over-the-top public display before you zoned out," Rollo said

"Don't be weak, child, focus your mind," the voice was smashing into my head once again. I couldn't focus, there was too much going on, but the voice was trying to tell me something. From my experience, it was most likely something that would save my life.

I got up from the table and made my way to the door. I needed the chaos to quiet down so I could focus. I was almost at the door when a woman jumped in front of me to block my path. It was the woman who brought our drinks to the table. My eyes were drawn to her smile, she had an aura that seemed to pull me toward her. As much as I wanted to back away something was keeping me in her presence.

"Going so soon? You have only scratched the surface of Persephone's Garden," she spoke as more of a demand. Her voice had a certain pull to it.

"I'm okay, just looking to get some air," I tried to walk around her, but she stepped in my path again.

"You're here with the delicious Norsemen from before. I could never forget them so strong and wild, they have such a forbidden beauty about them," she smiled and looked past me to the table. Whatever I was planning on doing went right out the window when I heard her words.

"What do you know about how strong and wild they are?" I could feel the heat building coursing down to my hands. Everyone had some explaining to do before I lose my temper.

"Well, I know the brown skin one with all of the tattoos is a beautiful prince," she said. Before she finished my dagger was at her throat.

"You might want to watch what you say next, I'm kind of on the edge right now." The woman wasn't frightened, I think her smile got bigger the harder I pressed the blade to her throat. Like she was feeding off my anger.

"I told him if he ever came back, I would not let him leave again. Maybe he enjoyed our time more than he would like to admit," her smirk was infuriating.

"What the fuck are you talking about? Who are you?"

"Poor girl, and you call yourself a Roman, you don't even know what you have walked into," she started laughing uncontrollably; it was sinister and evil.

I pushed past her and ran outside. I needed to figure out where I was so I could get us out of this mess, and then I will deal with the lying Norse sitting at the table laughing and having a good time.

Kole better have an excuse the size of Mount Olympus, because if anything less and we can end this journey right now after I kill him.

"Think child, stop playing games," the voice rang out again.

"What games? I'm trying to remember but the truth is covered under too much," patrons walking by were staring at me because I was clearly talking to myself.

"Well, burn it down till you get to the solution." I closed my eyes and grabbed hold of the fire. I had to see things clearly, whatever I was missing was right in front of me hidden behind all of this distraction.

"Think, you know the name, now piece together the story," the voice rumbled in my head again, but this time it was calmer, and I could tell who it was.

Mars was trying to warn me. It was him all along, he must be stronger in our lands. What name was he talking about? I dug deeper. I had to find what I was missing and like a slingshot, the answer smacked me right in the face.

"Persephone!" I said out loud.

Persephone was a goddess that was kidnapped by Hades and forced to marry him. She was forced to stay in the underworld and could never return to Olympus, but according to some stories, Hades was a terrible husband and spent so much time away from the underworld, she was basically his prisoner.

To entertain herself, she would have warriors visit her in the underworld and give them flowers that they could crush to return to the mortal world. The problem is Persephone was beautiful and insatiable, most warriors never wanted to leave. What they did not know is that if you spend too much time in the underworld, you can never leave.

The soldiers were trapped after spending three days with Persephone, and word around the underworld spreads fast. Persephone's guests were always found by Hades and dealt the most unbearable punishment.

This is her garden in our world. This is where she picks out her next victims, and the longer they stay, the more likely they are to be caught in her web. She uses the sirens to do so, they dull your senses and keep you drawn in. It makes sense, the sirens fed on everything, every emotion inside this tavern.

That's why I lost so much time here. The goal is to make sure we don't leave. It also tells me that Persephone may have had male and female lovers, which was a completely separate issue to be pondered another day.

I looked up at the sky and it was pitch black outside. We have been here for hours, and it didn't feel nearly that long while I was inside with the others. I ran back inside. I needed to snap everyone out of it before I punch my fiancé in the face for not telling me about this mysterious woman. Only Kole and Kare were at the table when I got back

"Where is Rollo?" I was almost out of breath from fighting my way through the crowd.

"He went up to his room to get some sleep, I didn't want to leave here until you came back," Kole said. I was having a hard time not flipping out on him every second I was in this place.

"We need to warn him, this place isn't safe."

"What do you mean?" Kare must have drunk too much wine, she could barely sit up.

"How many nights were you here the first time?" I grabbed Kole by the vest, and I could tell he was getting worried. "How many?" I was raising my voice now.

"It was one night. Rollo, Ivar, and I stayed one night and left the next day."

"Are you sure Kole? This is life or death."

"I'm sure, I did lose some time briefly but I'm sure it was one night," he said. "What do you mean life or death?"

"This place belongs to a goddess named Persephone, and she uses it to lure warriors back to the underworld so she can trap them, use them, and give them over to her husband Hades when she is done," I explained.

"So that's why I didn't want to leave the first time I was here," he put his hand through his hair. His calm understanding was only infuriating me more.

“I met your little girlfriend on my way outside, you want to tell me what was so amazing that you didn’t want to leave the first time?” I couldn’t stop thinking about how hard I wanted to punch him.

“I will explain how I was tricked by this place, but we should go get Rollo, and then we need to get out of here.” He was trying to get up, but I held him down in his seat.

“Rollo will be fine, you have to stay here for three nights before you are eventually stuck here, so if you’re telling me the truth then he will be fine.” I was waiting to see what his reaction would be, but he remained calm.

“I was warned the last time I was here by that woman, but this time I was prepared. Even though we only stayed one night, I think we should find another place to stay,” he said.

“We can’t leave now, your sister can barely stand, and you already let Rollo go and enjoy himself, so now we are stuck here. While we have time, you can tell me what happened between you and that woman.” I crossed my arms and waited for a response.

“In my defense, this was before I even knew you existed.” He was smiling but this was so far from a joke to me.

“Don’t play games with me, Kole. It doesn’t matter, you could have mentioned it before I stepped foot in this awful place,” I interrupted.

The longer he took to respond, the more agitated I got, but honestly, I’m not sure I even want to know. The thought of him being with other women before me wasn’t the problem, it’s the fact that it was this woman in my face taunting me about something that I had no knowledge of. I was pissed and embarrassed. I needed answers, and we weren't going anywhere until I got them.

"I'll explain everything that happened while I was here, but let's take Kare and find a room where we can talk and get some rest," he said. We gathered our things from the table and spoke with the woman next to the steps. She showed us up to one of the vacant rooms and left us alone for the night.

10 - It Is Not What It Looks Like - Kole

Every time this place came up in a discussion, I knew that I was going to have to face this at some point. I wanted to have a good time but Octavia was right, I should have mentioned what happened the first time I was here. Persephone trying to add warriors to her lineup made so much more sense. She used the women here, sirens as Octavia described them, to keep us entertained with food and drink, luring people through the simple pleasures of life.

I spent almost the entire night trying to explain to Octavia what happened the first time I stayed in Persephone's, her body language the entire time was frightening. I was not sure if she would try to tear my head off, light my body on fire, or both. She was clearly unhappy about everything that occurred, but she knew that I was technically held captive here against my will.

The All-father came to me and he saved me because otherwise I would have probably been captured. In hindsight, he only saved me so that his end game could remain intact, but I wasn't about to look a gift horse in the mouth. Either way, I was walking on a tight rope and one word would send me tumbling over.

"I'm sure that this isn't something that you like to find out, let alone in this way, and I should have told you. For that, I am sorry," I soothed and tried to bring her close to me with a hug as she placed her hand in the middle of my chest, essentially stopping me.

"You could have told me, but you decided to hide this. Now is not the time for secrets."

"In my defense, I didn't know what I was dealing with. If it wasn't for Odin, I would have never made it out," I stressed.

"Did you like it?" she asked, and I knew that I should never answer a question like this, but I had no way out.

"Is there any way to answer this without you hitting me?" I asked.

"I'm going to hit you regardless, this determines how hard and how many times." I still couldn't tell if she was joking or not.

"I was under a spell, so none of it was real, and as soon as I realized what was happening, I got rid of her." I avoided the question but what else could I say?

I tried to move closer to her and she responded with her fist, but behind the punch was a smile.

"Out of all the relationship problems we could have, I have to find out an ancient goddess is trying to capture my husband before I even get to meet him," she teased. "I guess I should be flattered."

It looked like I was making some steps towards being back in her good graces. We couldn't have anything between us that Marcus could use, we had to be perfect.

Kare was laying down in the small bed in the corner of the room. She fell asleep as soon as her body hit the bed. I wasn't going to mention to my mother how much I let her drink, I would never hear the end of it.

Octavia was getting comfortable for bed. I walked over to make sure Kare had furs to cover her. I couldn't believe how much she had grown in such little time. I needed to protect her, but at some point, she was going to have to look out for herself.

In Alexandria, she was going to be a handmaiden to Octavia. No one can find out the truth of our relationship or it would be used against us. The plan was dangerous, but it was all we had. I kissed my sister on the forehead as she slept peacefully.

I climbed into the bed and nestled up next to my future wife and queen. I could see the weight of the coming days was sitting heavy on her shoulders, exactly where she kept all of her other problems.

"Are you okay?" I asked. She took a while to answer, like she was analyzing all the different ways this could go wrong.

"I'm not sure what I am. Ever since that vision on the road to Midselium, I have been dying to come home, but now that I'm here, I don't know how to feel," she muttered and rolled over in the bed to face me. "Do you really think we have a chance at taking the city back?" she asked. It was a valid question. We could only assume that Marcus has been able to fortify the city by now, not to mention sway the people towards his cause. However, they didn't know the rightful queen was alive, and I was going to do everything in my power to show them.

"I think we do, all we need to do is stay together and stick to the plan and we can't lose. Don't look at me crazy when I say this, but we have some gods on our side." It was an awful silver lining, but a lot of Odin's and Mar's plans were tied to our success.

"No matter what."

"No matter what," I repeated.

I pressed my lips against hers and I could still taste the hint of fruit and the warmth of wine on her lips. She was mine and nothing in this world or the next would stop us from making her whole again. I couldn't wait to meet the girl she was before life steered her into nothing but tragedy.

She rested her arm on my side, her hands cool to the touch. I listened to her breath softly and steadily until she dozed off, and a few moments later I followed.

Ω

The sunlight peaked through the window and landed directly in my face. I felt well-rested, but I could easily take some more sleep. Octavia and Kare were still sound asleep. The day ahead of us would be strenuous, so I decided not to wake them.

I strapped on my vest, grabbed my axe, and left a note for Kare on my way out of the room. I needed to check on Rollo and make sure he was okay. I needed to fill him in on the new developments, first one being that he needed to find a new place to stay or he would be a prisoner in a Roman underworld. His room was a couple of doors down. I decided to knock this time and he answered quickly. He was alone, just like last time with a smile on his face. He walked across the room to pour himself a glass of water.

"Good morning."

“Good morning... I assume that your evening was enjoyable,” I replied not knowing how else to describe it.

“It was almost better than the first time. See then, I was caught off guard but this time I was prepared. These halls will remember my name, they should build a statue of me in this place,” he joked with mirth in his voice as he prepared for the day.

I decided that this was the best time to tell him that his dreams of being a figure in Persephone’s would end in him being a captive in the underworld. When I was done telling him about the warning, he seemed completely fine taking everything in stride but he wouldn’t stop smiling.

“What about this entire situation is funny, Rollo? I’m curious.” I knew I would regret the question as soon as it left my lips.

“So, you mean to tell me that the goddess heard about my exploits and decided, out of all of these warriors in this country, I am the one she wants to be locked in her underworld love dungeon?” he laughed.

“I honestly don’t know why I was expecting any other response from you,” we laughed together and made our way back downstairs.

Persephone’s was still alive even in the early hours of the morning. Warriors, soldiers, and travelers were already drinking. I couldn’t help but wonder how many of them would never leave this place.

We walked back down to the docks to check on the company, the outpost had barracks along the docks for them to sleep. Rollo and I wanted to know if there were any word from the army on the way. The captain had a letter from the three armies presently making their way to the city, the plan was still on track. Octavia, Kare, and I would be able to leave to sail to Alexandria tonight.

"So, run me through what we need to do next. This is your plan." I turned to Rollo.

"You sure do ask a lot of questions for a king. Maybe that crown is squeezing your brain too tightly," he joked.

"I'm not even wearing a crown, Rollo. Whenever you're done joking around, can you please explain to me how we plan to avoid this blowing up in our faces?" I crossed my arms over my chest.

"Relax, my friend. You and Octavia will leave to sail to parlay with Marcus in Alexandria while we get into position. When Kare gives us the information from the inside, we will position ourselves around the city to catch him off guard. I will lead an army on foot, following Gio who will disable any scouts and camps we come across in the night so that we remain undetected."

He pulled out a map of Gracia. I didn't even know that he had one. I've never seen my best friend so invested in anything. He was almost excited, and the determination made me so proud. He was going to be a great king when this was all said and done.

"We will cut off the supplies between this city and the island below, then when we get the signal from you, we can take him by surprise from all sides," he explained.

“How do you know that you will be able to come at him from the island below? What if they are still loyal to him?” I asked, and his response was just another amused smile.

“I will take care of that. Octavia told me that Marcus killed the king of that island the night he planned the attack on her villa. Once the people learn the truth about our plan to take him down, they should help, or at least provide passage to the bottom half of the city,” he stood back and admired his plan on the map.

I had to hand it to him, the plan was the best chance we had at this moment, not to mention the only one that made sense. I still didn’t trust Gio, but our motives are temporarily aligned. If I could find Delphi first, she would be more than happy to tell me about his weaknesses and having that information would be helpful if he ever decided to cross us.

“Let’s do this brother. We are one step closer to ending this and going back home,” Rollo stressed sounding how I felt, that this must work for the good of everyone we love and care about.

“Prepare the boats, we will be leaving for Alexandria at midday.” I shook his hand and headed back up to the tavern. It was time to take Octavia home. Octavia and Kare were awake and packing up their things.

“Rollo and I went over the final details of the plan, prepare to depart at midday for Alexandria.” I was waiting for her to agree, though I had no clue where her head is at this morning. No doubt she still has a vicious cycle of thoughts and feelings running rampant in her mind, keeping her anxiety as high as I've felt it each day we've gotten closer to her home.

She took a couple of deep breaths then secured her daggers in the holster on her thigh, the gold gems beaming under the sunlight.

"We need supplies and Kare needs Roman clothes to pass for a handmaiden," she responded calmly.

"Really?! I'm so excited, the clothes look so comfortable!" Kare beamed, almost jumping up off her seat.

"No problem, we can buy some provisions on our way to the boat," I told her.

"And one more thing Kole," Octavia called out, making me pause.

"What is it?" I asked.

"We need to bring a gift as a sign of good faith during the parlay."

"Damn, and here I thought my axe in his throat would be the greatest gift," I tried to hold in my sarcasm, but I was failing miserably. "Don't worry, love. I don't have a problem presenting a gift. This plan is all about achieving our goal, after all. He won't rattle us."

Ω

I didn't know what we would need on the trip, but I decided to think about what was important. I grabbed two of everything, which was my way of covering the necessities. I let Octavia and Kare handle the gift for Marcus. I saw them enter the blacksmith hut then after that head to the dressmaker. I was on the boat helping the company secure everything to the hull. We would be leaving as soon as the girls get back to the docks.

I walked over to Rollo and hugged him. At first, he tensed up. I thought I would have years to grow old with my father, but days later he was gone. Life was short, even for royalty, so I needed to make sure we had nothing lingering between us.

"May I ask why you are hugging me? Did I miss something?" His arms were sitting loosely at his sides.

"Stop talking for two seconds, Rollo. If the gods will it, we will see each other soon enough, but I would be a fool to believe there was no risk." He understood what I was saying. His shoulders eased and he brought his arms up to hug me back just as fiercely.

"The gods claim to be with us, but we are carving out our own destiny. We will succeed, and if we don't the great hall is prepared for us both, brother." We reluctantly broke the hug. I wouldn't choose anyone else to back me up at. At one time, it would have been my brother to have my back, but the guilt of Kyut's betrayal came and went like the vicious tide during a full moon.

I considered my punishment lenient because what he did was punishable by death. He was my blood and he spit in that blood for pride and a false sense of honor. Regardless, Rollo was constant and loyal, and I trusted him with my life.

Kare and Octavia walked onto the dock. All eyes turned in their direction. Kare was dressed like a Roman; it was so foreign to me but, in a way, she wore it as naturally as Octavia.

She wore a light green robe that hung loose on the shoulders. It was looser than I normally approved of, but she seemed comfortable. The robe ran all the way down to her feet, gold trim lining the outside. Her curls were sitting perfectly, as they always did. I noticed the two gold clips that kept the curls out of her face. She stopped at the beginning of the dock and smiled. It was clear that she approved of the clothing.

"What do you think, do I look like a proper Roman woman?" She opened her arms and gave us a spin.

"You look like you need more clothes," I complained shamelessly.

"And what is wrong with her clothes?" Octavia was right behind her wearing the dress I had made for her back in Lundr.

My eyes were fixated on the sigil that was to be ours after we get married. I still remember the first time I saw her put it on, when I asked her to spend the rest of her life with me and she agreed. The axe and spear sigil bounced right off the fabric just as fierce as the fire dancing in her eyes.

"She fits in perfectly, all she has to do is follow my lead, and since she needs to wait on me at all times, I can keep an eye on her," she reassured. She was carrying something wrapped in a golden fleece I assumed it was the gift for King Marcus.

"Did you take a visit to the stables and shovel what the king deserves into the fleece?" I could only hope someone shared my thoughts.

"I purchased the best spearhead I could find from the blacksmith. It is made from a precious metal trimmed in gold, in my opinion a very suitable gift." Octavia wrapped the spearhead back into the fleece.

"You both look amazing. Don't listen to Kole, he never knows how to conduct himself around beautiful women," Rollo smiled.

"Are you done talking out of your ass Rollo?" I laughed as I rolled my eyes.

"I've been around you before you were king of Lundr, don't forget that," he reminded me.

"I'll see all of you soon, the plan will work, and we will see this through. I gods will it and, most of all, we will it." He grabbed us all and we shared a group hug.

Octavia, Kare, and I boarded the boat. The company pushed off from the dock. We were sailing right into the enemy's hands. I had no idea what to expect, but we wouldn't fail. It wasn't an option. The gods had their own reasons for us to succeed but this meant so much more to me.

I understood why Octavia was so amazed by Najora because Gracia was completely opposite. It was clear that we lived in completely different worlds. No offense, as beautiful as Gracia is, I can tell I'm nowhere near home anymore. The water was rough and dark, almost black depending on how the light was touching it.

The horizon was eerily dark, almost a blood orange. That deep color lingered over the fields full of dry leaves the same color as the sky that skipped across the coast to the rhythm of the wind.

Octavia was standing up at the front of the boat staring out into the water; I could feel her tapping into the fire before her hands gave off a slight glow. I didn't know what to say. I remember how I felt when I was so close to my revenge, but this situation was far more complicated.

“Are you okay? Your hands are glowing,” I pointed out.

“I’m fine but something is wrong, like the essence here has been sucked out.” Her hands started to glow brighter. “Look what he has done to this place. The fields were full of life, colorful flowers that grew all along the river. Animals joined together for food and boats traveled in and out of the city keeping the trade alive. Now, all I see is a barren land, and all I feel is Marcus choking the beauty out of my home.” She never took her eyes off the horizon as she spoke.

About an hour later, we arrived in the bay of Alexandria, and I could not believe what I was seeing. It wasn’t a city I would ever want to visit. It was in ruin.

11 - The False King - Octavia

He has destroyed it. My home, the legacy that my family built after the war, has succumbed to this ruin, and it was one of the worst things I have ever seen.

The Sirius banner used to hang above the docks to welcome all the ships that entered the city. Now, it was replaced with the Bellator banner. He stripped away our existence. I couldn't find any piece of myself in this place. All of it completely washed away and it was all my fault. I lost a fight, and losing it claimed my brother, my sister, and my home.

The emotions were getting the best of me, it was so hard to accept this, everything about this place was completely foreign to me. The very identity stripped away by the imposters that claim to be its savior.

We docked at the port but before we could walk off the boat, soldiers were blocking our path into the market. Lightning bolts covered their shields and breastplates.

"No time to prepare. Marcus knows we are here. We all know our parts, let's make this happen." Kole's rendition of a motivational speech would have to do for now. He was the first to address the soldiers. Kare and I followed close behind him.

"Stop where you are and state your business." I recognized the voice as it was the same one that tormented Floria and I anytime they were in our presence.

The demon spawn of the imposter that was sitting on my father's throne. I stepped from behind Kole so I could see his face when his eyes glanced past Kole and connected with mine. His body went rigid once his gaze fell upon me, almost as if he was staring at a ghost.

"Greetings Lucius, you look like you've seen Hades himself. It's been a long time, but it feels good to be home," I smiled. It took him a second to gather his thoughts, but I was certain that he was already aware I was alive.

"Octavia, bless the gods you are back, we thought that you were taken prisoner and killed by the Norse. So why do you sail here with one by your side?" Lucius asked cautiously.

"This Norse is to be my husband, but I'm here to talk about a parlay for peace with your father. I assume he is still in charge. Would you be a nice soldier and take us to him please? Look, we even brought him a gift." I presented the golden fleece and opened it so he could see what was inside. I was trying to remember the passive gestures my mother would make when she didn't want to be bothered.

"A generous gift indeed. Follow us up to the villa, your men can rest in the barracks down by the docks."

"Thank you, soldier," Kole said.

"I'm a general, Norsemen!" Lucius snapped in return. Kole held up his hands in defeat with a smile on his face. He was enjoying this way too much.

We took the path through the market. The trek was so depressing. It used to be full of life, laughter, and trade. Now, it was a barren ghost town. Only certain shops remained open, and the streets were riddled with homeless residents picking food off the ground and kids with skin gripping their bones from not eating. The sight of it pulled at my heart.

The commotion drew our attention to the center of the market. A Roman trader had men, women, and even children in a single file line with restraints around their necks and ankles. He was walking them up on the stage one by one. If I understood what was happening correctly, he would take payment from the highest bidder. I heard rumors of the slave trade, but I was never alive to see it in person. My father abolished the act in his first few years as king. He believed you could have servants, but they needed to be compensated for whatever service they provided.

Marcus was the kind of man that would consent to this. His need for power and control was the exact reason why he didn't see anything wrong with having slaves. His soldiers are roaming free in the streets, rounding up the homeless. When the citizens weren't moving fast enough, they started to use brute force.

We continued through the market, diving deeper into debauchery and indecency. I watched men, women, and children on the verge of starvation being beaten by soldiers because they had nowhere to go.

My feelings were all over the place, but I never imagined this. He has taken everything that was meaningful in Alexandria and snuffed it out so that he could control it. I was starting to unravel. I wanted him to feel the same pain he caused me and killing both his slimy sons in front of him would be a start. Vengeance was burning holes in the calm façade I was trying to maintain. He was going to pay for what he did to Tiberius one way or another. I felt the fire start to build toward the surface. Everything I was seeing was going to set me off, until I felt a hand rest on my shoulder, and it snapped me out of my own thoughts.

"I know this is torture, but it is not time yet. Your hands are glowing," Kole whispered into my ear. I took a deep breath and attempted to calm my soul at his words.

"Thank you." I thank the gods for him. Even when I felt I was going to topple over and explode, he was always there to center me. He was going to be an amazing husband and king.

The cobblestone road up to the villa wasn't any better. In the alleyways between buildings you could see soldiers laughing, drinking, and forcing themselves on women. They didn't even try to conceal what they were doing. I couldn't hold my tongue any longer.

"You're not going to do anything about the soldiers beating citizens or defiling women in public?" I yelled to Lucius.

"The soldiers have free reign under my father's rule. They deserve to be able to enjoy themselves as long as they keep the city protected." He did not even look back as he spoke.

"The city is covered in filth and blood. I can honestly tell you that they are doing a terrible job," Kole interrupted.

"Who cares about the leeches that live down here, they have been living off the rich for years. The royal family stands above them all and they obey," Lucius responded.

“And now I see why you aren’t king,” Kole said. Lucius stopped the soldiers and turned to face Kole. There was no space between them, their faces practically touching, but it was clear neither would back down. Lucius’s body was tense, clearly agitated from all our remarks. If this was a part of Kole’s plan to play it cool, I was losing hope. We haven’t reached the villa yet and he was already picking a fight.

“I don’t know how you were raised in your country, you dog, but here we have our ways.” This was not good at all. I could feel him reaching for the dark power buried deep inside him. We will never get into the villa if he kills Marcus’ son on the doorstep. I jumped in between them.

“Kole, save your questions for the one in charge,” I tapped his shoulder to calm him down. He flashed that infectious smirk, the one that signaled to me that he was in control. He wanted to poke Lucius and see how far he could go. Evidently, he found the soft spot.

A giant structure caught my eye, something that was not built in the time my father was king. It must have been another of Marcus’ evil additions. I hadn’t seen the villa since the massacre that night. Some of the shops right outside were rebuilt from the fire, but the rest were left to rot as we passed through. The giant doors inside my family’s home were replaced with Bellator banners in every direction. I looked up to the spot where my vision showed me my parent's fate. That sick bastard touched every other part of the villa except that one.

The destroyed Sirius banner was still in the same spot and the spear marks that held their bodies were still carved into the wood. Not killing him on the spot was going to be so much harder than I expected it to be. I was hoping to see some semblance of the home that was stolen from me, but it was all gone.

“Stay here until I inform my father you are here. Then, he will decide where he will receive you,” Lucius stopped us at the villa entrance.

“Make sure you tell him it’s me because this is a reunion to die for,” I tried to hold in my smile. Lucius left the room to retrieve the false king.

“That was an awful joke, it wouldn’t feel right if I didn’t let you know,” Kole said.

“It wasn’t my best okay, I didn’t have a ton of time to cook up a better one, give me a break.” Kole made sure to get all of his laughter out now. I made sure to check every direction to avoid an ambush. I had no idea if the parlay would be honored but it was best that we do not get caught off guard.

Ω

Lucius returned shortly to inform us that the king would be waiting to receive us in the throne room. My memory betrayed me. Everything has changed since I arrived. I wasn’t sure if I remembered how to get to the throne room. Luckily Lucius was leading the way.

Like the rest of the city, the lightning sigil replaced all the spearhead sigils my father displayed. The longer I was here the more enraged I became. Nothing remained but disrespect and neglect. How did these people sleep at night knowing the city was imploding on itself? The villa was barely being taken care of and everything around it was crumbling. When Marcus was done here, he would go back home and leave Alexandria in ruin. Just a pitstop in his plan to conquer the world.

The walk to the throne room was mentally exhausting, I had no idea what to expect. From time to time, Kole would look back at me and make sure I was okay. I hope that everything going on in my head wasn't written all over my face.

We agreed to show a united front and I did not want to be the weak link in the chain, especially if the chain would be directly responsible for our success. Kare walked close behind me. I was impressed with how well she fell into character. No one in the room paid her any attention, which was great. When the time came for her to sneak out and deliver a message, it would go unnoticed.

We reached the council chamber which looks like it has not been used for a long time. The council table was covered in dust and trash all over the floor, more disrespect to the history of this house. I wondered if there is any part of this villa that deserved his attention. The double doors to the throne room flew open and my question was answered. All the city's prosperity was shifted to this one room, the lightning banners hanging in the room were bigger than I had ever seen. Gold place settings were sprinkled all over the small tables in the room, tables that were not here when my father ruled.

The two servants standing at the base of the steps were nude and their entire bodies were painted gold. They avoided eye contact with anyone, which I assume was an order from the tyrant in charge. I felt their pain, embarrassment, and shame.

It was not uncommon for servants to be on display for a celebration, which they were compensated for. This was a perverted notion of power over people with no voice, and it was disgusting. I tore my eyes away from all the disrespect to my heritage in the room, only to look up to the throne and be caught off guard once again.

The gods have chosen that I am to be the most tormented in this world. I was being tested every waking moment of my life. They probably sat back and laughed at the way I responded. I locked eyes with the traitor and murderer Marcus, wearing my father's crown over his midnight dark hair. It was shorter now, but he looked older. His beard was a dirty stubble, and his eyes were a dark hazel, almost blood orange like the skyline as we sailed in.

Behind him stood his son Titus, a spitting image of his devious father. His hair had grown, dark and greasy almost attached to his head. Standing next to him, arm intertwined with his, was the beautiful vision of Alexandria: my sister Floria.

Ω

She was here, she was right in front of me attached to that monster. But why? She knows what he is. Why would she still stand next to him after everything that he has done? Our home is in ruin, and our family was stolen from us. Yet there she was, standing there in a beautiful dress looking down at me and standing next to the enemy. I couldn't tell if she was surprised to see me or upset with me. Lucius stepped forward to announce us, but I could not take my eyes off my sister.

"Introducing King Kole Alexsson of Lundr and his fiancé, our princess, Octavia Sirius." Marcus stood up off the throne and folded his hand together in front of him.

"Thank the gods in Olympus, the princess has returned to us alive and well. The people have wept for you. We thought you suffered the same fate as your brother." How dare he bring up my brother. Before I could respond, Kole stepped in.

"Thank you for your welcome, King Marcus. Octavia has been longing to return home for some time, and I could not wait to support her in her return." He gave a slight bow, he was so much better at this than I was.

"I heard rumors of the princess returning to the outpost days ago, you made no effort to hide your identity on your way back to us," Marcus answered snidely.

"Why would I hide? I was taken. I did not leave of my own accord, and unfortunately, no one was sent to look for me. Luckily, Kole found me." I grabbed his hand because I knew it would provoke a reaction from him. After a slight glimpse of anger, he was back to his arrogant demeanor. "Floria, I dreamed about seeing you again. I heard rumors that our parents were killed, and all I could think of was you being here alone with no family." Floria was attempting to speak but Titus interrupted and pulled her back behind him.

"Your parents were traitors, and she is not alone. She has her husband. I am her family, I am her everything now. And why am I not surprised that you followed the same treacherous path by tying yourself to the enemy?" Titus was seconds away from being engulfed in my flames.

"I am no enemy of yours at the moment, but we have a lot to discuss, which is the reason for the parlay. Maybe you should let the adults talk, my friend," Kole responded condescendingly and crossed his arms across his chest.

"Maybe I should put a muzzle on the Norse dog that this traitor dragged in off the street," Titus' hand was over the hilt of his sword, and I knew Kole was not far from his axe, even if he hadn't moved.

"Enough Titus! Our guests are here under rules of parlay, we shall show them hospitality. Lucius, gather their things and show them to their rooms." Marcus spoke calmly but strongly.

"Your majesty, would I be able to have a word with my sister? We haven't seen each other in a long time. We are due for a conversation." Titus's face scrunched in anger, but Marcus waved his hand to his son to release Floria.

"Are you going to be okay?" Kole leaned over to comfort me. I could see the concern in his eyes. This is the reunion I've been fighting for since we shared that vision.

"I'll be fine, and after we speak, I will join you... but I need to explain to her everything that has happened." The guilt washed over me because I knew everything that was going on due to Kole's vision and I still chose to finish the journey with him instead of coming straight home. I will always wonder if I made the right decision. Maybe I should have run back here as soon as I had the vision, but I would have been killed if I came back with no allies. She may not forgive me, but she would have to understand.

"I'm not trying to upset you, but you should hold off giving away our entire plan until you know her intentions," he was speaking quietly.

"What are you trying to say, you think I can't trust her?" I couldn't hide the brief anger in my voice.

"No, I mean that her husband could try and force her to spill our secrets. All I'm saying is be careful, my love. I'll be waiting for you in our chambers. Don't worry about me," he replied soothingly and kissed me. The soldiers escorted him out of the room.

I turned my attention back to the task at hand. The room was empty now and the silence was deafening. My sister was not weak, I didn't expect her to be, but we had a lot to discuss.

She walked down the steps slowly and with purpose. The innocent flower that I left here in Alexandria was no more, and before she spoke, I could feel her anger.

"So, we should talk."

12 – Don't Tell Octavia – Rollo

Being a king was going to be way more difficult than I expected. I've only been on the job a couple of weeks, and I was just trying my best not to mess it up. My army was waiting to sail down the river, but we had to travel through Roman lands. Assuming that Gio played his part correctly, I should be able to get to my destination without running into anyone.

I prayed to the gods I wouldn't have to tell Octavia that he killed every Roman that crossed his path. My instincts tell me he would do what suits him best in that situation, regardless of any deal we made in the cave. Whether that decision is good or not Odin only knows.

The army from Lundr arrived on foot right outside of Perseus. Since I regrettably couldn't stay at Persephone's another night, I found a tiny room elsewhere to accommodate me. We had to make our way to the opposite coast so that I could sail to an island called Cosa. At least that's the name on this map. Kole and Octavia should have arrived in Alexandria already. By the time I'm done convincing our new allies to join us we should be ready to make our move on the city. I had no room for error, and I couldn't gamble with all of these lives in my hands. Taking Alexandria could be done without the allies, but why risk the causalities? It would be much easier if we were able to surround them on all sides.

When I return to my family, I can tell them I played a part in unifying this world, and although my father won't be here, I know he will be proud of me when I see him again in Valhalla.

The men were slightly worried about Kole heading behind enemy lines. At first, I was offended. It seems everyone tends to forget that I am a king, as well. I was going to have to find a way to remind them that I am just as important.

Ω

I met with the ground warriors early in the morning. If we left now, we could get to Gio's location by nightfall. I needed to ask him some questions personally about his progress. Hiking through Roman lands with this size company should be impossible with all the scouts that Marcus has. I may get an answer to my question before I am prepared to.

I took one last look at the town that almost trapped me in the underworld forever. Perseus was an amazing place. The next time I am there I will have to decide whether to punish or tip the blacksmith for his information on Persephone's. How many people has he sent there to be subject to that same miserable fate? What if he was somehow working with Persephone? A question for a different time, I suppose.

The countryside was completely different from the city. It was nothing like Najora, but it had its similarities. The flowers bloomed on the hills, creating a beautiful portrait that seemed to spread for miles until they hit the forest.

The sun was high, and the temperature was exhausting. I had to ditch all the furs within the first couple of hours of the journey. How does everyone deal with this kind of heat daily? It was so dry and depressing. I was lost in my own complaints, rambling to myself like a madman before my captain was waving to get my attention.

"King Rollo, it looks like we are approaching one of the Roman scout points."

"Finally, some action. How far out, captain?" I asked, grateful to be doing something other than waiting.

"It looks like there is some smoke a couple of miles to the south." He pointed ahead in the direction of black smoke shooting into the sky.

"Well, it's now or never. Let's see if Gio is a friend or foe." I really, really hoped he was a friend.

It didn't take us long to reach the first scout point. It was completely burned to the ground, nothing remaining was salvageable. I couldn't decide if that was a good or bad thing. Gio and his crew didn't leave any stone unturned.

The tents that housed the scouts were ripped to shreds. He had no need for the food, so it was all left behind to burn. Blood was splattered all around the area making it hard to tell whom it belonged to. But there was one thing missing: the bodies. What did he do with all the bodies?

My soldiers looked on in disgust as we walked through the camp. Clearly some of them were starting to regret the deal we made with the devil. For the sake of the mission, they kept all their opinions to themselves. We pressed on since there was no need to waste time with this mess. If we wanted to catch up to him by nightfall we had to keep moving.

My thoughts rushed to Kole and how he was doing in Alexandria. It must be way more interesting than this. I didn't even have anyone to talk to and I don't always make the wisest decisions when my mind has too much time on its hands. I needed some action.

We passed a few more Roman campsites and another scout point. It was all the same, burned beyond recognition and no bodies left over. What were they doing with the bodies? None of this made sense, unless the Romans don't believe in placing people in these camps. I should have come across dozens of them up to this point.

The sun was making its descent and the smell of freshwater lingered in the air. We couldn't be much further now. Gio would have found a place to sleep during the day, either a tent or a cave, anything that would keep him out of the sun.

I sent a couple of men to scout the coast. Maybe the cave I was looking for was down by the water. The waters were rough, but it would provide plenty of coverage from the sun. It was far enough off the coast that there was no risk of being washed away. It also gave Gio a clear view of his obsession, *the moon.*

"King Rollo, look!" A member of the company pointed to a giant cloud of smoke coming from the east side of the coast.

"Let's move!"

The fire burned high in the middle of the beach, black smoke filling the sky and eclipsing any light from the moon that was left. Standing in front of the blaze was Ambrogio, his hair pulled back into a ponytail laying perfectly down his back. He wore a black tunic and a Roman breastplate covered in blood.

The irony was there but judging by everyone's mood a joke would not be helpful right now. His family stood around the rest of the blaze staring into the fire. All of them were standing completely still like perfect pale statues. Something was off, like I was intruding on a private moment amongst family or friends that I had no place in sharing.

"Gio, what's going on?" He turned to me slowly, his fangs exposed, dried blood smeared all over his mouth. At first glance, he was terrifying, his gaze almost unfamiliar.

"We have much to discuss, my young king, but now we pay our respects to the dead and mourn my children that were taken from me by that witch." I didn't know what to say but, out of respect, I decided to hold my questions until he was ready. I assume he was referring to Delphi. Whatever happened here she had to be at the center of it.

The bodies burned and the ashes began to blow away over the dark waters until there was nothing left but embers crackling in the darkness. I still didn't understand what happened, how Delphi managed to take anyone down. Gio must have underestimated the reach she had.

He said things would get complicated, but this was not what I was expecting. If we didn't get this under control, it could put a major hitch in our plans. If the spirit could do this type of damage without warning, we are in for a tumultuous journey, one with the potential for true carnage and tragedy. I certainly didn't give the spirit enough credit if she could have this kind of influence on our plans..

I instructed my company to make camp here and secure the boats. As soon as the sun came back up, we were heading to the island. I took a seat next to Gio as the rest of his crew moved things inside the shelter they created. I couldn't help but notice all the new faces around. None of these people seemed familiar from the time that we spent in the Delphi caves.

"Are you going to tell me what's going on or are we just going to sit here in silence all night?"

"Rollo, has anyone ever told you that you talk too much?" His voice was cold, lifeless.

"All the time and yet it has never stopped me before. The only time I'm not talking is when I'm listening." I wanted to back off, but the plan was bigger than us and I needed to know if this was going to be a problem. Gio let out a long sigh. I could tell he was annoyed but then he started to speak.

"As you could tell, I haven't had a problem taking care of camps and any scouts that I have come across. The Romans had no idea we were coming, we caught them all by surprise. I attempted to negotiate with the soldiers we encountered but most of them responded as I figured. I had no choice but to use force to bring them in line."

"What do you mean by use force? I haven't seen a single body at any of these campsites," I asked as he locked eyes with me. The blood had hardened around his mouth.

"I gave them the same chance I gave the intruders that ventured into my cave. Either join me and let the gods decide if they are worthy or die." Now the unfamiliar faces started to make sense. Everyone here must have survived the bite and now they were loyal to Gio, a part of his unconventional family.

The gods declared that their lives will not be wasted in death, they can be used for a purpose. I wouldn't agree that this life was an upgrade. I would much rather see Valhalla than be robbed of the sun. Immortality didn't sound terrible, but Gio made everything about it look miserable.

"Quick question, and this is probably not important but, what did you do with the ones that died?" I braced myself for the answer that I didn't want.

"We buried them of course," I could see a smirk pulling on his face, "after we drained them of all the blood in their bodies." There was the answer I did not want to hear. Octavia was going to kill him and me, and then maybe him again for good measure.

"How about we just keep that between us?" I suggested. This still didn't explain what happened here at the coast, but Gio continued.

"We reached the last scout point a couple of miles back and the soldiers chose to die instead of joining me, except for one young scout. He pleaded and pleaded for his own life. He told me he was only here because his father was too old to answer the call to arms. Think of me how you want but I have no interest in killing children. He had no business on the battlefield in the first place, so even though it was against my better judgment, I let him go and we moved on," he clarified as he rose from his seat and put his arms behind his back, staring at the moon, his long-lost love *Selene*.

"We reached the coast, and we figured it would be more of the same. Why would anyone be expecting us? I accounted for every soldier thus far. But when we arrived, in the center of the camp was the same young boy I released. His eyes were bright green and his voice was hollow."

"*Delphi,*" I said under my breath.

"Somehow that bitch managed to possess the boy. He looked at us and his face twisted into an unnatural smile from ear to ear almost ripping his lips apart. The soldiers ambushed us and killed a few of my children before we wiped them out. Delphi had shared my weakness with the soldiers, and if anyone else knows it puts us at a slight disadvantage."

I had no words for what happened. We underestimated the angry spirit and now she was the only thing that knew how to kill our secret weapon. Too much of the plan relied on Gio, which means that securing another ally was very important.

"I can say this, young king, mercy is for the weak. It is a festering limb that must be severed to preserve the body, and I plan to sever every Roman that crosses my path. I will not let them take anything else away from me. The sooner you and your friends accept this, the easier it will be. These animals are beyond saving."

He stopped pacing and walked into the shelter without saying another word. Octavia was going to be furious, but what chance did we have if Delphi was able to possess anyone? Against my better judgement, I had to think about Gio's words. Was it worth showing mercy if it put the whole plan at risk?

13 - Rollo The Besotted – Rollo

“Don’t take it personally. We are not used to losing one of our own unless it is by our hands, and even then, it becomes unspeakable.” The voice that spoke to me was soft and comforting even though it startled me. I looked up and saw a woman who looked awfully familiar.

The woman had dark grey eyes, the moonlight hit them perfectly when she looked at me. The tunic she wore was black and went down to her waist falling over black pants still covered in mud from the battle. A rather impressive sword was strapped over her back. She had fair skin and long black hair. The winds on the beach were blowing her hair into her face, and when she reached to tuck it behind her ear, I could see the faint outline of a scar. I was transfixed staring at it, wondering how she got it. I couldn’t stop myself from staring at her in general. I felt like I knew her.

“Not much for words, your majesty? I can tell you are trying to assess if we have crossed paths or not. I can tell you that we have. The Delphi caves are my home.” Just like that, I remembered her. She was the woman that smiled at me when I presented my plan back at Delphi. I had to try to salvage the moment, my silence was probably very awkward.

"I remember you, no way I could forget that smile."

"I'm sure there are plenty of other things to remember," she replied and sat down next to me.

"You already know my name, do I get the pleasure of knowing yours?" I asked.

"I rarely give out my name seeing as most are not alive long enough to use it." The response caused me to tense until I realized the awful attempt at a joke. "My name is Marcella. It is very nice to meet you, even though the circumstances are not ideal," she smiled.

"Don't take offense but that is the first time anyone associated with Gio has made a joke." The sense of humor caught me off guard.

"I know. We can be a serious bunch. How was it?" she asked.

"It was terrible." We both laughed, and I was glad to finally have someone to talk to, even if it was just for a brief moment.

"Even though it was an awful joke, it is nice to meet you as well, Marcella. I don't take offense to Gio's mood, I know how it feels to lose someone close to you because of a decision you made."

The memory of what Ivar did to my father was forever stained on me. Killing Halfdan helped, but it would never heal the wound in my chest.

"I'm not foreign to loss either. It's actually what led me to Ambrogio in the first place, which is why I know in this mood he is of no use to anyone."

"How long have you been with him?" I tried not to seem too eager for company.

"A woman never tells her age, my king." She offered up a leisure smile.

"Even if a king commands it?" I teased.

"Since I am obliged to follow a king's command, I can say that I am more than four times your age." My eyes widened with surprise.

"That's impressive. You look great for your age, an image of perfection." I could see her trying to hide her smile.

"Are you flirting with me, Rollo?" she asked.

"Has a Norse king ever flirted with you before?"

"I have not met any, you would be the first actually."

"Then yes I am, the first and only Norse king to flirt with you. Not that any of them wouldn't flirt with you after one look at you. No way would they be able to help themselves."

"How charming. We have to enjoy the little things at times like these," she joked, not able to hide the smile this time.

I wanted to ask her more questions, but I didn't want to be rude. She seemed to be enjoying my company and time was not on my side as the sun would be rising eventually. Even though I didn't want to ask, it was now or never. I didn't know when I would see her again.

"You mentioned that loss led you to Gio. I know it isn't any of my business, and you can refuse if you would like, but how did you two cross paths?" She locked eyes with me and then looked up at the stars.

"I was a young girl, not much younger than you are right now, living amongst the Romans. In that time, the land was called something different, and we knew very little of the Norse. Gods and humans walked the earth in tandem, and as you know the gods were not kind. My family was poor, and we lived on the outskirts of a very large city. Day after day, my sister and I dug through the trash for things we could sell or eat."

"What was your sister's name?"

"Her name was Ilithia. She was two years older than me. My mother died while we were young, and this was the only way we knew how to survive. Every night we would pray to the gods to give us a miracle. We prayed for them to guide us to food, money, or anything that would keep us alive so we didn't have to rummage and steal."

"Where was your father?" I asked. Her body language changed like a sense of disgust was associated with the mention of her father.

"He was a loving man while my mother was alive. He was my life and my refuge. I would have done anything for him, and my sister felt the same, but when my mother died, he cursed the gods and fell into darkness. He didn't care about anything but drowning his pain. My sister and I spent more time on the streets than at home, but all the money we would bring back my father would spend in the tavern or at the brothels."

As she told the story, the light-hearted time we were having turned serious and dark. I felt guilty for even bringing it up, but I wanted to learn more about her. Gio and his followers came off as monsters but maybe all of them just had a story they needed to tell. Maybe there was beauty behind the beasts.

"My father's fall into darkness was spiraling out of control until Ilithia reached her breaking point. He found us one night outside of the hut where we slept, and he tried to take the money we earned that day. My sister was enraged, the years of stress that piled on her came crumbling down, and she snapped. She tried to fight him off, tried to make him feel something, a fraction of the pain he was causing us every single day. Ilithia was screaming and punching him over and over, trying desperately to keep him away from the money, but even while he was drunk, she didn't stand a chance. He threw her to the ground and stole the pouch. He turned to limp his way back to the tavern to spend it on his usual vices."

"No one was around to help the two of you? I would never let a man physically hurt two women, no matter if they were related." I was furious just thinking about it.

"This was a different time, Rollo. Romans are cruel and blind if the problem affects someone with lower status, and we were the lowest of the low. My sister didn't give up. She pulled herself onto her feet and jumped on my father's back trying to wrestle the pouch away from him. It felt like they tussled forever, but Ilithia managed to rip the pouch from his hands. She turned, grabbed my hand, and ran for the woods hoping to get as far away from him as we could."

She started to get restless while she sat, like the more she divulged was making her uncomfortable. Her voice was low as she forced herself to finish what I was assumed was the tragic end of the story.

"My father grabbed a handful of my sister's hair to stop her from running. She turned to fight him off again, but he used all his strength and knocked her off balance. Her head landed on a rock and her body was instantly motionless. My father grabbed the pouch. I like to think he assumed she was unconscious, but he didn't even check on her. I ran to her side and shook her over and over, but that was the last time I would ever see her again. The rage I felt overwhelmed me beyond anything I have ever felt. A father is supposed to protect his daughters from the cruel world, but anytime we tried to pull ourselves up out of the gutter, he was an unshakable weight that sent us crashing down. Like my sister, I too reached a point of no return. I grabbed a knife and attacked him. I didn't stand a chance of hurting him, but I was blinded by the anger."

She was staring directly into the fire and her sadness was turning into cold anger right before my eyes.

"I took the knife wanting to cut him into pieces, but I was a child. Realistically there was nothing I could do. My father was already angry, and my attack did not help the situation. He caught my hand as I swung the knife and then he slapped me to the ground. The knife was still faceup in my hand as I fell and managed to slice open my face when I hit the ground."

That answered the question of the scar. Her own father was the one that gave her a wound she has now carried with her for hundreds of years. I felt the yank on my heart. I don't know what it would be like to not be able to look to your parents for protection. My father was not a gentle man, but I always felt protected. Marcella stared into the fire.

"The blood was running down my face and my clothes, but I wouldn't stop. I wanted him to feel the pain he caused. I told him he was the reason my mother was dead, and as soon as the words came out of my mouth, he lost what little sense he had left. He punched me to the ground and started to kick me over and over. Somehow, I managed to force myself to my feet and I fled into the woods. I ran until my body gave out. I had lost so much blood and the bruises my father left caused my entire body to ache. I'm not sure when but eventually I collapsed in darkness."

"I'm so sorry that you had to experience something so gruesome. I know I have been quick to judge your kind, that I can admit." I wanted to find a way to comfort her.

"You wouldn't be the first and you will not be the last."

"What happened next, after you ran away from your father?"

"That I am not sure. I woke up inside a cave. Then, Ambrogio introduced himself. Being a child, I really didn't understand the danger that was staring me in the face. There was not many of us then, but it was our little family. I lived amongst them as a human for years until I had grown into the woman I am today. Ambrogio commended me for my loyalty and offered me the chance to become something more. I could become immortal, never to die, but I would have to give up the sunlight. I will admit that he left out a ton of other things but my decision was all the same. I had come to enjoy this life and I had nothing else to live for, so I accepted.

The bite was excruciating. I could feel my insides eating themselves and then my heart stopped. It was terrifying. I thought I was on my way to meet my sister and I welcomed the idea of seeing her again, but before I could cross over to the underworld, I was sent back. Now I stand before you hundreds of years later, cursed to some but powerful to most. And like you, I am craving a home as I did when I was a child."

I could not stop staring at her in amazement. This story was borderline unbelievable, and I wouldn't have believed it if she was not sitting in front of me right now. Maybe Gio isn't just an ancient psycho. He had managed to do some good in his life. Even though he was cursed, he provided a second chance for Marcella because the first one she was given was already cursed.

"Can I trust you?" I asked her.

"I could ask you the same. The only certainty that I can give is that we both want peace and to live in tandem in this world without fear of being hunted or alienated."

"Did you ever see your father again?" I asked hoping that she had some closure.

"How about we save that conversation for another day. This one has gotten dark enough, don't you think?" More humor, I think I just fell in love.

"Agreed." I nodded to her in agreement. Before we could continue the conversation, an arrow flew past my head and slammed into the wood behind me. A few inches over and I would be dead right now.

Marcella and I got up from the fire and looked down the coast. A handful of Roman soldiers were on horseback riding straight toward us, bows and arrows trained on our location. There couldn't be more than a dozen of them. We should have kept going up the coast to check for another camp.

"Get inside the shelter, I can take care of them," I yelled back to Marcella. She rose to her feet and pulled her sword from the holster.

"And let you have all the fun? They killed members of my family, I will see this through. We fight together, your majesty."

She was running down the beach before I could react, faster than anything I have ever seen. She must have caught the Romans by surprise, as well. By the time they could notch the arrows, she was ripping them off their horses one by one. She was grabbing soldiers with one hand and tossing them aside with no effort. She was miraculous.

Other members of Gio's crew joined the fight, fangs protruding from their faces. The soldiers did not stand a chance. I watched as she ripped them apart limb by limb. Blood squirted from the missing body parts and the men writhed in pain on the beach before they were put out of their misery. I never got the chance to even move, but then I heard more rustling in the grass from above. Four ropes dropped down by the shelter and more roman soldiers slid down the ropes.

"Finally," I smiled to myself.

My day just got more interesting. I needed to see what these Romans could do and, judging from the men dead on the beach, I didn't have much hope it would be a challenge.

I reached just below the surface to tap into my power. The lightning spread down my arms to the palm of my hands as I adjusted my grip on my hammer. One soldier made it down before the others. He charged me with his sword pointed directly at my heart. With my axe in my left hand, I knocked away the sword using his momentum against him and smashed the side of his head with the hammer in one smooth motion. He was dead before he hit the ground.

I jumped on the balls of my feet to get loose as two more soldiers made their way down the ropes. They pressed their attack at the same time forcing me into the defensive stance. I evaded and parried their strikes just waiting for the moment.

One of the soldiers dropped his shield guard briefly enough for me to make my move. I threw my weight into the shield knocking him off balance. The other soldier swung his sword trying to catch me as I recovered. I dropped to my knees and sliced open his leg with my axe.

Neither man noticed the clouds rolling in just above us. Before the two of them could regain their footing, I called down the lightning from the sky. A violent crack slammed into the beach and the soldiers were burned beyond recognition. The last soldier witnessed what happened to his comrades and decided to run in the other direction.

“Face me, you coward!” I yelled.

He was running full speed down the beach stealing glances back at me and then he ran directly into Marcella’s chest. He was knocked off his feet like he ran into a stone wall. The soldier was crawling in the dirt trying to get away, but it was no use. She lifted him off his feet by his throat. She looked past him to me, the life in her eyes nonexistent as her fangs extended.

She was a predator, completely absent of compassion or mercy. Blood was dripping down her face and, before she ripped into the last soldier, she smiled. Every muscle in my body was trapped between terrified and aroused.

What was I supposed to say to her after what I had just witnessed? The beach was riddled with the dead, so we pushed all the bodies out into the water. The sun would be coming up soon, and she would have to stay in the shelter with the others.

"You are impressive, Rollo. I can see why Gio would want an alliance with you." Marcella walked up next to me on the beach.

"I've never seen anyone move as fast as you. Thank the gods you're on our side. I wish I could stay and talk with you longer, but we are leaving at sunrise for the next part of the plan."

"It was a pleasure that we got to speak. Hopefully when this is all over we can spend some more time together," she said with a comforting certainty.

"Oh, that would be my pleasure," I agreed jovially, trying to hide how eager I was. She smiled and planted a kiss on my cheek, surprising me.

"Take care of yourself and that maniac who somehow managed to sleep through the entire attack. Most importantly, make sure you don't forget me," I mischievously joked though deep down I truly meant it.

"How could I forget the first and only Norse King to flirt with me?" She smiled so brightly, completely failing to hide the amusement in her voice.

I gathered up a small portion of the army and we prepared the boat to sail to Cosa to secure another ally. However, as we pulled away from the shore, I could not stop thinking about her. Her beauty, her kindness, the faint scar along her perfect face… and I couldn't forget the glimpse of the monster underneath it all.

14 - The Flower Has Thorns – Octavia

I've dreamed of this moment ever since I was rescued from that god-forsaken box. My little sister needed me. She needed to know that I was still alive. She needed to know that I was coming back to save her from this mess.

The woman that stood in front of me now was not the bright flower that I remember. This place has sucked the life out of everything. Kole was going to be my husband and my new family, but why I'm not allowed to have what remained of my old one I am having trouble understanding.

Floria was looking right through me, like I was a foreigner. A piece of debris that was dragged in from the rough waters. How deep would this punishment go? This was the only piece of my old life I had left, and I wasn't going to give it up, no matter how angry she is with me.

Floria walked past me to a small table with a decanter and a few cups sitting on top. She helped herself to some wine.

"Would you like a drink, sister?" I nodded, and she poured a second cup and left it on the table. An insult but one I was willing to accept under these circumstances.

"Thank you, but we need to talk. There is much I need to tell you." I walked over to retrieve the cup she politely left me.

"You want to tell me how you left me here and rode off into the sunset with your new prince." I was taken back by the spitefulness in her words. I wanted to feel bad for her, but it made me angry that she would accuse me of just leaving.

"Is that what you think happened? You think I did all of this for a husband? Do you think I watched Tiberius die in front of me for a man!? Are you out of your mind, Floria?!" I could not read her expression; she was cold as a winter gust. "They made me watch him die and locked me in a fucking box for days!" The tears were forcing their way up. I was trying to hold them back, but these memories would forever haunt me.

"Do you think it was all flowers and celebrations for me here? I watched that monster murder our parents, and then I was forced to marry my amazing husband," the sarcasm was evident in her voice.

None of this could have been easy for her, we have both experienced life-changing trauma.

"No one's pain is more important than the other, but don't think for a second that I left and didn't think of you. You are all I have left, and I refuse to lose you too." I reached to grab her hands but paused as I noticed bruising on the inside of her forearms.

We locked eyes. The stoic and cold demeanor was slowly crumbling behind her eyes.

"What is this, Floria?" I was trying to speak calmly but anyone could hear the violence brewing behind my voice.

“Nothing that concerns you, just the pains of being married to a monster.” She pulled away and pulled down her sleeves.

What I was feeling now could not be contained. The only thing I had on my mind was putting Titus’ head on a pike.

“How long has he been hitting you, Floria?” I asked.

“He hasn’t stopped since the day we swore to marriage. I have learned to deal with his treatment for the sake of my survival. I thought my entire family was dead. What else did I have to live for? Maybe I deserved this since I did nothing to protect them. I told myself if I just rode this out I will be on the throne one day and I’ll be able to take care of it myself.” She put her head down staring into her cup.

“I promise you I am going to get you out of this. You just have to trust me.”

“How do you plan on getting me out of here?” She still wouldn’t look up from her cup.

“I can’t say right now, but I have a plan. You just have to be ready when I say so. Can you do that?” I grabbed her shoulders.

I needed her to understand that this is not what she deserved. I was the one that was supposed to protect us, and I failed them, but I would not fail her.

“I guess some things don’t change after all,” she spoke with more venom than before.

“What is that supposed to mean, Floria?” I was reaching my limit for her sarcasm all too quickly.

"You are here for three seconds, and you are already making this about you. You never cared how your actions affected others. Did it ever occur to you that I don't want to leave? If this all plays out as expected when Marcus leaves, I will be queen, something that wasn't in the cards for me before."

"What are you saying? I have never wanted to be queen, and you of all people know that." I couldn't believe what I was hearing from her. No one has bucked tradition more than me. Why would she think I thirsted to steal power from anyone?

"But you will be anyway! Whatever Tav wants, she gets. Countless hours of mother pining over you, making sure you were ready to be a queen just because you were born before me. The only one to pay attention was me and in return what did I get?" she yelled.

"I'm so confused right now. I know you're angry, but I don't deserve this, not to mention everything you're saying makes no sense. I want you with me. If I'm selfish for that, then so be it. All I want is to protect you and save you from the monsters who blew up our lives and murdered our family." I was astonished with how she was more concerned with losing her seat of power than escaping her torment from our enemies.

"I love you Tav, with all my heart. That's why this hurts so much. I thought everyone was dead and that I had to come to terms with this life. I never knew I had the desire in me to rule but I want it, I want to be queen."

I thought I was going to burn this cup in my hands. I don't know why she is acting this way, but the only thing keeping me from losing my temper is my love for her.

"For the sake of us being back together, I'm not going to feed into this nonsense." Her time in this mess must have warped her brain.

"It's not nonsense, it's the truth," she stressed.

"The truth is that I'm here now and I need you to be ready. Can you do that?" I can't believe I had to plead with my sister in order to rescue her from this nightmare. Did she really believe that being a prisoner queen was better than being free?

"Okay, I'll be ready. Let me show you to your room before someone gets suspicious. Lucius will come and bring you to dinner."

She rolled her eyes, and I decided that I was going to ignore it. I gave her a giant hug but I wasn't surprised that she didn't squeeze me back. We are going to need time to heal and mourn properly.

It must have been some failed attempt at a joke when Floria and a couple of soldiers escorted me back to my old room in the villa, reminding me that this was not a safe place for me any longer.

This was clearly a move to unnerve me, but I was nothing but focused. Titus abusing my sister was the only thing on my mind. What made him think he had any right to ever put his hands on her? My gut was leading me to believe he was the masked assailant that I fought the night I was kidnapped but losing a fight to him would deal a terrible blow to my ego. I still didn't have proof but finding it would not be difficult. If I knew Titus, he wouldn't be able to hide his gloating.

My room hadn't changed much, everything was still in the same place. Kole and Kare were looking out my window talking amongst themselves. They must not have heard me walk in, so I decided to give them a minute. Watching them admire the view brought a small dose of warmth to my heart. Moments like my future husband and sister-in-law smiling, tiny glimpses of peace were what I needed to hold close to my heart if I ever thought we had a chance to get out of this mess. I had to hold on to the happiness while I was in the lion's den so that when things get out of hand, I remember what we are fighting for and that we will be strong enough to get out. We will prevail no matter what the gods see fit to throw at us next.

Kole must have heard me eventually because then he turned towards me, flashing that big, beautiful smile that I fell in love with long before he asked me to be his. Guards would be retrieving us to join Marcus at dinner soon, so unfortunately, this warm reunion would not last. We had to prepare to dine with a madman.

"How was the conversation with your sister?" Kole asked. I didn't know how I could even sum it up. We needed more time to sort out everything that has happened between us, one conversation was barely productive.

"We have a long way to go," was the answer I settled on.

"Do you think we can trust her?" he asked.

I know he was just trying to be safe but every time he asked me that I wanted to punch him in his gorgeous face just for insinuating the thought.

"Of course, we can trust her. She is a prisoner here just as much as we are. We are going to stick to the plan. We are all getting out of here," I snapped at him.

“So, you told her everything?” He kept pressing.

“No, I told her I have a plan and when I say so she should be ready.” He didn’t say anything back and I knew why. Deep down, maybe I didn’t trust her because I never told her what the plan was, but I would never admit it. She was my blood, she would have to trust me.

“Let’s just get ready for this riveting evening ahead of us, but first Kare, have some of the soldiers escort you back down to the boat. Have one of the soldiers write letters to Gio and Rollo letting them know what we have seen so far and that when we have more information, we will send another message.”

“What if they ask me why I need to go back to our boats?” Kare asked.

She did have a point, but soldiers were easily fooled by pretty girls. They think we are all dumb and helpless.

“Tell them your silly queen has lost something and you want to check the boats to retrieve it so I don’t throw a temper tantrum. Just run your hands through those perfect curls, no guard will say no.” She nodded and laughed as she walked out of the room.

I grabbed an old dress out of my closet. I couldn’t believe my clothes were still here completely untouched. Kole opted to wear his vest and some pants. He wanted the raven sigil to be on full display for Marcus if he was going to be taken seriously as a king.

He didn’t wear the tunic underneath. The warm climate here was not his favorite. He had yet to stop complaining about the heat, but I think what irked him the most was the guards taking all his weapons. At least if I wanted to ignore all the nonsense coming from Marcus, I could stare at Kole's muscles and how his biceps tensed underneath the raven tattoo that stretched all the way up to his shoulders. It felt like forever since I got to touch him. I was miserable being so close to him and not being able to just rip off his clothes. Like a plate full of food being held just out of arm's length.

Focus Octavia...... I still couldn't believe how distracted I can get when it comes to him. He must have seen me daydreaming because he gently rested his hand on my shoulder, startling me.

"You ready for tonight?"

"Am I ready to sit across from the man that killed my parents and his demon son that is beating my sister? Of course, another passage in the amazing story of Octavia." I rolled my eyes.

"Everything will be fine. Remember what I said. He's going to try to rattle us, but we are here to find out information. We don't need things to escalate," he warned me.

"I don't know how you can be so calm in a time like this."

"It's because I'm dreaming for the day I get to teach all of them a lesson for what they put you through," he kissed me softly, temporarily distracted until we heard a knock on the door.

It was time for dinner, and I had a feeling it was going to be the longest night of my life.

Kole and I made our way down to the banquet room with armed escorts at our backs, of course. Lucius hasn't let us out of his sight since we arrived outside of the privacy of our room.

Even then I assume he had guards right outside the door. They managed to not destroy this room. It must be where the fake king eats all his meals. Marcus was sitting at the head of the table when we arrived. Titus sat to his right and Floria next to her husband.

The table was covered in food, but I was so nervous that my appetite was nonexistent. The fireplace burned bright, bread was sliced and placed next to a bowl full of oil, meat was perfectly rolled and displayed, grapes were spilling out of the bowls, and candles lit up the entire room.

The Sirius banner that was previously hung above the fire was now missing, another slap to my face. I was starting to keep count of all the offenses I was taking just being here. Two chairs next to Floria were pulled out, making it obvious where they wanted us to sit, but at this point, I was done being told what to do. I walked over to the chair that was pulled out for me and dragged it to the other end of the table directly across from Marcus.

I wanted him to look me in the eyes while he tried to tell his lies. Kole didn't have words. I know we decided not to antagonize but a girl has her pride. He sat in the seat next to me and made himself more than comfortable. A flash of annoyance danced across the king's face, but one could barely notice because it was gone in an instant. I looked over to Titus and I could see that, even though my actions didn't provoke the father, I got a rise out of the son. Titus proved more and more to be an asset in our plans if he his skin was so thin, and his temper was so easily provoked. Marcus waved his hands and the servants proceeded to fix our plates for us.

"I am so glad that you two could join us for dinner. I trust you are comfortable with everything, princess," Marcus said.

"I am, thank you. It feels amazing to be home. I know that if others had their way, I wouldn't be alive to see it," I responded.

The door cracked open again and Kare walked in. We could only assume that getting the message out was a success. She walked to the other side of the table to grab a seat before Marcus stopped her.

"Excuse me, young lady, but we don't allow servants to eat at this table. You can take your food with the other servants in the kitchens."

"She is not a servant, she is my handmaiden, one I trust the most. I will not allow her to be treated like a slave," I snapped.

"Well, unfortunately, princess you don't make the rules here now," Titus answered.

Kole was getting agitated in his seat. I could feel that darkness pulsating from him and he was staring at Titus. Out of the corner of my eye, I saw Marcus squinting toward Kole trying to figure out what was going on. He must have felt the power, as well. I found it hard to believe he wouldn't be able to sense it.

I rubbed my hand on his leg under the table to try and calm him down before this dinner had a terrible ending. Kare nodded to us and walked away from the table without protest. I owe her the world for playing this part almost too well but stirring up a problem now would mean more eyes on her. She needed to keep a low profile if she was going to be able to sneak in and out to send messages back to our allies. The mission is bigger than all of us but the way we were being treated stung.

"I know you have been away from Alexandria for some time, maybe the customs out west aren't as civilized," Marcus took a drink from his cup as he spoke.

"If you mean we don't let guards beat on innocent people in the streets and have slaves do all our dirty work, then yes we are not very civilized," Kole answered followed by a smirk. "So, if you are done insulting my culture, maybe we can get down to business."

"A man that likes to get straight to it, I can respect that." He waved his hand and everyone cleared the room except the guards. "Would you like to explain why your countrymen ran into this great Roman city and killed my people?"

"I don't know where you are getting your information, but my father ordered no such attack. Perhaps someone was trying to make it seem like we attacked to disrupt the peace," Kole answered cautiously, somewhat insinuating we knew more than he let on without.

"Wouldn't that be convenient, the attacker inside our house telling us he was framed," Titus sarcastically replied .

"If my father wanted to upset the peace, then why is my wife-to-be still alive? Why was she allowed to live and walk among my people? Surely the head of a princess would send a strong message." Kole sat back in his chair.

I was happy to remain quiet. I wanted to hear how they would weave their lies.

"I was here that night and I know what I saw. Maximus and I fought side by side that night. Only your kind could be so ruthless," Marcus practically screamed as he slammed his fist on the table.

This man clearly had no limit to the extent he would go to cover up his part in this. He has no idea that we already know the truth, and honestly, I wanted to keep it that way.

"I don't know how many times I have to tell you that those men were not sent by us, but we are talking in circles. The bottom line is we are here to parlay."

"We are here to honor the parlay and that is the only reason you are still alive," Marcus said with an arrogance only he could accomplish.

I was losing my patience with all of this talk. He wasn't going to admit what he has done without a little more of a push.

"What happened to my father?" I blurted out. Marcus and Titus looked at each other, probably trying to make sure their lies align.

"Unfortunately, during the attack, Maximus accused me of being a traitor to our country," he said calmly.

"And why would my father claim that the great Marcus is a traitor?" I wondered if he could sense my sarcasm.

"On the words of a dead man, he attacked me, and I had to defend myself. The country was going to fall into disarray, so someone had to step up," he replied calmly, as if he had no care in the world.

"Well, that makes this easy then. You had to step in because all of the Sirius line was presumed to be dead. Technically, Floria here should have become queen when she married your little boy over there. For some reason, you decided to steal the throne from your own son. But besides that small note, you should have no problem stepping aside and returning the throne to the rightful heir, Octavia," Kole suggested with a smile.

"You really take us for idiots, don't you?" Titus was on his feet, clearly livid.

"You want us to just give over the throne to Octavia, which would make you a king," he walked over to Kole and leaned over him to say, "you will never be equal to us, you filthy dog."

Kole put his head down. He gripped the arms of the chair until pieces of the wood splintered. I could see the blood from his hands running down the chair of the arm. He looked away from the others and fixated on me. His eyes were pitch black, the familiar smoke seeping out the sides. He was slowly losing control and would eventually give up the whole plot soon unless he regained it.

"Marcus, out of respect for the parlay, your son still lives. But if he speaks to me like that again, I cannot promise restraint. You have been warned accordingly," his voice was cold.

"Titus, have a seat," he gestured for his son to sit back down. "It's time we all gather our resolve. Kole, I respect that you speak with a king's authority, but you have no power here. Although I don't approve of his methods, Titus is right. I in good faith could never just hand over the throne knowing that it would ultimately be under Norse rule. Our way of life would cease to exist."

"Is that what you think of me? You think that I would give away everything that I am just because my husband is Norse? If that's what you think of me, Marcus, then you don't know me at all," I interrupted.

The notion that I was a going to sit in the backseat while Kole ruled was offensive to me.

"Not only does he not wish to command me, but I also will not allow it. I am my own person and am more than capable of defending myself." Kole gave them a shoulder shrug as he knew it was the truth.

I looked over to Floria for confirmation of my character, but she had been quiet the entire evening. She has been conditioned by these men to not say a word or she would be punished.

"We can go back and forth all night but those are my terms. Not his, mine. The throne belongs to me and should be returned to me." I sat back in my seat and waited for a response.

"So, to avoid a war that I would eventually win, you want me to give up one of the biggest cities in Gracia to be ruled by you and your Norse boyfriend... am I understanding that correctly?" Marcus said methodically.

"That sounds about right, although he is much more than a boyfriend. Please don't underestimate our intentions or capabilities. We have allies, Marcus. It will not be easy for you to brush us aside as you would a small child whining for attention. There are no children at this table, so I would advise you tread very carefully," I assured him.

"Nothing in this life is easy, however, I do find it hard to believe that you have three armies worth of allies," he drolly replied.

I didn't need to answer. I smiled because Marcus made his first mistake. I finished the rest of my wine without a word, and I think he got the hint.

"Father, please tell me you aren't actually considering this? Once you return home, this kingdom was supposed to be mine," Titus whined to his father, like the very type of child I just described.

"A good ruler always considers his options, even if he doesn't plan on accepting. With that being said, I have matters to attend to. Please make yourselves at home while I mull over your offer," he concluded while getting up from the table. "Might I suggest you take a walk and visit the new arena. It is a staple of entertainment." With that, he made his way out of the banquet hall followed closely by his guards.

Titus and Floria lingered before he forced her to leave with him. Kole and I sat in the banquet hall in silence. We were not sure if this was a failure or success, but one thing was for sure. Marcus thought he had the help of three armies. What he didn't know is that Rollo was on his way to secure Gaius' daughter to our side. By now, he must know that his plan to have a mole in the Norse kingdom was a failure. I had a good feeling about all the advantages we had.

"All things considered, that wasn't too bad. I'm going to end up portaling Titus into the middle of the river, but it wasn't that bad," Kole said jokingly.

15 – MY SISTER'S KEEPER - KOLE

The arrogance of these men has no limits. This entire situation was getting tiring, though I could only imagine how Octavia was feeling, being that this is her home. I thought the first dinner was going to be the height of the visit, but there was plenty to come after that. Marcus was playing with us. Leading us on any chance that he got. It had been days since we laid out our terms and he has yet to give us an answer. He hasn't even tried to acknowledge our presence at all.

Every night he made another excuse as to why he hadn't had time to grant us an audience, and that's if he even decided to show his face. This game of his has put us all on edge, and I was starting to get worried there is more in the works than we understand. We came here to get information about his strength, but I couldn't help but think in some way Rollo was right. He needed to keep us around to see how strong we are, as well.

I had no choice but to play along with this game to keep my girls safe. Kare had managed to slip in and out with no problem, so at least I know we could still warn our allies. I was willing to play along for the time being, but my gut was telling me that something bad was going to happen. I can't believe I was going to say this, but I would kill for a vision from Odin right now. It was clear there was little to no connection to him in these lands. I started to lose that reassuring feeling the moment we left Perseus. The push of darkness that I usually felt from him had calmed to a light brush inside me.

Octavia convinced me that we should just enjoy the day and try to forget about the procrastinating asshole. We decided to take a nice stroll through what was left of the market.

"How do you deal with this weather every day? I feel like my skin is going to fall off."

The heat was unbearable here, unwavering in its intensity. No matter what I wore, my clothes would just stick to me.

"What's wrong with the heat? It's not even that bad this time of year," Octavia said with mirth in her voice.

"It gets warmer than this?!" The mere thought of more heat was terrible. The Romans were odd, indeed. How this temperature was considered mild I couldn't understand.

"This used to be one of my favorite places when I was a kid. Tiberius and I would come down here and watch the ships come in," her voice cracked some as she spoke.

"That's not something that the little girls do," I teased.

"I was hoping you would have learned that I am not like any of the other little girls," she said sending me a warning glare.

"Oh, believe me I know. I still thank the gods I found you all alone in a musty old box."

"Yeah, those were the good old days, and to think I was going to kill you on the spot," she smiled.

“Try to kill me you mean, emphasis on try,” I corrected her.

“I was never one for the details,” she laughed.

The market was just as dull and lifeless as it was when we arrived. No blacksmiths, no traders, or fishermen. It was just a ghost town, a shell of itself from what Octavia had described. I couldn’t hold it against her. This place was under siege, and with my help we would be the ones to liberate it.

“Where are we going anyway?” I asked.

“We are going to see this monstrosity that Marcus has built instead of taking care of all my people,” she answered.

It was clear he wasn’t trying to hide this arena. It was the biggest thing I had ever seen. I did not want to admit it to Octavia, but it was beautiful, like something dropped on earth by the gods. The arches and pillars were high enough to touch the clouds. I was speechless and I could tell that Octavia was impressed as well, although she would never admit it. We stood outside of the walls mesmerized. Neither one of us had said a word. We could feel the roar and rumble of the crowd from the outside. Maybe that’s why the market was so empty. The whole thing piqued our curiosity to say the least. What could possibly be so important that everyone has rushed inside?

“What is going on in there?” I asked.

“I have no idea, but I doubt I’m going to like it. Let’s go inside,” she suggested and grabbed my hand to drag me inside.

The stairs were made of a cold brownstone, all perfectly laid out in place. The roars only got louder as we weaved our way to the source. We reached the light at the end of the hallway. All I could see was a sea of people screaming and cheering. I couldn't understand how something like this could exist. How could you fit so many people in one place? It must have taken a thousand men to build this.

Octavia grabbed my arm and pointed down towards the middle of the arena. The sand was coated with blood. You could almost smell it, and trails of it were coming from the tunnels below. I couldn't understand what was going on and what was the purpose of this.

"This is what Marcus deems as entertainment," Octavia spoke with so much vitriol.

"What am I missing here? What is this supposed to be used for?" I asked.

"Wait a few more minutes, I have a feeling we will find out." Three men were escorted by guards, chains on their hands and feet.

The crowd was going wild, almost like a pack of animals calling for blood. The men were placed on their knees and, out of the tunnel on the other end, a man dressed in full Roman war gear walked out dragging his sword across the sand. Once he reached the prisoners, he threw the point of his sword down into the dirt and removed his helmet. The crowd was in a frenzy. It was the general that gave me an attitude on the dock, the son of the elusive king.

"Lucius," Octavia said out loud.

"I don't understand, is this some kind of execution?" I asked.

"I don't know, my father would never make a spectacle of this sort of thing. He did his duty, but it was never for sport, it was for justice."

Lucius fed into the cheers of the crowd. They were showering him with love. He picked up his sword and sliced off the head of the first prisoner. It felt like the arena was going to collapse on itself. The Romans were losing their minds as the prisoner's blood spilled all over the sand.

"What the fuck is happening?" I waited for her to answer but Octavia looked so disgusted and distraught.

"I can't believe he built this to kill people for cheers. It's the only way they can feed their sad egos. We need to stop him, Octavia!" I had to scream for her to hear me over the crowd. She was already on her way back down the stairs.

"We need to end this," she replied gruffly, her face tense and cold.

I've seen her in so many different moods, but this one was concerning. The last few days have been a test of our patience, but I knew she was reaching her breaking point. She stormed into the throne room expecting to find Marcus handling whatever business he claimed to be responsible for. Only we didn't find Marcus, we found Floria pacing back and forth. She looked nervous. I felt terrible for the predicament she was in, all the abuse she was taking just to make sure she could stay alive. If only she knew how badly Octavia wanted to come back to rescue her, then maybe she wouldn't take all her anger out on the one person she had left. I knew this conversation wouldn't be a good one, Octavia was too fired up.

"Floria, where is Marcus?" she asked.

"Why would I know where he is? It's not like he or Titus keep me in the loop," she snapped back before walking over to the table to pour a cup of wine.

"I need to talk to them, and I am tired of waiting and playing games. We need an answer from them now." I could feel the ripple of the flames coming off her.

"If you need answers from them then you need to get them yourself. I can be of no help to you," she replied curtly and continued to drink. "You told me to be ready, so I'm staying out of the way. I will be ready for whatever plan you and your husband are making. Even though I believe it to be a fool's errand." She tilted her head back to empty her cup.

"You make it seem like this is where you want to stay. I tell you I'm here to help and all you do is sit around in silence drinking every minute of the day." Floria was still ignoring her. If it was anyone else, she would already have a dagger at their throat. "Ugh, this is not helping at all." She turned back to me. "I need to find them but as usual they are avoiding me. What should we do now?" she asked.

"I'm not sure but I was thinking about taking a walk down to the docks. I heard it can be very interesting at night," I implied as discreetly as possible.

I hope that she could understand the hint. Kare still hadn't returned from the docks, and I wanted to make sure she was okay. But I had to make sure that Octavia was calm enough for me to leave her alone.

"I don't know how you could think about taking a walk at this time but knock yourself out. I'll deal with this so-called parlay." She had a tiny smirk on the side of her mouth, so she must have gotten the message.

"You two play nice, okay?" I laughed.

Ω

I was finally able to get out of the villa without a group of guards following me. Whatever had gone down in the arena must have had them all distracted. It felt like for once I could breathe. These Romans were so particular about where I was able to go. So much concern that the scary Norse would stir up some trouble, the whole thing just made them look weak. I didn't want to seem too eager to head straight down the docks, so I decided to do a little sightseeing on my way, but my main focus was to find my sister.

Most of the city was in ruin except for some parts which retained its character. Romans were obsessed with statues. Dozens of them were scattered all over the city, some engaged in battle, others staged as triumphant warriors. I couldn't read Latin, so I had no idea what the words meant. All of this infinite knowledge and power and Odin didn't think to gift me with an ability to read Latin. I cringed thinking about how unprepared I came into this situation. I knew we would have to lean on Octavia to guide us through her people's lands and customs, but I had hoped to be of more use given my gift of sight.

The locals walked by without saying anything, but I could feel their glares behind my back. My surroundings weren't my own. I needed to be more careful. I realize that a Norse staring at the Roman statues was not a great way to keep a low profile, if that was even possible. Everything from my attire to my mannerisms screamed I don't belong here.

The giant raven on my vest probably didn't help my case, but I refused to wear Roman clothing. It would just feel disrespectful to my father. A king doesn't bow to anyone but his queen and the gods. Life lessons that I would never be able to discuss with my father. I would have to accept that a giant part of this was my fault. I should be learning under my father's tutelage instead of playing king in a foreign country. Maybe it was my fault for not paying attention to the laws that I was next in line to enforce. Stories end in tragedy in every culture. I took one last look at the heroes and continued to move through the market.

I made sure to stop by all the market carts that were still open. Maybe a couple of Roman souvenirs would cheer Octavia up. The guards that should be on patrol were enjoying themselves a little too much at the tavern. Plenty of them were laughing and falling over themselves, completely drunk.

The sun was barely peaking over the horizon when I finally reached the dock. There was still no sign of Kare. I was starting to get worried. She should have been on her way back to the villa by now. Something wasn't right. The boats were all aligned along the docks, but I couldn't find the raven sigil anywhere. If I knew Marcus, he would have placed our boats all the way at the end of the dock out of spite. Another way to show me where my place was in his city. He would pay for all the little pokes to my ego eventually.

My heart was slamming in my chest, and my thoughts were spinning out of control. If I lost my sister in this place, it would be my fault. How would I be able to face my mother? How would I be able to protect my people as king if I couldn't even keep an eye on my own sister? Boat by boat, still nothing. I was living in my worst nightmare. I made it to the end of the dock before I finally found our boat stashed away as I predicted.

Sitting on the main deck drinking and laughing with the rest of my men was Kare. My heart finally rested in my chest and my fear was pushed away.

"Thank the gods, Kare. We were expecting you to be back already, I thought something had happened to you." I ignored most of the others drinking with my little sister, though I noted all of the men too comfortable in her company, as any good older brother would.

"Kole, I'm fine. I'm sorry I just wasn't in a hurry to head back into that villa. They treat people like animals, I needed a break so I wouldn't lose my cool," she spoke to me with purpose. "I didn't want to be the one to ruin the mission."

Her demeanor seemed to relax when she was around her own. I certainly couldn't fault her for needing some time away from the villa and all the madness that accompanied Marcus and his kin.

"I want you to know that I love you and appreciate everything you have done. I don't blame you for not wanting to come back. I'm just glad you are okay." I smiled at her. I didn't mean to get all emotional, but I already lost one sibling to this mess.

"I sent the ravens to everyone already. They are still waiting for more information from us, but I gave them an update. I instructed the soldiers to send ravens if anything happens to us while we are in the villa. Soldiers like to talk a lot down here," she said confidently.

"That's a good idea. I'm going to hang out in the market for a little longer, but it's getting dark. You should be heading back soon otherwise people will wonder why you aren't helping the princess," I joked.

"Okay, let's go, but we can't walk together. I have some things I can bring back to Octavia, so no one gets suspicious." I scrambled back through the market just looking and picking things off different carts until I finally saw Kare making her way back to the villa.

I was on the other side of the road, but I was able to keep an eye on her. She was walking quickly down the road with no problem until two soldiers stumbled out of a tavern I passed earlier. It was clear that the men were intoxicated but they didn't appear to be a threat to Kare as she was passing them. I must have spoken too soon because as she kept walking the soldiers called out to her.

"Hey, handmaiden!" Kare kept walking, doing her best to not acknowledge them.

"Hey, we called to you," the soldier yelled.

Kare kept walking but the soldier was trying to catch up to her. I wanted to believe she could handle herself, but I kept myself close just in case this got out of hand. I didn't want to intervene because that would only make things more complicated for Octavia, but my patience as of late was very thin. The soldier grabbed Kare on the arm to stop her from walking. I moved closer so I could hear the conversation.

“Why are you in such a hurry? You should come to the tavern with us and have a few drinks. We could show you a good time.” I was doing everything I could to curb my anger.

“No, thank you,” Kare said nicely, “I have to return to the princess. She gets cranky when I don’t return right away.” She turned to walk away but the soldier grabbed her again, this time with more force. I could see on her face she didn’t appreciate it.

“Who cares about the whore queen. She thinks she can come here and take over just because she was passed around by the Norse. As soon as she is gone, Alexandria will be a better place,” the soldier was laughing and stumbling while he spoke.

“Those words are not necessary. However, you may feel about her, I need to return to the villa now. Have a good night, gentlemen.” She tried to pull away again.

“Hey bitch, I didn’t say you could go.” This time the soldier grabbed Kare by the hair and dragged her into an alley. He was going to pay for it dearly once I got my hands on him.

Kare elbowed the soldier in the chest forcing his grip to loosen on her hair, then she turned and kicked him directly in the groin. The soldier fell to the ground gasping in pain. She was reaching for her weapon, but she couldn’t grab it in time. The soldier grabbed her by the throat and pinned her against the wall.

“I’m going to send you back to your princess in piec.......” Before he could finish his words, I snapped his neck and his lifeless body fell to the ground.

"What the hell took you so long?" Kare was coughing and holding her throat.

"I thought maybe you could handle it. Clearly we have more training to do." I grabbed her hand, and we ran out of the alley back to the road only to find four more soldiers waiting for us. All of them had their eyes trained on us. This is the worst thing that could have happened.

"Soldiers, before you do something you will regret, how about we just forget about what has happened here tonight?" I was doing my best to diffuse this situation.

"How could we forget about you coming into our home and attacking us? How could we forget you showing up here again thinking that you make the rules because you managed to infect the queen?" the soldier spat at me.

"We didn't attack anyone, you and your slimy friends just tried to rape me," Kare interrupted.

"Why would any of us need to rape a handmaiden? You should consider yourself lucky that we would even want to touch you. We could have you whenever we want, I'm sure you would enjoy it anyway," he smiled.

"I'm warning you to watch what you say next," I was on the edge of losing it. Nothing I hate more than cowards picking on someone they think is weaker than them, and they seem to come in large amounts around here.

"And what are you going to do? You may be a guest of the king, but I will skin you like the animal you are and send you back to all the other dogs so they know who their master is," the soldier spat.

I tried to take Kare's hand and walk by. I wasn't going to get through to them by talking and the insults were testing me even further.

"Where do you think you're going, dog? I'm not done with you." He put his hand on my chest blocking my path and he leaned in close to my ear. I could smell the wine on his sour breath. "If it was up to me, I would kill you now, then I'd take your princess and your handmaiden and let the boys get a taste of the spoils of war."

I pushed Kare back behind me and grabbed the soldier's hand and squeezed until I could hear the bones break. I tapped into the power, allowing the darkness to well up inside me. At this moment, I was done hiding from these Romans.

"What the fuck is wrong with his eyes?" the soldier screamed, still holding his broken hand.

"The time for words is done. You can leave now, or I'll send you to your beloved underworld." My words must have meant nothing because instead of running they attacked me all at once.

It was more challenging than I thought it would be. Legs and fists were flying at me from every direction. I tried to parry and block what I could but the soldiers wouldn't relent, and I lacked my weapons. They weren't afraid enough yet, but I could change that. I reached deeper and grabbed even more power. The next kick that came instead of blocking I threw my elbow into it, breaking the bone instantly.

I needed to get some distance between us, but teleporting would give away all of my abilities, and I didn't want anyone reporting what they had seen back to Marcus. I tackled the closet soldier and drove him to the ground away from the others before he could get up. I slammed my fist into his face knocking him unconscious.

Two men charged toward me, but I could hear more steps coming our way. Someone went to get reinforcements. I needed to end this now because it was only going to get worse. I grabbed a sword off the ground and made quick work of the two soldiers in front of me. I did not strike killing blows, but they would bleed out shortly, a part of me wanting them to suffer. When I looked up again, six more soldiers were surrounding me.

"I'll tell you like I told the others, let us pass and we can forget any of this happened." I was ready to open portals for them all and drop them out of the sky.

"That won't be necessary, Kole." I recognized his voice before I saw him. Walking in between the soldiers was the general, Lucius. "You are not in a position to negotiate."

"The dead soldiers around you may make you consider otherwise," I said calmly still holding the sword at attention.

"You are impressive, but if you don't surrender then I'm going to open the handmaiden's throat from ear to ear," he smiled.

I looked behind him and two men were holding Kare with her knife to her throat. I don't know how I was going to get out of this, but I couldn't risk her life in the process, even though Octavia was going to kill me anyway. This was definitely not a part of the plan. I threw down the sword, there was no other way out of this.

"Good choice. Take the girl back up to the villa, we need to have a conversation with her and her queen. But you Kole you have broken the rules of parlay and therefore I can arrest you." He walked over and put chains around my hands. "And what am I to do about my dead soldiers here? If I'm not mistaken, you savages believe in blood for blood." He waved his hands and from the bottom of the road being dragged in chains were my crew members from my ship. "You killed three of my men, so how about I let you watch me kill three of yours? That's only fair, right?"

He forced three members of my crew to kneel down and one by one he slit their throats. Their bodies jerked and spasmed as blood poured out all over the road and I was forced to watch the whole thing in horror.

"This is all your fault, Kole. I have to say thank god my father would never agree to your terms because you are an awful king." Lucius threw a right hook directly into my jaw causing me to fall to the ground. I picked myself up off the ground and I could feel the blood dripping from the side of my lip.

"You better hope your father kills me because if I see you again, I'm going to rip your heart out," I spit blood all over his breastplate.

"You will die, don't worry about that. Everyone is going to be here to watch it, even that bitch of yours."

The soldiers picked me up. I expected them to walk me back up to the villa, but they took a turn down an alley. I was surprised to find out they were walking me toward the biggest building in Alexandria, the stones and pillars stretching to the heavens, but we didn't go toward the stairs. The men dragged me to a passage that led underground.

The walls were lined with metal bars. Men sat in the corner of the cells, dirty and bloody with buckets of hay in the corner. I could still hear the cheers and roar of the crowd underground as they threw me into a cell and locked it behind me.

Lucius meant for my death to be a spectacle, but I had a few tricks up my sleeve. All I needed was time to think, which being in this dark cold cell alone is exactly what I had time to do. Maybe I will be able to gain some upper hand being down here, but my only concern was what trouble my actions have caused Octavia and Kare.

16 - THE FLOWERS COVER THE SPEAR – OCTAVIA

I looked down into the city from my balcony. I could tell the city was winding down. Neither Kole nor Kare ever came back from the docks. I was starting to get very worried. I should have never let him go down there by himself. I know he can take care of himself, but he didn't have any weapons and he didn't know anything about Alexandria. After my brief conversation with Floria, which led nowhere might I add, I started searching all over the villa for Marcus or Titus to no avail. How did he manage to avoid me this entire time?

The only thing I found was more guards and my drunk sister (again) roaming the halls pretending that everything was okay. She was drinking so much and pressing me about my plans. I wanted to tell her, but the timing wasn't right. I needed to find the others.

Maybe Kole and Kare were already in the banquet hall since it was almost time for dinner. I couldn't shake the gut feeling that something bad was going to happen. We never went this long without checking in with each other.

My homecoming has been a nightmare since our boat docked. When were the gods going to cut me a break? A loud bang snapped me back to attention. I turned to see three guards standing in the doorway.

"Can I help you goons with something?" I asked them barely acknowledging their presence.

"Marcus requests your presence in the throne room."

"Well, it's about time. Is my husband back yet?"

"I was instructed to bring you to the throne room, nothing more."

I wasn't happy about being summoned by Marcus, aside from the fact that I have been looking for him for hours. The game that he was playing was getting old and today was the last day I would tolerate it.

On my walk to the throne room, I rehearsed the speech I was going to give him in my head. We had been here long enough. We weren't going to learn anything new at this point, so we might as well accept that he will not surrender and war was going to be inevitable.

My palms were sweaty, and I was getting nervous. Still, no word from Kole or Kare. The thought of it was twisting my stomach into a knot. It wasn't like either of them to just disappear. I walked into the throne room and the guards took their place at the entrance blocking the doors. I scanned the room looking for any sign of them. The knot moved from my stomach to my chest. Something was very wrong.

"Octavia, I'm glad you were able to meet us. Sorry about the last couple of days, the kingdom requires much attention." Marcus was pompously sitting on the throne.

"I can see that. I have been looking for you for hours and no one could tell me where you or Titus have been." Titus was standing at the base of the throne with an evil glare on his face. His expression was intense, like he was holding the anger of a volcano beneath the surface.

"We had some important things we needed to take care," Titus spoke coldly.

"Then what is your answer because what you're doing to my city is barbaric and wrong. I'm tired of your games." I couldn't hide my tone, but everything that I have seen was starting to boil over. "Either surrender the throne or we can dismiss this parlay and prepare for what comes next." I needed him to take me seriously. He still looked at me as if I was the girl that he kidnapped, but that girl has been gone for some time.

"Interesting that you bring up dismissing the parlay. Maybe you should have a seat so we can talk. By the way, have you heard from your fiancé today, princess?" Marcus smiled.

My heart was in my throat. It took me a few moments to gather my resolve because ever since he left my side to go down to the docks, I could feel that he is missing. I could feel that the bond that connected us somehow moved further away.

"My husband took a walk down to the market. He finds our Roman culture fascinating. He likes to learn of our stories and traditions. A real man is not afraid to embrace change," I said.

"So, there is nothing else that you need to tell us, princess?" Marcus asked.

"I've said what I need, the ball is in your court," I responded.

Marcus raised his hand and the guards dragged in a woman. The clothes she was wearing were covered in dark dried blood. I saw her curls covering her face and that brown skin that reminded me of Kole. My heart dropped from my throat back down to the pit of my stomach. The guards threw Kare down at the bottom of the throne, her hands and feet were in shackles.

"What the fuck do you think you are doing Marcus? Release her now." I could feel the fire underneath the surface. I was not going to let the same thing happen again. I couldn't protect Tiberius, but Kare wouldn't suffer the same fate. Titus grabbed Kare by the hair and lifted her head so that I could see her face.

"You see, I would release her if she wasn't involved in a crime earlier today. Blame that she shares with your beloved Norse king, who for some reason put his head on the line for a measly handmaiden." He stood up from his seat and he was on his way down the steps. "Now, why would he do something like that? I think you all have been lying to me since your boat landed on these shores. Your arrogance will be your undoing, princess. Your father used to say the same thing," he smirked.

"Don't you dare speak as if you knew my father or his thoughts of me. What crime has she committed, and where is Kole?" My hands were starting to glow, but I was trying to keep it together.

"Your king is rotting in a cell waiting to be judged for killing three of my soldiers to protect your handmaiden, who shouldn't have been absent from your side anyway," Titus responded.

“Now is the time you start talking about why you are here, because the killing of my men violates the terms of parlay and he will be punished. If you tell us everything, maybe we will let you live until we can find you a proper husband,” Marcus chimed in.

“Where the fuck is my husband, Marcus?” He had a smug look on his face, he found me amusing.

“Princess, please, there is no need for yelling,” he waved his hand and the guard picked up Kare and took her away.

“What are you doing with her?” I took a step toward the throne and the guard put a knife closer to her throat.

“If you stay where you are, no harm will come to her. She will be placed in your room under supervision until it is time for her to be judged, but you shouldn’t worry about her. You have some explaining to do.” Marcus turned his attention back to me. “I’ll lend you some advice princess. You should really be careful who you trust.”

The smile that stretched across his face was wicked as the small girl walked into the throne room brushing past me and locked arms with Titus. Her face didn’t change as she settled in next to my captors.

My sister, my blood, and the last connection I had to my past, stood with the monsters that separated us. I didn’t want to believe it. Kole warned me about how deep Titus’ manipulation could go, but this was something I could never have prepared for. Either way, whatever her reason for the betrayal, I was in no state of mind to consider forgiveness. Maybe I needed to accept she had made her choice.

Kole was in a cell, Kare was being contained to my room, and I was all alone with no way to contact any help. Titus and Marcus stood on the steps next to the throne basking in the pain on my face. It felt like they were on the verge of laughter.

I was aware of the heat on my hands as they started to glow. The humming in my head began. It was faint, but I could hear the voices. I was unaware of anyone in the room. All that I could see was the one who stabbed me in the back. I couldn't take my eyes off Floria, but she kept her eyes on the floor hoping that she could escape what she has done.

"Kill them all!" The voice was pounding.

"Trust no one, end it now!" They got louder.

I was starting to lose it. Everything that I'd been holding on to was overflowing and it was aimed right at my sister, who still hadn't raised her head to look me in the eye. I could smell the stench of burning wood as my hands started to sink into the table leaving charred marks shaped like my fingers.

"What the hell is she doing father? Her hands are melting the table!" Titus shouted.

"I'm not sure, but I've had enough of this spectacle. Put her in chains. A couple of days in her room should calm her down until the trial begins." Marcus urged the guards to grab me. "You see, when I questioned your sister about your intentions, she suspected you were here to steal what we have built. Unlike you, none of us are traitors. We love this Roman way of life, we would never allow you to come in and take it." He started to walk away. He let out a deep laughter from his gut as he made his way out of the throne room, leaving me in the midst of my breakdown.

The voices were screaming as they approached me. The first guard reached for my arm and I closed my fist over his. The smell almost made me gag as his skin started to melt. He tried to pull his hand away, but I wanted to make sure he felt as much pain as I did.

When he finally pulled his hand free, he ran across the room screaming in pain. I made a move towards the throne, but three more guards grabbed me. They beat me to try to subdue me, but I was lost in rage screaming over all the voices in my head.

"Look at me!" I screamed at my sister.

"Look at me!"

"Look at what you have done!"

"Look at me, Floria!" I screamed until my voice was hoarse and the guard slammed the base of his sword into my head. I fell to my knees, and they dragged me back to my room kicking and screaming, and locked me in.

Ω

Kare ran to my side and hugged me as I screamed my sister's name. This type of betrayal hurt worse than any wound. I closed my eyes and tried to give myself over to the despair because I was sure this would be the final straw. This is what would take me over the edge. Maybe I should just burn it all down. There is nothing left for me anyway. Nothing but pain and anguish and even after everything the gods felt the need to take Kole away as well. So, to hell with all of it. I was going to let it all go. I reached down to grab the flames. I was going to burn every Roman I could find that tried to protect Marcus and Titus. I would put both their heads on spikes above his precious arena.

I walked over to the door and, to my surprise, found it unlocked. I ripped it open expecting to have to fight some guards, only I wasn't in the hallway of the villa, I was in the wasteland of the dead soldiers. At least that's what it looked like.

The sand was rough under my feet, the heat unbearable. There was nothing in sight until I heard the cold voice coming from all directions. After our journey to Midselium, I would never forget the god of war's voice.

"This is quite a mess you have created. Now instead of thinking with your head, you are letting your emotions get in the way." The god's voice roared in my head.

"With all due respect, if you're not here to help me, I'm not in the mood to be chastised." I didn't have time for this nonsense, I had a city to burn down.

"Why do think I'm here? I was unable to reach you in the Norse lands, but here I am strong. You have come a long way and proved you are the right choice, but there is much to do." A chair made of bones appeared and the god sat down. I didn't presume to ask him to conjure me up a seat, as well.

"Everything is falling apart. I'm sorry if I don't see the road to success like you do. It must be my mortality." I was hoping the sarcasm wouldn't get me killed.

"As I said to you before, in these lands, I am stronger. While I am not allowed to directly help you, there are questions that can be answered, if you know how to ask," he said. He remained silent which was my signal to ask questions.

"How am I supposed to finish what we started without Kole and no way to signal to the others?" I asked in a panic.

"You are the fire of Rome, start acting like it. You are not out of options. You need to trust the ones who have earned it." I couldn't do anything but roll my eyes. This was going to be unbelievably difficult, and my track record with riddles was terrible. If it wasn't for Kole, I would never figure them out.

"What is that supposed to mean?" I threw up my hands.

"You want another answer, ask a different question, but time is running out my child." Again, how convenient. I had a zillion questions and now I had a time limit. I was not going to get all the answers I wanted but I needed to stick to the most important questions. Mars couldn't tell me specifically how to win but if I had the pieces that I needed to win then he didn't have to.

"Where is Kole?" I asked.

"Your beloved king is in a cell under the arena waiting to be judged, but do not fear for him. I can feel him, his rage won't allow him to be broken so easily." I felt a weight lift off my shoulders. He was alive and, if I knew him, he wouldn't give up.

It was torture to be separated from him. All I wanted to do was be in his arms so we could weather this storm together. Mars must have known that the answer helped me. I felt at ease with the energy that was coming off him.

"What about our allies?" I asked.

"A storm is on its way to Cosa and, if the land holds, the queen will have her support," he replied and sat back in his chair.

This one was going to be a lot harder to decipher. the storm must be Rollo... but what does he mean if the land holds? Ugh, everything was a damn puzzle, it was exhausting.

"I hope this has been helpful my child, but I must go. You have the tools, and you have the power. Trust your instinct, follow your gut, and you will be victorious."

Before I could ask anything else of him, I was back in my room, the glowing in my hands fading as I was staring at the door.

17 - DEATH AT A PARTY – ROLLO

The sea was against us the entire way. I didn't feel much of a connection to Thor over these waters, which was a terrible omen. There was no use praying for safe travels at this point. I didn't know what I was walking into once I reached this island but getting killed on sight was definitely on my mind.

The rough water was trying to make sure that we never made it to shore. This was too important for me to fail, so even if I had to swim there myself, I needed to get the help I promised. No matter how much I was worried about my boat being flipped by these waters, the only thing I could really think about was Marcella. I've never met anyone like her before, but the image of her ripping those soldiers to shreds was burned in my head. Beautiful and dangerous, I wasn't sure if I was interested or afraid. Intrigued was most likely the word.

"How much further till we reach land?" I asked.

"We can see land from here, my king. We should be docking soon," the captain called out.

"Is it safe to dock at this speed? The water could smash the boat against the rocks." I couldn't downplay how nervous I was.

"We have no choice, we either dock or the waters will carry us away," the captain yelled over the violence of the ocean.

Water was crashing into the boat from all directions. The captain was right. If I waited any longer, we all might drown. The boat plummeted towards land fast. It was now or never. I had to trust my crew because this would be such a crappy way to die. We tied a rope to a giant metal anchor and threw it overboard. It slowed down the boat as the side of the hull slammed into the port nearly capsizing the ship. The hull scrapped against the side of the dock. There was noticeable damage to the boat hopefully I could borrow some supplies to make repairs. We weren't dead but it wasn't the entrance I had planned.

What looked like the royal guard was waiting on the docks. I assume they were wondering how I was able to even make it to their shores. It was decorated with royal blue fabric up and down the pillars. Waving in the vicious wind was a blue flag with a golden three-headed fork. I knew it was a weapon of some sort, but I didn't know the name. I should have asked Octavia if there was anything I needed to know about her neighbors on this island. What if they kill visitors on sight? What if they eat people? This could get out of hand fast. Let's just hope my overactive imagination is getting the best of me.

The soldiers approached us cautiously waiting for us to say something. Now that I am king, I had to be introduced formally every single time. I wish I'd brought my crown with me. It would make me feel more king-like. I just felt like a guy with a hammer saying he was king. It didn't make a difference to the Romans, but these are the conversations I use to distract myself from all this responsibility.

The crew stayed behind to make sure the boat was tied down. If not the rough tide would sweep it right into the ocean. They also needed to assess the results of my dramatic entrance. I walked up the docks until I ran into a group of soldiers who stopped me from going any further.

"Announce yourself, Norsemen. Why have you traveled to our shores?" The rain was smacking me in the face, I could barely lift my hood to respond back to them.

"Is there somewhere we can go to get out of the weather and speak? This doesn't seem the right time or place to have this discussion." The soldiers stood perfectly still like statues, and I could see that my request made no impression on them at all. The Romans were so serious all the time, it was exhausting.

"I am King Rollo of Ragnarsson. I am here to speak to your queen on behalf of princess Octavia." The mention of her name gave the soldiers pause. I wasn't sure how they felt about her here, but she was the only connection I have to this land. Judging from their body language, the soldiers seemed to relax enough to escort us to the main house.

As the soldiers escorted us, even though the weather was terrible, I observed the surrounding lands. Cosa had so much potential. This island must be beautiful without the extremes of a storm harassing it. The wind was blowing the rain sideways. The force wasn't unbearable, but it left nothing to be desired.

The guards walked us to what I would assume was the main house. It was built from a light-colored wood that was flexible in the wind. Every gust bent the top of the wood, but it wouldn't break. I've never seen this type of wood in Najora.

Once we were inside, I felt like I was interrupting some type of celebration, but it was nothing like a Norse feast. This was very different. You could hear the storm raging on the outside, but no one inside seemed to care. A rhythmic drum was controlling the movements of the crowd. All different types of people were dancing around the room, spinning, twirling, and exchanging dance partners as they pranced around the room. Dark skin, light skin, blonde hair, and dark hair. There was no end to the different combinations. It was like none of them had a single care in the world.

The men were shirtless, wearing nothing but a light material around their waist. The women wore the same material. Some elected to cover themselves, others didn't care to do so, and neither decision would divert my eyes.

The energy in the room was infectious, similar to how I felt every time I stayed at Persephone's, which depending on whom you ask could be good or bad. I wanted to meet the queen alone, I didn't want to give off the wrong message. The guards stripped me of my weapons, so it was just me and my alleged charm.

"My queen, you have a visitor. He says he is here on behalf of the missing princess Octavia." At the sound of her name, the queen snapped to attention. She had long blonde hair and piercing blue eyes.

She stood tall. From the center of the room, I was looking up to her as she walked down towards me. We happen to be the same height. Good thing my ego was less fragile than most. I was completely outnumbered with no weapons, but still confident enough in my ability to appeal to any man or woman if need be. The queen didn't say anything once she approached me, she just kept glaring. I could see flickers of a roaring ocean, a sign of her royal blood. The gods have passed their gifts down through her blood.

"How do you know of the princess Octavia? I was told that she didn't survive the ambush. An ambush that I was told was carried out by your people." For the first time since her guards announced me, she broke her stare. "For you to even be here is foolish Norseman." The thought of having to explain everything from the beginning just seemed exhausting, especially since I had some of the information but not all of it.

"First and foremost, thank you for allowing me in your home Queen…" I looked to one of the guards to help me with the name.

"Cassia."

"Yes, Queen Cassia."

"I wouldn't thank me yet. We still aren't sure if these faces are the last ones you will see, Norse King." She looked to her guards to help with my name. I couldn't help but laugh.

"Rollo." She nodded for me to continue. "I am aware of the ambush of Alexandria and, while I know the men that attacked were dressed like my countrymen, they were not sent by us," I told her.

"I'm sorry to interrupt your majesty, but why should I believe the word of a stranger over one of our own?" A slender older man asked. He was dressed in gold fabric as he emerged walking slowly toward the center of the room. The queen rolled her eyes as the little man spoke.

"Sorry Rollo, this is Julius. He is an advisor from Alexandria," the queen said. She spoke his name kind of dismissively, so I opted to start my story.

I started from the beginning and made sure not to leave out any detail since Ivar tried to have us killed in the woods. I informed her that Octavia is alive, but she was kidnapped the night of the ambush by Marcus who was working in tandem with Halfdan.

The deeper I went into the story, her temperament changed. She was completely engaged anticipating getting an answer I'm not sure that I had. She was just hungry for all the information she could get. When I finished, I was tired of hearing my own voice. I just hope I didn't forget anything, the fate of the plan depended on it.

"You make some very bold claims and, while parts of your story fit the timeline, it is treason to speak against the crown in this manner, especially with no evidence," Julius said. It was clear who Julius was loyal to.

"I'll be the judge of what is treason, Julius. You are an advisor sent here without request, might I add. That being said, it is an amazing tale Rollo. You surely have captured an audience. Not every day do we get to stand in the room with someone who has been to the land of the gods. Your claim to have communed with your gods and one of mine is quite an accomplishment as well. You could be one of the most famous

Norse in the world. So, why are you here fighting for a land that is not yours?" she asked.

"Because I have lost people that I love as a result of power and glory hungry leaders. If Marcus succeeds, he will march directly into Najora and start a war that no one wants. He values our lives lower than animals. The actions of others have forced me into being king, a role that, if I can speak plainly, I was not ready for." Her face softened after I spoke.

"I too have been forced into this to keep my people from suffering. I have no proof, but I believe there is some foul play responsible for the sudden death of my father. However, I will not help you unless I know that we have a fighting chance," she said.

"My queen, what you speak of is blasphemy. You can't really believe this dog whom you have only just met might I add. He is here to separate the crown so he can take the land himself. Our lord, King Marcus, is leading us into a united age, all countries under the Bellator banner just like the gods of Olympus," Julius said proudly.

"Oh, I know we have a fighting chance, and I have no care to rule this land. I have a kingdom of my own to run and that is enough for me but if you joined us, it would give us a clear advantage over Marcus," I spoke directly disregarding every vile word that spilled out of Julius' mouth.

"My queen, you should have him killed just for the thought of turning on Marcus. Don't forget you have sworn loyalty to him," Julius yelled. I thought it was a perfect time to stir the pot just a little bit more. Julius was obviously a Marcus puppet.

"Queen Cassia, right now Octavia and her fiancé, King Kole of Lundr, are in Alexandria at this very moment for parlay," I smiled and continued, "we had hoped to end this feud with no bloodshed, which further validates my point of not wanting to take any lands from the Roman people. The gods have set us on a path of peace, not tyranny." I had a feeling that I was making a great impression on the queen.

All this talk of liberation was pushing her closer to our side. I know she is smart enough to see that Julius was an extension of Marcus. She didn't strike me as the type that liked to be told what to do.

"This King Kole, he is a Norse as well?" she asked.

"Yes he is, and he is my best friend and one of the best men I know. He has sacrificed much to make sure that the princess returns home," I answered.

"With all that in mind, their marriage would technically make him King of Roman land. What would stop him from taking our cities? A king's ambition knows no bounds when in the name of power." Cassia waited intently for my answer.

"If any of you know princess Octavia, she is not one to be controlled. She loves her home very much and she only wants the best for her people. Our hope is one day we can live in unison and recognize both our cultures and respect them as such." I made sure to direct my statements towards Julius again. Watching him squirm was entertaining.

"This is madness! And Marcus will hear of this. It is treason to conspire against the king." He forced his way through the crowd heading towards the door. He waved his hands and a few other people rose from their seats at his command.

“Make yourself comfortable, Rollo. With all of this new information, I have some business to handle before we finish this conversation,” she snapped her hands, and the guards grabbed Julius and three other men that were sitting in the crowd.

“Sweep the city of any other moles Julius has planted here. His spies bear his mark. I won’t have them telling any more of my secrets. We have pressing matters to discuss, and I would rather speak freely.” She made herself comfortable again at the front of the house.

My shoulders tensed, and I braced myself expecting her guards to round me up next. Would she lock me up as well just because she was paranoid?

“Rollo, I will have a room prepared for you. We have much more to discuss and, if I like your plan, maybe we can talk about our next move.” She signaled the musicians. The music started playing again, her people poured their drinks as the guards rounded up more and more of Julius’ spies.

The guards escorted me to a room upstairs. My furs and weapons were laying neatly on a bed. I laid down to try and process what my next move would be but, for now, since my weapons were returned to me, I could say that Cassia was on the road to trusting me and joining this fight. I hope Kole was having the same success in Alexandria. I laid down staring at the ceiling expecting to be up the entire night, but I was exhausted. Even though Cassia was rounding up spies, the party continued, so I closed my eyes and let the soft rhythm of the drums carry me to some much-needed rest. I dreamed about home, the clean cool breeze, the laughter of the people, and on the edge of my dream was her face. The faint scar, empty eyes, and the monstrous grin.

Ω

I was ripped out of my sleep by a stranger shaking me, and without looking I had my knife to the man's throat. It took me a minute to come to, and I let the man go. Maybe I wasn't as comfortable as I thought.

"Maybe we shouldn't have given you your weapons back," the man muttered as he backed away from me and stood in the doorway.

"Sorry, I don't do well with surprises. Is there something you need?" I asked. I was already embarrassed enough so moving past this would be great.

"The queen requested your presence downstairs. It's time to get answers, and she would like you to be there." He walked out before I could answer. I assumed that meant it was not optional.

It sounded like the storm had settled. I wonder how much of that was natural. Did the queen somehow have a way to manipulate the weather the way my father did? The house was all but empty at this point. There was no music or chatter just the sound of fire cracking inside an empty hall.

Cassia was standing in front of the fire poking at the embers, her royal guard was behind her standing at attention. She was dressed in an ocean blue dress with armor plates on the shoulders trailing down her arms. Next to her, someone was tied to the chair completely naked, but I could not see the prisoner's face. Whatever was going on, I wasn't sure why I needed to be here.

"Rollo, thank you for joining us. I hope you were comfortable in the room we gave you," Cassia said with a wide smile on her face.

"Of course, I was very comfortable. Thank you for the room. I managed to snag a few moments of sleep. Apparently revolution is exhausting." I laughed to soften this mood. I kept trying to look past her, trying to get an idea of who was tied up.

"My father was preparing to leave that day Alexandria was ambushed, and he kept saying something felt off. His connection to the gods was strong, he had a knack for reading omens. Even as a kid, he would know whenever I was lying just by looking at me. Something about the way my energy shifted." She walked past the prisoner in the chair toward me, I tried not to show how uneasy I was, but I had to be prepared for anything. Fighting her is not what I wanted to do but I would rather not be caught off guard. She paid no attention to me and just continued her story.

"He told us that something didn't feel right about this trip, so he would be sailing there alone and, when he arrived safely, he would send for my mother and I to join him. Alas, he left that day and never returned. A couple of days later, my mother receives a message from Marcus stating that my father and King Maximus have been killed in a Norse ambush. Not only that, but the boy Tiberius and his sister were also dead." She made her way back to the fire and started to poke at the embers again. She turned and walked back toward me completely expressionless. This whole thing was creeping me out.

“Can I just say very quickly that I don’t do very well with heat,” I joked, my defense mechanism in tense situations. The queen’s face remained expressionless as she continued telling her story.

“My mother was so distraught with the news of my father that she fell ill. She was so in love with my father that losing him was crippling, and life without him was unbearable for her. So, one night, she walked into my room. She thought I was asleep, but I could feel her staring at me. She kissed me on my forehead, then snuck out of my room without saying anything.”

“She didn’t say goodbye?” I asked. Cassia shook her head in disappointment.

“She walked to the edge of the island and jumped into the rough water off the coast and never returned.” You could tell that she still wore the scar of her mother leaving. I knew exactly how it felt to not be able to say goodbye.

“Now, I am the queen, and on the day I was coronated, Marcus arrives at my shores forcing me to swear loyalty to him because of an impending Norse threat.” I saw where this was going and I really didn’t like it. She returned to the fire and grabbed the steel rod. “And just when I think I have it sort of figured out, you arrive here telling me that the princess and her Norse fiancé are in Alexandria to parlay to end this threat, so here is what we are going to do.”

She grabbed the chair and spun it around so I could see the prisoner’s face. Julius was sitting in the chair unconscious his hands were tied and he had shackles on his feet. A royal guard grabbed a bucket of water and threw it onto Julius snapping him back to life. The man gasped and was shaking his head back in forth trying to figure out where he was.

“What do you think you are doing, release me now Cassia!” he yelled.

“Not until I hear the truth. You were present the night of the attack, correct Julius? So, you are going to answer my questions or this is going to get ugly.” She took the steel poker and laid it on top of his leg, Julius screamed in pain as the light stench of burnt flesh smeared the air. She removed the steel rod after a couple of seconds and returned it to the flame.

“Rollo, have a seat please. We all need to have a conversation, and I pray you too are being truthful.” She had a cold, impatient look on her face. Two guards grabbed me and forced me down into a chair across from Julius. He was fighting to free himself from the restraints.

“Julius, I hope by now you can tell how serious I am. I advise you think carefully about my next question. My only ask is that you please answer truthfully, or it is going to be a long night for you.” She paced back and forth with deadly precision.

“You are a disgrace to Gracia, and you will pay for your……” Cassia’s fist connected with his face almost knocking him out of the chair before he could finish the sentence. He sat motionless for a bit, and I was afraid that she might have killed him with that punch, but then he spit blood onto the floor and groaned in pain.

“How did my father die that night?” she asked.

"We told you, he was killed by the Norse in the ambush, most of us were lucky to make it out alive. Thank the gods Marcus was there," he struggled to talk.

"See that's the part that I don't buy. Countless people were attacked and killed including two Roman Kings, but somehow you and all of Marcus' pathetic followers managed to avoid death." She had a curious tone in her voice. "Rollo, if your people were to attack, in all honesty, do you think it would have been easy to kill two Roman kings without a king of your own being present?" Her eyes raced over to mine.

"Honestly, I've seen our kings fight and, if yours was anything like ours then no, we surely wouldn't have managed to kill any of them without him present," I answered truthfully.

I remember vividly when Kole fought King Styr. I had never seen anything like that type of power and strength. No chance he would be taken down by common men. I wondered how Julius would come up with a lie to back up his story.

"You see where I'm going with this, Julius," Cassia turned back toward him.

"Marcus is a great warrior. The gods were with him that night. He saved us all it is unfortunate what happened to the others." Julius' voice was frantic.

"So, you're saying that my father and King Maximus were inferior to Marcus, and that is why he survived. Sorry, I'm not buying it." Cassia stuck the steel rod through his shoulder and out the back of the chair.

Julius shrieked in pain to the heavens and then Cassia yanked the steel rod from his flesh. Blood started to spill down his clothes and his eyes rolled to the back of his skull as he tried to stay conscious. Cassia came around the front of the chair pausing in front of him letting him bleed just a little bit more.

After a couple of seconds, she took the hot tip of the rod and burned the edge of his wound in the front and back to seal it closed. Julius continued to scream as his flesh burned against the metal.

"Now Julius, stop lying to me or I'm going to stab you and close the wound over and over again. Trust me when I say I could do this all night and not tire of your screams." She returned the rod to the flames.

"Rollo, you have given me your entire testimony, in amazing detail I might add. My gut tells me that you are being truthful, which is why you are just sitting, not tied up like this traitor." She smiled at me with a manic look on her face before she turned and struck Julius in the face again.

The man would not relent, and Cassia proceeded to stab him anywhere she could think of. At this point, even I wished that the man would confess because the smell of flesh was nauseating. Julius kept slipping in and out of consciousness. In order to wake him up for more torture, a guard would throw more water before the process would repeat all over again.

"Wake up, Julius. You will be able to rest soon. I tire of this game and, if you don't speak plainly, the next one is through your heart. Now, tell me what happened to my father."

Julius was covered in blood, burn marks all over, and the chains around his feet were digging away at his skin. I don't know how he managed to keep this up.

"You let me go and I'll tell you everything you need to know," he struggled to force the words out.

"Start talking and I will strongly consider giving you peace," Cassia said.

"Marcus had a plan to unify the country and eventually take over the lands out west. He claimed that the gods spoke to him and wanted him to reclaim this land, but first he needed to move pieces off the board." The last words he said seemed to enrage Cassia and she was raising her fist to strike him again.

"Wait," I yelled to her, "let him finish. I'm not sure how much more punishment he can take, and we need answers." She glared down at Julius and decided to heed my advice.

"Marcus' dream of uniting Gracia under one king would never happen with Maximus and Gaius in the way." His bloodshot eyes traced up to meet mine. "He shared the same sentiment with a Norse king, Halfdan. Together, they needed to wait for the right moment to stage an attack that would convince the people and keep both our leaders in the dark." The pain must have been intense, Julius was trying to speak through it.

"So, that's why you waited until the celebration days, you knew we would all gather in one place," I said it out loud to myself.

"What Marcus did not count on is your father sailing off on his own, but he has spies everywhere. It wasn't long before he located him. Your father docked on an unmanned coast to conceal his own arrival. He was never supposed to make it to the celebration." Cassia's face was flushed with anger and confusion, jumping furiously between the two. "Somehow Gaius managed to survive the attack. He killed six men, and then made his way to the villa in Alexandria. He burst in the doors and accused Marcus of being a traitor before dying from his wounds."

"So why did no one help or do anything about it?" Cassia was frustrated.

"The attack began immediately after that, and it distracted everyone from the accusation. All that were present jumped into action to defend the villa." He was talking and periodically spitting the clumped blood out of his mouth.

"Octavia has talked about that night. She said that she fought someone that overpowered her, but I've seen her in action. She is not without skill," I said.

"Marcus had his son Titus and his men dress like Norse to make the attack more believable. He killed the kings boy Tiberius. The plan was to kill her as well, but someone must have failed that part of the plan."

"Why would Marcus trust you with all of this?" I asked.

"He needed someone he trusts to keep tabs on our newly ordained queen," he refused to look at Cassia.

It was all starting to make sense. This is why the gods decided to take action when they did. In their own sick way, they managed to save us, though I still did not approve of their methods. Julius was breathing a sigh of relief after finally confessing to all the lies he was forced to keep.

"After the chaos died down, Marcus had the people turn on King Maximus for not retaliating immediately. He was able to sway the crowd and put them to death, completing the last part of the plan." Cassia was staring at the floor., She hadn't said a word since she learned the truth of her father's death, but Julius continued to speak. "We have done what the gods instructed us to do, and if you savages would have done your part, we wouldn't be here. I assume that whoever orchestrated this with Marcus is no longer with us?" he asked.

"You would be correct, I killed him myself," I nodded.

"Figures, we should have never relied on any of your kind. Something like this is too complex for your simple minds. All you care about is fighting, drinking, and dreaming of your false promise la-," Without warning Cassia slit his throat.

He was fighting to get his hands free to cover his throat, but his hands were bound. He struggled to speak but the blood leaked from his mouth and his wound until he went limp in the chair, never to say another devious word again. I can't say that I blamed her for killing him. He was a coward and, to be honest, he got off easy compared to all the lives he has ruined.

"Now, you are at peace," she whispered in his ear before she wiped the blood off the blade on her sleeve. "Rollo, I'm sorry for the nature of my hospitality thus far. You are free to roam the city as you please." She grabbed a cloth to wipe the rest of the blood off her hands.

"Thank you, Cassia. I'm sorry to hear about your father, warriors always deserve an honorable death, though none of this surprises me. There has been no end to the amount of treachery displayed by such disgraceful and dishonorable cowards since this colossal shitshow started. I only hope those of us who have lost can band together to honor our dead by exacting justice against those who have earned our retribution." I hope she knew that I was being completely sincere.

"I will have plenty of opportunities to do right by him when my armies join you and take down this traitor." I looked up quickly to make sure I heard her correctly.

"So, you agree to join us?" I wanted to hide my surprise. But let's be honest, I can't believe I actually pulled this off.

"Don't look so surprised. When you are ready to strike, let me know. I will begin preparations." With a slight nod, she made her way out of the room.

Her guards carried out the lifeless body. It was a bloody interrogation, but Julius finally filled in all the pieces we were missing. When I reunite with my friends, I can tell them the truth. The truth about that night, the reason that Ivar and his traitor father decided to have us killed in the woods. Nothing Marcus promised would have been worth that type of betrayal. He almost ripped our entire nation apart for some false sense of power. Now I just needed to wait for the signal. We were going to end this once and for all.

Ω

I'd spent the next couple of days trying to catch up on some of the much-needed sleep, but it seemed like the party in Cosa never stopped. Cassia informed her people of the changes that were going to be made in the wake of removing all of the men that were loyal to Julius.

The mood from the crowd was joyous, like a dark weight was lifted and everyone could finally breathe. Even the weather responded to the mood, the storm that tormented the island when I arrived calmed to a light breeze and a strong sun. This place was amazing. I understand why the locals were so happy. The island was such a peaceful place. If I wasn't on a mission, I'd be working on my tan or lack thereof.

"Take a walk with me, Rollo." Cassia looped her arm underneath mine and we walked through the city.

"Seems like Julius took the bad weather with him to the afterlife," I joked.

"It may seem so, but I'm afraid that I am responsible for that," she said. I wanted to ask what she meant, but I did not want to overstep and end up strapped to a chair myself.

"My family is decedent from the Roman god, Neptune. He has complete dominion over the ocean in his lands. It is said that this island was a piece of his underwater kingdom and that, over time, it made its way to the surface. How true that is I wouldn't know. Legends have a way of becoming embellished over time, though I'm sure you have experienced this of your own folklore."

We headed down towards the beach. The sand was getting into my shoes, and it was something that I would never get used to, no matter how beautiful it was. I knew I would spend days trying to get rid of it completely.

"So, why would all the storms be your fault?" I asked.

"When my father died and I became queen, my powers started to develop, but I had no one here to guide and teach me." She put her head down. I knew that look, the reoccurring pain of losing her parents flooding to the front of her mind.

"If it makes you feel better, I almost killed myself and my best friend when my powers started to grow. Our paths are very different, but we have to stay strong and learn as we go. Kole always tells me that if we open our imaginations then we can manipulate our powers to fully control them instead of them controlling us." I wish I could steal that advice and call it my own.

"Not all of us have been touched by the gods though," she said. "But he sounds like a wise king, I look forward to meeting him."

"Please don't tell him that in person, it will go to his head, and I've seen it up close. It's big enough already." We both laughed.

"Now that I have full control over the island, and I don't have to worry about spies reporting everything I say to Marcus, I can focus on making my father proud. I assume the beautiful weather is my mood improving. For once since his death, I feel like I can breathe freely and make decisions for myself."

We stopped and turned to the ocean, the water was calmy rising up and down the beach. I felt like it was a privilege to see Cosa this way instead of how it was when I arrived. It was bright and innocent, untouched by all the turmoil that was happening in the rest of the country.

We stood on the edge of the water in silence. Taking my time to appreciate how much I missed the peace and quiet. The memory of home tugged at my heart. I was thrust into this responsibility and, though I would not change my path, a simpler life wouldn't be off the table.

"Do you mind if I ask you a question?" She spoke softly.

"Yeah, go ahead. Speak your mind," I answered.

"When you and your friends made it to Midselium, did you see any of the other gods?" Her eyes were blue as the water we were standing in, but I couldn't tell what she had riding on the answer.

"No, we only saw the gods that we were descended from, which was followed by a story. A rather long one, actually," I joked. "Odin and Mars told us that not all the gods agreed with their plan to heal the rift between them. What that means for the future I have no idea, but we know that they are dedicated to fixing their mistakes."

That was as honest as I could be. It didn't bode well for us knowing that Odin could only find two allies to heal a blood feud between immortals, but I wasn't the one making any decisions.

"Do you think we can win?" She asked sincerely.

Kole was certain we could win and that was enough for me. I grabbed both her hands to reassure her.

"Yes, I believe if we all work together, we can win." She took a step closer until the space between us was swallowed up.

"Then let's make sure we win, pretty eyes." She planted a kiss on my cheek, which completely surprised me. I thought she was about to lean in for the real thing, but I was saved by a soldier running towards us in the sand. My mind was completely wrapped on Marcella, I did not want to give her the wrong idea.

"My queen, we received a message from Alexandria that says it came from someone named Kare," my head snapped at the mention of her name.

"Does that mean anything to you?" She asked me.

“That is Kole’s sister, she is with them in Alexandria. What does it say?”

The queen ripped open the message and then her eyes met mine, but this look was different. It was bleeding with urgency.

“What does it say?” The suspense was killing me.

“It says come now!” Her blue eyes shined bright.

“I think that is a signal to go if I’ve ever seen one.”

18 - LOCKED UP – KOLE

The blood of my crew was on my hands. I would have to go back to their families and explain how their lives were taken by a spoiled child playing general. When the opportunity presents itself, I will make sure their death is repaid, but for now I needed to maintain my focus.

The floor of the cell wasn't stone, but the sand was hard and rough. It was pitch black at night you could barely see your hands in front of you; all I could hear were the groans coming from the other prisoners. The guards have been bringing people in and out of these cells for days. I had no idea how long I'd been down here. When you can't see the sun, it makes it tough to keep track of the days. No wonder Gio was so miserable, he was completely unaware of the time that passes and being immortal probably didn't help to ease the frustration.

My thoughts would wander from time to time but always fell back on Octavia and my sister. I didn't know what had become of them since I was taken, but I had hope that they are okay. If I know Octavia, she would be making damn sure of it. Nonetheless, my actions put them all in danger. I should have killed everyone in that market for good measure. It played in my head over and over that there had to be something that I could have done differently. Any option I could come up with put either Octavia or Kare in danger. I wasn't sure what they had planned for me now and, to be honest, I didn't care... but if one hair was misplaced on either of their heads, I would burn this entire city to the ground with no hesitation.

Dust from the walls started to fall from above and I could hear the familiar sound of the crowd filling the underground hallways. Must be time for the king to sentence more of the prisoners to death, lining them up and killing them on their knees with no honor. There is nothing more despicable or dishonorable than preventing any man or woman from fighting for their place in either this world or the afterlife, no matter where they believe they go after death, though I guess I shouldn't be surprised given the cowards who are calling the shots.

I heard footsteps coming from the far side of the tunnel as guards funneled in and started to unlock the cells, dragging out prisoners one by one. I tried to get onto my feet in preparation that my cell would be next. If they were going to take me then they should be ready for a fight. Instead, they dragged the other prisoners past my cell and out the other end of the tunnel barely acknowledging my existence.

"Too afraid of the big bad Norse!" I yelled. "Probably best you leave me here, I wouldn't want to fight me either," I taunted.

"You sure do have a big mouth, dog," the hair on my neck was at a standstill. Even in my short time here, I have grown so tired of the voice. "Have you always been all talk or is this based on some newfound delusion that you will make it out of this alive?" Titus walked slowly in front of my cell. I wanted to rip him in half, but I knew he was here to try to agitate me, so I decided to play along. Maybe I could get some information from him about the others.

"This must be my punishment then, sitting in this cell listening to the voice of the king's brat," I barked. Titus' company alone was torture and that smug look on his face was an exact replica of his father.

"Oh, your punishment will come, don't worry," he replied with a sneer.

"Is there a reason for this visit? As you can see, I have some straightening up to do here in my cell, I wasn't expecting company," I joked.

"I just wanted to see the face of the alleged chosen one knocked off his high horse, and his bitch won't be far behind." The giant smile on his face melted off when he realized that he slipped and said too much. Now at least I know Octavia is alive. I just needed to keep him talking to find out about Kare.

"Did your brother tell you what I did to all of those soldiers without even trying? I thought you all were supposed to be warriors." I smiled. "I wouldn't even be here if I didn't give up willingly, it's kind of pitiful actually. Two of your guards could barely deal with an unarmed handmaiden," I continued.

"I wouldn't worry about her either, she is with your bitch locked away. Once we make an example of you, guess who will be next," he countered with his signature evil grin on his face.

That was all I needed to know; they were alive, so all I had to do was figure out a way to get us all out safely.

"Again, while this has been an amazing conversation, I would rather speak with the person in charge, not his blood slaves," I turned my back to him trying to hide my smile because I know what dismissing him would do to his fragile ego. The Romans couldn't stand that I wasn't afraid of them.

"Disrespect me all you want for now dog, but when your throat is opened on the sands, and your blood is washed away from this land just like that weakling Tiberius, none of this will be amusing." My blood was boiling at the mention of the name, but I could not let him provoke me, so I stood firm until he left.

Ω

Thanks to Titus and his visit I could start thinking about how I was going to get us out of here. The plan didn't have to be perfect, but I had to know what was waiting for me outside of this cell.

Marcus was smart but he was arrogant, and the apple didn't fall far from the tree. In order to spur his hatred for the Norse even more, he was going to make sure my death was the biggest spectacle this city has ever seen. I could always just get out of here but leaving Octavia and Kare wasn't an option.

First things first, now that all the other prisoners were gone, I didn't have to pretend to be trapped. I closed my eyes and reached down for the darkness. The feeling was all too familiar as the power swept through me. A black door opened in front of me and I stepped through. Just to be safe, I only aimed for the outside of the cell, keeping the irritating chains in place for now. I started to walk towards the end of the tunnel, heading closer to the raging sound of the crowd begging for these cowards to take another life.

The stone on the way up to the arena was covered in blood. The heat made it impossible to ignore the terrible smell; it clung to the inside of my nostrils turning my stomach. At the end of the stairs, other prisoners were watching the executions through the gate, waiting for their turn to be fed to the slaughter.

How many of these men were actually criminals? And how many of them just happened to offend the new king and his weak sons? As much as I wanted freedom for them, I couldn't blow my cover to save everyone. I pushed past the prisoners so I could get to the front. I expected the guards to be keeping watch, but they were just as obsessed with the entertainment as the crowd was. They weren't paying attention to any of us.

From this gate, you could see the whole arena except what was right above me, which just sounded like more crazy fans. I counted three guards at this gate, two at the entrance to my left, two more to the right, and three right across from me directly underneath the area where I assume all the important guests sit.

The space was decorated with wooden tables and chairs, wine casks, goblets, and more food than you needed, especially when you were watching men get killed. That must be where Marcus sits, and I was almost certain that he would make Octavia and Kare watch me get executed while he enjoyed an afternoon snack. He was too proud and too much of a showman to place me with other prisoners. I would be out there to be killed alone. I was going to be an example for anyone watching.

If I could open a portal, maybe I could get to the balcony in time and get us all out. Escaping the city would be difficult, but once we were all together we could figure it out. It wasn't fool proof but if we can get away, we can regroup with Rollo and the others and try a different strategy. We would lose the element of surprise, but what other choice did we have?

I returned to my cell, resigned to wait until it is my time to shine. With Odin's blessing, I could pull this off or at least take as many Romans as possible with me before I welcome the gates of Valhalla and pray that Octavia forgives me in death. I pulled on the darkness searching for any remanence of the All-father, but it was as quiet and as dark as a tomb.

Ω

I waited in my cell for days and nothing happened. Why did everything here have to be so dramatic? I might kill myself out of boredom at this point. The guards had been bringing me bread and water periodically, but now the time between my rations were increasing. Days would go by sometimes without food or water, or what I could assume was days. Whatever they wanted to do to me they needed me weak enough to be confident they could pull it off. *Cowards.*

The water was hard to ration because I had nowhere to hide it but the food I could keep in my pants. The guards didn't care whether the tray they retrieved was empty or not. I planned to ration the food to accommodate for the days the guards seemed to forget to bring me anything. I didn't know when they would come for me, but Marcus would be expecting me to be starved and weak, waiting to be relieved of his torture. Unfortunately for him, I would be far from weak. I would be a caged animal waiting to strike.

A loud bang came from down the hall, the sounds of keys hitting the guard's belt. He wasn't carrying the usual tray, so I wasn't going to be eating today. Thank the gods I ate some of the bread I had saved up earlier. Four more guards made their way down into the tunnels, all of them converging in front of my cell. Whatever was coming next I wasn't going to like it.

The guard opened the cell and stepped in. Instinctively, I took a small step back before the other guards filed into my cell. The guards didn't speak. They just all stared at me while we waited for someone to make the first move. What was Marcus planning to do?

This must be all a part of the plan to break my spirit in captivity. Marcus and his tactics grow in dishonor as the days drag on. If he thought this was going to break me, maybe he didn't know anything about the Norse at all. I could just take the keys from the first guard and teleport out of here but, in order for my plan to work, I had to make them believe they had the upper hand. I planted my back foot and braced myself.

All five guards attacked me at once, throwing punches and kicks in every direction. I managed to block most of the strikes but, after a few seconds, I fell to the floor and curled up in a ball to protect myself. I closed my eyes and focused on the dark rage that I had brewing under the surface. The guards continued to punch, kick, stomp, and spit on me, but I remained focused on the ravens. I let them engulf me to distract me until the soldiers finished their orders. The barrier between the real world and my darkness was folding in on itself. The raven swirled all around me, protecting me, empowering me, promising me my revenge, whispering that all I had to do was endure.

I kept my composure and let the darkness absorb everything. The power calmed and soothed me as the chaos from the attack continued. At some point I would feel the pain of the beating I'd taken, but for the most part, I was fine. I didn't even know that soldiers were done. I pried my eyes open and realized I was being carried up the stairs towards the giant gate leading into the arena.

The crowd had simmered to a small rumble, everything sounding muffled which I assume was a result of the beating. When I was dragged onto the sand, the sun burned my skin bringing me into view. The crowd went from a small rumble to a giant roar.

Citizens in the crowd were stomping and cheering at the top of their lungs, but I couldn't understand what they were saying, it was all too loud. They threw food and drink in my direction as the guards carried me out. The sun was high and unbearable. I could feel the weight of it sitting on my shoulders, but I could also feel it underneath my hands and knees. the sands left a burning sensation as the guards placed me in the middle of the arena. The pain from the attack started to settle in as my meditation wore off. Nothing felt broken, but I was sure that I was not a pleasant sight.

I looked up to the royal balcony where I expected to see Marcus, but it was empty. My heart plummeted into my stomach, Kare and Octavia aren't here. Maybe I had underestimated Marcus. Was I the one that was arrogant, thinking that I was the hunter in this scenario? I sat in the middle of the arena on the sand, just waiting and praying to the gods that I didn't completely miss my opportunity.

19 – A TERRIBLE SHOW – OCTAVIA

The guards kept me locked in this room for days with no information on Kole. I tried to stay calm. If it wasn't for the vision from Mars, I probably would have burned down the villa already.

Kare spent most of the days sleeping and crying. She told me about what happened in the market, she believed that all of this was her fault. Kole wouldn't let anyone touch his sister nothing she could have done would have changed that. I know it was a difficult decision to make, but if it was the world or Kare it was an easy choice for him. I would have done the same, screw the parlay.

They brought us food and water every day, but we were never allowed to leave the room. I bet Titus and his slimy brother enjoyed finally putting me in my place. Little do they know I only allowed this place to remain intact because I couldn't risk them hurting Kole if I lost my temper. I would never forgive myself and it would be impossible to face his mother if he was to die as a result of my actions. Kare started to rustle around in the bed startling me. I wanted to try to get her to eat something being as she was going to need her strength.

"Kare, you need to eat," I insisted.

"How can I eat with my brother in a cell because of me?" She muttered.

"Kole is not in the cell because of you, none of this is your fault. You were just trying to get back to the villa, you weren't provoking those men," I assured her.

"I should have returned earlier but the people here just hate us so much. Playing the part is exhausting. I wanted to be around my own, I was being selfish," she said shamefully.

"It is exhausting and I'm sorry that this is the type of introduction you have experienced here, but this is not how it was under my father's rule. I understand why you didn't want to come back," I remarked as I walked over to wrap my arms around her.

"We will get through this, but I'm going to need your help. We are practically sisters after all and, as you can see, I'm in dire need of someone that I can trust," I smiled. "All we need to do is find your brother. I have an idea where they are keeping him. Once we free him then we can leave this place and regroup, maybe come up with a different plan," I said.

"Reinforcements should be here soon," she said calmly. Maybe she was starting to lose it. Why would she be so certain help was coming if we have been locked in this room for days? She hadn't been able to send any messages from here.

"How do you know anyone is coming Kare?" I asked.

"I told Kole down by the boats before those assholes attacked me that I instructed the crew to send more ravens if they didn't hear from us. It's been days since I have been down to the docks and the guards love to gossip amongst themselves. Someone has certainly let it spill that we have been captured." I jumped up, grabbed Kare's head, and planted a giant kiss on her forehead.

"Kare, you are a genius," I called out. I ran over to the balcony hopeful that I would see some boats on their way to the city. I knew it was a long shot but now I had a big glimmer of hope. "That means Rollo is going to come, we just need to be ready when he gets here." A flame in my chest sprung to life.

"How are we supposed to be ready while we are locked in this room?" She was clearly still too worried to see the bigger picture.

"We won't be locked in here forever. Marcus is going to let us out when it is time for your Kole's punishment. They told me that in the throne room. Once we get to the arena that will be the time to make a move." She didn't look too convinced but this had to work. "When the time is right, we need to all get away from the guards and teleport out of the arena together. Hopefully Rollo will be here by then, but if he isn't the three of us can manage until help arrives."

"This seems like a long shot Tav, I have to be honest with you." Her shoulders drooped, and she turned away from me. This glimmer of hope should have lifted her spirits.

"Is there something else wrong?" I asked.

"I didn't say anything because I didn't want to upset you," she confessed in a low and uncertain whisper. I was so confused about what she could possibly have to tell me.

"What do you mean?"

"As I said, soldiers talk and, while I was down at the docks, I heard rumors about your sister," she replied. The mention of her name caused my fists to tense up.

"You heard rumors about Floria?"

"Yes," she said reluctantly, "soldiers would say horrible things about all of us so that wasn't anything new, but some spoke of her being jealous of you because now you were coming back to steal her crown," her voice broke as she spoke.

I took a step back and tried to recall the conversation I had with Floria when I arrived. She didn't even have a crown for me to steal. She was being abused by Titus but, somewhere in between all the pain, maybe she did believe that being queen would solve all of her problems. How did I manage to ignore what she was saying? I've been so wrapped up in saving her I didn't even notice how different she was, and now we are paying the price for my ignorance.

"I'm sorry, Tav." Kare startled me out of my own thoughts.

"It's okay, Kare. Floria made her choice, and I will deal with that later." I had to focus on what was happening now. "You're right, it does seem like a long shot, but it is all we have. You just make sure that you are ready to move when I say so, okay?" Before she could answer, I heard the click of the lock and the door swung open. Every time I saw him, I wanted to put my fist right through his face.

"It's time, make yourselves presentable. We have a show to attend," Titus snickered and walked out of the room before I could respond.

A part of his show, that's what he thought of us. A minor inconvenience in his plan, something that could be easily handled and, if necessary, snuffed out. The guards surrounded us as we walked down the halls of the villa.

My restraints were removed but Kare wasn't so lucky; they kept her hands shackled. Marcus did not want the people to see me chained up even if they do not believe I am the rightful ruler. I haven't seen Floria since the throne room, but I knew she would not be too far from her husband, chasing behind him like a well-trained puppy. Kole spared his brother, but I was not sure I would be able to forgive her if something happens to him or Kare.

Marcus met us at the entrance of the arena. He was wearing a golden cape lined with the fur of a lion and my father's crown sat on top of his head, his hands resting on the hilt of his sword.

"Good day princess. I hope you can appreciate what I have built for this city. In the age of the gods, this is where men became heroes and where criminals are served justice."

"If this is where criminals are served justice then it shouldn't be long until you're chained up and thrown to the middle of the crowd," I smiled.

"You have spirit, Octavia, you always have but I'm not sure you realize the magnitude of the crimes committed by your betrothed. In due time, you will see what we do to those who resist the new age, and maybe that will shift your attitude into shape," he hissed coldly.

"I doubt it," I retorted with a sneer on my face.

He waved in the direction of the steps signaling me to make my way upstairs. He was directly behind me, the guards following close behind. I could see the sunlight peeking in from the staircase as we entered onto a balcony that was heavily decorated.

Chairs with gold trim and red cushions were fashioned around tables lined with fruits, vegetables, and multiple casks of wine laid out for guests. I stopped at the door while the others filed in. Marcus sat in the biggest chair in the middle of the balcony. I was waiting for Kare to come up so I could keep her as close as possible. It would be easier to escape if she was by my side.

After the guards, I expected her to walk through the door next. Instead, I came face to face with Titus and Floria, attached to his arm exactly where I said she would be. I couldn't contain my look of disgust. I waited for her to say something to me. I waited for her to explain to me why she thought this was worth it, but she walked past me as if I didn't exist before taking a seat next to her husband.

The dagger that she stabbed through my heart wasn't enough, she managed to twist it and finish the job she started in the throne room. The last piece of my family shattered into pieces. What has happened to us? How have we come this far in such a short time? I wanted my family back but inch by inch it was being taken and I've been powerless to stop it.

The unexpected roar of the crowd slapped me out of my trance. Whatever this was, it was going to begin. Kare walked in a few moments later. I pulled her over to the end of the balcony to sit next to me. The color drained out of her face when she looked at me.

"Kare, what's wrong? Are you okay?" She couldn't squeeze the words out, all I heard was a whimper before she covered her mouth to stifle her cry. I didn't understand what happened between us being downstairs and now, but whatever it was she was terrified.

The crowd was going insane, but I was trying to block them out to find out where this reaction came from.

"Kare, please talk to me, tell me what's wrong?" She was still trapped in silence as the tears ran down her eyes. I realized she wasn't looking at me, she was looking past me towards the center of the arena.

The part that I completely ignored while I was waiting to make sure she got up to the balcony safe. I turned to find my future husband, my love, and my king down on his knees. Chains were locked around his wrist and the only thing keeping him from falling over was the guards holding him up.

The blood from his face was leaking down the front of his clothing and he was so bruised I almost didn't recognize him. Faintly I could feel the power sliding right under the surface of my hands. How dare they do this to him? Just like that, I wanted to burn all of this down again. I watched in anger as they pulled his hair so that he could look up to the balcony and Kole did something only he would do in this situation. He brandished that big, beautiful smile even as the blood dripped down his lips and turned his teeth red.

I glanced over to Marcus and the anger on his face was brief, but it was there, the first slight crack in his fortress. He always managed to reel himself back in and keep his composure no matter what but slowly Kole was peeling away the layers.

I locked eyes with Kole down in the arena and gave him a slight nod hoping that he would understand that when we had a chance we had to go. He gave me a reassuring nod and now we just had to wait for the right opportunity. How could I not love this man?

20 - The Nightmare Returns – Octavia

This pretentious, arrogant asshole was really going to push every button I had. It was like he was put on this earth to test my resolve. An unrelenting punishment from the gates of Olympus, but I told the gods a long time ago I am no longer their plaything.

Marcus rose out of his seat and signaled for the crowd to quiet down. I was certain he was about to make another false declaration to these people to fortify his miserable god complex.

"Welcome citizens! I can hear the roars of your favor all the way in the villa, I assume that you are enjoying the arena I have provided," he stopped speaking waiting for the crowd to get through the applause. "I have a treat for you, sent directly from the gods themselves. As some of you may know, the princess Octavia has returned home and, while we are so happy that she is alive and well, her time away has caused her to stray from the ways of Alexandria." The crowd responded to his taunt with disdain.

"This is the part when he tells everyone in the city that you like to lay with animals, Octavia." Titus laughed but my eyes went directly to Floria, giving her every chance to redeem herself but, as usual, she was mute.

"The same men that kidnapped her and killed our dear Tiberius, forcing her to marry this Norse savage. She has been twisted by his lies and deceit. He used her grief and convinced her to bring him here under the guise of a parlay. He was hoping that she would be able to reclaim her birthright and deliver it directly into the hands of our enemies," he declared and made sure he turned and smiled at me. "Like the savage that he is, he murdered three of your soldiers in the market. This man spilled Roman blood in our home. For disrespecting the rules of parlay and throwing dirt on my gracious hospitality, he must be punished."

I'm not sure what I expected but when the crowd cheered in agreement it almost felt like a slap in the face. This was my home, the people I have known since I was a small girl running through the market with my siblings, and yet they have turned their backs on me. How deep does this hate run that without even a chance to speak for myself I'm being painted as a traitor for falling in love?

"The arena was built for your entertainment, and I have more than succeeded in that promise, but it is also here for the people to witness the justice of the crown. Kole Alexsson, you will be sentenced to death for violating the terms of parlay. May your blood on the sands serve as a message to any others looking to overthrow the crown." Marcus spoke to the crowd proudly.

Marcus was raising his hand to signal the execution. If we were going to move now would be the time. I looked down towards Kole waiting for him to open a portal up to the balcony. I grabbed Kare's hand in anticipation. I never took my eyes off him, but he wasn't looking in our direction, the bloody smile still stretched across his face. Before Marcus could drop his hand, Kole started to speak.

"Am I not allowed last words in this country?" he asked still smiling. "I know I am foreign to this land, but I figured I would ask." Marcus slowly dropped his hands.

"Now would be a good time to ask your gods for favor because you will not be in the land of the living for long." He gestured to his soldiers to allow Kole to speak. The guards still held onto him but removed the knife from his throat.

"It is true that I arrived in Alexandria with your princess, and I have every intention of making her my wife, but being your ruler is not something that I want," he addressed the crowd. "She loves her home more than anything and would never allow it to be taken from her. Since we have been together, she has been educating me in the ways of your history and your customs." The crowd grew silent as he spoke.

I was trying to figure out where he was going with this. Once the guard lowered the knife, he should have been ready to get us out of here as fast as he could.

"Your history speaks of great and honorable heroes, but to kill an unarmed king would not be favorable in the eyes of your gods or mine." Now he ignored the crowd and looked straight at Marcus. "I issue a challenge to any Roman warrior here today. If it truly is the will of your gods then here is where I will fall, but if it is not, you will have to face me yourself and prove that you and you alone are the rightful king," the crowd gasped and for a moment it was silent in anticipation of an answer from the balcony.

Marcus mulled over the decision, but the crowd became impatient. They must have felt the unrest coming from their fearless leader, his silence failing to give them confidence.

"Do not allow this dog to dictate the terms father, just kill him and be done with it," Titus said.

"I cannot just kill him and be done with it, a Norse king just laid out a challenge. The rest of the country will not respect our rule if I just kill him now." I was trying to hide my smile, seeing them so thrown off was refreshing. I don't know what the plan is, but Kole's little stunt delayed his execution, and in some way, he managed to win a tiny portion of the crowd.

"While you are brave, young king, you are not worthy of a challenge with me, but in the spirit of entertainment and since I have a love for the people, I will allow you to see how you fare against our warriors." The crowd went into a frenzy. I'm sure that the cheers could be heard all the way up on Olympus.

The people have become blood hungry for this barbaric display. Out of the corner of my eye, while everyone else was focused on the frenzy, I saw a green flash sweeping all along the outer rim of the arena. It was gone in an instant, but I know what I saw.

"Bring him his weapons, and let the games begin," Marcus called out and returned to his seat. I wondered if he understood exactly what he was doing.

There was not a single warrior he could bring out that would bring Kole down, but in due time he would find that out for himself. My king was as smart as he was fierce, I just wish I knew what the plan was. The guards unshackled him and handed him his axe. I admired his restraint as he could have killed them all in seconds. The same guards that carried him out here were most likely the ones that put the bruises all over his face.

"I really don't see why we would give him his weapons back when we could just kill him right now and end this nonsense, who cares what these people think." Titus was trying to convince his father.

"You have much to learn, my son. He challenged our honor. I would be perceived as a weak fool if I was to take the easy way out. That is not what kings do. In order for us to rule, we must make sure our lands are at peace with the new regime, not wondering if I'm afraid of a tiny Norse." Titus wanted to respond but instead walked to the table and poured himself another cup of wine. Marcus signaled to the crowd to begin.

Ω

Kole eyes went pitch black before the warriors were sent out and I could see the power flowing through him right under the surface. He was tapping into the darkness, swimming in the bliss of the ravens. I thought maybe now was the time he was going try to open a portal up to us, but nothing happened. He stretched his arms out wide like he was basking in what was remaining of the sunlight. "What the hell was he doing?" I said to myself.

The horns blared and two warriors were released from opposite sides of the tunnel. The first wore a brown tunic and a leather breastplate, sword in one hand, shield in the other, with a cloth tied around his head to keep his hair in place. The second warrior was a much larger man dragging a giant war hammer. He was shirtless with a messy tangled beard that hung way past his stomach. He was filthy covered in sweat and dirt. I could only imagine how bad he probably smelled.

Kole dropped his arms and sized up the two men walking slowly towards him. His eyes returned to normal and the bruises on his face began to fade. That must have been what he was doing, he found a way to relieve his pain with Odin's power. I could feel him all the way up on the balcony, the darkness brushing against me giving me goosebumps.

His arms were shiny from sweating in the heat and his biceps tensed in anticipation of battle. I didn't know he could impress me any more than he already has. Getting the best of these two should be simple, but I was still nervous after what happened to my brother. I would never underestimate an opponent again, no matter how certain victory was.

Kole was smiling as the men circled him, taunting them to attack. It worked all too well, pushing the big warrior to charge with his war hammer raised over his head. He brought it down with as much force as he could, leaving a small crater in the arena floor but it was too slow. Kole rolled out of the way and slammed the base of his axe into the back of his head. The attack wasn't enough to do any damage, it only angered the bigger warrior and forced him into another rash attack.

While he was trying to get the hammer out of the ground, the first warrior advanced on Kole swinging his sword. His speed was decent, but I could tell Kole was toying with him. He parried every attack, leaving a small enough opening for his opponent to think he was making progress. I really wish he wouldn't play around like this and just get this over with, but the crowd was enjoying every minute of it.

Every swing of the hammer and the sword had the crowd gasping with anticipation. They begged for a killing blow, but Kole dodged every time leaving them disappointed but not entirely disinterested. Kole retreated to the far side of the arena, a safe distance away from the warriors so that he could address the crowd. He was not taking these men seriously at all.

"Is this all Alexandria has to offer?" The crowd was yelling at the top of their lungs. I couldn't tell if they loved him or hated him. "How about I end this now? Is that what you want?" They responded in what sounded like an agreement.

The warriors charged him at once and his eyes went black the power of the All-father surging at his will as he sprang into action. He lowered his shoulder into the warrior's shield knocking him off balance and rolled to recover in just enough time to avoid the hammer. On his way back to his feet, he landed a punch on the knee of the bearded warrior, the sound of the bone breaking vibrated throughout the entire arena. He grabbed at the knee screaming in pain on his way to the ground. Kole spun around to find the other warrior swinging his sword at his neck. He ducked underneath the strike and slipped behind him. He grabbed the cloth that was tied on the warrior's head and yanked him to the ground. The crowd was chaotic, I could barely hear myself think as the fight went on. The bearded warrior tried to get up, but his knee kept buckling under his weight, all he could do was crawl.

"Do you yield?" Kole screamed to the warrior as he held the warrior down on the ground. Whatever the man said next it must not have been a surrender because Kole raised his axe and separated his head from his body.

He didn't bother to ask the bearded warrior if he would yield. When Kole approached him, he somehow managed one last swing from the ground. With no strength behind it, Kole caught the strike and wrestled the hammer free from his grasp. He raised it high over his shoulders and smashed the bearded warrior's head. It burst under the hammer like a piece of fruit. I thought I was going to throw up everything that I had eaten.

Kole barely broke a sweat. He raised his axe to the crowd as they cheered, reveling in the violence of this spectacle. His eyes were black and smoking which was familiar to me but may have caught the others off guard.

"Is that all you got?" He yelled to the balcony.

Kole walked back to the center of the arena with his axe over his shoulder, a smile on his face even bigger than it was before waiting for a response.

"Impressive, my young king. Maybe you can be of some use in this arena. I shall think about sparing you and keeping you as one of my guard dogs. You can sleep with the other animals and come at my beck and call," he shared a snide laugh with the guards on the balcony. "But let's see how you deal with more of my best, since you seem to enjoy the spectacle." Marcus was raising his hand signaling for another challenger and four more came out from the tunnels.

"Give me a challenge Marcus or come and fight me yourself. I won't waste any more energy on these weak men, they shouldn't have to die because you are afraid," Kole taunted.

"Do you see how he disrespects our warriors, Alexandria?! He doesn't even see them as his equal in combat. This Norse wants to wash our existence away, but we will not allow it!" Marcus turned his attention to the crowd.

"Then come and stop me Marcus but know this: if these men attack me, they will all die and their blood will be on your hands," Kole countered. Marcus raised his hands and signaled for the attack.

The four men all converged on Kole at once. He closed his eyes and grasped the darkness as he did before. All four were striking at once but none of them could land a blow. Kole dodged and countered anything that managed to get close to him. He was a man amongst boys, punching and tossing any warrior that was in his path with incredible strength. The crowd reacted to every close call, every swing of Kole's axe, and every drop of blood that he spilled. The four men did not last long, the time for joking around was over. Clearly Kole was done playing games with Marcus and his pitiful men.

He stood in the center of the arena surrounded by the dismembered body parts, covered in blood and filled with rage. I didn't recognize him, but I could feel his presence stretch all the way across the arena. A dark cloud of massive power loomed over all of us. I could feel his purpose, his hunger, and his will to make sure that we all get out of this city alive. I hated how long it has been since I was able to touch him, really touch him and have him the way that I wanted. The gods know it's been an eternity. Even in the midst of him fighting for his life that part of me was never cut off from him. The feelings that his presence demanded from my body was always in the forefront. "Now is not the time Octavia" I chanted to myself.

The sun was descending in the sky forcing the guards down in the arena to light torches to brighten up the darkness. Still standing in the middle of the arena waiting and taunting our captors was my husband to be. I looked over to Titus only to see his face twisted in rage, while Marcus' face was still stoic, lacking the overwhelming emotion his son was showing. But it was impossible for him to ignore the massive amount of power that I felt.

"Seems like the only thing being punished is the number of warriors you are losing Marcus," I smiled.

"One more word from you and I'll cut your throat myself," Titus snapped.

"You will do no such thing," Marcus interrupted. "I must say that your king is most impressive..." Before he could finish his thought, Kole was slamming his axe against a shield and the crowd responded in unison.

"Looks like the people are starting to see who the real warrior is," he screamed while slamming the axe against the shield. "I am Kole Alexsson, I am the blood of the raven. I have walked in the company of the gods, so tell me Alexandria, am I not a king?" He incited the crowd further, slamming his axe on the shield. To my surprise, it started to feel like they were beginning to rally for him. "Have I not shown you how deep my blood runs? Do I not fight for the love and honor of your princess? I am still standing. Have your gods not deemed me worthy?" I would have to remember how fickle the people are if they could turn on their king this easily.

I could finally see why Kole decided to pursue this spectacle instead of just portaling us out of the city. He means to gain the favor of the people so that we may still be able to salvage our original plan, saving my home and destroying the Bellator family in the process.

Titus was so livid, I thought his head was going to explode. His entire face was bright red and the veins in his neck protruded with anger as he watched their plan completely fail. He was out of his seat yelling at his father, bringing a giant smile to my face.

"I told you we should have killed him when we had the chance. Now the people are starting to turn against you as you sit here patronizing this false sense of honor." Titus was face to face with his father now.

Marcus was still unmoved. I envied the way he was able to keep his cool. This whole punishment was crumbling right in front of him. Marcus turned to me and smiled.

"I must admit this was never a part of the plan but I have something else in store for your King. I am certain you are going to love this," he got up to address the crowd once more. "You seem to have won over some of the citizens, so I will extend an olive branch to you. Show the people you are really here for them." I couldn't understand how he was still so confident, none of this made sense. "I was saving this for a better occasion, but when would be better than right now?" His smile was devious as he addressed the crowd. "Now that I have a Norse king wanting to take the seat in a Roman city, it will only be right that he dispose of the Norse scum we had in the cells below. Show us that if we allow you to be a part of this city that you will do what needs to be done."

He waved his hands and out of the tunnel directly across I saw what I thought I would never see again in my life. The mask, the same mask covered in dried blood, the mask that haunted my dreams and destroyed my family that faithful day. Tiberius's face flashed before my eyes and the words he spoke to me before he killed him.

"Witness your demise." Those three words I would never forget, three words that he was going to pay early for. My hands were pulsating and glowing, I could feel the flames dancing from the pit of my stomach and coming to life under my skin. My fingers clenched the handles of the chair, and I could smell the wood beginning to singe. I needed to make him pay or I was going to explode. Before I could get up, the guards wrapped chains around my hands and feet securing me to the chair.

"What the fuck are you doing? Let me go now," I screamed and rocked violently in the chair trying to break the chains, but the guards held me in place. The chanting in my head was low and steady.

"Kill him."

"Destroy him."

"Burn him."

Marcus was drinking a cup of wine smiling. He wanted me to lose control to feed his ego, but I still didn't understand the motive, unless he believes the masked man could actually kill Kole. I decided I wasn't going to stick around to figure it out. I was going to be the one to kill him. I lit the fire in my hands and grabbed the chains causing them to heat up. The heat shot up the links until it reached the guard's hands making them too hot to hold. As soon as they dropped them, I worked my way out of the chair.

"I wouldn't go any further if I was you." I turned toward the voice. Titus was holding Kare with a knife to her throat. I expected her to be afraid, but the only thing on her face was anger. I knew she considered herself to be a warrior in her own right and loathed being used as a pawn in this fight.

"Sorry, Tav." The look on her face showed a ton of guilt, but she had to know I didn't blame her for anything. She wouldn't even be here if it wasn't for me.

"It's okay Kare, it's not your fault," I said.

"Now have a seat, we have a show to finish, even though I'm not sure why we are having the show in the first place," Titus sneered as he pushed the knife closer to Kare's throat.

I wouldn't get the satisfaction of killing him myself, but I hope that Kole made it unbelievably painful. I was sure that Titus was the man in the mask. I could almost feel it the more I was around him. This whole thing was incredibly weird. Either way, whoever was wearing it was going to die.

21 - Raven Of The Arena - Kole

I was going to make him regret not killing me when he had the chance. He was a coward and a pretender. How many times did I have to call him out before he came down here and fought me himself? He raised his hand, and I heard the gates behind me open from the tunnels. Strolling out was something I thought I would never get to see.

The terror that kept Octavia up night after night, the one that stole everything from her, and now that mask was walking straight towards me. Was this supposed to be some sort of trick? Why would he dress them up as Norse and deliver them directly to me? Regardless of how they were dressed, they weren't my countryman, and I don't give a damn about this crowd. Whoever was wearing that mask was not going to walk out of this arena alive.

"I don't know what your king has promised you, but I guarantee you he does not value your life, or he would not have sent you out here to face me." Whatever his response was it didn't really matter, he was going to die anyway.

"You speak as if you know the outcome. Nothing you do here will matter once you fall. We will kill your handmaiden and sell off your queen, and you'll be just another dead dog," he shrugged and pulled out his sword. I pointed my axe at his head because I needed him to understand that this wouldn't be like any other battle he has fought.

"It's your funeral. The only thing you need to know is that, before I kill you, I'm going to rip off that mask and Octavia will decide your fate." I was saving my strength hoping that Marcus would come down and fight me himself, but the man in the mask would have to do. My only regret was that Octavia wouldn't get to do this herself.

The rage I felt when I looked at him was hard to describe but I knew every bone in my body wanted to rip him apart. The game I was playing was no longer important. Three more soldiers appeared behind him. I should have known he was going to be too much of a coward to fight me on his own.

I decided not to hold back, so as soon as one of the soldiers rushed to attack me, I summoned up the darkness and opened the black portal directly in front of me. Instead of walking through it myself, the Roman ran into it completely disappearing until I opened a portal in the sky. The others were confused until the screams of their comrade came from up above as he plummeted from the sky. I took a step back and his body crashed into the sands killing him on impact. His death didn't seem to rattle the man in the mask, but I had plenty of time to make my point. The rest of the soldiers were apprehensive to attack me again. I think they finally realized that I wasn't the one that was trapped with them, they were trapped with me.

This seemed like a great time to thin out the numbers so I could focus on the masked man. I advanced on the remaining soldiers, slipping past their shields and landing blows on them both. The masked man tried to attack me from behind. He yelled before he attacked. Instinctively, I opened another portal and jumped into it. I appeared above one of the soldiers not too high but just enough for me to bring my axe down cutting off his sword arm. His blood sprayed all over the sands as he reached for the wound to stop the flow, but it was no use.

I was growing tired of the games. The more I fought and gave myself over to the power, the more invincible I felt. My thoughts were deafening even in the midst of battle; it was almost an out-of-body experience and the person I watched I hardly recognized. It was a surge of power derived from pure darkness, but I have never felt so enlightened.

The last soldier attacked me, snapping me out of my own thoughts. He was swinging his sword high and low, looking for any opening, but I was too fast for him. I kept my feet moving and I studied him, waiting for a chance to make him pay. He dropped his guard for a split second, and I landed a kick in his chest creating some space in between us. I grabbed my axe and hurled it directly at his head. He managed to dodge it, which I expected, but by the time he turned back to face me, I had my hands around his throat. I know it wasn't his fault that he was here, he was just following orders, but the mercy in me was long gone. I reached into his chest and ripped out his heart before throwing his body aside. I knew in my heart that the act was barbaric, but the power fueled my anger releasing me of my compassion.

Now there was nothing in between me and the man that has caused Octavia so much pain. I was going to give him the same mercy that he gave her brother.

"You're a demon, an abomination of the gods," the masked man yelled.

"I am your demon, and this will be your underworld. I warned you this would be your funeral and I plan to make it a luxurious event," I roared and pointed my axe in his direction. I wasn't sure but I believed that I could sense some fear in him. "Do not fear death, you can die as so many others have right here in this arena that your king built. Look up towards your ruler that decided to sacrifice you," I nodded towards the balcony where Marcus sat. I expected him to be nervous, but he managed to keep his cool even though I have killed everyone he has sent my way.

While my attention was on Marcus, the masked man was already arm's length away preparing to attack me. I raised my axe to counter and our weapons met in the middle with a force. He was a lot stronger than I expected him to be, but that didn't matter. I owed Octavia his head, and what my love wants, she gets.

I pushed off creating some space between us and picked up a sword from one of the dead soldiers. I pressed the masked man with my axe in one hand and the sword in the other, trying to see how he would respond to a different style. He was quick, managing to block my strikes and coming close to landing a counter. This wasn't one of Marcus' useless soldiers. This man had some skill. He moved with purpose and precision; my victory would not be immediate. I swung my axe high, and he blocked it with his sword. He brought his shield to my chest causing me to stagger backward. He charged towards me as I regained my balance with an overhead swing of his sword. I met his swing with my sword and it snapped in half, a shard of the sword dragged across my face, the warmth of my blood fresh on my cheek.

"I can add that blood to this mask, dog. Maybe after I kill you, I'll dip the entire thing in your corpse," he choked out. If it was meant to antagonize me, it worked. I dove deeper into the darkness, relenting almost all the control I had left. Nothing mattered but finishing what I started.

Everything slowed down, the sounds around me were muffled, the pain in my joints and the gash in my face faded, and the tunnel vision pointed straight towards that mask. I let all of it go: the pain, the desperation, the hunger, my love for Octavia and my family, all of it was lost in the swarm of ravens and an immersible amount of power. I was aware of my movements, but I could not say that I was in complete control. We fought ferociously; trading blows one after the other. The sound of the steel clashing together vibrated through the entire arena. He was a much better warrior than I expected.

My sweat and blood splashed onto the sands as we held our positions in another stalemate. If this was going to end, I had to make a move. I thought about the strategy I used to defeat my father and how it saved my life in the last fight. The man in the mask wasn't half as strong as my father, but he had seen what I could do already. He was aware that I could open portals, but I had another trick up my sleeve. Instead of trying to match his strength, I relinquished some of my position and he took the bait. He saw it as an opening and brought his elbow directly into my jaw and a thunderous kick to my chest, knocking me back exactly as I planned. There was no better time than now. I dropped the sword, grabbed my axe, and threw it directly at his chest. He laughed and dodged it with no problem, but he never took his eyes off me.

"You thought just because you flash your devil eyes it would make me forget that you tried that move earlier, maybe you are as dumb as you loo-," blood sprayed out of his mouth interrupting his final words as my axe slammed into the center of his back.

Behind him the two portals I opened were fading away, one to catch the axe and the other to spit it back out without him knowing. The masked man fell to his knees reaching for the hilt that he would never be able to reach. It took a lot of effort to quell the darkness, but I managed to bury it beneath the surface and gain some semblance of myself. I looked up to the balcony and, for the first time, Marcus looked unsettled. The stone wall he built was beginning to crack and it was only a matter of time before I toppled it over.

I still owed them one more thing before I claimed my victory. We needed to know who was behind the mask. Octavia would be able to put a face to her nightmare and I hoped that what I have done will bring her some peace. I pulled the man up by the back of his breastplate and forced him to face the balcony. I locked eyes with Octavia. I wanted to share this with her. I wanted her to know that I would go to the ends of this realm for her because I knew this was for her healing, not mine. I ripped the mask off his face and smashed it under my feet, it would never be used again. I recognized the messy dark hair, but I couldn't be sure. I leaned forward to see his face. Bleeding out of the mouth slowly was Lucius Bellator.

My head snapped to Marcus. No wonder that wall was beginning to crack. His son was going to die all because he wanted to make a spectacle of me, and it had backfired in the worst way. I couldn't hear what they were saying but Titus was livid. He was on his feet an inch away from his father's face, yelling at the top of his lungs. A green flash swirling around the balcony caught my attention briefly, but it was gone just as fast.

"People of Alexandria, as you can see, I have liberated you of the scum that has tormented you. To my surprise, he is not one of my people but one of your beloved princes." The crowd could care less about who was dying in the middle of the arena, all they wanted was blood and I quenched their thirst. I needed to make sure that they can see what the king has done. "Before you die, look up to your princess. Your life will fade as the light in her eyes did every day she had to live with what you did." I held his head in place until he took his last breath. I don't know if it brought her what she was looking for but at least we know that the monster that changed her entire life was gone for good.

Lucius' body fell to the dirt and the crowd was in a frenzy. I put a chink in Marcus' armor without an army. As his eldest son continued to berate his father, I was wondering how much more he can take. Anger was a rushing stream and, with enough pressure, the dam was going to crack.

22 - What A Plan – Octavia

Lucius?!

The entire time he was the one Marcus decided to use in the attack. What kind of monster would put his own son in the way of danger like that? How did he manage to defeat me in a fight? The more I thought about it, the more it didn't make sense, but nevertheless seeing Kole smash the mask and watching Lucius take his last breath took a weight off that I didn't realize I was carrying.

I stared at Kole as he let Lucius' body fall and reveled in the cheers of the crowd that have completely turned on their king. He gambled his life to push off his execution and somehow turned it into a positive for us. Titus was completely distraught; his brother was dead, and it was very clear who he blamed.

"You spent this entire day catering to these people for a show and what has it gotten us?" Spit was flying out of his mouth while he was yelling. "Now my brother is dead because of you. You killed your own family for nothing, and his blood is on your hands." Marcus was either ignoring Titus or he really didn't care, I couldn't be sure. I know that his eyes never left

Kole, who was standing in the arena basking in the praise that should have been his.

"What the fuck is wrong with you, old man? Say something! Tell me what you are going to tell my mother? Make sure you tell her that you spoon-fed your own son to a Norse so people would like you!" He walked around so his father could not escape his gaze. "You are pitiful. Maybe the gods never chose you at all. You're a washed-up old man attached to the past. It's time for you to step down and let me handle this since you obviously don't have the stomach for it." Before he could finish, Marcus' hand wrapped around his throat. I shifted back in my chair because this is not what I expected.

I have been waiting for Marcus to show even a slither of emotion, but I always expected it would be directed towards us, not his own son. Even as he held him by the throat, he never broke his calm resolve.

"Your voice is exhausting. Never forget everything you have, I gave you. Now you stand before me throwing a temper tantrum like the brat that you are." His voice was cold and direct when he scolded his son. "You've never understood how to play this game. The gods have chosen this path for me, and I will walk it. If it was up to me, I wouldn't have a son that is so weak willed and thin skinned as you." He lifted Titus off his feet and held him in place like he was lighter than a feather. "This Norse killing your brother means nothing to me, and this display was not to make these people like me... it was to make them respect me as their king. Your brother knew the part he needed to play. Why do you think he was in the arena? He will be welcomed by the gods for what he's done for Gracia. My only concern is that now after I kill the Norseman, I will have to work over these people all over again before I move to the west and finish carving out my new world order."

He took a deep breath and tossed Titus across the balcony like he was nothing. His body slammed against the stone with so much force it knocked him unconscious. Then, Marcus turned his sights to me.

"Do you understand how small you are in the grand scheme of things, princess? Your parents, your brother, even my own miserable son will not stop this if the gods will it. After I kill your king, I will wipe this land clean of them. You cannot keep a limb if the wound has festered. It is always best to cut it off completely." As he spoke those final words, I saw the familiar lightning streak illuminating the whites of his eyes. He turned to face the arena. I saw Kole stand in attention, probably a response to the overwhelming power that I felt as well.

Clouds funneled in from all directions and you could hear the thunder from within. Marcus raised his hands, and out of the sky, lightning rested gently in the palm of his hands. It responded to every movement of his finger like he bent the will of the element. Rollo displayed his skill with control, but he couldn't hold it like it was a pet. He smiled and jumped off the balcony leaving all of us alone. I ran to the edge because I was sure the jump would hurt him, but he was enshrouded in the lightning, and it was guiding him down until his feet softly touched the sand. I really couldn't believe what I had just seen, and I knew I needed to get down there quick because Kole was not going to be able to fight him alone.

Titus was still unconscious as Floria jumped from her seat to check on him. I still was unable to fathom how she could still feel anything for a man that treated her this way. How is there nothing left of the girl that I grew up with? Everything she used to stand for was gone, and as much as I wanted to fix her, I had bigger things to worry about. She has shown me her allegiance. Saving Kole was more important than dealing with her right now.

"There was a time that I would have done anything in the world for you, and you returned that with betrayal." I forced out the words.

"You will never understand what I have been through, and as usual, you are selfish and thinking about yourself," she spat at me.

"You are still missing the point, Floria. The only reason I am here is because of you. I was happy in Lundr. The only thing I wanted to get back was you, and now you're a stranger to me." I could feel the tears wrestling to the surface.

"It's always been about you, Octavia. I was going to have something for myself, and you burned it down." The words stabbed me in the chest. I could not believe what she was saying, but I couldn't waste time. I had to help the others. I was on my way to the staircase before I turned back toward her.

"I hope we all survive this because then you are going to have to live with all the blood that is on your hands. You call me selfish, claim that I am here to take your crown...completely missing that you are the one being selfish all over a power you never had and likely never will. Mark my words: you will regret the day you chose power over blood." I freed Kare from her restraints. "I need you to find our weapons. They took them away from us when we docked, they must be somewhere down by the boats." She nodded and ran down the stairs. Something about just leaving felt unfinished, I needed one more look back at my past. "Now you really are alone. I hope that monster keeps you warm at night." With those words, I headed down to help my new family.

The arena was in complete chaos. Some citizens were fleeing, while others tried to get closer to the action. Guards tried to take control of the situation, but no one can make sense of what was happening. My only concern was to make it down to the arena before Kole tried to fight Marcus alone.

I made it to the giant fence that led you into the arena. Just as I suspected, Kole was already trying to find an opening in Marcus' defense. He charged with his axe. With one swing of his hand and little effort, Marcus sent him flying back across the sands.

"I have allowed you to breathe for long enough. Your arrogance will be your undoing, little king." He ran over to Kole faster than my eyes could even see and lifted him off the ground by his vest before throwing him effortlessly across the arena. He slid on the sand directly next to my feet. I reached down to help him up, but after all the fighting he has been through, he was leaning a lot of his weight onto me. I could only imagine how weak he was. The mere fact that he could still fight was amazing.

"Took you long enough," he smiled at me.

"We are staring down one of the oldest warriors I know, and you are smiling at me right now."

“I think you underestimate how gorgeous you are,” he responded.

“If we survive then you can explain it to me,” I smiled back.

Marcus was walking towards us, the wicked smile spreading across his face. He was covered in lightning, but it wasn’t like what we’ve seen with Rollo. This was more powerful, and it created a barrier around him burning everything in his path. He had complete control and every intention on unleashing that power on us. It was terrifying, and it reminded me of how intimidating Styr was when Kole fought him in the holmgang.

“You claim to have walked among the gods, but I fought in the great war side by side with the gods, and I have spilled more than a fair share of your savage blood. I could easily add one more to my belt.” His eyes went completely white. The hair on my arms started to raise and goosebumps swept all the way down my spine. I have never felt any force of power like this before.

“How the hell are we supposed to fight him like this?” Kole sounded exasperated.

“We just need to buy some time; help is on the way.” Marcus was still slowly walking towards us flashing his strength with every deadly step.

“How do you know help is coming?” he asked.

“Your sister is a genius, that’s how. I’ll explain later, just know we’ll have lightning of our own to match his soon,” I explained with a smile on my face, “Let’s keep him busy for now. We can attack him from opposite sides.”

"You don't have any weapons." Just as he finished speaking, Kare came running and dropped my daggers and my sword behind us.

"Perfect timing, Kare. Now get to higher ground," I told her.

"I can help," she yelled.

"Yeah, you can. Find your bow and get to high ground. When you have an opening, you fire," I retorted. For the first time since before Kole was taken, she smiled as she nodded and ran back down the tunnel. I strapped the holster to my thigh and grabbed a spear that was laying on the ground.

"Let's do this."

We ran in opposite directions, forcing Marcus to choose whom he was going to attack while one of us could sneak around the back. He zoned in on me as his target, his bright eyes tracing my every movement. Just my luck. I reached within and felt the fire flicker to life right beneath my skin. My hands started to glow into a light flame that streaked down the spear as I had done before. I wasn't sure how I was going to be able to get close to Marcus. I just knew if he got his hands on me it could end very badly.

I charged him with the spear letting the flame guide me. He didn't move to stop me, he just watched as the spear was pointed straight at his heart. I was so close but, just as I was in striking distance, a streak of lightning came off his body and shattered the spear in half.

I froze in disbelief which left me wide open for the king to counter my attack. I couldn't move fast enough, and his hand connected with the side of my face knocking me off my feet. The pain was instant. I wasn't shocked that he managed to hurt me with no effort, but how was I supposed to land a blow on him? He stood over me and a low devious laugh came from his core.

I could hear Kole rushing him from behind. He must have seen exactly what happened to me because, when he swung his axe, he anticipated that the lightning would protect Marcus. The axe was zapped out of his hand, but he was already looking to follow up his attack. He landed a punch to his face and planted a kick in his chest, but Marcus seemed completely unfazed. He grabbed Kole by his wrist and held him in place. Kole tried to get away, but the king held him tight. I knew what was coming next. I have seen this move before from Rollo.

The clouds rolled in right above them both. Kole was fighting to get free of his grip, but he was not going to get loose in time. I looked around the arena for anything that could help. I spotted a shield picked it up, then turned to run full speed at Marcus, putting my shoulder behind the shield. As expected, when I got close, the lighting off his body shot towards the shield, but it absorbed the shock. I slammed all my weight into Marcus, knocking Kole free.

"Get back!" I yelled.

Kole backed away from Marcus and I rolled to his side as a giant streak of lightning crashed into the sands of the arena. The crater left behind was devastating and would have been even worse if he managed to hold Kole in place.

"We can't keep doing this. It's not working, we can't even do any damage," I was rasping, already out of breath even though the fight has only just begun.

"He has to have a weakness, everyone does, we just need to find it," Kole stressed.

"That's easier said than done when you are also trying not to get killed!" Sometimes this man can drive me to drink.

"I'm aware of that, my love, but what choice do we have at this point?" He got back on his feet and wiped the blood from his mouth.

Kole's eyes went completely black. He was looking toward Marcus, so I could only assume he was using the Odin sight to find anything that could help us. Marcus could care less he felt like there was no way he could lose.

"The gods have forsaken you, little ones. I allowed you to believe that you have had a choice in any of these matters. You let the gods warp you and manipulate you for a few party tricks, but you are unwilling to do what needs to be done to obtain absolution." He twirled a mass of lightning in his hand like it was a toy as he spoke.

"This game is for the ruthless, survival of the fittest, not for two kids who want to play hero. While you may have some help, I know that the other gods are ready and waiting to finish what was started so long ago. This world is to be ruled by me under one king just as the Gods of Olympus, and anyone that has a problem with that will be forced into submission or removed from this world." He was moving closer, and a second energy mass appeared in his hand. "Now, who will I be killing first? The savage king or his traitor whore?"

My anger got the best of me, and I was running at him before he finished speaking. I don't know what I was going to do, I just wanted to kill him. My hands were engulfed in flames, and all I could see was red. In the center of my rage was Marcus with this arrogant smile. I needed to cause him pain.

He shifted his weight and threw the mass of lightning, but I managed to dodge it easily. I picked up a sword that was left on the ground and slashed upward. Marcus dodged it again. I continued to press him, swinging the sword in any direction I could, but Marcus was too fast. He caught my wrist and planted his knee into my stomach. The air was sucked out of my chest, but the adrenaline kept me from heaving up all the food I'd eaten.

Marcus summoned more energy in his hands. He brought the energy up to my face, and I knew if he brought it any closer, he could burn my skin off my face. I willed the flames back into my hands in a sense of desperation and grabbed his wrist trying to burn him enough to loosen his grip on me.

Even though I could feel the heat burning his skin, he would not relent. Kole dropped out of a portal beside Marcus and swung his axe in an attempt to free me, but the king was too fast once again. He abandoned the energy mass to catch Kole's arm and slammed his head into Kole's nose, causing him to stagger back.

He turned and centered his attention back on me. The energy mass reappeared but, instead of aiming at my face, he aimed the ball of light into my chest. The force launched me back across the arena. I rolled violently across the sand until I slammed against the wall, a wave of pain came crashing over me as my body ricocheted off the stone.

A heavy thud landed next to me seconds later. I could see Kole trying to will himself back to his feet from the corner of my eye. We continued to attack Marcus over and over, but we were getting nowhere. He was too fast and too strong. We didn't stand a chance, but we couldn't give up. To make matters worse, it was clear that Marcus was just getting started.

"What are we supposed to do, Kole?" I struggled to speak as blood mixed with my sweat.

"I hate to admit it, but I might be fresh out of ideas," he replied with trepidation in his voice as he was getting back up to his feet.

"It can't end like this. We haven't done all of this to lose when I'm so close to getting my home back."

"I made you a promise and I will see it through, no matter what." He smiled again.

"No matter what," I replied to him.

"I'm glad you are sharing a moment. I think you are both foolish but it is clear that you care for one another," he spoke coldly. "While it is admirable, I believe I have had enough fun for the day, and in the interest of time, I will just kill you both at the same time."

He raised his hands. Everything around us responded to his will. It felt like he was altering nature right in front of our eyes. The lightning shield grew bigger and bigger, burning the sand and vaporizing anything that was around him. The dark sky was illuminated with streaks of lightning, the thunder rumbled through the entire area, and the sand trembled under my feet.

I looked to Kole. A tiny part of me was hoping that we could hold each other and prepare for the end, but I knew he would never surrender this way.

"It's a shame you will never see each other again. As children of different beliefs, you will not share the afterlife. You should have cherished life instead of adopting this pointless mission." His eyes went completely white. I could feel his power building, the scale of it felt terrifying. He was going to destroy everything just show us that he could do it. I felt Kole grab my arm.

"Run Octavia!"

"What?"

"You need to run, get out of here. Take Kare and find the others. Live to fight another day," he pleaded.

"In what universe do you think I would leave you here alone?" The thought of his request pissed me off so much. I could not believe what I was hearing.

"I know you won't but I'm begging you to reconsider."

"If you know I won't leave then you know it is a waste of time to even ask." He weaved his hand in mine and smiled.

"You're so stubborn," he said.

"You should talk." He pulled me closer and kissed me. I had forgotten how soft his lips were, how much I yearned to be held by him. It's been an eternity since I was able to fall into his arms and appreciate how much I missed him. We have been so wrapped up in all this chaos, I forgot everything that I gained. He was my center, my lifeline, and my king.

He broke our lips apart and his eyes were black, the familiar smoke rising out of the sides. I knew what he was going to do but before I could oppose, he was pushing me through a portal.

"I love you, Octavia," and his face vanished as I fell backward into darkness.

Ω

I reappeared outside the gate. He must have been unable to focus because he didn't even portal me far. I was going to have some serious words with him when this was all said and done. I ran back through the tunnels heading towards the arena when I heard the explosion. The aftershock knocked me off my feet as the wind shot through all the tunnels.

Fear swept completely over me, but I was still in shock from the explosion. The ringing in my ear was unbearable but I knew I needed to get to Kole now. I had to save him from himself, and then kill him for taking me out of the fight.

The tunnels started to rumble. I assume they were going to collapse soon. I needed to get back on the inside. The ringing in my ears started to settle, and I swear I could hear screams but not the type I expected. I could hear war cries and metal slamming against each other. If Marcus caused the explosion, why would there be any fighting? Everything should have been destroyed, including my husband.

The room stopped spinning long enough for me to get on my feet and run toward the middle of the arena. I pushed my way through the gate stumbling through the piles of destruction. The entire wall of the arena was crumbling. Someone managed to bring it down, but who I couldn't say.

Out of the corner of my eye, a Roman guard was rushing at me with a sword. I grabbed my daggers and braced myself, but before he was able to reach me, an arrow struck him in the throat knocking him to the ground. I looked up and saw Kare in the stands smiling at me before she resumed letting off arrows three at a time. I couldn't see what she was shooting at, but I have never been more confused. Why was she smiling? Where were Kole and Marcus? What caused that explosion?

"You just going to stand there or are you actually going to help?" I knew that annoying voice anywhere. I never thought I would be so happy to see that giant head and that messy hair. He was covered in his element and carrying his hammer.

"Rollo! Thank the gods you're alive."

"I should be saying the same to you, but we can talk later. We got to get back into the fight." Two roman soldiers rushed him, but he killed them both with ease and barely a thought.

I stepped out from behind the debris and found the arena covered with soldiers, some Roman but mostly Norse. Rollo had made it here in time with the army, and now this battle was going to shift. He was running through Romans, knocking them left and right, leaving nothing but scorch marks in his path. Marcus was on the far end of the arena fighting off as many Norse as he could, but the soldiers didn't stand a chance against his powers. They posed as nothing more than a distraction. I had to find Kole, so I kept searching the arena for any signs of him. He had to be alive in here somewhere. Kare was masterful, shooting arrows all over the arena, taking down as many soldiers as she could. Just like she practiced with Rollo, explosions and distractions were happening all around her, but she was deadly and focused.

More Roman soldiers poured in through the hole on the far side of the arena, but they weren't a part of Marcus' army. I was trying to get a clear look at the sigil, but everything was moving too fast. In the middle of the soldiers stood a woman with blonde hair and eyes as blue as the sea. I hadn't seen her in many years, but I knew who she was. She was carrying a giant trident instructing the soldiers to get into position. It was queen Cassia of Cosa. Rollo managed to get her to join us.

She was much taller than I remembered. She impaled soldiers with the trident with tremendous force. Her blue eyes could be seen from across the arena as she indulged in the battle. She was fierce as the ocean, the same as the god she descended from. If the world didn't lie on our shoulders, I would have had time to admire her tactics.

This battle was beginning to turn in our favor. Marcus was running out of allies and, though he was powerful himself, he would not be able to take all of us. I reached within and brought the flames to life. I fire spread through my hands and engulfed both my daggers. I joined the fight helping in any way that I could, cutting down anyone that was looking to defend Marcus. Even though we had the numbers, more Roman soldiers kept filing into the arena, wave after wave of them. Rollo and I were back-to-back fighting off as many as we could.

"Rollo, where is Kole?" I asked while fighting off another wave.

"I don't know, I thought he was will you."

"He tried to save me, and I haven't seen him since. Please tell me Gio didn't turn on us because I do not see him here." I know they all trusted him but now wasn't the time to say I told you so.

"He's here, I wanted to keep him back until we really need him. He is the secret weapon, after all."

"I think this justifies as us needing him, Rollo. We are losing ground. Marcus is pulling soldiers out of his ass apparently," I yelled, and just like that I finally laid eyes on him.

Kole was in the middle of Roman soldiers, his eyes pitch black, killing anyone that was brave enough to come within his vicinity. He looked up and we locked eyes. I didn't have to explain to him how upset I was about him sending me away. I knew he meant well, but if we are going down, it will be together. I was just happy that he was alive, and I can tell that he felt the same. He mouthed *I love you,* and we jumped back into battle together.

Rollo sent a streak of lightning through the air burning the soldier next to him beyond recognition. That managed to get Marcus's attention. Almost like the familiar power called out to him. He stopped what he was doing and headed straight toward us. Cassia and her army were able to keep the Roman soldiers storming into the arena at bay while we prepared to take on Marcus again, but this time was going to be very different.

"So, you manage to get some reinforcements. All this means is the people of Alexandria will have more bodies to clean up when I'm done," he said coldly.

"I wouldn't be too confident about that Marcus; you are completely outnumbered." I sounded way more confident than I was.

"Numbers mean nothing to me. There are gods and men, and I have been chosen by the gods to cleanse this land. This will not be the day I die. If this is how you plan to waste your time, then so be it," his voice thundered through the air.

"I guess no one told this guy about how much the gods leave out," Rollo smiled.

We lined up as Marcus marched towards us with almost a dozen soldiers behind him, their weapons trained on us. The green flash I saw earlier was still dancing on the upper decks of the arena. Again, it disappeared instantly forcing my attention back to Marcus.

Another blur crossed my eyes. I could feel it before I could see it, and one by one the soldiers behind Marcus were falling to ground bleeding. I looked toward Kole because I had no idea what was going on, but Rollo was smiling.

"You mind filling us in on what is happening," Kole said.

"You will know soon enough, this guy loves an entrance," he shrugged his shoulders.

The soldiers were dying faster than I could track what was killing them. Blur after blur, the soldiers were dropping so fast that Marcus didn't even notice his ranks were thinning.

"Any last words before I kill you all?" Marcus asked with an arrogance to rival all others.

"I was going to ask you the same thing," Gio replied and appeared behind one of the soldiers, ripping into his neck with his canine fangs. His shirt was soaked in blood and that monstrous smile was on his face. Four more of Gio's family appeared and ripped into the necks of his soldiers and drank their fill.

"Looks like you just lost even more Marcus. You sure you're not ready to surrender?" Marcus turned and the sight of Gio was the first time that he seemed to be worried. It was clear that he was aware of what was staring him down. He was probably one of the last Romans to even know of his existence. His face shot back to us, he looked furious, completely enraged.

"Do you know what you have done, you stupid children?" he scolded us. He was between anger and fear.

"You mean by coming here and reclaiming what was stolen from me?" I answered.

"This creature is the biggest abomination that has ever walked the earth, a vampire parasite and you plan to hand the city over to him."

"You killed your own people, sacrificed your son, and planned to wipe out an entire race, but somehow I am the biggest problem." Gio wiped the blood off his hands and was face to face with Marcus. "I see one hundred and fifty years hasn't changed much," Marcus raised his fist to strike Gio, but he was so fast the punch was not even close. He continued to taunt the king, knowing it was getting under his skin.

"I see the infamous Roman temper hasn't gotten any better either, but it won't matter after tonight. My family and I will finally be free and not forced to live under your thumb." Marcus was done with all the talking. He sprang into action with all his fury aimed at Gio, but Gio was still too fast.

He moved quickly to our side and settled In next to us. He would have to wait to fight Gio, the rest of us had a score to settle. Kole, Rollo, and I stepped into his path, and we attacked him from any angle we could find. Weeks of anger radiated from me as the voices and the battle hum got louder and louder.

"Kill him."

"He must not live."

"He took all of it from you. Everything."

Kole was swinging his axe and opening portals all over so Rollo could jump through and somehow find a way to get behind Marcus. While he was busy trying to evade their attacks, I ignited my daggers in both hands and cut into his flesh any moment there was an opening. Blood covered his armor as it streamed out of the wounds and ran down his legs from the damage I had done, but Marcus was still standing unfazed.

Marcus was shooting balls of energy trying to land a blow on any of us, but we stayed in motion, the three of us never staying put in one spot. He was getting so frustrated, but we just kept weaving in and out of our attacks. Marcus shifted his approach and, instead of trying to attack us head-on, he tried to predict where we would be. He launched the lightning at us but didn't wait to see if he made contact with us. He turned quickly and fired an energy mass directly where Rollo was.

"Holy shit, this is not good!" Rollo yelled. The energy mass was heading straight towards him. There was no way he would have any time to dodge it.

He reached out his hands to stop the mass. I could see his eyes illuminate, he was tapping into his power to try to lessen the blow, but the mass began to grow smaller and smaller. Somehow, he managed to absorb the energy as the mass got so small it disappeared.

"Did you guys see that?" Rollo was shouting, almost cheering that he managed to not die.

"That's it, I have a plan." Kole was speaking to himself, and he nodded to Rollo. "Give up Marcus, you're just wasting your time," Kole was smiling even though I thought it was premature to celebrate a victory.

His eyes were black, and I could feel him reaching out with his power, grasping for something, though I didn't know what.

"How do you figure? You aren't any closer to winning, young king. These are scrapes, but nothing you have done will put me down." He laughed.

"I know how we can defeat you Marcus, I'm giving you one last chance to surrender. Maybe my future wife and the gods will take it easy on you." I got chills every time he called me his wife but now was not the time to lose focus.

"Delusion must be a basic trait for your people. No matter how many allies you have, I will never surrender to a dog and his bitch," he spat. The smile drained off Kole's face, his eyes returning to the smoky black state which meant that Marcus had sealed his fate.

"When you see it, you strike," he said to me without warning.

"Wait what?" I asked.

He nodded towards Rollo and they both charged at Marcus, completely leaving me out of the plan.

What did he mean by when I see it, and how would I know? We really needed to work on this communication thing.

I wasn't sure what was different about this plan because all the maneuvers we have tried thus far weren't working.

Kole charged the king and let his axe fly, the lightning around Marcus deflected the blow as expected. Kole slid inside of his guard and began to land a flurry of punches against Marcus' armor, it sounded like he was punching a brick wall. He was laying every ounce of strength he had into the punches. Marcus dismissed his punches and grabbed him by the throat and lifted him off his feet.

The same energy mass that launched me across the arena was building up in his hand and he was aiming it straight for Kole's chest. I couldn't stand and watch him get hurt, I started to make a move to free him.

"Not yet, Octavia," he let out a hoarse scream as Marcus gripped him tighter. My heart was racing.

"I'm not going to let you die," I was moving closer, but he held up his hand signaling me to stop. I don't understand why he kept trying to take me out of the fight.

My hands were covered in flames, and I was not sure who I was angrier with. Marcus' hands were a bright white but as he lifted his palm, Rollo brought down his hammer in an attempt to free Kole. Once again, the lightning sparks jolted the hammer out of his hand. I could see that Rollo was expecting that. He reached down and grabbed the energy mass, absorbing it into himself.

The light grew dimmer and dimmer in Marcus's hands, Rollo's eyes were glowing so bright it was blinding. His breathing intensified as he absorbed more, but the fatigue of all that energy was noticeably affecting him. He would not be able to hold all of that for too long, Marcus was too strong. Kole's eyes shot to mine, he lifted his hand, and shouted with whatever voice he had left.

"NOW!"

A portal opened in front of me, and without a second thought I stepped through. The darkness wrapped around me and spit me out right behind Marcus. He didn't notice me until it was too late. He assumed that the lightning would protect him as it had the entire time, but Rollo let go of his hand and threw a punch with everything he had, distracting Marcus just enough. The flames skated from my hands all the way down the hilt of both daggers, and I planted both in his back.

The king roared in pain. Then, a giant wave of energy knocked us all off our feet. Marcus rolled around the sands in pain bleeding all over. He couldn't reach the hilt of the daggers and none of us wanted him to make a last-ditch effort to try to kill us, so we decided to stay back until he accepted his end. I underestimated how stubborn he was, as he refused to go quietly. He writhed in pain as he tried to remove the dagger.

"You think this is over, you stupid children. This is only the beginning," he yelled as blood poured out his mouth from his stab wounds. "My gods will avenge me, this is bigger than all of you, and I will see that my vengeance is had." He managed to get himself up on his feet. I was amazed that he could even continue to speak. "You have reset all we have worked for, and the gods will not take this lightly. Something is coming, and it will finish what I started, I promi......" Gio was attached to his throat, his sharp canines tore into him and yanked like a rabid dog. Marcus was silenced and fell to the ground, his head barely attached to the rest of his body.

"You were right, my young queen, his head was worth it," he smiled.

23 - It's Not Over – Rollo

"Okay, honestly that was gross." I couldn't hold it in. Watching Gio rip his throat out was not nearly as enjoyable as I thought it would be. Marcella peaked her head out from behind him, her hair hanging free and reckless from all the fighting. I would recognize her anywhere. I could do without all the blood splattered all over her face, but she was still unusually perfect.

The remaining army must have seen their leader fall because the fighting had finally stopped. We finally had a moment to breathe. Our victory was hard fought but the destruction of this city was extensive. The arena remained standing, but the structure was in pieces. It would take Alexandria years to recover from this battle. I wonder if the Romans would leave that part out when they told the story about everything we accomplished. My own personal chapter in Roman history would be an amazing story for my kingdom. Octavia brushed up against me and I wrapped my arms around her. I was genuinely happy to see that I had made it in time, and she was in one piece.

“Thank the gods you’re okay, I thought I was going to be too late.” I wrapped her tighter.

“Your best friend has a talent for letting everything come down to the wire, and you shouldn’t be thanking me. Kare is the one that saved the day,” she said. Kare was on her way over to us being followed by Cassia. I turned to help Kole, who still had his hand rubbing the bruises Marcus left on his throat.

“Thank Odin you’re still in one piece brother,” I hugged him fiercely, “hell of a plan by the way.” A sly smile stretched across his face.

“Thank you for leaving me out of the plan, once again,” Octavia yelled.

“Sorry about that, Tav. Me and Kole have practiced together for years, we really don’t need to tell each other what to do out loud anymore. We have to get used to having another person working with us,” I said. “Once he realized that I could absorb Marcus’ power, the plan just seemed to be obvious,” I shrugged.

“Obvious to everyone but me I see,” she pouted. Kole didn’t look to apologize; he just walked over and planted his lips on hers before she could finish complaining.

I tried not to stare but they were right next to me. I cleared my throat loudly hoping that would break up their embrace as the others made their way over to us at the center of the arena.

I don’t even know where to start with all the introductions. We had to be the most unlikely group of allies the gods have ever seen. Now that the present threat was gone, we needed to sit down and hash out all the demands we agreed upon in the event of our success.

The seven of us stood in a circle looking from left to right. Most of us knew each other in some way, but there were some new faces. I decided to break the silence since no one was jumping to introduce themselves.

"Okay, so where do I start," I thought out loud and took a step forward. "Let's start with the new faces. Cassia is the queen of Cosa, the island just south of here. Octavia and her obviously know each other. Marcella is one of Gio's oldest family members, I met her on the beach before I sailed to Cosa." She flashed a smile my way which made me feel unusually warm inside. I looked around to make sure everyone was still keeping up with me, but mostly to make sure no one noticed if I was blushing. "Cassia, Marcella, this is Kole king of Lundr, and his future wife Octavia, the new queen of Alexandria. The girl with the bow and arrow, and excellent aim thanks to her rigorous training, is Kole's sister, Kare." I had to throw that last bit in, just to tease Kare as I would my own sister. She rolled her eyes in response. This was so exhausting, I wasn't sure why I volunteered to be the one that filled the awkward silence with the sound of my voice. "Everyone else, we all know each other, so no need for introductions. Any questions?" The circle remained silent as we all traded skeptical glances with one another. I decided to give up trying to bridge the divide between this odd collection of allies. "I'm glad all of you are so excited about the victory, please feel free to contain your enthusiasm," I said sarcastically.

Ω

The icy mood was beginning to thaw, and the others started to have small separate conversations with each other, which was encouraging for the time being. If this was going to work, we would have to get comfortable around each other. Until suddenly, a vicious wind whipped through what remained of the arena and the bright green light swirled through the rubble.

“Did you see that?” I asked Kole.

“I thought it was only me. That green light has been appearing and disappearing all day,” he said cautiously.

“I’ve seen it, too,” Octavia agreed from behind me. Something wasn’t right, the wind got stronger, so strong that it could have knocked you off your feet if you weren’t prepared.

“What now!” I yelled. I looked to the others, but everyone was trying to keep the sand out of their eyes.

The bright green light we saw earlier was thickening into a mist trailing over all the dead soldiers in the arena. Fear raced up my spine because I knew what was coming. It was all too familiar. A lifetime ago we sat in the cave and listened to Gio’s tragic story, and he described this mist precisely.

“It's Delphi,” I screamed, “she’s here!”

The mist was pouring in seeming like it had no end. It continued to sweep across the arena surrounding us. Whatever the spirit had planned for us, it couldn’t be good. Gio’s entire body went still as he watched the spirit enshroud the arena in green mist. I could see the pure dread in his eyes.

The bodies of dead soldiers began to rustle all around us, slow movements and eerie moans coming from the corpses. The bodies struggled to make it back up to their feet, their dead hands clutching the weapons that remained with them as they died.

“What the fuck is going on? Who is Delphi?” Cassia asked.

“When I say it is literally the longest story ever, that is no exaggeration.” I looked back towards her as I gripped on the hilt of hammer.

“You think a few dead bodies are going to scare me? Hell of a show bitch, but the only thing you have done is upset me more,” Gio was snarling. “I’ll find a way to snuff you from this world for the fate that you bestowed upon me.”

“I’m not sure taunting the spirit is the best idea, we really don’t know how to get rid of it, if that is even possible,” Kole bellowed.

Then a cold familiar voice spoke through all the madness, drawing our attention. Walking toward us was the recently deceased king, his eyes replaced with the green mist and his head barely attached to his body. Even the wound Gio left him with was still bleeding. Delphi spoke through the dead king’s mouth.

“It has been a long time, my child, but the time of escaping your fate has passed,” the voice responded lifelessly.

“My fate?!” Gio shouted in anger, “you are the one who damned me to this life, robbed me of love and purpose. I only gave you what you deserved in return.”

“So, we are just going to ignore the fact that she managed to possess a dead king?” I asked.

“SHUT UP, ROLLO!” They all yelled in unison, and I put my hands up in defeat.

“One can’t fight what is destined for them. You made choices that led to where you are now, and since you do not see that, it is a mistake to allow you to remain in this world,” Delphi spoke. “What is worse, you have involved these other misguided souls with your madness.”

“All I wanted was Selene. Time after time, you and your miserable group of puppet masters used me as a pawn. The gods are my maker, and you are their messenger. Fuck destiny, and fuck you most of all. From now on, I will write it myself, and the first item on my agenda is to wipe every inch of your spirit from this world.” The veins bulged in his throat from all the yelling as the dead soldiers began to close in around us.

“So be it, my child,” Delphi raised her hands and the soldiers attacked us all at once.

All of us reacted at once, bracing ourselves for the unstoppable wave of bodies. The dead soldiers screeched as they attempted to rip through our defenses. The corpses were fresh, the blood from their wounds still leaking all over the sands as they rushed in a blind rage.

There was nothing left of their souls, just a relentless hunger for death and destruction. I called forth the lightning and swung my hammer in any direction. The soldiers were easy to dispatch, but we had killed so many that Delphi had a lot of dead at her disposal.

“There are too many of them,” I screamed to the others, but no one was paying me much attention as the bodies just kept coming and coming, trying to break through the defense we created. We needed a new plan, or this was going to be the end of us all. The mighty chosen warriors taken down by an ancient spirit with a vendetta that doesn't even belong to them.

Gio was cutting through the bodies in a blind rage, his fangs extended past the curve of his lips and a vicious growl coming from the pit of his chest. He was a feral animal, his claws ripping through the bodies like nothing I have ever seen. I was impressed, maybe slightly terrified, but all of this wasn't enough. I could see the fatigue weighing on everyone.

Then the answer hit me like a ton of bricks. We had an ace in the hole and she was standing right in front of me. I was just too stupid to remember.

"Octavia," I called to her.

"Rollo, I'm a tad bit busy trying not to die, this better be important!" She cut off a Delphi soldier's head.

"Remember in the wasteland when you went all crazy from hearing the voices?"

"Seriously Rollo, exactly how is that relevant at this very moment?" she grunted as she continued chopping into zombie-like soldiers.

"Oh, I don't know, maybe the Roman princess that has power over the dead could be of some use while we fight a bunch of dead soldiers. You know what, you're right, why would that be relevant?" I said sarcastically.

She scowled at me before she closed her eyes. The flames erupted around her hands, and she slammed the palm of her hand against the sand. The flames shot directly into the ground.

I didn't know if this would work, but it was the only option we had left.

The flames fissured and spread through the ground to the feet of the soldiers all around us. The bodies started to convulse and twist in unbearable pain, bones breaking as the limbs spasmed under the weight of her fire. Once she managed to reach all of Delphi's soldiers, the dead around us stopped attacking.

Their attention shifted to repelling the flames from taking over the bodies. I would never get used to seeing Marcus' head barely hanging to his body. Delphi was struggling, trying to will the soldiers back under her control, but she was losing ground quickly.

"Octavia, keep going, you almost got them all!" The flames trailed far and wide taking over any soldier that it touched.

"I can't take anymore, it's too much," she yelled. The flames reached out to touch the rest of the soldiers on the other side of the arena, and then out of nowhere, they began to fade. All my hopes began to vanish with it.

24 - A Death Deal – Kole

The flames just stopped short of full control and my eyes shot straight back to Octavia. She maintained control over the soldiers she reached, but her influence couldn't go any further. I can see how exhausted she was, we all were, and I honestly could not see an end game here. There must be a way to win. Even though Delphi didn't seem to be something that I could reason with, I had to try. We just needed to find out what she wanted, besides Gio dead of course.

The more I thought about his story, I realized that he became a victim the same way we did. Yes, he's made some rough choices, but he has paid the price and then some. Should he have to pay this ultimate price for just searching out his purpose? Falling in love and doing whatever it took to be with his love was that what he was paying for? It all felt way too familiar. Octavia willed her power deeper into the ground to force the soldiers to surround us, keeping a barrier between us and the others. Giving us a tiny moment to regain some of our strength. I looked across the sands to Marcus, the green mist still spilling out of his eyes as his head hung awkwardly, barely attached to his neck.

"This fighting is futile. Just hand over the vampire and I can atone for the mistake the gods have made. Nature requires balance and Ambrogio is a mistake of the huntress. He was never meant to exist outside of her service."

"Why should I have to pay for your sins? My life ended the moment I ventured into that cave... where was the balance then?" Gio wiped the blood off his face with his sleeve.

"What is done needs to be undone," Delphi said coldly.

"What if we balance nature another way?" I interrupted.

"How about we take this green smokey bitch and burn her from existence?" Gio snarled.

"I mean, technically you tried that," Rollo countered.

"Gio, can you relax for a second? I'm trying to find a way out of this for all of us," I was almost pleading with him to stand down.

"And why should I do anything to help the ones that stole everything from me? Do you understand what that feels like?" His eyes were pinned on mine communicating more than just the words he was saying, and I could tell he was on the brink of losing it.

The calm and collected king I met in the cave was gone. He was generally afraid of what was going to happen next. The mask he wore to hide the pain of the past was cracking into pieces, showing us glimpses of the man that was terrified for his future. He didn't realize how much pain we hid every single day; if anyone understands it's the three of us.

"We can find another way to achieve balance in nature."

"Kole, have we not learned our lesson making deals with gods and spirits?" Rollo glared at me.

The holmgang was my fault and it was a mistake that I would pay for every time I sat on my throne, but either way, I was all out of options. It was either we die or live to fight another day.

"Gio got his powers from the huntress, while the goddess Selene's essence lives inside the moon. Technically, if she was to bless someone with powers the way Artemis did, the scales would be balanced." I waited for Delphi to agree with my logic. "Technically, there would be two beings infused by the essence of a god, and like Gio has his weakness, this being should have one, as well. Right your wrong without taking a life for nothing."

"Are you insane?" Gio grabbed my vest. "You would let her subject someone else to this curse? Do you know what you are asking?"

"I'm asking for your life to be spared, and in the process to bring a piece of Selene back to this world. Is that worth anything to you?" I asked.

"You have no idea what will come of this. The decision you make is for the safety of your people, but I warn you this will not be a happy ending. All actions have consequences, no matter how well intended they are, trust me on that," Gio warned, returning to his calm demeanor before walking away.

"Believe me when I tell you Selene is in no space to refuse as her life has never been her own. We are not done here, vampire! I have accepted nothing yet," Delphi snarled. He turned and addressed the spirit inhabiting Marcus as if he had given up on everything.

"Do what you will, but no more blood from my family will spill," he promised and stepped out from the protection of the circle against all our better judgment. Marcus' eyes flashed a bright green.

"I accept your deal, but this isn't over. Pain will be delivered for your disrespect and disobedience, and you will be seeing my imprint from this deal one way or another," Marcus spoke and then the green mist left his body, and the corpse went lifeless, as did the rest of the soldiers. Gio didn't even acknowledge the last words from the spirit as he walked away.

"Gio, watch out!" Kare screamed.

A Delphi soldier that somehow snuck past us was charging at Gio from behind with a sharpened piece of wood just like the villagers in the cave. Before Gio could turn, Kare jumped in the way and the jagged piece of wood was hanging out of her stomach, blood instantly pooling from the wound. I snapped the soldier's neck and managed to catch my sister on the way down.

"No!"

Kare fell to the ground dropping her bow. Blood was soaking her clothes, my hands, and the ground underneath her. She was bleeding too much and losing color by the second.

"Kare, please don't leave me! I can't do this alone, I need you," my voice quavered as emotions slammed into me like a tidal wave, tears crashing down. All the power I had, and I was losing people I love over and over.

First my father at my hands, and now I would have to go home and explain to my mother how I failed to protect her baby. Rollo arrived by my side. I barely noticed when he grabbed my shoulder and knelt next to me.

"Kare, please!" I cried. She was trying to speak but her voice was so rough and hoarse I could barely understand. "Don't try to speak, everything is going to be fine, little sister." I knew I didn't have much time, all I could do was just be here, but it didn't make it hurt any less. Her perfect skin and beautiful bouncing curls was the only way I wanted to remember her, not bleeding out in a Roman arena. She shouldn't even be here, and she wouldn't if I didn't agree to this plan.

Another Alexsson death and it's my fault. Maybe my brother was right about me, maybe Odin was right. I'm a selfish monster on the path to destroy others to get what he wants.

"Help her!" Rollo was yelling at Gio and Marcella.

I was ignoring all the commotion around me. Kare struggled to breath as I held her in my arms. She managed a smile, and it shattered me into pieces. What world could I live in where she didn't exist? What land could I rule without my baby sister? She lifted her hand and rubbed the tears streaming down my face.

"Rollo, she's slipping away," my voice was cracking under all of the tears, "I don't know what to do. Tell me what I am supposed to do!"

"I have an idea Kole, but I'm not sure if it will work," Rollo replied. I couldn't understand what he wanted to do until I saw him waving over to Gio.

"Gio, help her now. She saved your life and Kole negotiated for your life, you owe us everything," Rollo demanded.

"You need to be sure. I don't want to promise you anything but letting this beautiful flower die would be a tragedy," Gio replied, looking deep in thought. I needed Kare alive regardless of the circumstances. I couldn't lose her. Without even considering it, I made my choice.

"Do it," I agreed, looking back down at Kare. She was completely slipping away. "Do it now."

"No Kole you can't," Octavia yelled.

"I can't let her die, Octavia!"

"You can't subject her to this, to being exactly like him," she pointed to Gio.

I didn't know what she was going to be but, despite how I felt about the vampire, he had done nothing but show up for us when we needed him to.

"Octavia, whatever grudge you have against him will not rub off on Kare. Gio has gained our trust, and if he can make sure my sister lives, then that's what I'm going to do," I said the words strongly and for the first time in our relationship this was non-negotiable. I could feel the tension as soon as the words left my mouth.

But I knew she was not going to tell me to let my sister die. I didn't look back at her for the okay, no more people were going to die because of me.

"Gio, do it!"

Gio kneeled next to her and stroked the curls that were almost lifeless and whispered in her ear.

"Your new life awaits you, my dear," he murmured and lowered his fangs to her arm. A sense of dread took over me, something telling me I was making a mistake.

“Wait! Wait!” I reached to stop him, but Rollo grabbed my arm.

“We can’t stop now, she’s running out of time, brother.” He gripped my arm tighter stopping me from moving.

“Rollo, take your hands off me.” The darkness was skating right below the surface of my skin. I was staring Rollo in the face, and I could see that he was prepared to fight me if need be. He cared about her just as much as I did but maybe this was another selfish decision.

Did she deserve to live a life in darkness just so I could see her alive? What if the gods decide that she isn’t worthy and she dies anyway? He managed to distract me long enough for Gio to pick his head back up and lock eyes with us in silence.

“It is done, young king. Now we wait for the gods to judge her,” he said softly.

“Well, how long does it take?!” I screamed to him. Before he could answer, Kare’s eyes flew wide open, and she screamed to the heavens. Her nails were digging into the sand as she twisted her body back and forth in pain.

I dropped down to grab a hold of her and tried to comfort her, but she just kept convulsing and screaming, it was unbearable to watch. I felt the darkness flooding inside me, and all of my rage was pointed toward Gio.

“What the fuck did you do?!” I roared to the vampire.

“I’ve done exactly what you asked me to do, young king,” he said it way too calmly for my liking.

"She's screaming and trying to rip herself apart in pain, that is not what I asked for," I balled my fist up into his shirt. I didn't know how to kill him, but I was going to rip his heart out and see if that would stick until Rollo came over and loosened my grip on the vampire.

"Kole, calm down please," he begged.

"Why should I be calm? Look at her, Rollo!" Kare was hunched over in a ball moaning in devasting pain.

"Marcella told me that this is what she went through when she was bitten as well," he explained and pointed to this mysterious vampire Rollo has come to know so well. He continued to hold me back from moving forward.

I knew I could trust him but seeing her this way was not very convincing. I wouldn't be able to forgive myself if she died. I looked over to Octavia. She was disappointed in my choice, she wore Kare's pain the same as me. She was dying to say I told you so, but she wouldn't rub it in just to be cruel. Gio walked back over to me and spoke softly.

"Transformation is different for everyone. All we can do is wait. I won't pretend to understand what you feel but I know this will not be easy. I thank you for the kindness that you have shown me, I have been alive a long time and haven't met very honorable people like yourselves." He scooped his hands underneath Kare and picked her up off the ground. Her breathing had slowed but she was still alive.

"The sun will be coming up soon. We need to get inside, and when your sister wakes, I have a lot to go over with her." I surveyed the destruction that was caused by the battle and Delphi. While I was happy to bring down the tyrant, Octavia's home would take some time to recover from this.

I almost forgot that she was still kneeling on the ground, exhausted from taking control of all the soldiers. I ran to her to make sure she was okay.

"Are you okay, my love?"

"I'm fine," she replied, our previous exchange was still wedged between us like a mountain. "How is Kare? Is she going to make it?" There was genuine concern in her voice.

"Only time will tell, Gio is taking her back to the villa to make her more comfortable."

"I know you had to make that decision and I wouldn't have let her die either, but her being anything like Gio doesn't sit right with me, even if he helped us win the day. It seems like we always have to give up something in order to keep our heads above water," she complained. I wrapped my hands around her waist to help her up.

"You saved the day again, my queen, and I will continue to give up anything for you and the ones close to me." I smiled and pulled her close to me.

"Everything is destroyed. This was not the way I wanted to win back my home, all of this senseless death, not to mention another deal was made. One that we have no idea how it will turn out." She was right and that is something we would have to deal with eventually, but for now I was just happy to be reunited with her.

"I love you so much. Do you know that, Octavia Sirius?"

"I love you too, my king," she returned my smile with a much-needed kiss. For too long I have been unable to touch her, feel her lips against mine, and I was not going to let anyone separate us again. Even if she silently hated how much we had to risk getting to this point.

"While we are all enjoying you licking all over each other, it's been a long day. Can we go back to the villa and relax? Besides, we have much to discuss," Rollo remarked. Octavia smirked at him, paying him no mind as usual, but I could tell something was still bothering her.

"The job is not done. Titus and Floria are still here somewhere, we need to find them. The rest of us can go back to the villa and get more acquainted with each other, and I need to formally thank you all for your part in this," Octavia addressed everyone.

"I will be with Gio waiting for Kare to wake, I can't do anything until I know she is okay." I kissed Octavia one more time admiring her strength before I followed after Gio.

Ω

I sat at her bedside for hours waiting for her to wake up. Every minute that passed I punished myself. Rollo explained to me how the bite works from what he learned from Marcella's story.

Kare had experienced more pain before I got here, and when I walked into the room to find her not breathing, I almost fell into pieces all over again. They assured me this was all a part of the process; she would have to venture to the brink of the afterlife and then come back. I wondered if she would make it to the gates of Valhalla. Since she was not meant to stay, the All-father would turn her away. Would she see my father there? I hope not, that would be an unbearable tease.

Octavia and Rollo passed by multiple times to try and get me to eat but I had no appetite. I was empty, a hollowed-out version of myself. The only thing I could do was reflect on all I have done and all the lives that have been lost at the base of my choices.

The alleged chosen one, the new King of Lundr has killed his father, banished his brother, slaughtered hundreds of Roman soldiers, led his crew to a foreign land to fight a senseless battle, and caused his baby sister to lose her life. I'm the reason Kare lays before me lifeless. I'm surprised I can still lift my shoulders given the weight of all this tragedy sitting upon them.

How could I have fallen so far so fast? It felt like yesterday when I was just a prince training and drinking with my best friend. Taking every single moment for granted. Maybe my story would end like the Roman tragedies Octavia told me about. There was no doubt that I have brought change to this world, but would my choices be the ones that will unite us? And would any of us be here to enjoy the change?

I would give anything for a sign from Odin right now. His absence was noticeable This deep into the Roman lands I could barely feel that reassuring presence, and I didn't want to admit it, but I needed some of his skewed guidance. I heard a noise behind me at the door and turned to find Gio in the doorway.

"Can I speak with you?" he asked tentatively. I got up and walked over to him.

"I wanted to thank you again for what you have done here today. You could have turned us all over after the battle was won, you didn't need any of my people anymore. Why did you save us?"

"Because it was the right thing to do. You aren't evil, Gio, no matter how you wish to be perceived as such. You were used by the gods the same way we were. The only thing we agree upon is that this land doesn't belong to either side. I want to live in peace with everyone so we can all thrive together," I explained and walked back over to the bedside. "It is exactly what Kare would have done, she has always been more kind than me." Gio tapped me on the shoulder.

"For what you have done for me, I promise you that I will be a mentor to Kare for as long as I live. I am alive because of her and that is not something I will forget, you have my word." He stood with his hands behind his back.

"I know in the arena Rollo said that you owed us everything, but why did you save my sister? She doesn't mean anything to you." I didn't expect a straight answer.

"On the contrary, despite how the rest of you may feel, she is the most interesting out of all of you," he said quickly.

"What does that mean?" There was a hint of offense in my voice, which he must have picked up on because he started smiling.

"From the moment your wide-eyed sister ventured into the Delphi caves, I could sense that she was a vision of hope. She was pure and untouched by the blight in this life," he divulged and looked past me to her as she still laid peacefully. "Letting something so beautiful be taken on my account seems completely misguided, so I wanted to help her... but before we venture down this road, there are things you need to understand," he spoke strongly, which snagged my attention.

"There are things you need to know, as well. My sister is not a killer, and she won't be one of your controlled soldiers killing whenever you feel the need to," my voice was stern because I wanted him to know exactly what I meant. His face twisted in confusion.

"I can tell you one thing, my young king, your sister will kill. It is something engraved in our nature to be predators," his eyes traced softly over her, "but she will not be a killer for sport, merely for survival."

I thought he was done talking but he continued now with a more purposeful tone.

"You sit here and talk a tall order, Kole, but remember as you said we are not so different. I have no intention of controlling Kare." I turned my head regretting ever speaking the words. "Monsters and heroes are more alike than you think. You kill with no remorse to protect yours, the same as I do mine."

I honestly had no answer for him. I'd killed my fair share to protect my home, family, and my wife.

"The vampire is the abomination when he kills, that's what the gods have ordained, but I will not let anyone view her as a monster. I won't let her be subjected to the slavery of persecution as I was," he promised, his eyes staring intensely.

"Then I guess at least there is something that we can agree on," I reached out to shake his hand and he responded in extending his.

“There is only one thing you need to remember. Though she will be different, she needs to be reminded that she still has family. Remind her that she still has people from her old life that love her,” he urged as he looked me in my eyes.

“That won’t be a problem,” I answered.

“Aww, you guys missed me,” the voice was like hearing heaven on earth even though she sounded horrible. Gio and I spun around to find Kare leaning up smiling at us. Some of her color was returning but she was moving slowly.

“Thank Odin you are awake, I thought I lost you,” I ran over to hug her, but Gio stopped me before I could reach her.

“I know you are excited, young king, but as I said: Kare and I have some things to discuss,” he snapped his fingers and a woman walked in behind him.

“What is she here for?” I was completely confused.

“What happened? Why am I so hungry? You guys have anything to eat?” Kare questioned. Gio stretched out his arm and stopped me from approaching her.

“If you go any closer to her, she will kill you off instinct. Unless she gets her hunger under control, and I am the one that can help her with that. You are going to have to trust me.” He brought the woman over to Kare, took a knife, and slid it gently over her wrist into the cup that was on the table.

“What is going on?” Kare was frightened, and her eyes shifted to me as she naturally backed away from the cup.

“It’s okay, just drink and everything will be clear in time,” Gio soothed and gently pressed the cup to her mouth, and once she got a smell of the contents inside, she drank without resisting.

I watched as her eyes rolled back in complete euphoria, more color came back to her skin and her curls becoming full right in front of my eyes. If I wasn't sitting her watching it, I wouldn't have believed it.

"She is in good hands, but we have so much more to discuss. Please go eat and get some rest. From what I've learned from the others, you have been locked in a cell for weeks and you spent the rest of that time fighting. You need to take care of yourself." I took one last look at my baby sister, then against my better judgement I left her with him.

Gio was in a better position to help her, so I had to let him take over. I didn't realize how exhausted I was until he said it.

I left them and made my way back to my room to get some much-needed rest. But I knew sleep wouldn't come because talking to Gio revealed something I had been wondering since I met him. I finally figured out what Gio's weakness was, and now the same thing could harm my sister.

25 - Finally! – Octavia

I made sure all the others found rooms in the villa before I decided to head back to my room. I gathered a few men that I knew I could trust and tasked them with searching for Floria and Titus, but deep down I didn't want them to find her. Once they do, I will have to look her in the face and decide her fate.

Would I be strong enough to pass judgment on the only family I had left? Would I be strong enough to show mercy as Kole did with Kyut? The guilt was stifling because finding her dead may be easier than dealing with the problem, but all of that would have to take a back seat for now.

The only thing I needed to do was see Kole. Marcella got word from Gio that Kare was awake, and he was working with her, explaining some of the things about her transformation. I needed to check on Kole and make sure he was okay. He was locked in a cell and then forced to fight for our entertainment, all at the hands of my people. I know he would never hold that against me, but I had to make sure that he understood how sorry I was about everything that happened, especially with Kare.

I wasn't proud of my reaction to Gio changing her, but deep down I was conflicted about the choice he made. Gio was as complicated and dangerous as a pet snake. If we took care of him, he would be loyal, but he could strike at any time as that is his nature. I decided to add that problem to the long list and deal with it later. At this moment, I just needed to see my future husband.

I pushed past the giant hallway taking in all the defiled remnants of Marcus. Even though he was gone, the stench of his stay lingered in this house. Years of history wiped out faster than I could wrap my head around it. It would take even more time for the citizens to heal from everything they have lost.

I stopped right outside of my door. I'm not sure why I hesitated, but I stood right outside the door afraid to enter. Nothing about this place felt right anymore. How was I ever supposed to feel comfortable here again? Only the gods know how many enemies I have managed to create by taking over the city, so I needed to tread carefully. I reached down and grabbed one of my daggers and slowly walked inside. I was not going to be caught off guard anymore. Whoever made the mistake of breaking in chose the wrong room.

The door creaked open slowly against my palm as I crept into the room. I glanced over the vanity, and it was empty. Another look over to the bed, it was empty as well. Whoever it was must have been giving themselves a tour of my bathroom. I pressed myself against the wall trying to keep myself out of sight. Footsteps approached before the person came into view. I jumped from behind the wall and swung the dagger upward ready to kill. His arm came up and caught the dagger mid-swing.

"That is a terrible way to greet the man you love," Kole teased with mirth in his voice and a smile on his face.

"By Olympus Kole, you knew I was here. Why didn't you say anything? I could have killed you," I yelled. He was still smiling at me, that giant beautiful smile that I could never get tired of. I lowered the dagger only to realize that he wasn't wearing any clothes.

"The reason I didn't say anything when I heard you come in is that I thought this would be a much better greeting," he said calmly.

"It is a much better greeting. Actually, I just wish that I was more prepared for it," I implied and moved closer to him to lay my hands on his chest. His skin was so smooth, he was still wet from the bath he had just taken.

"How are you doing?" I asked.

"Much better now," his lips grazed my forehead and the rest of my body shuttered softly. "I feel like I haven't touched you in a million years."

"You haven't. Don't worry, I've been keeping count."

"How about we fix that and deal with tomorrow's problems after you come down from the clouds?" He lowered his mouth down to mine, and his teeth grazed my bottom lip.

I felt the heat run deep in my body. I wanted to live in this moment forever. I wanted him more than I wanted air. I got my wish because, before I could say a word, his mouth pressed against mine as we fell into the familiar rhythm, our tongues having perfected it from our time spent together.

My body was hungry for him and every touch from his hands sent me into a frenzy. A frenzy I tried to contain but small moans escaped me as he caressed my breast with his hands.

"Kole," his name barely making it through my lips.

"I hope you're not telling me to stop because that would literally kill me."

"I would never tell you to stop," I grabbed the length of him and slid my hands back and forth across him slowly, watching him react to every stroke, watching him devour me with his eyes, watching him worship me. I kissed his neck and then his chest as tiny gasps and moans were stifled in his throat.

"If you keep that up, you're going to end this celebration early," he drawled. I tried to hold back the smile.

"Sounds like a challenge."

"That is not what I meant," his breathing became more intense.

"Show me how much you like it," I demanded, stroking him faster and faster. His head fell back over his shoulders. He relinquished control and decided to give in. Watching him live in this pleasure was driving me crazy. Heat was building between my thighs as my nipples hardened, sensitive from rubbing against the tunic I was wearing.

"I can't hold it much longer," his body started to shutter so I stroked him faster and harder.

"Show me, my love," I whispered to him as he found his way to the finish, moaning. As his muscled tensed and spasmed in my arms. The weight of the world seemed to fall off his shoulders and while he was vulnerable, I could see that he was nothing less than perfect.

"You are a blessing from the gods," he said to me softly before picking me up off my feet. "And you were right. Let's throw another celebration, and I know exactly who the guest of honor will be," he walked over and sat me down on the edge of the bed.

He walked around to the other side of the bed and climbed in behind me, the anticipation kept me in limbo. I was counting the seconds until he would be touching me again. He slid in behind me, both our legs hanging off the bed and my back placed against his chest.

"How am I supposed to see that handsome face from here?" I leaned my head back and his cheek grazed my lips.

"All you need to do is relax and let me touch you. It's been so long, and I can't think of anything else," he kissed the side of my neck and sent a chill all the way down to my toes.

His left hand traced around me, cupped my breast, and pinched my nipples, forcing an unexpected cry to leave my throat. He was on a mission, his hands never stopped exploring every part of my body trailing the heat back to my center. Silently I begged him for what I knew was coming next, but he continued to tease me, forcing me to stay suspended in pleasure.

"Please," I cried out to him hoping that he would give me what I needed.

"Don't rush a masterpiece, Octavia." I didn't have to see him to tell that his eyes were on me, taking note of my every reaction to his touch forced out of me.

"Please, why do you torment me?" my voice was cracking under his touch.

I couldn't take the teasing anymore. I needed to feel him inside me. His hand brushed my hips as he made his way down my thigh slowly creeping towards his goal. He floated his finger over my center sending a jolt of nerves back through my body. The moan that left my mouth this time was much deeper.

Kole gave me no time to react before he slid a finger inside me, slowly moving it in and out while his thumb traced small circles over my clit, engulfing me in complete bliss.

"You feel so good," he whispered, his lips resting right by my ear before he proceeded to place his lips back on my neck. I could feel him pressing against my back. He was ready long before I expected him to be. I reached back and grabbed his hair to make sure he could hear me.

"Is that all you got?" I said making sure he could see the smirk on my face. A low growl in his chest and a devilish grin flashed before Kole picked me up and laid me on my stomach and gently laid his body on top of mine.

"Let's see if I can show you what I got," he said before slapping me on my backside. Kole pinned my hands down under his. It was strong but gentle at the same time. It was possessive, exciting, and unbelievably sexy. He started kissing my neck down to my shoulders and in the middle of my back before he slid inside of me. He smelled like citrus flowers from his bath, and I just wanted to pull him closer and let him have all of me. His body moved slowly at first making sure I could feel every inch of him, every thrust striking another nerve deeper than the one before. I couldn't hold my voice anymore, there was no need to hide how much I needed him.

I turned my head back to get a glimpse of him at work he was focused on me and only me. Beads of sweat glistened off his brow and his chest as his muscles moved in unison. He was taking in every part of me, leaving nothing to be discovered, and the thought of his lust warmed me up even more.

"Harder," I smiled knowing that was exactly what he loved to hear.

"My pleasure, my queen." His hands gripped firmly on both sides of my hips, and he pulled me back onto him, each time harder than the last until my voice was nearly hoarse from screaming his name. He pulled me up, so my back was flushed against his chest when he placed his hand lightly on my neck and I grabbed on to his arm allowing him to keep me upright.

I moved my hips back against him as he continued to slam his body against mine delving deeper inside me, bringing me closer to paradise. My nails were digging into his arms as he gripped my neck a little tighter. My legs shuddered as he toppled me over the edge, paying me back for what I had done to him earlier and I couldn't be more thankful. He released the grip on my hips, which I was sure would have a nice bruise the next day and we crawled into the bed to hold each other. He looked at me with passion burning in his eyes, but it was beginning to simmer giving us that brief moment of clarity.

"We did it, Octavia," he kissed me. "Your home." I snuggled up against him and laid my head on his chest.

"You are my home," I said. The smooth breeze from my balcony kept us cool in the night, but even I couldn't ignore the burnt smell from all the destruction that we have been through.

Rebuilding Alexandria would have to start tomorrow because now nothing mattered but being in his arms.

26 - Small Talk – Kole

I was going to let this dream carry on for as long as I was able to. It was my first night sleeping in a bed since Marcus locked me in the cell underneath the arena and I couldn't have asked for a better night.

Octavia was still sound asleep. At some point in the night, we managed to detach and make ourselves more comfortable, but now that I was awake, I wanted to be close to her again. She rolled over to face me, but her eyes were still closed, her body breathing steadily and peacefully. Her hair hung loosely around her face. I wanted to brush it back behind her ear, but I did not want to wake her.

We still had some work to do but being in charge could wait a couple more minutes, especially for her. She saved us all and sacrificed so much to get to this point. The pain of Floria's betrayal would not wash away easily, and if anyone knew what that felt like it was me. It was a pain I would have done anything to spare her from feeling. Kyut's words played over and over in my head.

"I will never forgive you, you will never be my king," I hear them echo through my mind as I recall the memory.

When I needed him most, he insulted me and cast me aside, and even after all of that, I spared him when I have killed for less. I looked down at the woman that would be my wife just to admire the one decision that I made that I was certain was not a mistake. We had completed step one and now we had to move forward to finish the task.

A knock at the door jolted me out of my own head and caused Octavia to rustle in bed.

"Is the dream over already?" she forced out after a long yawn.

"Apparently it is. I'll take care of it, you take your time," I kissed her on the forehead and jumped up to grab the first pair of pants I saw. I opened the door to the only face that I would allow to disturb my time with Octavia.

"Sorry to wake you but I wanted to let you know everyone is gathering for breakfast and then heading to the great hall," Rollo was brushing his hair out of his face.

"Okay, we should be down soon, keep everyone entertained. I know it's your favorite thing to do," I joked.

"I have had enough entertainment to last me a lifetime. Crazy kings, psycho spirits, Kare almost dying, should I go on," he replied sarcastically. The reminder of my sister zapped all the color out of my face. Rollo looked at me with concern, he must have noticed. What hurt even more is that I could not see her again until the sun was down.

"Do you think I made the right choice?" I searched his face for some acceptance.

"I think you did what needed to be done. I would have never let my sister die if there was a way to save her."

"But to subject her to that type of life seems selfish." Deep down I was mostly worried Kare would never forgive me.

"If anyone can handle it, its Kare. I have met other members of Gio's family, they are not all bad. Maybe she can shine some of that light on him, he is kind of grim," he laughed.

"Thank you, brother," I reached out to hug him, but he raised his hands to keep me away.

"Whoa, don't you dare hug me. Put some clothes on first. I love you, but not that much," he teased, not even trying to suppress his laughter as he walked back down the hall.

Ω

It took us some time to separate from each other. We felt like so much time had been stolen since our ship docked in Alexandria. Against Octavia's protest, we managed to get out of bed and head down to the great hall to grab some breakfast before responsibility came back to slap us in the face. Octavia found an old gown of hers in the closet. She examined herself in the mirror surprised that the fair-colored gown still fit her after all this time. She looked perfect in anything she wore. I, on the other hand, had to salvage something that one of the guards was wearing. The clothes I wore while I was imprisoned were all but rags now. The rest of my clothes were on my boat, so I had to make do. I left my cloak in the room, it was way too warm to wear inside the villa. The climate here was abysmal.

The cleanup inside the villa had already begun. We had a long way to go but the citizens were working together and making progress. They took pride in their home. Walking slowly down the hall, most of the Bellator banners were already being taken down. It didn't erase history of what occurred here, but it was a start. I squeezed her hand to reassure her that I was here for her. We were going to right this wrong, and I would be with her every step of the way.

"No matter what."

We could hear the commotion in the room before we walked in. It seemed like everyone was getting along in our absence, that in and of itself had to be a win. Trying to keep everyone happy was going to be tedious work, and to be honest it was work that was never going to be finished.

All the conversations stopped as we walked into the room. Eyes all over the room shifted onto us. Everyone was staring, and it was starting to feel uncomfortable. I know the outfit wasn't my best, but there was no need to stare. Before the insecurity of this Roman outfit set in, they all raised their cups in salute as we stood at the threshold.

These fellow kings and queens did us the honor of acknowledging everything we have done to get us to this point and the gesture would never be forgotten. We were going to work together to heal this fractured land and create a world where all will be safe and prosper.

"We thank you all for the gesture, but it is unnecessary. We did not do this alone. Without the rest of you we wouldn't be here right now," I said confidently.

"Well of course we know that. I am the one that saved your ass, after all," Rollo laughed before drinking from his cup. The seat at the head of the table was left open, I assume for me.

"Why don't you take that seat," I smiled at Octavia.

"Why me?" she asked in surprise.

"Because this is your home, I didn't help you get it back so that I could sit at the head of your table," I explained and pulled the chair out so she could sit. I took the seat to her right. Rollo sat on the left, followed by Cassia a little further down the table.

The empty chairs along the table were for Gio, Marcella, and Kare. I couldn't wait until I can see her again, I hoped she was okay. I know the adjustment wouldn't be very easy, but she was strong, and I had faith she could master this like she mastered everything else.

"Cassia, it's been a long time. I'm sorry about your father, he didn't deserve what happened to him that night," Octavia spoke.

"It has, my fellow queen. I haven't been to Alexandria since we were kids, and I certainly did not expect to return under these circumstances, but here we are," she lowered her head. "We have all experienced loss and pain, but I am thankful that your friend journeyed to my shores. Without him it would have taken me longer to get to the truth," I looked towards Rollo and gave him a nod of my approval. He set out to secure an ally and he was more than successful.

"Rollo has become a most trusted friend to the Romans in such a short time. I wouldn't be here without him," Octavia said.

"I spent some time with your friend Rollo. He talks too much but he is a valued ally," Cassia teased as Rollo snarled into his cup.

"We have much to learn from each other, Cassia. While I was doing a lot of talking, I observed the ways that you live on Cosa that can be applied to the rest of the kingdoms. The way the people live reminded me of home. It was peaceful and carefree, a life that suits the type of king I want to be," he replied earnestly as he lowered his cup.

"While I am glad, we are here working together. I'm sure that it wasn't Rollo's charm that led you to help us," I searched her face for answers.

"As I am the queen of Cosa now, I have to make sure I look out for my people and their well-being," I shifted in my chair waiting to hear what Rollo promised her. "All will be welcome in Cosa, Norse and Roman, but I would like to make sure that we are allowed to rule as an independent nation. Our time under Marcus has left us distrusting. I would like to work on rebuilding that trust, but we need to do that independently," she said with a resolute face.

"We have no issue with you ruling your land how you see fit, but in order to maintain a lasting peace, we have some suggestions that I would like everyone to hear. Some of the atrocities that I have seen in my time here cannot be allowed to happen anywhere else," I responded.

"I will listen as a favor to Rollo, he assures me that your intentions are pure."

"Sounds like a plan, but we still need Gio here so that we are all on the same page. For now, let's eat and toast to stability," Octavia raised her cup to the table.

"Now, Rollo, tell me more about these ideas you have after your visit to Cosa."

27 - HOUSEKEEPING – OCTAVIA

For the rest of the day, we took a walk around Alexandria to see how the repairs were coming along. Kole suggested we lend a hand. As crazy as Marcus was, he was right about one thing: in order for this transition to go smoothly, I needed to have the support of the people. So even the smallest gesture helped. It was our fault parts of the city were in pieces in the first place, the least we could do was help them clean up the damage we caused.

Kole was across the market helping a family carry supplies to rebuild the roof of their store. The same Romans that cheered as he was chained and beaten in the arena. He held no grudges against them, all he wanted to do was help. How did I find a man that was so powerful and confident, yet he seemed to never put himself above anyone else? How did he carry the weight of the world on his shoulders and never crumble?

Somewhere between admiring him for helping, I started to notice the way his biceps tensed when he lifted something, and it sent that flutter through my body. No man has ever made my body tingle just from watching him work. The day I spied on him at the lake I wondered what those hands would feel like skimming the curves of my body. A time before I knew how important he would be. I was drawn to him even before I understood why, and now my life wouldn't be complete without him. He never looked to minimize me and giving me the head of the table in the great hall was another testament to the type of man he was. Although a small gesture to others, I know he wanted me to know that I was his equal. He would not only see me as his queen, but I would also be seen as *THE* queen.

When Marcus locked him underneath that arena, he stole a part of me. It was a part that I would never let go of again, and the gods know I could never get enough. He looked my way briefly and smiled as the sunset danced across his brown skin. He was a work of art, a perfect sculpture and he was mine, all mine. I decided to join in because sitting and admiring Kole was not helping anyone but myself.

It took some time, but we managed to clean up most of the market and get some of the shops back up and running, but the sun was going down, which meant that Gio would be awake soon and Kare would be joining him. I know the reunion wouldn't be easy for Kole. I imagined he was about to meet a completely different version of his sister.

I have yet to come to terms with what she will be, but I would have done the same thing to save Tiberius without a doubt in my mind. I lost a sibling right in front of me and it is not a pain I would wish on someone else. He looked up as the sun began to disappear behind the horizon and I can tell the wheels in his head were already spinning off the handles.

"Vampire."

What did that even mean? It's what Delphi called him among other things. Abomination, eternal mistake, none of it was positive. If I know Kare, she will make the most of her new life, but at what cost? Would she still be as bright and bubbly as she was before or a miserable monster like her maker?

Ambrogio was not a great benchmark. He was smart, and calculated even, but watching him interact with Delphi, you could see there was a lot of unresolved hate and despair. Things I assume don't melt away when you have an eternity to sit with them. The animal I saw rip Marcus apart was now a part of Kare. A part I never wanted for her.

"Are you okay?" I searched his eyes for some answers.

"I'm okay," he tried to force a smile.

"I've made so many decisions thinking that I was doing it to protect all of you," he started, and I could see the emotion building behind his eyes. "What if Odin was right? What if everything that I've done was just for me?" He was staring at his hands.

"Why would you think that? Everything you have done has kept us alive." I tried to reassure him.

"But at what cost? I wanted to bring you home. I wanted to unite the lands. I wanted to save my sister," I could see the intensity as he spoke. "All of that I decided, so again I ask at what cost?"

"The cost of being a king, a cost of being my king," I grabbed his hands and pulled him closer. "You remember what I told you in Midselium?" a sneaky grin crept up his face.

"I said that you should take control more often," he grabbed me by the waist and pressed my body against his.

Normally I would feel awkward about being pressed so close to him in public, but he was intoxicating. There wasn't much I would say no to at this point.

"Whenever you're ready to be serious," I said. The grin went away, and he looked me deep in the eyes.

"You told me you don't care what the gods say, you will not be controlled or ruled over unless you will it so," he repeated word for word.

"Exactly, so if I didn't agree with your decisions you would know. I didn't hold my tongue when you decided to save Kare, I wouldn't hold it now. You just need to know that I won't be silent if I think you're doing something wrong, but I will always have your back," I pressed closer to him leaving just enough space for my hand to rest on him. It didn't take long to feel how excited he was, but now wasn't the time.

"You ready to go inside? We have a lot to discuss," I tried to divert his mind off the physical.

"I'm ready for something else," he laughed.

"Kole," I said his name seriously, trying to lock down the smile that was trying desperately to leak out.

"I'm ready," he ran his thumb softly on my cheek before kissing me. "Thank you for the pep talk."

Ω

I decided to walk around a little bit while Kole went back to the room to clean up for dinner. I knew if I went with him, he would get delightfully distracted, so I told him to meet me in the great hall once he was ready.

The progress being made in restoring the villa was amazing. The Bellator stench wasn't completely gone but this was a step in the right direction. I wonder if Kole expected me to hang banners with the axe and the spear sigil. Before we left Lundr, we didn't have a chance to discuss anything. I didn't even know what his opinion is on the matter. Did he even want to stay here or not? Lundr was his home. I wouldn't expect him to just abandon them after so recently being named king.

Now that I am queen, I've never been more conflicted on where I wanted to carry out my rule. I'm finally home but it feels like more of a graveyard. The ghost of my family sweeps through these halls reminding me of everything that I lost. Anger welled up in my chest because I didn't lose anything, it was taken from me by a fucking traitor. Literally ripped out of my hands and, even though he was dead, I didn't feel any better. Maybe it's because I didn't get to kill him myself. His son was the last stain on this earth, and he would pay for the sins of his father. Once I catch Titus, I couldn't put into words what I was going to do to him, especially since he managed to poison my sister's head.

I stopped by the garden to see if any progress was being made. This was one of my favorite places growing up and those savages didn't even keep up with it. Roses, poppies, tulips, and other wildflowers used to brighten up the villa no matter what time of day, and now all that was left was dirt and empty flowerpots.

This would be one of the first things I want to be restored. Floria loved the garden as much as my mother did, she told me when I was young this is where she came up with her name. My sister was supposed to be the flower that blossomed through our home and, up until I returned, I thought she would live up to her name. I bent over to press my hands in the dirt. It was dry and lifeless, exactly how I felt every time I looked around at what used to be a safe place for me.

"Sorry to interrupt you, my queen," the soldier startled me. I turned with my hand on my dagger. I know it was an aggressive response, but trust was not high on my list these days.

"I just came to tell you that we haven't located Titus or princess Floria."

"Why are you still here? I need them found."

"We have searched the entire city, my queen, and no one has seen them. We assume that someone who was loyal to Marcus is hiding them." I was trying to keep my temper in check but just the mention of their names infuriated me.

"Listen to me, I don't care if they are hiding on Mount Olympus, you need to find them or find someone that can give me information on how to find them," I implored. I could feel the fire reaching underneath my skin.

"I'll get to it, my queen."

"Thank you," I tried to dismiss him but not in a rude way. I was angry, but it wasn't his fault. I should have dealt with them when I had the chance.

"You look like you want to punch something," Kole commented as he slipped into the garden without me noticing.

"Of course not, unless you are volunteering yourself to get punched," I forced a smile.

"Anything for you, my love. Take it easy on me though," he joked.

"Why would I do that?"

“You should have sympathy for me, I was locked in a cell for days,” the smirk on his face told me all I needed to know.

“Don’t you dare compare your days in the cell to my days in that box.”

“I’m just saying I won all my fights once they let me out of the cell,” he shrugged and laughed.

“You’re not making a good argument for me to resist punching you, my love.”

“Let’s save it for later,” he winked.

“Are you done? Everyone is waiting for us.”

“I’m done for now but wait until you hear about what I have planned. You’re going to have plenty for me later,” he taunted and wrapped his arm around my waist, and we walked together to the great hall.

28 - Rebirth – Kole

My heart was pounding in my chest nonstop all day waiting for this moment. Every single hour waiting for the sun to go down so that I could see my little sister again. Would she be the same or did I ruin her life? She would have plenty of time to resent me considering she is immortal.

"Vampire," was the word that Delphi used.

In no world would Kare be considered a parasite. Gio made a promise to me, and a big part of me believed him. Was it the wrong place to put my trust? Maybe, but what other choice did I have? Letting her die was never an option.

Octavia and I were the first to arrive in the great hall. It amazed me how quickly it was restored. Marcus had terrible taste, but it seemed that the hall was returning to its former glory. I didn't have anything to compare it to, but this clearly was better than the misery the tyrant king put this city through.

The table was already set with grapes, bread, and wine covering every inch of the fine wood. Octavia requested that it be a round table, she didn't want to sit at the head and seem more important than everyone else while we discuss the terms of the new treaty. Decorating had to be one of the Romans' favorite past times because everything was so over the top. Gold leaves trimmed all the chairs and the edges of the table, the servants must have robbed the throne for all this money. I can see where Gio gets his ostentatious behavior from, it was ingrained in him from his days as a Roman. Seven chairs, one for each of us that were so integral in winning the city back. I had a plan to cement this precarious peace we have constructed in the short time we've come together.

It wasn't long before the others started to find their way in. Rollo was first and he was deep in conversation with his new muse. I didn't know much about her, only that her and Gio were close. Whatever they were talking about must have been entertaining. Nothing else in the room mattered to them, it was the same way I looked at Octavia when I met her. I know he can take care of himself, but I hope he knew what he was getting into. And if he was successful, the first thing I would do is run to him for advice on how to reconnect with Kare.

Cassia made her way in after them wearing armor. I wonder if she ever wore anything else. My palms were sweaty, and my nerves were firing off inside my body. How long was Gio going to make me wait? I know he liked to make an entrance, but I wouldn't describe myself as patient right now.

"Relax, my love, they will be here soon," Octavia whispered and placed her hand over mine. The anticipation did nothing but stir up my anxiety, a feeling that I was becoming all too familiar with. I decided to begin. Hopefully it would distract me long enough to calm the storm of anticipation I was going through.

“Let’s begin. Marcella, for the time being until Gio returns, will you be able to speak for him?” She nodded. “I want to reiterate to all of you how thankful we are for your efforts against Marcus. All of us have been affected by the actions of the ones that we trusted. I am here to reassure you that Octavia and I have a goal to break that cycle. When the last great war was fought a peace was put into place and we are here to not only uphold that peace but to make sure all are included, and all have a voice.” I reached for her hand for comfort. “Ever since the gods led us to each other, we have wondered what the end game was, and along the way we have crafted a dream that can benefit us all and garner in new peace. Not just for the two of us, but Norse, Romans, and vampires.” I looked over to Marcella to make sure that the words were not offensive, but I really didn’t know what to call them. A shadow appeared in the doorway halting my speech.

“Sorry we are late, and I swear this time it wasn’t my fault,” Gio was standing at the entrance with the usual smirk on his face.

“Strolling in late like you’re the only one that’s important, not much has changed,” Rollo laughed.

“Seeing as I saved the day and the beautiful Kare, I think that I am the most important,” he drawled as I recognized standing right beside him my little sister dressed in Roman robes that suited her, just like everything tends to.

I jumped out of my chair ignoring everyone else in the room. She was the only thing that was important to me.

“Okay. I see that everyone is ignoring me now,” Gio said sarcastically.

“Give it a rest, man, for two seconds,” Cassia snapped and rolled her eyes. I didn’t know her well, but I think I already liked her.

I walked over to Kare slowly. I didn’t mean to treat her so foreign, but I didn’t know if anything would set her off. She looked even more beautiful than before, like somehow the transformation enhanced her traits.

“Are you okay, sister?” I asked distinctly.

“Don’t I look okay, brother?” She answered.

“Of course, you do,” I started to break down immediately. “I'm sorry for everything, I just.... I just couldn’t let you go. I'm sorry,” I cried as she reached up slowly and brushed the tear from my eye.

“Don’t apologize Kole, I know why you did it and I'm not upset with you anymore, anyway,” she moved closer to me with some hesitation, and she embraced me.

Her hands were strong, but I hugged her back. She was cold to the touch, and she didn’t smell like home. She didn’t feel familiar as she once did. What exactly had she become?

“I promise you, I am okay. More than okay even. The colors are brighter, my hearing is amazing, and I feel so strong. Gio has been an amazing help. I know the sacrifice you’ve made, brother, and I don’t take it lightly. You are my family and that will never change, but I have a new life I have to pursue now.” She spoke plainly but I could feel that the words weren’t easily said.

She walked past me over to Octavia and Rollo and reached to embrace them as well. Octavia tensed and flinched at her approach, but the uncertainty didn't last long. Tears fell from both their eyes. Though we have opposite opinions on what was done, for now, we are all happy that she is here.

"Well, now that we all made up, can we get back to the task at hand? I've grown fond of all of you, but I much prefer the weather in Cosa," Cassia tilted up her cup to all of us. I shook off the reunion for now and went back to my seat.

"When we started this, promises were made to all of you. Octavia and I intend to keep them all, but in the interest of preventing segregation again, there are some things we would like to suggest, if that is okay with everyone." I addressed the room.

"What are some of these suggestions?" Gio was looking around the room. "Oh, and before we begin, would it be too much trouble to ask for something to drink," he tried to hide his smirk.

Octavia waved over a servant and whispered something in her ear, she backed away in shock at first, but then she nodded and left the room.

"First thing goes for everyone, and Kole and I agree it is not negotiable," Octavia looked to me for confirmation, and I nodded in agreement. "Slave trade of any kind is forbidden; all servants are to be compensated for their service." The table nodded in agreement.

"Seeing as you love attention, Gio let's start with you," I said as the attention at the table shifted to him. "We are ready to honor all of your requests that were promised. You and the vampires can live out in the open and rule as you see fit," I couldn't help but smile. I felt like I was breaking a generational hatred between him and the people who shunned him.

"Beautiful, my young king. I can see the celebration now." He was flashing his fangs and raising his cup.

"Hold on a second, Gio. Kole and I have some additional requests," Octavia interrupted.

"And just like that the fun is over," Gio slumped in his seat.

"We have no desire to do what the ones before us have done. I don't want to control your population. Those that are willing may join and live among you, but we would appreciate it if you stopped killing random travelers. No need to keep your secret since you will be living out of the shadows," Octavia continued. "You can occupy the land around the Delphi caves if you want or take a piece of the land outside of Alexandria for your own. Is there anything that you do not approve of?"

"You two have kept your word to me and, in the interest of keeping my promise to Kole and making sure Kare safe, I agree to all of the terms." A servant returned and placed cups in front of him, Marcella, and Kare.

I glanced over to my sister. She picked up the cup and raised it to her mouth. Her body went rigid at the scent but then, as the liquid made its way down her throat, she relaxed almost into a sense of pleasure.

"Cassia, Rollo informed us of your demands. Cosa will be allowed to rule on its own without interference. The only request we ask is that Norse and Romans alike are allowed to live in amongst you in peace," I said.

"I thank you for keeping your word. Rollo was right, both of you are very honorable and I am so happy to have met you.

Everyone is welcome on Cosa, no matter the culture. Especially since it was he who lead me to the truth about the fate of my father," she raised her cup in agreement.

"The truth?" I asked. Rollo's shoulders went tense, and he slowly dropped his cup back down to the table. He clearly had something that he forgot to mention.

"You have something to tell us, Rollo." All eyes drifted towards him. He smiled nervously, so Cassia spoke instead.

"Marcus had an advisor and spies all over Cosa when Rollo arrived. Once he told me the story of you two making a move, I questioned the man. With some persuasion," she paused and glanced over to Rollo, "he revealed to me what took place that night at the villa." She told the story from the beginning all the way to the painful end, leaving us in complete disbelief when she revealed who was actually under the mask that faithful night.

"You killed the Bellator boy, so clearly that is why it slipped my mind," Rollo explained.

Everyone assumed that I killed the masked killer, but Marcus paraded his own son and sealed his fate once he entered that arena with me. I slammed my fist against the table, even in victory he found a way to outsmart me.

"Yes, but I killed the wrong Bellator boy. If it is true that his son Titus wore the mask, then that means Tiberius' killer is still out there," my eyes shot back to Octavia who surprisingly was taking this information better than I expected. "Are you okay, my love?" I asked.

"More than okay. The job was not yet finished, anyway. Now this just adds more motivation, and it fills in a lot of the gaps from that night," she spoke so calmly it was frightening, a slight shimmer of flames danced through her eyes. "I won't let that ruin what we have accomplished. We will catch them, but for now let us celebrate. We are all on the same page and agree to the terms," Octavia raised her cup.

"Before we do that in the spirit of celebration, I have a couple more suggestions, if that is okay with you, my queen," I interrupted. Though the news of Titus was unexpected, my plans didn't change.

"Ugh, hurry up. I want to celebrate this victory at some point," Rollo groaned.

"Trust me, it's worth it. I know I should have talked to you in private before, especially considering this new information," I made sure to give Rollo a death stare. "But what am I if not spontaneous," Octavia looked at me sideways. I knelt to the side of her chair and grabbed her hand.

"Wait, didn't you do this already?" Rollo said.

"Shut up, Rollo!" Kare yelled.

The familiar banter warmed my heart and forced a smile out of me. I looked directly into Octavia's eyes.

"I know we have both experienced losses in our homes, things that defile everything that we have ever known. I don't want to live in the torment of horrible moments and memories that we are going to regret. Instead of choosing to abandon my home or yours, let's build our own."

"What do you mean build our own?" she asked.

"We made our own sigil and I told you it only exists if we make it so, and I think building a new home will solidify that.

The axe and the spear, the raven living in the fire between our two worlds, a country made up in the sense of unity, and a table full of representatives to run it." I don't know what I was expecting her to say but, if I learned anything from my proposal, she is never quick to answering life defining questions.

"A table full of representatives?" Gio questioned.

"You are all kings and queens in your own right. We should all be a part of the conversation when it comes to making change, a representative from every kingdom will allow all of us to remain on the same page." I smiled at the others and turned back toward the woman I love.

"I think it is a fantastic idea," Kare spoke out. "You both deserve it, and Tav is going to look like a badass in her new kingdom," Octavia looked at me, her eyes glistening trying to hold back the tears.

"I think you are the best thing that has ever happened to me, and I can't wait to build a new home with you." She jumped into my arms and kissed me. The rest of the room erupted in applause, and I took that as a yes from everyone.

"One more thing," I yelled.

"Odin's beard Kole, what else do you want?" Rollo threw his hands up in frustration.

"We are going to sail to our new home, and you are all invited to the ceremony." I was waiting for someone to pick up on the hints.

"What ceremony?" she asked.

“I’m finally going to make an honest woman out of you, my love,” I smiled as the rest of the room continued cheering.

29 - Bachelor Party – Rollo

I managed to find my way down from the villa back to the market. Everything looked the same in Alexandria, the roads lead to other roads. All the buildings looked the same, except for the giant pile of debris that used to be the arena. At least that's what Kole called it. The battle with Marcus was sort of a blur, honestly, but this was a time for celebration.

I remember Kole proposing when we left Lundr, but we set sail before they could even celebrate. Now, it just felt surreal that it was actually going to happen. Like it was going to be official and, even though the family has fractured a bit, adding Octavia to the group was a good way to get things back on track. The skinny girl covered in dirt that we pulled out of the carriage in the woods was going to marry my best friend. The way they met would be an amazing story for all our kids, if we lived long enough to make any.

It would take a couple of weeks to get the boats ready to sail and Kole wouldn't tell us where we were going, which was more annoying than he knew. I couldn't wait to go home. I'd had enough of traveling to last me a lifetime. I just wanted to sit on my throne and, for one second, not count how many things have gone wrong since we left Midselium.

There was one great thing about Kole delaying our trip. I got to spend more time with Marcella. I said her name slowly in my head making sure I didn't miss a syllable. Only being able to talk when the sun goes down is frustrating, but that was something I was working on.

"You seem to be unbelievably focused," Kole managed to sneak up on me.

"I'm admiring our handy work," I pointed toward what was left of the arena.

"Marcus was a madman, but I can't ignore how beautiful it was," he looked at it with some kind of admiration.

"A weapon can be ugly and beautiful depending on who is wielding it," I remark, something my father used to tell me in between drinks.

The reality is he would have never seen me become king anyway even with that fact it didn't lessen the pain any. It wasn't a part of our culture, but one could dream. "You ever going to tell me where we are going, or do you expect me to sail blind?" I asked.

"Is it really bothering you that much? It was meant to be a surprise, but I guess it wouldn't really matter to you considering you have already been there." I couldn't hide the curiosity on my face. He started to pace back and forth, which apparently has become a norm for him. Must be the way he dealt with the stress.

He was always adding things to his plate. I admired him for that. He was willing to take on everyone's problems while somehow maintaining his own. He even managed to find the person he was meant to be with in the process. But technically the gods gave him a head start.

"Okay, I'll bite. What do you mean I have been there already?"

"Take a walk with me," he suggested and started to lead me toward the broken arena. I decided I would indulge him.

"I would think you wouldn't want to be anywhere near this place again, it doesn't exactly inspire great memories." We walked through the shattered tunnels out into the sands at the center of the arena

"There is always a method to my madness, brother. We have one more thing to take care of, and then I will tell you everything you want to know. Besides, this should be fun," he smiled.

"What are you talking about?" My attention was stolen by the noise. I could hear them before I could see them. Footsteps and a lot of them coming from every direction.

"What exactly did you just lead me into?" I asked.

"Well, it was the only way I could get these cowards to show their faces. They think this is their best chance to kill me for what I did," he explained, speaking so calmy. He was just waiting very nonchalantly.

"Who are we referring to again?" I reached for my hammer.

"The last of Marcus' disciples, of course," he smiled.

"Why are you so happy, and how did you know they were coming?" I asked. He pointed to his now pitch-black eyes.

"Odin sight, of course. Do you want to keep talking, or are you ready to finish them off so I can go and get married?"

"Surely."

I willed the power from inside. The lightning coursed through my core before it danced down my arms and covered my hands, spreading to my hammer. Maybe I should give it a name, but that didn't seem important at the moment as the remainder of Marcus' soldiers filed into the arena. I couldn't tell how many were left and it didn't really matter. I needed a nice warm-up anyways, then I would finally be able to leave this place.

I never thought I would see the day when I have had enough of the battle rush. I wanted to decompress in the worst way. But in the spirit of supporting my brother and not dying, what's another battle? If I was going to do this then I might as well try something new. This was the perfect time to work on a new move, and just like that a fantastic idea popped into my head.

"Hey Kole, you down to try something? I got a fantastic idea."

"What do you have in mind?"

"Just open one of those fancy portals above my head and point it toward them." He nodded.

"This is going to be so awesome," I said to myself.

"What is your plan?" he asked again.

Just like we practiced in the woods, I quelled all the power from my hands down to my feet and I kicked off the ground right into the portal.

My body swirled into the empty void. Seconds later daylight appeared, and I was flying full speed straight towards the guards, spinning with my hammer like a violent storm. I took out more soldiers with one shot than I expected. There was no way to hide my excitement. I hit the sand, landing on my feet this time and not on my face. I was really getting good at this.

The rest of the soldiers were heading towards Kole. He was holding his own, as usual. I could see the smirk on his face. He was getting very crafty with the portals, almost a borderline expert. The soldiers couldn't even get close to him at this point. We played these scenarios in our heads for years as kids, sharing the battlefield back-to-back, protecting each other. I could think of no better feeling then going into battle with my best friend. Well, actually that's a lie. There was one thing that felt way better.

"How could be smiling right now?" Kole yelled.

"Just reminiscing about Persephone's, that's all." Oh how I missed that place.

"Really? Right now? At this very second?" He couldn't help but laugh.

"What? I like to live in the moment."

"How about we stop messing around and finish this?" Kole nodded and immediately took out two men with a single swing of the axe.

The rest of the soldiers didn't put up much of a fight, but Kole made sure to spare one of them. He held the last survivor by the throat and pressed him against the only wall in the arena that was still standing. I took a seat in the sand and let him work.

I would have just killed him, which is probably why I wasn't in charge of this endeavor.

"Now that we have gotten all of the extra mess out of the way, I have a few questions for you, my friend. Answer truthfully and I'll ask my wife if you should live. She has a much bigger heart than I do, but if you lie, my friend over there is going to smash your head in with that fancy hammer." I made sure to give the man a nice wave, no sense in being impolite.

"Okay, let's begin. How many more are loyal to Marcus?" The soldier didn't speak, so Kole squeezed tighter.

"Kole, I think you have to let him go in order for him to speak," I gestured towards his hands.

"Oh wow, silly me," he released him, and the soldier almost coughed up a lung. We waited for him to catch his breath to answer the question.

"Why should I tell you anything, Norse dog," the soldier forced out his response while rubbing his neck.

"Rollo, did we literally not just go over this? Maybe he needs a closer look at the hammer," Kole laughed so I made my way over to him, twirling my hammer in my hands.

The severity of the threat must have become apparent to him, so he started to stutter the answer that we needed.

"We were the only ones left in the city. The rest of his supporters fled during the battle."

"Now we are getting somewhere. Where did they run to? Do you have another place where you plan to meet?"

"No, this was the last push to avenge our king," he lowered his head in defeat.

"The prince Titus and his wife have also disappeared. What do you know about them?" Kole asked.

"They left the city the day after the battle. Rumor is they are hiding somewhere north of here, but I do not know where." He shifted onto his knees and continued to spill everything that he knew.

"Did you know that Marcus sent the wrong son to die at my hands in the arena?" Kole was pacing again, it was getting very unsettling.

"Marcus convinced his son Lucius that the gods had bigger plans for him, win or lose. It was all to keep you off the trail of the real leader of the ambush."

"That is such a dumb plan because now I have to kill them both. Why did Marcus trust any of you with his plans?" Kole asked.

"He didn't. After he was defeated, soldiers began to talk. Eventually someone uncovered the truth about Lucius. The gods must have a higher plan, there is no way they would allow you animals to succeed if it wasn't a part of the plan," he spit at our shoes.

I couldn't believe that this man was telling us everything we wanted to know while his comrades lay dead all around him. I don't have a prejudice toward the Romans, but their warriors were so weak. Spoiled hypocrites. Honestly, I would have never given up any information that would put someone I cared for in danger. The gods would bless me for dying with honor, but that is where we differ.

These Romans that were loyal to Marcus were always out to save themselves, which made a girl like Octavia so interesting. She set herself apart from these men as did Cassia. They were built with warrior spirits something that we all shared. It is what made Octavia so perfect for Kole. Selfless meets selfless or stubborn meets stubborn. Whatever it is, it works.

"Rollo, you awake?" Kole bounced me out of my own head.

"Yea, I'm good."

"Then what should we do with our friend here? Keep in mind he just tried to kill me." It would have been easy to kill him, but from this day forth I wanted to try to turn a new leaf. Everything did not have to be solved with death. We needed to be better than the ones that came before us and learn to show some mercy.

So, I walked over to the soldier and thought about all the pain we just endured in the battle with Marcus. I thought about how they stuck with him even after his defeat and tried to avenge that madman again. Then, my hammer slammed off the side of his head before he fell to the sand. I'll turn over a new leaf some other time.

Ω

We walked out of the broken arena and already I needed to take a bath again. The sand was such a pest. Once it gets on you, it's impossible to get rid of, no matter how hard I try. I took a seat on a bench and took off my shoes to pour out the sand.

"Now that you almost got me killed again, you going to tell me where we are going?" I asked Kole.

"Like I told the others, I want to be close to both countries, a true beacon of peace," he couldn't stop smiling. While it was annoying, it was awesome to see him so happy. "Octavia and I are going to build our new home near the entrance of Midselium, and I want to hold the wedding ceremony there before we build. And you are going to be standing right next to me when I do."

Out of all the places I thought I would hear, that was not my guess, but it makes sense. I was with them on that journey as they fought the urge to stare at each other and as we hiked up the treacherous path. I witnessed them being drawn to each other's presence and the need to protect each other from the very beginning.

Kole even told me about her spying on him at the river. Neither of them were worried about coming on too strong. At the holmgang when he almost died fighting his father, I had a feeling she might leave in order to save herself. Kyut made himself very clear that she would not be treated very well without Kole's protection I wouldn't have blamed her for leaving. But when she heard him cry out in pain, she was willing to stay and be with him to the very end. I could only hope to have a love as pure as theirs.

Kole was waiting for my response. Instead of talking or making a joke, I walked up to him and hugged him, because standing next to him as he cemented his place in history would be my honor.

"Congratulations, my brother." I was holding back my tears, but it was a losing battle.

“Thank you,” he replied, hugging me tightly. He pulled away from me and tried to smile to hide the tears.

“Now, tell me more about this idea you learned from Cosa, the one you mentioned to Octavia a couple of days ago.”

30 – Do I Or Don't I – Kole

"A dome?" I said surprisingly.

"Yea, a dome," Rollo nodded. Why didn't I think of that? That would be a great way to make sure that Kare could have a safe place to enjoy, and we wouldn't be forced to only meet at night if she didn't want to. It would also help with the royal relationship between us and Gio. If we could find a loophole, we would be able to spend so much more time together. The decision is too fresh to weigh the right and wrong of it, but she was alive, and I needed to have some faith. Seeing her last night was encouraging, but she was noticeably different.

I still couldn't get the image of her rolling around clutching her body to fight off the transformation. The pain looked excruciating, something I would never wish on someone I cared about. How would everyone back home react to her new transformation? I would have to introduce our new ally to the people eventually. I could only hope he wasn't immediately judged.

Octavia has never been a fan of Gio and his kind but she and Kare had grown so close; I didn't want this to fracture their relationship. Rollo must have felt me having a war in my mind, the silence must have spoken volumes.

"Everything is going to be fine, Kole. We can make this work. Cassia is going to show us how to build the dome and Kare will be able to live somewhat of a normal life."

"I know, don't mind me. I just want to make sure it was all worth it." I put this decision on my pedestal right next to being forced to kill my father to be king. I was running out of space on the shelf.

I needed a chance to find out if Octavia is okay with this. Before we got to Alexandria, we were talking about finding Gio's weakness, but now that same weakness could kill my sister and I couldn't allow that to happen. Gio unintentionally revealed details of what could kill him, but it was something that I need to keep to myself. I wasn't even sure that I was going to share it with Octavia. It won't take others long to find out what can kill vampires. The more people that know, the more danger Kare would be in. We all had something to lose if we have a falling out. Not to mention Rollo's fascination with Marcella. He thinks we haven't noticed but he could not stop staring at her across the table as we discussed terms.

"I know you're not going say anything, but what is the deal with you and Marcella?" I asked. He looked at me surprised as if I pulled that idea out of thin air. "If you were trying to hide your interest, you're doing an awful job. Maybe stare less next time," I laughed.

"Believe it or not, I was trying to play it cool, but something about her makes me nervous," he was smiling. "I'm not sure what it is, when I'm around her it's like she can see right through me, so I try my hardest to not mess it up by saying something stupid... and yes I was staring because she's literally perfect." He spoke with disbelief.

"Then tell her how you feel. She's a little old for you, but I think you should see where it goes. We all deserve to be happy." I said with amusement in my voice.

"I can't just tell her how I feel. She's almost a hundred years old! What could I say to her that she hasn't heard already?" He threw his arms in the air.

"That's not the point. Maybe she is not looking for something she hasn't heard already. Just be yourself. You're a warrior, a king, and an amazing man." I put my hands on his shoulders to make sure he knew I was being sincere.

"Maybe I'll take your advice, considering you're about to walk down the aisle."

"Descendent of the All-father of wisdom and you are still just considering," I shook my head. "Let's finish getting our things together, the company is working on the boats and now you know where we are headed. Spend some time with her before we leave. I'm not saying I can see the future, but I think this will be great for you."

31 – Speechless – Octavia

Kole spent most of his time trying to plan everything perfectly. It had been weeks since we fortified our alliance, and he couldn't wait to tell everyone our plan was to get married near Midselium.

Building a new home was terrifying but the painful memories that Alexandria brings were exhausting, and the longer it took for the soldiers to find Titus and Floria just added weight. My temper flared every single time I heard their names, especially since my tormentor in the mask was still walking free and breathing.

I thought that the gods would give me peace and allow me to feel the satisfaction of that revenge, but while they throw salt in my wounds, they can't destroy what I have in my heart. The happiness outweighed all of it, and I was overflowing with it. I couldn't wait for Kole to officially become my husband at the same place I fell in love with him.

He saved me from my kidnappers and was kind to me even though I tried to kill him. We shared a vision together that dramatically changed the course of both of our lives. When everything was taken from me and I felt powerless, he never left my side. He found out I was a princess and treated me all the same, never looking at me like a prize that needed to be sheltered. I wasn't a treasure meant to be stored away, I was a flame meant to burn bright. He would always protect me, but he respected me enough to know that I can take care of myself. I could not wait to be tied to him forever.

While there was so much joy, we still had a problem that we could not agree on, and I didn't want this one issue to ruin everything that we have built together. He tried to bring up how I feel about Kare being a vampire but I was dodging the conversation as much as I could. I was not ready to accept that Kare was now tied to that monster. Gio had proved to be a man of his word, and without him who knows if we would be standing here right now, but he was still a monster and I did not want that for her.

She was such a beautiful soul and one of the brightest parts of my experience in Lundr. Yet now she would be stuck with him, another spectator to his cruelty. It wasn't fair, but even I could admit it was better than the alternative. Vampire or not is still better than dead. With that being said I felt for Gio, don't get me wrong. What happened to him was awful, and if someone ripped Kole from my arms and I was never allowed to see him again, maybe I would be a monster as well. That never granted him permission to be so ruthless and heartless when it pertained to others' lives.

For the good of the people, I want to try to get my feelings under control. Luckily for him, I'm in a great mood. Love is in the air and I came up with an idea to hopefully thaw the coldness from his chest.

“You almost ready?” Kole burst into the room with his beautiful smile.

“I sent a boat ahead to start setting everything up. I also sent a message to everyone back in Najora to meet us.” He walked over and wrapped his arms around me. “In a couple of days, we start our lives together. You starting to get cold feet yet?” I shifted the flames to my hands.

“Does that answer your question?” I smiled.

“Did I ever tell you how hot you are?” He couldn’t hold the sly smirk back.

“That was the worst joke I’ve ever heard,” I scoffed playfully.

“Not my best but the facts remain the same.” He pressed his lips against mine, tasting sweet like fruit.

I managed to pack everything that I wanted to take but most of my room was left untouched. I was going to start a new life and I didn’t need to bring any of the old. I instructed the soldiers to take all of my things left over and distribute it to those who lost everything due to our battle with Marcus.

“Are you sure you don’t want to take any of your Roman clothes? I prefer you to not wear anything, but I assume it could get awkward for everyone else,” he shrugged jokingly.

“They all have the spear sigil on them, and I don’t want to wear anything that doesn’t represent us both,” I explained and watched his face light up as he moved closer.

“Have you thought about what you are going to wear for the ceremony?” he asked.

"I have, the dressmaker has been preparing it for me the last couple of weeks. I can't wait for you to see it, but that won't be until we are standing on the altar." He walked over to the bed and sat down, the energy shifting briefly from the playful mood we were in.

"Have you put any thought into what type of ceremony you would like to have?" The question shouldn't have come as a surprise, but it did.

The fate of a kingdom was on my mind. Titus and the mask, my missing sister, and where we would live. I never considered what type of marriage ceremony I wanted to have. It felt disrespectful to my family to completely shed the Roman tradition, but to be honest I was not a traditional Roman anymore.

"I haven't had much time to think about it, did you have something specific in mind?" I deflected the question back to him to buy me some time to gather my thoughts.

"No I haven't, but what I do know is that the Norse ceremony could be a little much for someone that was not raised as we were. I have no idea what a Roman wedding entails." I would never tell him to scrap every detail of his culture from the wedding, and I was relieved that he didn't assume that I would. Another notch added to the long list of things that make him perfect.

"How about we meet in the middle?" I proposed.

"I'm listening, beautiful." I prayed to Olympus he would never stop complimenting me.

"We have decided to build our home and embrace both cultures. How about we do the same for the ceremony? It seems like the perfect way to start," I suggested.

“That is a great idea, I couldn’t have said it better myself… so it’s safe to say we can skip the drinking of ritual blood part of the ceremony,” he laughed. I couldn’t help but look at him horrified.

“Please tell me that you are kidding?” He just kept laughing, amused by my expression I assume. “Um, yes we can definitely skip that part.”

“I’m going to finish getting the last-minute things we need. We are going to leave first thing in the morning,” he turned to me on his way out. “I noticed you haven’t been to see Kare since she turned outside of all of us talking in the great hall. I know it’s hard because of the way you feel about Gio but don’t push her away. She needs to know she still has you,” he implored. I dropped my gaze to the floor. It was so hard to face him when it came to this subject. Especially since I was so conflicted on how I felt.

“I’m sorry, Kole. I don’t mean to push her away. Things are just very complicated, but I will make sure I say goodbye before they leave tonight.”

“Thank you,” his gaze lingered for a moment before he left the room.

The way I felt wasn’t personal, but Kole was right. If I wanted Kare to avoid becoming a bitter angry monster like Gio I had to make sure she knew I was still here for her. I was being selfish and only thinking about myself. She is the one that died. Her life would never be the same again. She was going to live forever while the rest of us would eventually grow old. The thought of watching people you love die over and over was a wound that I imagined would never heal.

As the centuries pass, it is understandable why you become detached, but as long as I am here, I won't let that happen. I let one sister down, I was not going to abandon my new one. I stormed out of the room because now I was on a mission. The sun was going down, so I should be able to find them somewhere.

The villa was alive this time around, a completely different feeling than when I arrived here. Further proof that Marcus was a blight on the existence of this city. He was probably jealous of my father this entire time. Alexandria was one of the biggest cities and, when I was growing up, it flourished under his care. Trading ports always had boats docked, merchants sold their entire stock, and the people had plenty of money to take care of themselves. Marcus had these people living in filth while he gorged himself up in the villa. Once we removed him, it's like the heartbeat returned and the energy shifted, just walking down the hall I could feel it emanate.

Rollo and Marcella were sitting on a bench enjoying a drink. I didn't want to ask what was in her cup. The nature of it would always make my skin crawl, but I was going to try for Kare. She didn't ask for this. Despite my feeling of his company, it was about time Rollo decided to spend some time with her. All the staring was starting to make us all uncomfortable. I haven't known him very long, but I've never seen him behave this way. He always carried himself with so much confidence, but around her something was different, almost as if he is unsure of himself.

The mighty warrior had finally met his match. I chuckled inside as I made my way over to them.

“Have you guys seen Kare?” I hated to interrupt them, but I didn’t see them in the room.

“No, her and Gio left a few minutes before you got here. Everything okay?” Rollo asked.

“Everything is fine. I just wanted to make sure I got a chance to talk to her before we leave.”

“It’s about time,” Marcella said under her breath.

“Is there something that you need to say to me?” I could feel the fire streaking underneath the surface. She put her cup down, her grey dark eyes inches away from mine. I noticed the scar that ran along the side of her face.

“I said it’s about time. We have been here for weeks, and you haven’t said a word to her,” she responded with very little emotion.

“What business is that of yours?”

“Octavia, calm down,” Rollo moved to put his hands between us.

“Shut up, Rollo!” I could hear the silent beating of the war drums. “What business is it of yours? Last time I checked, we just met you.”

“It is my business because now Kare is also my family. I’ve heard what you think about us in the cave, but I never thought you would shun your own.” I reached for my dagger, but this time Rollo stepped in between us.

“Kill her!”

"She's a parasite!"

"Abomination," the voices were deafening in my head. I was losing it, and the more she spoke, the better it was going to feel when I killed her.

"Seems like I struck a nerve, there must be some truth to my words," she flashed a devilish smirk.

"You better shut your mouth, you have no idea how much I love that girl. Especially after everything that I've lost," I couldn't hear how loud my voice was over the drums.

"And that is your problem, you think you're the only one that has lost something. We may be immortal, but did you ever think about what our lives were like before we turned? Did you ever think that maybe we have lost just as much as you?" I wasn't sure but I thought I saw tears in her eyes; if there were, she wiped them away quickly. "I lost my sister and I would do anything, including ending my own life, to see her again. If you love her the way you say then I suggest you start showing it, because once she is detached from everything that she loves only the gods know what she can become." There was a fury in her eyes I did not expect to see.

The voices began to fade, and my body relaxed, Marcella's words replaying in my head. The words were the slap I needed to bring me back to reality. My hate for Gio clouded all of it and I was taking it out on Kare. It led me to think about how this started, how I only feel this unquenched anger when the voices are blaring in my head. Was it me or was it Mars? It had to be him, whatever he feels towards Gio is deep, borderline vengeful. It's embedded in who he is, and he was passing it to me. The deeper I dive into my nature the feeling becomes more intense.

"You bastard," I said in my head.

I calmed the storm building inside me and prepared for the guilt wave that was going to crash into me after what I had just done.

"I'm sorry, Marcella. Reacting like that was not my intention," I admitted sheepishly.

"I'm not the one that needs it, my queen. I'm over a hundred years old, not much offends me," she sat back down and grabbed her cup. "Just be the sister that connects her to her old life, and Gio and I will be her guide through the next."

Wise words from a vampire and, as much as I wanted to punch her, she was completely right.

"Rollo, make sure you keep her around," I smiled to them both. "My apologies again," I backed away and made my way outside the villa.

Ω

I have never been so embarrassed in my life. Regardless of how beautiful she is, technically she was my elder. I shouldn't have snapped at her like that. I was going to have a conversation with Mars about this because I can't walk around wanting to kill anyone that he thinks deserves it. I didn't know that this was a part of the deal when he bestowed this so-called blessing on me.

At every single turn, these gifts can betray you. First, I almost killed Kyut when I lost my temper. Now, I feel like a volcano ready to blow every time I see a vampire. I had to fix this because I can't keep living this way. I was in the middle of practicing my apology speech when I saw them.

Kare and Gio huddled in a corner in the darkness separated from everyone. The drums came flooding back to the front of my mind, like a massive Roman legion marching toward the enemy. He must have heard me as I got closer because his face whipped around, and his fangs were stretched out of his mouth and covered in blood. Sitting in between him and Kare laid a servant, her body limp in his hands barely breathing. No more time for patience, no apologies, no remorse. I ripped my dagger from the holster and charged directly for the monster himself.

I rushed Gio and barreled directly into him. I tried to put all my strength into it, but he was back on his feet in an instant evading my dagger. The ground scorched under my hands which were completely engulfed in flames.

"Octavia, what are you doing?" I could hear Kare, but I couldn't see past the blind rage.

"I told you if you hurt anyone, I was going to kill you. The ink on our treaty isn't even dry yet and you're showing her what a monster you are. I will not let you turn her into one," I picked my dagger up of the ground and rushed him again, trying to hurt him in any way I could but he was too fast. He managed to evade me before I even got close.

Kare was hysterically screaming, begging me to stop, but he has taken it too far this time. He took a half a second and glanced at her, and that left me an opening. He wasn't ready for it, and my fist connected with his jaw knocking him to the ground. He tried to get back up, but I was already on top of him punching him with every ounce of strength I could muster up.

Battle drums slammed in my head with every punch. It was intoxicating, and it was exactly what Mars wanted me to do.

Gio tried to cover his face, but I did not stop punching. It felt like I was hitting a stone wall but still I would not stop. My knuckles began to bleed but the flames healed them instantly. The reoccurring pain fueled my anger. He was going to be dealt with right here and right now. I must have been losing my mind because I could have sworn that he was smiling.

"Octavia, stop!" I heard him but the drums were louder.

"Octavia, stop!" My arms had no feeling left and I kept punching. I felt a hand on my collar, and someone pulled me off and wrapped his arms around me, pinning mine to my sides. "Calm down, what are you doing?" I couldn't hear anything outside of the rhythm of the drums and the fire that clouded my vision and filled my senses.

Four more figures appeared in front of us, in a low stance snarling with their fangs protruding from their faces.

"Octavia, you need to stop!" My eyes beamed to the one that was restraining me, and his eyes pierced right through me.

"I'm here, it's me, Kole. You need to calm down, take a deep breath." I wanted to comply. I wanted to calm down for him, but the image of Gio hurting that innocent girl was enough for Mars to keep the flame lit inside of me. I started to speak without thinking.

"We aren't even off the land yet and he is already killing people, and what's worse he is showing Kare how to do it," I looked down at Gio as he wiped the blood off his face. He was still smiling. "I will not let you ruin her, not now, not ever." Gio got back on his feet. His soldiers started to move in closer.

I twisted and tugged to get out from his grasp, but he was holding me in place completely. Gio raised his hand and the others stopped moving.

"I have tried to assure you that I would comply with your suggestions, and still you persecute me. Maybe you aren't as different as the ones that have come before you." I shifted my shoulders again to get out of Kole's grasp but to no avail. The drums started to fade but I was still no less angry than I was before.

"I saw you with my own eyes! Do you deny it?" I yelled.

"Look again, my queen," he said.

I had almost forgotten that I left the limp servant with Kare. I was so angry I didn't even think to check on her. Kole released me, and then I heard her soft voice.

"My queen, I'm sorry but you are mistaken. I volunteered to help Gio," the servant spoke but she held her hands up in complete fear of me.

"Volunteered?" I asked in surprise. Gio brushed past me and made his way back to Kare as the girl finished her explanation.

"Yes, my queen. I was there when this Norse girl was being nursed back to health. I heard her story about the time she spent here and how twisted and wrong everything was when she arrived. I wanted to show her that all of us are not like the people she met. I figured this was a good way to show her that we are capable of compassion." The servant's words struck me like a hammer, and I had no idea how to respond.

"I was showing Kare how to feed without killing someone, and before you interrupted, I was going to show her how to heal someone afterward," he lifted his hands to his mouth and with his canine teeth punctured a hole in his palm. "Our blood has healing properties so that if we weaken a person after feeding, I can make sure that they have no lasting effects from us taking their blood. If you would have asked before attacking me, I could have told you." He wiped the dirt off his clothes and returned his hair to the perfection that it was before. I was speechless. I spun around and Kare's eyes met mine. I knew she wasn't going to welcome me with open arms after that. There was nothing but pain and disgust left.

"Kare, I'm so sorry, I didn't know," I pleaded to her, fighting back the tears. She backed away from me.

"I can't believe you would think that I would sit here while he killed someone. I know how you feel about what I am now, but I never expected this, Tav." I looked up to Kole and his face was stone. I didn't know what to say to anyone.

Trying to be a savior and I turned into the biggest villain. I turned into the monster that I assumed I was protecting her from. Kole slipped his hand into mine, a small gesture of support, but I know I put him in a difficult place.

"Gio, I'm sorry. I don't know what came over me, but I just snapped. I didn't mean it I swear." Kole grabbed my hand a little tighter signaling me to give it some time.

"No need to apologize. Your precious alliance is intact but I'm not the one that will hate you forever for this. I've had hundreds of years to accept how Romans view my kind, but Kare is new. This curse comes with a lot of benefits but there are many challenges ahead, and I wanted to spare her from the persecution for as long as possible, but here we are." Gio and

Kare didn't speak another word before they turned and disappeared into the night before I could offer any more apologies.

"What have I done?" I searched Kole's face for sympathy, anything to make me feel more than a complete failure.

"You made a mistake. Give her time, she will forgive you." He tried to comfort me.

"No, she won't. I pushed her away, and then I slammed the coffin shut. Why would she ever speak to me again?" I couldn't understand why he thinks she would ever speak to me again.

"Because she loves you. Kare has always wanted a sister and from day one she looked up to you. Just give it a little time before we assume," he pulled me closer to him sensing that I was seconds away from falling apart.

"I'm sorry, I'm sorry, I'm sorry," I slammed my face into his chest and cried in his arms until I had no tears left.

32 - KING TO KING – KOLE

Not what I was expecting a couple of days before my wedding, but since when has anything gone the way it was supposed to. I managed to get Octavia back to her room. After hours of tears, she managed to force herself to get some rest.

The rest of the night I was trying to convince Gio to stick around for one more day so that I could get a chance to talk to Kare about what happened. I've seen the influence of Mars take control of Octavia in Lundr when she almost killed Kyut but this was different. The rage I could feel coming off her was from a very dark and ancient place.

Usually, I can always bring her back quickly, but her eyes were lost in the flames. It was no coincidence she was losing control here of all places. Whatever was brewing here it was strong. Mars hates Gio. He considers him a creature that shouldn't exist. He is no different from Delphi, and if he could get Octavia to kill him and never lift a finger, he would be happy but I was not going to allow that to happen. I know Octavia would never consciously attack him that way without a reason.

Especially since she doesn't know how to kill him. There was no way she would go in without a plan.

I was so torn and placed in a very difficult postion. I'd grown to trust Gio, especially since he has taken the responsibility of helping Kare through her transition. But I wanted her to know that she was still my sister, and we were still family. Kyut threw me away the second he didn't agree with me, and I was not going to do the same. I had to have faith that in her heart Octavia didn't feel this deep hatred. I finally managed to calm her down and get her to actually get some much-needed rest. Her breathing fell into a steady rhythm next to me. I decided I was going to sneak down and have a conversation with Gio. The sun was still up, but they found a nice cave belowground that provided them shelter.

Ω

It didn't take me long to reach the cave entrance. It was unnaturally quiet as usual, reminding me of the Delphi caves, a place that I had no desire to revisit. The trail down into the cave was lit with torches making it easy to navigate. How did this guy manage to always make himself at home so fast? I'm happy that they had the torches for regular people, the rest of us didn't have the enhanced hunter abilities. A soldier appeared and stopped me from proceeding further.

"That's far enough, King Kole," the soldier said with a low growl in his throat. I was not excited to be met with this type of hostility.

"I came to talk to your King, and offer my apologies for my future wife's behavior. It was a misunderstanding." His body went rigid, and I could feel that he was not excited about the topic.

"You are lucky our king still desires an alliance because what she did should warrant a punishment." His words didn't come as a surprise, but he was brave to speak about Octavia that way in front of me.

"I'm happy that he still desires an alliance, and as much as I am enjoying this chat, is there any way I could speak to him myself?"

"He is resting, and he prefers to not be disturbed unless you want to bring an offer worth waking him for," the soldier dismissed me fairly quickly. "You are lucky you're all still alive." The threat was not something I appreciated and I was tired of this game already. I pinned the soldier against the wall and raised my axe to his throat.

"Would your head be a good offer?" I could feel my power swelling. All I wanted to do was talk, this was so unnecessary.

"Attacks from the King and Queen in the same day, this is going to be a glorious partnership," Gio's calm voice prompted me to let the soldier go.

"I mean no disrespect to you, but maybe we should work on how we talk to each other," I glared at the soldier, "what do you think?" His lips peeled back to expose his teeth and a low growl was rumbling in his throat.

"Leave us, Kole and I need to speak," Gio interrupted, throwing his hands in front of the soldier. He was still tense as he made his way down the cave.

"What brings you here, Kole? I told you I'm not the one who needs an apology," he had no feeling in his voice.

"I came to offer it, regardless," we walked side by side. "Octavia is still learning how to control her powers, as am I, and sometimes it gets away from us a little bit. I'm not making an excuse for her, but it plays a part in what happened."

"She has made no secret about what she thinks of me." He had his hands crossed behind his back.

"I will not disagree. The woman I know speaks her mind, but she is not irrational and hateful." He didn't seem to take my words with any belief, but he did burst into laughter.

"She could have fooled me, young king."

"Being in Alexandria, so close and connected to the vengeance of her people, intensified her ties with Mars. I believe he is using some of her feelings and amplifying them."

"You know if I didn't experience the gods personally, I wouldn't believe that," he smiled.

"Since I've heard your story, I know you can attest to their manipulation, and I wanted to offer my apology. She is resting now, but I was hoping she would be able to have a word with Kare before you leave tonight." He sat down and made himself comfortable.

"That is a decision she has to make. I will not force her to do so to ease your conscience." He spoke like a protector.

"I agree, her life is different now, but I want her to know that I will never abandon her. We are still family. Can you speak to her about it and send a message up to the villa with her answer?"

"I will ask on your behalf. You will have your answer soon. Now can I go back to sleep? I was having the best dream."

“What could you possibly dream about that hasn’t already happened? You’ve been alive like forever.” I joked.

“You have no idea what kind of imagination I have, young king,” he laughed and made his way back to his room.

“I’ll leave you to it.” This meeting went way better than expected.

33 - It Can Only Get Better – Octavia

I wanted to bury my head in this pillow and never leave this bed ever again. I made an utter fool of myself. I was supposed to be a queen, I was supposed to be the figure that the people look up to. I was supposed to portray a symbol of strength and grace, but today I felt like a spoiled hot head. I acted like the same people I fought against since I arrived here. The same Roman prejudice they expected from us.

My mother would be so ashamed of me. She had never lost her cool like that. I lost her too soon. I never got the chance to learn how to rule under her tutelage. I always thought I would have more time with her. Unlike Floria, I didn't spend my days following her and learning how to be a proper Roman woman. In hindsight, it is something I will regret forever.

A servant brought a letter from Kare. She was agreeing to speak to me *thank Olympus*. I had a long road ahead to fixing this and she was worth every second. Life was entirely too short to spoil this opportunity. If I was going to smooth things over, I needed to show a sign of good faith, not just to Kare but to Gio as well. I still wouldn't trust him, but I could find a way to thank him for helping. I know I was being too hard on him, but it was hard to ignore everything that I saw in that cave. The way he talked about life was as if it was just a waste of time and something he couldn't be bothered with. The sentiment didn't sit right with me. We trusted him with the battle, but that was something that fed his destructive ego. We used his vengeance the same way Mars was trying to use me. You reap what you sow apparently, and it was going to be the death of us all.

I got up off the bed and sat in the middle of the floor. To get to the bottom of this I needed to talk to the source. I closed my eyes and steadied my breathing before I dove down into the flames. The flame was burning bright in the darkness, calm and powerful. I wrapped my hands around it and allowed it to take over. I waited until I felt weightless, and then I was dropped in the middle of a wasteland.

I wonder why he always wanted to meet here. Surely there was more to life than a wasteland and the aftermath of battle. A fire broke out in the middle of the wasteland, so I knew exactly where I needed to go. The fact that he was making me walk there was beyond frustrating. In my mind, I expected to be welcomed by a celebration. I mean I did succeed in my own war. Gracia was back under control, Kole regained his home, and, in a few days, we would be married which would lead to a united land. Mars didn't seem like the type to celebrate but a girl could hope.

I found him sitting on a giant chair of bones. His helmet was in his hands, but he was in his usual golden armor. Can you believe that seeing a god was no longer exciting? It had turned into a necessary evil.

"Nice of you to reach out, my child," his voice slammed into my head from all directions, something I would never get used to.

"I wish I could say that I'm happy to be here. The last couple of weeks have been interesting, to say the least," I said sarcastically.

"This is a joyous time, my child. Your home is restored, and your family avenged," he held up his arms in triumph.

"Getting revenge for my family was amazing, although Titus is still alive. Restoring Alexandria will be very satisfying but our mission has grown past revenge." Mars put his helmet down and shifted in his seat.

"Is there anything more important than revenge? It is what has fueled you till this point, is it not?" He already knew the answer. I had to think about how I was going to answer this question. The last thing I wanted to do was offend him.

"It has fueled me, but I have gained so much more along the way. A husband, friends, and a family that has embraced me. Their protection is now what fuels me," I said with a straight face.

Mars looked at me with confusion almost daring me to keep talking. Like the big mouth I am, I kept talking.

"I'm sure you have been watching everything that has happened, and you are aware of how things have changed."

"If you mean changed, you must mean how I give you the power to take back your home and yet you give pieces of it back to that disgrace, Ambrogio," he barks, the flames shooting off his armor responded with him, almost reacting to his anger.

"It was necessary to the cause. We didn't stand a chance without his help."

"His help," Mars couldn't hold in his laugh.

"Is there something you would like to tell me?" I asked.

"No, nothing that I can share, but I will warn you. What you have done has spread. Gods talk, and the deal your husband to be made with Delphi will not be forgotten. As Odin and I told you before, they are not too fond of what we are trying to accomplish."

"Will the other gods be making an appearance to let us in on the gossip?" I asked.

"All I can say is they are stirring, which is more than they have done decades," he replies, his face emotionless.

I had to really consider if I wanted to tell Mars about our plans, but I found it hard to believe that a god could be kept in the dark.

"While the gods decide whether they want to interfere with our plans, we can move on to other things. I'm sure you are aware, but I figured I should formally tell you about the plans moving into the future," I peeked up at him trying to gauge his temperature.

"Are you talking about the union between you and the Norse? For a second Odin believed you would fight against destiny, but I assured him that when Romans love, we love hard and passionately... a fire that will consume anything that

is in its way," his flames burned with excitement just talking about it.

Why am I not surprised that the gods had a wager on if Kole and I would end up together? The thought of it offended me. Before I could curb my temper I was already snapping back.

"I know this whole thing seemed like a plan to you, but the reason I love Kole is that regardless of anything that has happened or has come our way, he has never not been on my side. In the face of gods, monsters, and spirits, he is my constant. Destiny did not shape him into being a great man, so I won't allow you to claim credit." I realized after I finished my sentence that I was on my feet pointing at him.

"You see how bright that fire burns, child. You are in the face of a god that can crush you with a thought and your love for him has you talking to me as if I'm another foot soldier." His words registered quickly. In the midst of me wanting to add more to the conversation, I pushed down on my temper.

"Kole and I plan to build a new home along the path to Midselium, allowing both Norse and Romans to be close enough to their home to be able to feel the presence of their culture. It's a first step towards healing all the rifts between us, the Norse, and even the vampires." Mars's shoulders grew tense at the mention of Gio and his kind. "Are you saying I can trust him or not?" I was starting to get agitated.

"I say nothing, child, but be aware and live with the decision you make." I couldn't hide the disappointment on my

face, so I decided I needed to wrap this up before I get myself in more trouble.

"I have some requests, if that is something that you will allow."

"I will never approve of your partnership with the animal," he remarks.

"Vampire," I corrected.

"Whatever. I assume that some compensation is in order. What is it that you want?" I took a deep breath and thought about what to say.

"Kare is a vampire now, and I can't keep having violent outbursts toward them. Save me the riddle because I know the anger I feel is coming from you, so in the interest of keeping peace, do you think you can help me?" The sly grin tugged on his face.

"I cannot curb my influence, child, it is who I am, and it is who you are. The fire burns bright in us all and it burns its brightest in the face of adversity. As time passes, you will learn to control it." He kept smiling

"What is so funny?" I asked clearly annoyed.

"If you are having that reaction to vampires, it means that deep down you still view them as a threat. Unfortunately, I can't help you with that. You need to decide if you trust the nature of the monster, or if you believe they need to be put down as I do." He spoke directly through me.

"Fuck me," I ran both my hands through my hair.

"Is there anything else, child? I need to return to Olympus. The sand here is starting to bother me." He shifted uncomfortably in his seat.

"I have an idea. You're not going to like it but it's something that I need, consider it a wedding gift."

I would have to wait to see if Mars would honor my request, but it was worth asking. After the news that he wouldn't be able to make me less murderous, I needed something to go right. The sun was starting to set, and I needed to meet Kare. They had a lot of ground to cover to get back home so they would be leaving very soon, and this conversation would determine whether I would have a maid of honor at my wedding. The door opened and Kole walked in.

"Did I miss something?" he asked.

"No, just having a conversation with the warlord," I pointed up to the sky.

"He have anything good to say?"

"That is yet to be seen," I made my way to the door.

"That is a godlike answer with little to no information, but I'm going to leave that conversation for another day," he laughed. I blew him a kiss on my way out the door.

I finally reached the throne room, which was completely restored. The color of the stone was returned to its original color. All of the gold that Marcus horded was moved back to its rightful place. It held some of the resemblance from the past.

We never hung the banners back up because I honestly did not know who lived here anymore. It didn't feel right hanging the Sirius banners because technically there was none of us left, and I didn't want to force the new axe and spear banner on these people. I would not be a conqueror like the villain before me.

Maybe we should just hang some nice colored banners with no sigil. Anything that would make this room look more colorful. Standing here it just felt completely empty, a void in the middle of a giant memory. A version of my history that can never be replicated again, this part of my life molded me but what I will become is still written in the stars.

“Something about it feels different, am I right?” the voice startled me briefly. Even though her tone has changed, the voice was the same.

Kare walked into the throne room slowly dressed in Roman robes, her curls bouncy and full of life. I noticed she was still wearing the golden clips I gave her before we left Perseus. Maybe Kole was right. Even though I am conflicted with what happened to her, maybe a path to forgiveness is a possibility.

My eyes rolled slowly over her as she closed the distance between us both.

“A distant memory I’m afraid,” I forced a slight smile hoping it would ease some of the tension.

“I imagine that I will feel the same way when I get to see Lundr again. I just hope that amongst the change I can find parts of my old life that won’t disappear.” Her shoulders dropped.

The words sat on my chest like a boulder. At the slightest bit of adversity I almost turned my back on the person that did everything in her power to make sure I was comfortable when I arrived in her home. I moved closer to her. Naturally I expected her to retract but she was as still as stone, a familiar stance from Gio.

"I'm not very good at this queen thing, and I know I will make mistakes but there is one thing I know for sure. No matter what changes, I will not forget everything you have done for me in this short time," she put her head down and tried to hide that beautiful smile that resembled her brothers so much. "You welcomed me as family immediately, and I risked losing sight of that because of someone else's vendetta."

"Do you mean Mars?" Kare interrupted.

"He has a particular sentiment towards vampires but that is no fault of yours. You didn't ask for this as I didn't ask to be influenced by him. These are the cards we were given." She walked past me towards the windows, and she was staring out at the moon.

"I have so much to learn moving forward, but even though I died, I have never felt so alive. I still feel like myself believe it or not, but stronger and more aware of what is happening around me," I was not sure where she was going with this. Yes, she looked the same and even sounded the same, but her movements and mannerisms were nothing like the joyous soul that I knew in Lundr. "Gio told me that I will be different but being a vampire doesn't change who you are, it only enhances what you were. I can literally hear the waves crashing against the docks from here. I can feel footsteps and listen to heartbeats when people are being untrue, it's fascinating." I was still struggling to understand what all of this meant. Did she think I was being dishonest? "I can feel how uneasy you are around me, but I can also feel deep down that you do not hate me," her words sent a wave of relief over the everlasting guilt.

"I could never hate you, Kare." I wanted to reach out and grab her hands so badly, but I was not sure if that was an acceptable gesture. Though she remained still she was flustered in gathering her thoughts.

"I don't mean to ramble, I just thought I should share some things that I have learned being around Gio and his," she paused, "my new family," she continued. "You have things inside you that are not fully in your control the same way we do, and in order to live in peace, we must be patient with each other. All of this is new."

"I'm glad that he is helping you. We have had our differences. Even though I do not approve of some of his methods, he kept his word, and none of this would be possible without his help." I walked over to the window and took in the sight of the moon with her.

There was no warmth coming from her, but I reached down and weaved my hand inside of hers. She did not protest.

"You will always be my family Kare, if you will have me," I spoke softly.

"I told you before Tav, I've always wanted a sister," she smiled, and I could see her fangs slightly poking out the side of her grin. The tears started to break through the barrier after I fought so hard to keep it together, "I'm so sorry Kare, for everything, and I will spend as long as I need to make it up to you." I know that my face was not pretty right now.

Kare reached up to my cheek and gently wiped the tears away. Maybe she was right, she was the same kind and selfless person I met in Lundr.

“We are all good Tav, don’t worry about it. Apparently I literally have all the time in the world.” A tiny laugh escaped me in combination with the tears.

“Was that an immortality joke?” I asked.

“My first one, actually,” she smiled.

I reached across and gave her a big hug. I could feel her body tense and I was sure she made a low growling sound, but I didn’t let go. I think I needed this more than she did. I couldn’t lose her. After Floria’s betrayal, I couldn’t afford to push away any more family.

“Are you ready to be my brother’s old lady?” She said playfully.

“As long as you decide to stand up there with me,” it was the best attempt I had in asking for moral support. I never dreamed of getting married, but I hoped that when it happened Floria would be standing by my side. Kare wasn’t a replacement by any means. She was someone I had grown to love, and the day wouldn’t be the same without her there.

“I would love to!” Her smile was bigger than the sun and for a brief moment the colorful and full of life Kare leaked through the stoic stone vampire that stood before me.

I had a lot of work to do when it came to accepting her transformation, but it was a sacrifice that I was willing to make for peace and for family.

“Wait until you see the dress.” I could feel the excitement beaming off her.

34 – Majestic Marcella – Rollo

I decided to leave Alexandria early. I figured I could be helpful with the wedding setup instead of sitting around. I could at least tell the others I had something to do with making this day perfect. I was having mixed feelings about being back on the trail to Midselium. So many memories, good and bad, but I wouldn't trade the experience. The man I am now wouldn't exist without the sacrifice I made for my people and my friends. That snake Ivar set this in motion the betrayal is one thing I would never forget. I hope that he was taking advantage of his days Kole gifted him.

My father had to be watching me from the great hall bragging to Thor about what I have accomplished. I literally killed myself. How many warriors can say that they have done something like that? How many warriors can say they spoke with the gods? I carry a hammer blessed by Thor as proof. Now after all of that I was going to attend my first wedding. Everything was going to change, but I wasn't losing my best friend, I was gaining so much more.

I've been trying to keep my mind busy on this trip with all this mushy marriage nonsense because I could not stop thinking about Marcella. Every minute that the sun was up and I couldn't be around her was draining. I only reason that I left Alexandria was to catch up with Gio and spend more time with her. How did this woman fill my thoughts so quickly? I felt like I could spend hours talking to her about anything.

All the history and knowledge she had was entrancing, and even under that beautiful, perfectly curvy figure was a ruthless side. Something faster and stronger than anything I have come across. I had to look deep inside myself and ask why that was so damn exciting. The thought of her hiding that natural animal under her gorgeous exterior drove me crazy. The sooner I get back on the road to Midselium, the sooner I can see her again.

We were only a couple of hours out and the timing couldn't be more perfect. The sun would be going down soon. Before she leaves, I told her to meet me in the clearing that Kole chose for his ceremony. I'm not sure if this is a good idea, but I was going to take his advice instead of trying to be cool. I'm going to tell her how I feel and, with Thor's blessing hopefully, she feels the same.

The company that departed to begin the preparations for the ceremony have made amazing strides in getting ready for the most important wedding in our history. A dock has been built right below the trail to Midselium so there was no need to take the long exhausting hike from Perseus. Markets and shops were being built; everything was in the early stages, but this was going to be a miraculous town once it was complete. Norse and Romans were working together in harmony trying to get this right for their King and Queen. I assume the name was a work in progress.

This is what it was all about. I had to sit back and appreciate that I played a part in this. A world with enough space for all of us to have a voice. Vampires, spirits, and everything else that will shake up this world. I decided to help some of the citizens with the setup instead of sitting around. I had to wait for the sun to set before Marcella would meet me, so it seemed like a great way to pass the time.

I know Octavia was going to love this, not one detail or piece of gold was spared. The clearing was decorated with the wildflowers from the fields of Alexandria. They managed to salvage some of them from the wreckage. I carried every bench and sat them down one by one behind each other. Wood pillars stood as tall as the heavens with vines and flowers growing so much that they carried over to the benches and lead all the way up to the altar.

The women were laying the flowers down the center aisle all the way to the front. Even I could appreciate how beautiful it looked. Octavia was going to cry her eyes out when she sees it. I took a seat to admire the handiwork. Lifting all these benches was no small task, but I could have never made anything look this beautiful. My thoughts started to slip back into the future. Would I have this one day? Was I capable of being lucky enough to have someone love me this hard? Would I ever love someone enough to go through all of this? I have no idea how long I was sitting down contemplating this mystery.

"Are you aspiring for this outcome, or does it frighten you?" My shoulders relaxed at the sound of her voice. I shifted in my seat and turned to see Marcella walking down the aisle.

Her beauty froze me in place, like time stood still as she made her way to me. Her hair was silky black hanging just over her shoulders and the flowers on the ground reflected out of those perfect grey eyes and the scar that I was beginning to love. She wore a thin grey dress that hugged her body perfectly, elegant and extremely sexy.

Suddenly, the thought of having something like this wasn't scary. I longed for it. But I only longed for it with her. She invaded my mind and tortured my thoughts, even when she wasn't around, and now standing right before me, her mere presence had me frozen like an old statue. I must be going insane. That has to be the only explanation.

"Speechless, I see. So you must be frightened by all of this," she said.

"No, of course I'm not frightened," I shook off that awkward feeling. "It's not every day a beautiful woman walks down an aisle towards you and you're not the one getting married," I laughed.

"Is that something you are looking forward to?" She asked before sitting next to me.

"If I meet the right woman, anything is possible," I smiled.

"And just like that a lucky lady becomes the queen of Ragnarsson," she laughed. I loved her smile and the way the fangs lightly scrapped her bottom lip. I had to force myself not to stare.

"Maybe I can take you there after the wedding. My home is amazing, I think you would love it." I tried not to sound too eager, but it was so hard for me to keep my cool around her.

"I would love to see your home. You have already seen mine, and I assume that your home is much nicer than the cave," she smiled flashing her fangs again.

"There will be no more caves for you now that you don't have to hide. You could come and stay, if that's something you would like to do," I could see the level of intrigue rising. "So, is that a yes?"

"I would love to!" she smiled back at me.

I almost jumped out of my seat in excitement, then I immediately realized how embarrassed I was for that reaction. But she didn't hold it against me, she just rested her head on my shoulder, and we took time to appreciate how amazing the decorations came out. If I could bottle this feeling up and have it every day I would.

We took a walk along the river. The trees shuffled as the cool breeze swept through the night. The moon illuminated the path. The bargain that Kole made with Delphi was forever plaguing my thoughts. We would have to pay that debt eventually, but for now it was just nice to be with Marcella.

Now that the fight was over, and she agreed to come back to Ragnarsson with me, it was clear that she was at least kind of interested in me. Talking to her was still unnerving and the butterflies in my stomach were on overdrive, but I have made progress.

"I have so many things I want to show you on the way back to my home," I tried to keep the excitement under control.

"Sailing will be difficult. You know I'm unable to travel during the day."

"Call me crazy or desperate, but I want to spend as much time with you as possible. We will travel by land and find shelter during the day, the same thing you did with Gio to get here," I grabbed her hand and locked eyes with her.

"Are you prepared to live in the shadows just to spend time with me, Rollo? You know I am promising you nothing more," she said softly. Clearly drawing a line in the sand but that wasn't going to scare me off.

"Being with you, I could never be in the shadows," I smiled. All she could do was laugh at my awful attempt to be smooth. "In all seriousness, I'm willing to live in the darkness in order to get you there safely, until I come up with an alternative, which is already in process."

"You're going to invent a way for us to be in the sun?" she asked, and I could tell that she was apprehensive, not wanting to put too much faith in an idea that wasn't real yet.

"Now that Kare is a vampire, I owe it to her to be able to come to see her family, and if you like what you see in Ragnarsson, I want you to be able to come back whenever you please." I could already hear my voice getting higher.

"That's very honorable, Rollo. You and your friends aren't like any that I have met. Unfortunately, many of us have lived for so long that all we see is the evil in the world, but maybe there is some hope for humanity after all," she smiled, as we continued to walk.

"Were you not once human?"

"What I was and what I am now are two different things Rollo."

The conversation had taken a dark turn, as it usually does whenever we are together, but there was one last thing I wanted to ask her. I know it wasn't any of my business, but the curiosity was going to kill me.

"Can I ask you a question?"

"You're a king. Ask away." She opened her hands in a gesture for me to start talking. I had to build up some resolve because I knew this was such a personal question.

"After Gio turned you, did you ever go back and look for your father?" Her body tensed at the mention of his name, and I immediately regret bringing it up.

"I know you have been curious about the subject. What took you so long to ask?"

"I didn't want to overstep, it seems like it's a touchy subject. I didn't want to be the one to bring back all of the pain," I hoped that this was less awkward than it sounded.

"Oh, it is a story about pain, but not mine. I only ask that you do not view me any differently than you do now after you have heard the story." I wanted to protest because how would that be possible.

I'm not sure what she could have done, but after learning what he did to her when she was a child anything less than revenge would be a blessing for him. In what world does he get to continue living his life after killing one child and abandoning the other?

“We have survived more than a fair share of nonsense. I’ve seen you rip a guy’s throat out and smile afterward. I doubt this story will turn me against you,” I smiled, and she couldn’t hide the smirk on her face. The way her long sharp teeth slowly crept on the edges of her lips fascinated me, like the pain of the bite could be exciting. I don’t know how my mind shifted to this so quickly.

“You’re staring again, Rollo,” she said snapping me out of the daze I was in. Now I could feel the heat rushing to my face. I wonder how many times she has caught me staring.

“Sorry, I don’t mean to stare, but you make it very difficult to concentrate.”

“Am I doing something specifically?”

“No, you’re just being you, and it suits you.”

“I’ll see if you’re saying the same thing after my story. Walk with me.” We continued down the river before she stopped under a giant tree and sat.

“After Gio turned me, the only thing I could think about was how Ilithia never got the chance to live again. All that rage was aimed at one person and one person only.”

“Your father.”

“Yes of course,” she nodded. “Throughout the first couple of months it was all I could think about. While Gio was trying to teach me control and patience, all I wanted to do was go back and give him what he deserved. The blood fueled my every desire, my every instinct. It turned me into a hunter, which is why I was so valuable to Gio. I quickly became his most trusted companion.”

“Companion?” The word immediately grabbed my attention. Not once did I consider that the two of them could be a thing. Why wouldn't they be a thing, Marcella was one of the most beautiful women I've ever seen. She looked up at me and she must have sensed what was going on in my brain.

"We have never crossed that line. He has known me since I was a child, anything more would be strange to us both," she laughed. Thank the gods was all I could say under my breath. "At some point, my rage calmed, and I became much more calculated and in control, and even though Gio advised against it, I returned to my home to pay my respects to my sister. She never had an official grave, but I would never forget the spot where she lost her life."

She had such a specific reaction to this topic. It was a brief moment of discomfort whenever she brought up her sister. She wasn't the same little girl running through the woods, but she still felt powerless since she couldn't save her. I know exactly how that feels.

"I hadn't expected to see anyone once I arrived but, as you know, the gods are cruel to many. Sitting in the same spot that he committed the vilest act was my father, bottle in hand as usual, but this time he had the nerve to be crying over the spot where he killed her."

I couldn't hide my expression. How could the man not feel any guilt after what he had done? I assumed that she killed him on sight and that is why she didn't want me to think any different of her, which I wouldn't have. I've killed more than a fair share for way less.

"Is that where you took your revenge?" I asked.

"Not quite," she shrugged and continued. "He didn't see me as I approached him. He was crying putting on a pitiful performance for no one to see. I could smell the alcohol from the distance. I wanted to rip his head off on sight, but the years had taught me patience. I opted to have a brief conversation with him. For whatever reason, I needed to hear what he had to say. I asked him what has happened that troubles him so, and he told me that in this spot his daughter was taken from him. His head was down, focused on the spot like a sad puppy. I asked if he had any other children and his response was no others that mattered."

I could not believe what I was hearing. I wanted to be a voice of support for her but if I met her dad, I would have killed him myself.

"I'm not sure what response I was expecting but, if I was being honest with myself, it caught me off guard. Either way, I was done with the games. I grabbed him by the collar and forced him to look me in the eyes before I told him who I was," her hands clenched into a fist. "Once his tiny brain realized that I was his long-lost daughter that didn't matter, he started to tremble in my hands. He felt as weak as he made me feel that night. I looked him in the eyes as he started to cry and beg for me to spare him. That's when I told him I was back from the underworld ready to claim his soul," Marcella got up and just stopped talking right when I was hanging on every edge of the story.

"So, what happened after that?" I can't believe she just left me on the edge like that.

"My king the rest is up to you. I can tell you the rest on our journey, if you are actually serious about walking in the night with me," she closed the distance between us and placed a kiss on my cheek. Her fangs grazed the side of me face as she pulled away. I think I love this woman.

35 - Family Reunion (Kind Of) – Kole

I was relieved to hear that the conversation between Kare and Octavia went so well. I needed them to get along for any of this to work. Life wouldn't mean much without having both of them in it.

We said farewell to the vampires last night as they departed for the Delphi caves. By the time we arrive they should be ready to meet up with us for the ceremony. I stood at the front of the boat embracing the cool fresh air. It was a welcoming feeling compared to how we arrived in Gracia. Eventually I was going to coil up like a raisin in the heat if I stayed any longer. The Romans were an odd people to live in such dry, exhausting heat when other parts of the world had such beautiful weather.

In a couple of days, I was going to be standing on an altar, pledging my love to the woman of my dreams, a gift from the gods themselves. To top it all off, I was going to be lucky enough to stop a war, bringing us all together in the process. Her ears must have been burning because her soft voice spoke from behind me.

"Are we almost there?" Octavia asked rubbing her eyes.

"Yea, we are almost there. We should be reaching our new dock in a couple of hours." I put my hand out to feel the breeze.

"It was a great idea sending everyone ahead to build this," she spoke about it like it was her idea.

"I'm a popular guy. There should be a lot of people lining up to see the most eligible man in Najora take the leap," I said jokingly

"Most eligible, huh?" I couldn't wait for the joke.

"Oh, of course."

"I mean it's you, Rollo, or your weird brother... doesn't seem like a lot of competition," she drawled and laughed. "Although, I did see a couple of warriors that could give you a run for your money," the smile on my face immediately shrunk, which led to even more laughter from Octavia.

"How about you just sit and relax? No other warrior would have given you this much adventure," I turned away to make sure I didn't look too jealous.

"I guess we will never know," she shrugged and walked back to her seat on the boat.

I knew that the dock would be brand new, but I never expected it to look this perfect. We sailed down the river and up ahead the people managed to build a beautiful wooden dock capable of docking multiple boats along the side of the river. It was so long it had to be about seven boats deep. The progress that was made in such a short time was amazing, way more than

I expected. The wood had Norse runes carved into the floorboards and Latin engraved into the post. Octavia ran up to the front and nudged up against me. Neither of us spoke, just admired everything that had been completed before we arrived.

Giant flags waved in the wind brandishing the sigil that would be a new staple in history. The axe laying over the spear, a testament of what we would inspire to be. Two different cultures coming together to show those before us and after us that this is possible.

"I can't believe this is all for us," I murmured unable to take my eyes off the flags.

"Your father would be so proud of you, Kole," Octavia whispered. She wrapped her hands in mine.

"I just wish I could share it with him. All of this is exactly what he would have wanted," I ran my hands through her hair.

"I know it's what he wanted, and that's why we are going to make sure that we honor him, not only for his sacrifice, but his vision," she assured me.

"I love you so much, Octavia."

"Oh, I know you do," she smiled and pressed her lips against mine, "I love you too."

"Let's go see the rest of the progress. We still have a few days before the ceremony, but my mother should be arriving soon with Rollo's family, and then Kare and Gio the night after that."

"Sounds good. Cassia should be here by then as well, but for now let's enjoy what we have in front of us." She jumped off the boat and was already on her way up to the market.

The market was coming together beautifully. The commotion was surprisingly refreshing. This is what a market should sound like, the complete opposite of the barren market we left back in Alexandria. Roman and Norse shops crowded the path up to the clearing. Runic statues and Roman pillars were displayed out front as the shop owners compared their stock. As we continued through, we noticed people carrying materials in a single file line heading towards the space where the ceremony would be held.

We were told we were not allowed to see the clearing yet. I told them to spare no expense on the decorations and, as much as it pained me, I had to trust that they knew what we would like. A tent was set up for us in the meantime until our house was finished being built. We haven't discussed whether it would be a longhouse or a villa, but I didn't have a preference as long as Octavia was with me.

"Have you seen Rollo yet? He should be here already," I asked.

"From what I heard, he has been seen courting Marcella every night, and he spends the day sleeping," Octavia smiled.

"I'm glad that he is spending time with her. He deserves some happiness just like the rest of us." I really wanted this for my best friend, even if I am a bit concerned with their predicament, her being a vampire cursed to live in the dark while he remains a mortal. He had been completely supportive of us from the very start, and it seemed like he forfeited some of his own dreams to make sure that I was happy, so I won't let my worries overshadow my happiness for him. Dropping everything to follow us back and forth couldn't have been easy.

“She is a firecracker, but I like her. She won’t take any of his shit, so she’s perfect for him,” she smiled. “So, what should we do to kill the time?” That immediately stole my attention.

“You have anything particular in mind?” I can tell where it was going from that sly grin on her face. She jumped into my arms before her mouth crashed onto mine, and I just prayed that no one decided to walk into the tent.

Ω

I would love to spend the entire day in the tent, but the horns were blaring from the docks, which meant that our families have arrived. I haven’t seen my mother since we decided to bring Octavia back home. I couldn’t contain my excitement at having her here to celebrate such a momentous occasion, and I know Rollo felt the same. He was so homesick; it was written all over his face. All he talked about was going back to Ragnarsson.

I didn’t even want to think about how I was going to explain to my mother what happened to Kare, but it wasn’t something I could hide forever. She was going to find out one way or another. Kare was slowly getting back to her old ways day by day with help from Gio, but clearly there was something different about her. I was so nervous. I was already sweating, and I haven’t even seen her yet. My mother could always tell when something was wrong. I had to do my best and button up my emotions until it was time.

A knock came from the outside of the tent, snapping me back to reality. I turned back and looked down at the blanket. Octavia was still asleep.

"You coming or not?" I can tell it was Rollo. I popped out the front of the tent still trying to situate my clothes. Last thing I needed was her to wonder what I was doing before she arrived.

"Why are you in such a rush, Rollo?" He turned and just stared at me.

"So, let me run down the list. I'm excited to see my family because, since I got on a boat in Lundr, we have fought and almost died in an arena against Romans, an ancient evil king, and a vengeful spirit."

"Okay, I see where you are coming from," I forfeited, lifting my hands in the form of surrender.

"Let's not forget that I did all of that while rallying vampires and yet another queen from a Roman island. I've been kind of busy man," he remarks with a smirk on his face, clearly proud of all he has accomplished up til now.

"I get it, Rollo. Let's go down and see everyone, Octavia will join us soon."

My mother was leisurely walking up the dock, appreciating the detailed craftwork that blended Norse and Roman cultures. I almost forgot how beautiful she was. She has been so strong since the Holmgang, and I could never forget all that she has sacrificed. I left her back at home to rule in my place and she was probably doing it better than I could. Nothing knocked her off her stride, she was a vision of confidence. Without my father, she would be the one I would have to learn from. As she made her way toward us, I was working my way through the many apologies that I needed to give for letting Kare get hurt. Rollo ran up to her and gave her a quick hello before running past her to his mother and sister, who were just as happy to see him.

They were all jumping around on the dock hugging each other. I was almost jealous. I walked up to my mother and wrapped my arms around, squeezing her close to me. She gasped but only for a second. She wrapped her arms around me and squeezed back.

The memories flooded back from the night before the Holmgang, and I couldn't hold back the tears. I missed her so much, but I had to be the king the land needed. Since the moment I left, I had no time to be a son. Her letter that she wrote held me over, but there was nothing like having her here embracing me like only a mother can.

"I'm so happy to see you, mother. I'm so grateful you could make it," I mumble through all the tears.

"I wouldn't miss this day for the world, my son. Your father would have been so proud of what you have accomplished. This place is amazing." She was looking around at the market we managed to build. "Where are Octavia and your sister?" The dreaded question that I was trying to avoid the moment I sent the letter telling her to come.

"Octavia is getting dressed, she will be down soon, and Kare will be joining us later. How are things at home?" Her body language changed, I could sense the shift in the energy coming from her. I knew I was not going to like the answer. Kyut better have kept his word because it was not likely that I would spare him a second time.

"Let's wait for your queen and speak in private. I know we are here for a celebration, and I'm not here to bring down the mood, but you still have responsibilities, son," she smiled.

Ω

Instead of waiting for Octavia to come down, we walked up to the tent to discuss whatever has transpired back home while we have been busy fighting battles. Anything to move the attention away from the secret I was keeping.

Rollo, Octavia, my mother, and I shared some food and ale. We were still awaiting answers from her. I know we have been gone for a while, but for once I was just hoping I wouldn't have any problems.

"When will Kare be joining us, Kole?" It was the second time my mother asked. The group attempted to hide the awkwardness in the room. We weren't sure how to really answer the question. How do you tell your mother that her baby is going to outlive her because of an ancient Roman curse? Let's not forget to mention that none of this was her choice. She was bleeding out in the arena, and this was a last resort. Clearly, none of us wanted to be the ones to break the news, so I continued to push it off.

"She will be here soon. You know how she is mother, no one controls her," I finished with a nervous laugh.

"If you say so. Octavia, you are looking amazing, as usual. I know it has been a long road for you, but how does it feel to know that your people are back in good hands?"

"Thank you, Astrid. It feels bittersweet. We went through so much to get here, but we made it happen, thank the gods," she answered gracefully.

"Which gods are we thanking?" My mother asked with a serious face that caused the whole room to fall into silence. No one moved a muscle as we tried to gauge the tension in the room. "Relax, children, I'm just joking; everyone is so tense. Isn't this supposed to be a celebration?" The sigh of relief swept through and relaxed the room out of suspension. My eyes fell on Octavia, thanking the gods my mother was not going to make this difficult. I shouldn't be the one to break the news until Kare was okay with me telling our mother.

"So, tell us what's going on back home. I'm dying to get back there, the weather doesn't really agree with me here," Rollo complained as he was rubbing the sweat off his head. My mother gave a deep sigh, and I knew that none of this was going to make me happy.

"I'll start with the good news. Lundr is thriving, and the people have really rallied behind the new king, with a little help from your amazing mother," she took a moment to bask in her success. It was a level of vanity that was rare when it came to my mother. "Rollo, as you may have heard, Ragnarsson is also doing very well. I am in constant contact with your mother and sister, and since you guys left it has been a very smooth transition into the new regimes. The talk of us living together in peace is being received well, for the most part. As you know, everyone cannot be pleased."

"Okay, that sounds amazing... so what is the bad news exactly?" Rollo interrupted. Whatever was going on, I could tell my mother was looking for a way to word it properly. The good news was good, but it seemed like the bad news was worst.

"It's Kyut," she said with a straight face.

"What do you mean? What has he done now?" My anger flared immediately. I had balled up my fist to stifle the darkness back down. I spared him, gave him another chance at life. It wasn't the one that he wanted, but it was a gift, nonetheless.

"A couple of months after I sent you the letter, he kept in contact with us. It seemed like everything was going as well as they could, up until a few weeks ago. I sent the messenger up there, and they never returned. I have even addressed some messengers personally to Ivar and still no response." Rollo and I looked at each other knowing that this could not be a coincidence.

A few weeks ago, we battled Marcus in the arena, and I made another deal with a power that I do not understand. We were on the same page, but neither one of us knew why it would affect Kyut and Ivar up north.

"Since then, we have had no communication with them, and I have no idea what is happening, nor will I send more men up there without being able to guarantee safety to their families." I didn't know where to start. Was Kyut just being vengeful or did something happen?

Did this have something to do with the Delphi? She told us there would be consequences, and I never considered it would reach as far as my land. And that snake Ivar could not be trusted. Odin wanted him spared, and that is the only reason he is breathing. I should have let Rollo knock his head off, too.

"Seems we both have missing siblings now, my love," Octavia said sarcastically. Every scenario was stampeding through my head. I could barely keep a lid on all my emotions.

Why did this have to happen now? Right before I was going to be married. Of course, he had to pull this nonsense.

"Kole, I can see that you are already taking the world on your shoulders, but for now everything is fine. Enjoy this time because you only have one wedding day, and life is too short. Trust me," she reached down and rubbed the gold arm ring that my father gave her. You could tell how much she missed him. "This time is about you bringing your father's dream to reality and spending time with your wife to be. We can deal with the problems later. I miss your brother more than anything, but I have to live in the present, and right now I just want to celebrate you and my daughter in law," she raised her cup. For the rest of the night, we filled her in on everything that took place in Alexandria (outside of Kare of course). I watched as she marveled at how brave we were. She also wanted to kill Marcus herself for what he did to me in the arena.

The night was better than I could have imagined. The only thing missing was my little sister, but I knew that was a problem that would present itself in a few days when she showed up for the ceremony.

36 - Wedding Of My Dreams – Octavia

Tonight was the night. When I wake up tomorrow, I would be Octavia Alexsson. Roman princess married to a Norse King in the center of her new home.

The days seem to drag when you are anticipating something that was going to completely change your life. So many things needed to be done, so I had plenty of time to keep myself busy. Astrid and I were able to spend a lot more time together than we did when I was in Lundr, and the mood was much better this time around, less stressed. She kept asking about Kare and, every time she did, I hated myself for not being able to be honest, but I didn't feel that it was my place to tell her secret. I was going to be family, but this seemed a little closer to the heart than what I was comfortable with.

Kole would have to eventually tell her since Kare would be arriving at sundown, but we never spoke on how the conversation would go. I sat on the edge of the bed in my tent, and I was fighting the urge to throw up, my stomach was in knots from my nerves. Who knew walking down the aisle with all the attention on me was the most terrifying thing I could think of, considering all of the battles I have fought up to this point.

Make no mistake, I've been looking forward to marrying Kole since the day he asked me, but now it was very life-altering real. What if I wasn't ready? What if the complications of ruling one day tore us apart? I would never be able to forgive myself if I let something like that happen.

"I know cold feet when I see it," I hear Astrid call out as she walks into the tent. I couldn't even think of anything to say to counter.

"Is it that obvious?" I looked up to her for some type of reassurance.

"I remember the day I married Styr. I could barely keep any food down. He was so handsome and so powerful, but that's not really important," she laughed. "I wasn't trying to bring two different worlds together in the process, so I can only imagine how you feel." She did her best to sound supportive. "But it was on the heel of the great war, we pledged a life together and didn't know how long of a life we would have.

"I'm not sure why I am so nervous. I know with every vein in my body that I want to be with Kole, but the deeper I go, the more obstacles I run into." I let out a deep sigh and rubbed my hands together to settle some of the nerves "How did you know that everything would be okay?" I asked.

"I didn't know truthfully. All I knew was that I loved him, and he needed me as much as I needed him. That was going to have to be enough." What a perfect answer to the most difficult question.

Kole was right, his mom was a natural, and that only reminded me how perfect my mother was. She will never get the chance to see me walk down the aisle. I won't get to see her smile at me the way Astrid is smiling right now.

"Don't get me wrong, child, ruling is not easy. Not for one second, but as long as you and Kole respect each other and stay on the same page, it will work itself out."

"I don't know if he told you, but I can be very stubborn," I chuckled.

"That is a trait we share," she winked before continuing. "Do you think I expected the gods to use my family and tear it apart? No, but my husband believed that he served them best until his last breath, and he wouldn't have done so if he didn't think Kole was going to be an amazing man and king," she placed her hand on mine. I have no doubt that your parents knew that you would be a gracious queen."

"Thank you," I whisper. I did my best to hold back my tears as she pulled me in close for the hug I did not know I needed.

A noise at the front of the tent caused us both to pull away. Standing at the entrance was Kare. She had a smile on her face, but when she saw who was standing in front of me, all color drained from her face. I couldn't pretend to know what she was feeling. It should be an amazing moment, but maybe she felt ambushed.

"Kare, my sweet daughter!" Astrid ran across the tent and threw her arms around her. "I'm so happy to see that you are safe, I missed you so much," she was kissing her on the cheek, forehead and hugging her harder and harder. I felt like I was intruding, but I wouldn't dare leave. Kare's eyes told me that she was not ready to be alone with her mother. "Everyone has been so secretive about when you would arrive but I'm just so happy that you are okay... even though you are freezing, we should get you some more clothes."

"I'm happy to see you mother. Don't worry about me, I'm fine, but you are squeezing the air out of me," she tried her best to put excitement in her voice. "I just came to help Tav get ready. The ceremony will be starting soon, and you can't be late to your own wedding," she was signaling me to get her out of this awkward moment.

"Of course, of course," Astrid let her go and walked over to the table to pour three cups of ale and passed them to us both. Kare looked at the cup cautiously, I wonder if vampires could drink, but that wasn't important. "Let's toast to family, peace, and the future with my girls." We knocked the cups together. My nerves were so bad I finished the ale in one gulp. Kare put the cup down and grabbed me by both arms

"Enough waiting, Tav. Show me this amazing dress you told me about." I almost forgot to get dressed. The mother-daughter reunion washed away some of my anxiety. I couldn't walk down the aisle in the rags that I had on right now. I walked over to a wardrobe and removed the covering from the top. I wanted it to hide it from everyone until the time was right. I had it made before we left Alexandria by the Roman dressmakers, who paid specific attention to every detail I needed. I revealed the dress to Astrid and Kare, and when both of their mouths hit the floor, I knew I made a great decision.

It was made with a white, lightweight silky fabric, one that I knew Floria would have loved. The dress was cut low in the front, just enough to gain my future husband's attention and make me feel sexy, but not enough that it made me feel naked. The body waistline fit perfectly and complimented every curve I somehow managed to maintain throughout this war. The silk continued to tail down to my hips leaving a high slit up the side of my right thigh, giving me plenty of space to move around. Being unable to move in the dress would have only added to my anxiety. Last but not least, a holster made of leather that wrapped perfectly around the top of my thigh for both my daggers. The true wonder was the beautiful embroidery along the waistline of the dress, fashioned with lace and diamonds.

"Tav, that dress is unbelievable," Kare said. I looked up to see how Astrid felt about the dress and found she was in tears, nodding her head with approval.

"You think Kole will like it?" I was concerned that maybe I had done too much.

"Octavia, it is perfect. Strong, sexy, and beautiful, everything that you are," Astrid forced the words through her tears. I slipped into the dress and tried to situate myself into the shoes I had made to go along with the dress. The shoes were the same color as the dress, covered in the same lace and diamonds.

The gods know that I wish my sister was here. I couldn't shake the feeling that it was criminal for her not to be involved, but there was nothing I can do about that now. I decided to wear my hair loose over my shoulders with the golden clip keeping it from brushing into my face. To honor Kole and his culture, I braided strands of my hair and slid golden rune beads to the end, just as their warriors did. I took a deep breath and turned to my mother and sister-in-law.

"How do I look?" Outside of all the screaming, cheering, and hugging, I think that means I did a good job.

I could hear the light tap of the drums playing and see the light from the torches shining over the trees once I stepped out of the tent. *This was actually happening*. I made my way down the trail as I was directed, reaching back to Kare for support. It was dark, but torch lights illuminated that path.

Everything looked normal until I reached all the flower petals scattered on the ground, causing my heart to skip a beat. Something familiar about them pulled at my memories like they were a part of something that I was missing. I bent over and picked up one of the pedals and realized it was wildflowers from the fields of Alexandria.

Someone thought of me enough to decorate this entire trail with all the different colors of my old home. I was going to cry before I even get to the altar. The attention to detail spoke about the love that I managed to garner from these people. I was lost in admiration on my way to the altar, the pillars were decorated with more flowers, and as I rounded the corner about to look down the aisle, I would have told you that nothing could be more breathtaking than what I was seeing.

Flowers and vines spread from pillars all the way down to the benches in perfect unison. the torches made everything bright and vibrant. Down the aisle at the center of it all was the man of my dreams waiting for me.

Ω

Kole was standing on the altar, his eyes fixated on me. All the guests turned as I emerged at the end of the clearing, but none of them mattered. The only thing I could see was him. He was dressed in a long black cloak with gold trim lining the edges and a loosely fit white shirt underneath that made his perfect brown skin sing out to every nerve in my body.

He flashed me that intoxicating smile that made me fall for him deeper every single time. The way he looked at me was impossible to put into words. If the music didn't start to play, it would have kept me frozen like a statue in the back of the clearing. I watched him shift his weight back and forth trying to maintain his composure, but his eyes never left me.

Every rise and fall of his chest curbing the hunger he had for me in his eyes. No one had ever made me feel like I was the center of the universe, but now seeing him this way made me feel more confident about nothing coming in-between us.

I took more steps, closing the distance between us. I could feel Kare walking behind me, and I trusted that she had my back. I clamped down on my lips to try to hide the fact that I wanted to smile until my face was broken. This is how happy this man makes me; he was right out of a fairy tale. After what seemed like an eternity of walking, he was reaching out and grabbing my hand helping me up to the altar. I had no idea how I was going to make it through this ceremony without bawling my eyes out.

The closer I got, I could see the runes that were stitched into his cloak, but nothing could distract me from how delicious he looked. I recognized all the familiar faces, which was only going to lead to me being even more emotional. Astrid sat in the front row next to Rollo's mom and sister, behind them Marcella and Gio. I could see Cassia's blue eyes shining from all the way in the back. All these people here to celebrate our love further proved I wasn't going to make it through this thing without my emotions knocking me off my feet.

"Are you okay?" Kare whispered from behind me. All I could do was nod, trying to fake all the confidence I could muster up. The priest stood before us, the robe covered in runes, but I looked down and saw he was holding the Roman marriage cloth. Couples in our culture wrap the cloth around their wrist to make it official.

"We decided on having both cultures, did we not?" I could see the smirk on Kole's face.

"Yes, we did, my love," I mouthed *thank you.*

"I would like to welcome all of you here on this glorious evening to celebrate the union of Princess Octavia Sirius and King Kole Alexsson, under the stars right outside of the land of the gods. They have both been chosen by the respective powers that be to lead us all into a new age of peace and prosperity. Octavia beautiful, fierce and strong, she has shown that she is a woman of understanding and principle. She has shown that even though you feel the world is against you and all is lost, there is still light waiting for you at the end. Octavia, I want you to know in front of all of the people that have come to support you today, we love and admire you, and we are lucky to have someone like you sit on the throne for us. With that being said, do you take this man to be your husband, to love and serve, to honor and protect, to support and provide until you take your last breath."

Another hit to the dam and the tears were going to flood this entire ceremony. I'm not sure what I needed but those words filled up any holes or doubts I had about becoming queen.

"I do," and I felt confident enough that I wasn't going to cry. I finally let the smile spread across my face.

"Kole, strong and valiant, a son and a prince to the people of Lundr. The moment Odin chose you to lead, you gave all of it away without a second thought. You are the bravest of us, and worthy of the challenge of wisdom that the All-father has bestowed upon you. You were chosen for a reason and your love for this princess helped complete what your father wanted to build. Thank you for you sacrifice, and you too are the best choice to sit on a throne for us. Do you take this woman to be your wife, to love and serve, to honor and protect, to support and provide until you take your last breath?"

"I do," there was that piercing smile shattering me into pieces in place.

Kole reached back and grabbed two gold arm rings from Rollo, one with the head of a raven, the other the head of a spear. Gently, he grabbed my wrist and secured it into place, and I did the same to him. Never to be removed unless one of us were to leave this world. The priest lifted the cloth over his head and launched a small prayer to Olympus before wrapping our wrists, cementing our union and making us officially man and wife.

"Great power and position demand great sacrifice, you have proven your worth more than we can count. Under the eyes of the Roman and Norse gods, I now pronounce you man and wife. Kole, you may kiss your bride." I swallowed the tension in my throat as his strong arm wrapped around my waist and pulled me close to him before his lips laid over mine. Amidst the cheers, we shared the most amazing kiss, one that I would remember until the day the gods take me from this world.

Ω

The roar of the crowd could have been heard in the heavens. A spectacle even the gods would be jealous of. As me and Kole made our way back down the aisle, the guests threw rose petals our way while reaching out to rub our shoulders in congratulations. They began clanking cups of ale and singing songs in a completely different language than I understood. Kare and Rollo walked behind us, guiding us to our seats.

The two thrones sat atop the clearing over a bunch of tables that were spaced out to allow for dancing in the middle, if that was something you were interested in. Floria used to say that I had two left feet and I never considered the fact that I would have to dance. Hopefully Kole would excuse me from that part. After fighting our way through the cheerful mob that was our guests, I was finally able to sit and kick off my shoes. They were gorgeous, but they were definitely not my style.

"So, my king and queen, how did I do?" Rollo could not wait to let us know that he played a small part in the decorations.

"Everything looks amazing, Rollo. Thank you for the major part you played in these decorations," I said genuinely. It was easier to let him revel in this instead of fighting him with it.

"It looks like Marcella needs some company, Rollo. Don't sit up here talking to a married woman all night," Kole laughed.

He must be really into her because he disappeared almost instantly. I reached out to grab Kole's hand. It sent a jolt through my nerves. Then, he pulled my hand closer to his mouth and planted a kiss on the back of my hand.

"I've never been happier," he said to me. "Now it's time to dance."

"Oh no, no, no, I don't dance, husband of mine," I empathically refused. He started to laugh uncontrollably.

"What is so funny?" I started to take offense to the laughter.

"I planned for this. I don't know why but I did, call me psychic, but I had a feeling you weren't dancing type."

"What gave me away?" He had my curiosity piqued.

"I mean, you look like you have two left feet," he teased. I punched him before he could admire his own joke.

"Let's go," he led me down to the dance floor and, as we made our way to the center, the attention in the room shifted. All eyes were on their king and queen.

I reached up over his shoulders and felt his strong hands on my waist. Kole gently rocked me back and forth to the hypnotizing drums. He was so much better at this than me. Dancing with anyone was the last thing on my mind but I could get used to it with him. It was so peaceful, so fulfilling. I never knew that you could lose yourself in this feeling.

The man of my dreams held me, dancing with me and staring into my eyes, telling me everything he wanted to do to me without speaking a word. I didn't even notice that others had joined us on the dance floor. Kole's mother was dancing, smiling, and twirling with one of the Norse soldiers. Kare and

Gio seemed to move completely in sync. It wasn't fair how effortlessly vampires moved. Cassia was lost in laughter with another Norse warrior I was not familiar with.

"Have I lost your attention already?" Kole asked me.

"No, just making sure everyone is enjoying themselves. I don't want to be the queen that throws a terrible party," I joked.

"Well, someone surely is," he gestured behind me.

"Finally," I said.

Rollo and Marcella most likely started out dancing, but now the only thing that was moving was their faces on each other. It was about time he made a move. She was immortal, but I doubt she would wait around for him forever.

"Can this day get any better?" I rubbed my hands all over his perfect arms.

"Yes, of course it can. We have a whole honeymoon ahead of us, and I plan on it being glorious," the smirk and the darkness that skipped in the back of his eyes sparked the fire inside me.

I grabbed a handful of his shirt so that I could bring him closer to me and slammed my lips against his. He tasted like ale and fruit, and his tongue danced around mine, completely forgetting anyone was around us until the guests started to cheer us on (again).

37 - A Glorious Gift – Octavia

You wait so long for this day, and it seems like it lasts for only a second. We were deep into the night and managed to have the time of our lives. At the end of all of this, we would be bonded forever. My hands started to glow, and I could feel the fire creeping up from my stomach, but I wasn't the one that was calling on it. It was forcing itself to the surface. Kole's eyes darted to mine.

"Are you okay?" he asked. He must have felt it.

"I'm fine, but this isn't me," I answered. I stared at my hands trying to figure this out. What could be happening that would upset me this much? I was having one of the best days ive had in a long time then it hit me. *"Octavia, you idiot,"* I said to myself. I know exactly what this is, and deep down I can't believe I actually pulled it off.

"Seems like you got something going on in that brain of yours," Kole said.

"I have a surprise and a peace offering," I smiled at him before making my way to the center.

“Only you could give someone else a gift at your own wedding,” he laid his hand in front of me and let me steal the show.

“If I could have everyone’s attention, please. I have something I would like to say,” I was going to have to maneuver around this without spilling the secret about Kare before she was ready for people to know. “In light of the events in Alexandria, although we were successful, we did suffer some losses. I treated some people poorly, and I’m prepared to start mending that relationship and make sure that you all know that that isn’t the type of queen I want to be.” I looked at Kare and nodded with a smile. “Gio, we have not always seen eye to eye, and as a gesture of my appreciation and remorse, I have a gift for you, one that I hope you will appreciate.” I closed my eyes and dove deep into the flames. Waiting right at the edge was Mars. He looked annoyed, but I knew that he would do what he promised.

The fire took over my body and shot out of me. I was watching as the light shot out of my body straight up towards the moon. I could hear the crowd gasping. I knew everyone was scared but it would only be a few more minutes. I was snapped back into my body as the light dimmed. I felt weak, but Kole was there to catch me before I lost my balance.

“What exactly did you do? You scared me half to death,” I could see the concern in his eyes.

“You’ll see,” I said through the strain in my throat. Gio was staring up to the moon like he could sense something had changed. It was pulsating, pushing the energy back and forth, like an animal trying to escape from a cage.

"What did you do?" Gio yelled, making no effort to hide his anger.

"Mars, hurry up!" I said to myself.

The light came slamming down in the center of the dancefloor knocking us all off our feet. When the smoke cleared, a woman stood in the middle radiating power and a white aura. Gio was in shock. The years of distrust, anger, and resentment washed away as he saw the love of his life standing directly before him. Her hair was still the same platinum that he described in his story. She had huge brown eyes, and Gio was not kidding. She was one of the most beautiful women I had ever seen.

"Gio, please accept my apology," I asked. He looked at me, and for once hope and gratitude was all that I could read of him.

"Thank you, my queen. I don't know what you gave to make this happen, but I am forever in your debt," he spoke gratefully.

"It's not permanent, but it's the least I could do for trying to kill you," I smiled.

"This will do plenty, thank you," he nodded.

"You made a deal with Mars, didn't you?" Kole asked.

"Yes I did. I tried to get him to help me with my temper, but we compromised on a gift."

"And the vampires?" he asked.

"It's a work in progress, but don't worry. I'm okay, Kare and I are okay."

“No need to explain. You are the hero today, and you probably will be every other day for the rest of our lives,” he smiled at me.

Selene stood in the center looking around, but I knew where her focus was. It had been hundreds of years since she and Gio were able to look each other in the eyes. If I was separated from Kole that long, I wouldn’t be half as nice. Kole and I returned to the throne and let them have their moment. I didn’t know how long she was going to be allowed to be here and spending it awkwardly with us probably wasn’t ideal.

“Are you really here?” Gio said softly. Selene’s voice was so soft, almost like music that would forever calm you.

“I am, my love, but not for long. The gods have granted me a short rope on request of the new queen,” she turned and gave me a slight bow. “I have been watching you and I see your struggle, my love, but the time for vengeance is done. You need to be a leader and a father to our children,” Gio’s face twisted with confusion. “It’s time for you to let the past go.”

“Why should I forgive what they have stolen from me? Why should I forgive them when the reason I am unallowed to hold you right now is because of them? Why should the last fleeting moments that I get to spend with you be wasted on talking about them?” He snapped.

“Because I know the man that you are, not the man that the years have turned you into, the man that I spent days talking with is the way I always want to remember you,” she ran her hands along his cheek, and I could see him shudder under her touch. Her touch was gentle, but it was strong enough to knock down the wall he placed around his emotions. The vampire persona was absent in front of his one true love.

"I came to tell you that you are done hiding and hating. Forget about what you have lost, look at all you have gained," she waved her hands gesturing the crowd.

"But all I have ever wanted was to get back to you!" I felt terrible because I could feel the pain in his voice.

"And I am here to tell you that you need to let me go. You can no longer live this way. I won't allow you to," I couldn't believe what I was hearing. I didn't bring her here to break his heart. I thought that a reunion would be healthy for him, but a breakup could send him into a frenzy.

"So, you seek to abandon me as well," he said quietly and violently.

"Never would I abandon you, but I want you to live. You are immortal, and you have spent a hundred years in misery. I want you to embrace it, embrace life. This world has been cruel to both of us but we both know not all stories have happy endings. I'm certain we will meet again someday, but until then you need to be free of the weight of the hatred that has burdened you." She kissed him and couldn't believe how sad this was.

It was not my intention to cause more pain. I thought I was giving hope. Selene turned to the throne to address us.

"Thank you for this time, Octavia, but while this was a favor to you, it also stands as a warning."

"What?" we said in unison.

"The gods are displeased and especially the spirit Delphi. She does not like to be outsmarted, and the deal you made was technically a loophole. Gods hate loopholes."

“I knew the gods would come back in retaliation, but can you give us any sign of what is coming?” Kole asked.

“I cannot. The stipulation of my visit won’t allow me to, but what I can say is that you have relieved Ambrogio of her wrath, and for that I thank you. But nature has found balance by unleashing another curse, one that is spawned from my essence, and the moon will be its anchor as the sun was his,” she turned back towards Gio.

“What do you mean a curse has been unleashed?” Kole questioned.

“That I can’t answer, young king. I’m sorry.”

“If you can’t tell us what it is, can you tell us where it is?” Rollo interrupted. Her shoulders dropped, and from that we assumed what her answer would be.

“That I cannot tell you either, but I am sure you both have an idea. Nothing is a coincidence, just remember that, young ones.” She walked over to Gio and he pulled her into his arms. “Live, my love, and experience all you can. Even allow yourself space to love again, if that is in the cards. I will always love you, and hope we meet again in the afterlife,” she kissed him, then looked into the crowd though I couldn’t see who or what she was looking at. Before he could say goodbye, the light dragged Selene back up to the moon. Leaving Gio on his knees, staring and contemplating what to do next.

38 - Party Killer - Kole

I can never say that the gods are inconsistent. Every time I think I have brought myself some time for happiness the nonsense has to crash the party. Gio was frozen in the wake of Selene's departure. He hadn't moved a muscle since she said her last words. Kare and Marcella were standing with him, offering whatever type of support they could. I'm not sure how effective it was.

"Out of everything I expected out of this night, a visit from the moon goddess was not on the itinerary," Rollo finally broke away from Marcella enough to speak to us.

"Another warning, why am I not surprised? She all but confirmed this has something to do with the random silence from up north." I was already ready to go on a tangent before Rollo stopped me.

"We didn't have a choice, Kole. Delphi would have killed all of us. She is another notch that needs to be dealt with, but we have to be smart." I had a confused look on my face because I'm unsure when Rollo became the calm and calculated one. That was typically my role to play.

"You're right, but it is not something we can ignore. Selene gave us the smallest amount of information possible. Aren't you the least bit curious what this new curse will create?"

"Of course, I'm curious, but we are here to celebrate you and Octavia. The problems can wait another day, or they can at least wait until we know for sure."

"Sounds like you're scared, Rollo," Octavia joked.

"Honestly, I am exhausted, but the good news is Marcella has agreed to come back to Ragnarsson with me, so I can check for myself what is going on up north. Why don't you try to let someone else save the world for once?" He started smiling. "Now, if you will excuse me, I have some business to attend to," he faced in Marcella's direction.

"Your business wouldn't happen to be an immortal brunette, would it?" I asked.

"That's exactly what it is," he laughed on his way back to the center of the dance floor. For one second, I believed that he was going to take something seriously. I figured it wasn't a bad idea to put Selene's warning in the back of my mind, considering I know that Rollo would fill me in on whatever he finds when he gets back home.

My attention was funneled back to my wife. After her encounter with Mars, she was weak, but her strength was slowly returning to her. I could feel it radiating off her. I was so wrapped up in what I was going to do about this stupid warning, I completely forgot to make sure she was okay.

"That was a very nice thing you did for Gio, even if it didn't play out the way we wanted it to. I'm proud of you," her face slid up to mine. She was going to have a hard time believing that her intentions were received in a positive way. No one could have predicted what Selene was going to say to him.

Gio finally decided to make his way to the thrones. His temperament was impossible to read. It wasn't the same cold, stoic demeanor. It was almost like he was holding himself together, fighting the urge to release all of the pain he'd been harboring for years. I got a glimpse of that pain in the arena as Delphi taunted him about the mistakes he made that led to him being cursed. Without the ability to take his rage out on anyone, he had bottled it all in and had been doing so for years. My only hope was that he could learn to address how he's feeling and not wait until it explodes, if not for me then for my sister's sake.

"I wanted to thank you again, my queen. Pardon my manners right now, but as you can imagine I have a lot to process." Octavia nodded not really knowing how to respond to his words. "You both have given me more in the last couple weeks then many have in decades, and for that, you will always be friends to me," he folded his hands behind his back presenting his usual stance. "This day is about celebration, and although I am feeling the pain of losing my love again, I know that I will see her again someday, but for now I will live my life as she requested. I hate to admit it, but I have learned a great deal from you two, more than I have learned from humans in years. As hard as it is to swallow Selene is right and I will honor her wishes. Starting with being a real leader to my family, old and new," he looked back at Kare, and she smiled in return.

"Thank you, Gio. It's been a long road but I'm glad this is where we ended up," I replied.

"Your sister has one more gift for you both, and then we will release you to enjoy your honeymoon," he waved for Kare to make her way up. Seeing my sister thrive in this life so quickly made it easy for me to take a step back for a little bit to enjoy. She made her way forward and smiled at Octavia.

"Remember we went shopping before we left Perseus? We went to the blacksmith to buy a gift for Marcus, though clearly, he never deserved it. After the battle, I stumbled across it in all of the rubble," she opened the box and unwrapped the spearhead out of the cloth.

It was made of pure gold and along the edges it was lined with various colorful stones. I can't believe they spent this much on that bastard Marcus, but that wasn't important right now.

"As a gift to you both for saving me and saving this land, I wanted to present this to the true King and Queen."

Octavia reached out and accepted the gift with tears running down her face. She passed the gift to me and reached out to pull Kare in for a giant hug, and I couldn't have been happier.

Ω

The way the guests just returned to the party after all of that drama was impressive. Everyone must have left their responsibilities at the door but, as much fun as we were all having, the party would have to end eventually. We made sure to stop by and talk to all our guests. We wanted to be the type of rulers that were accessible to the people, not the type that hides behind their comfortable walls.

After finishing the rounds, I grabbed Octavia to get her attention for my last and final surprise of the night.

“I know it has been an action-packed evening, but I have one more gift to give you.”

“What kind of gift?” she asked.

“Well, technically it’s a gift for us both, but I can compromise and make sure that you feel like it’s all about you.”

“What devious plan do you have now husband?” She smiled and looked at me curiously searching for the answer, but the word husband was all I could focus on. She was mine and all of me was hers. Finally.

“We need to leave. It is time for the honeymoon, and I have a very special place in mind.”

“I wonder where that can be... all we have done lately is barely escape death,” she laughed.

“I can never forget the first time, and I want to remember the first time as husband and wife in the same place,” the hint still didn’t register. I was going to have to lead her to the answer. “We are going to Midselium. We are going to let the villa take care of us and stay for as long as we want. Time moves differently there, as well, so the others won’t notice how long we are gone,” a devilish grin gleamed on her face.

“Yes, take me back to the place where I thought I’d lost you not once but twice, super romantic,” she couldn’t help but remind me of the time Rollo almost killed me. I know she wasn’t trying to be a mood killer, but she was destroying mine right now. “When do we leave?” she asked, and just like that, I was wrapped around her finger all over again.

“Right now.”

39 - Honeymooners – Octavia

Apparently, Kole has been practicing with the portals behind my back because, after we said our goodbyes to our guests and family, he opened a door right outside of the entrance to Midselium. The doors looked exactly the same but, now that I was more in tune with my powers, I could feel the energy emanating off them even more. It was a silent pull assuring me that I was indeed supposed to be here.

The fog rushed around us the same as before while we stood face to face with the massive doors that reached above the clouds. No need to read the runes and Latin carvings that we didn't understand, we already know what we need to do to enter.

"We only saved the world, you think they will deem us worthy," Kole laughed.

"Knowing the gods, probably not." We made a small cut on our palms and pressed them against the door. The visions came faster this time, almost like the door recognized who we were. My time in the cave watching Gio rip apart those travelers, my arrival in Alexandria, Floria's betrayal, being separated from Kole and watching him cut down the men in the arena, fighting

Marcus alongside my friends, Kole making the deal with Delphi, Kare's death, my fist pounding on Gio's face, reconciling with Kare, and at the end it all led up to us proclaiming our love for each other in front of everyone in our new home.

When the vision released us both, Kole stroked his hand through my hair, and I leaned closer to him for comfort. Reliving all of the memories wasn't a surprise this time, but it would take me some time to process. The doors to the land of the gods swung open accepting our payment, as if we haven't paid enough.

Ω

The mood inside was still barren and somber, something I hoped would change with time. The gods had their disagreements, and Midselium was clearly paying the price for their disputes. Being petty wasn't something exclusive to mortals, there was no reason why this place should be so miserable looking when all-powerful beings were in charge.

The omega sat in the same spot ahead of us. I wanted to visit the structure, but I wasn't really looking forward to another lecture right now. We were here to enjoy each other and relax, for once. Once the doors closed, we left all of the problems we had in the real world.

"Do you think Midselium has a beach?" I regretted the question as soon as I asked. There was no reason to get my hopes up.

"While we have everything we need, I think we may have to forfeit the beach," Kole answered with a smile. My shoulders dropped, and I can't believe I was actually pouting about it.

"Is the self-sufficient magic villa not enough, my love?"

"Don't mind me, being a queen has already spoiled me," I smiled.

"Well, let's see if we can spoil you some more."

"How could a girl say no to that."

The villa didn't seem as big this time around. I was certainly becoming accustomed to the fancier things. Most of the house remained the same. The pillars still stretched higher than your eyes could see, piercing the dusk-colored clouds above us. The weather was something we wouldn't have to worry about, at least.

The portal that we used to get home the last time was in the center of the main hall. The water was a radiant blue like the ocean, it was moving in circles almost like it had a life of its own. The staircases weaved in multiple directions leading to the many rooms I assumed this place had. But there was something new that wasn't here before. A small trail of flower petals leading back into the kitchen snatched my attention. It took a minute but the smell of whatever was being prepared in the kitchen slammed into our nostrils.

"Now how does the villa know that I love wildflowers?" I asked Kole.

"I'm not sure, but it is a very nice touch, way more romantic than me," he answered and followed the trail. "You worry too much. We are supposed to be here to relax and enjoy each other." He was right. Even though this was amazing, I was still a little on edge, but he didn't deserve the brunt of my attitude.

"You're right, let's get more comfortable," I suggested. He watched me walk up the stairs and I didn't need to guess what was on his mind. His jaw was tense, as his eyes scanned me up and down. I couldn't help but think about his arms pinning me to his chest. If I told him to take me right here on the stairs right now I know that he would, but the thrill of teasing would make this more exciting. No sense in wasting any time, I've been separated from him for long enough. "Maybe you would prefer if I wore nothing at all," I said softly.

Whatever fire that was brewing in him was ablaze. I'm not sure that anything could stop him as he made his way to the steps. He was pulling his shirt over his head as he closed the distance between us. I undid the knots that were keeping my dress clung to me and let it fall right there on the steps. He stopped right before he reached me and just admired every inch of me before scooping me up in his arms and carrying me.

There were plenty of rooms to choose from and I knew exactly what I wanted. At this point, telling my husband no would be torture for us both.

"Dangerous game you're playing, my love," he had a low growl in his voice, unable to hide how excited he was, and I would never want him to.

"Who says I'm playing games... and if I was, I can see that you are very equipped for the task," I nodded my head toward his pants. I could see how excited he was. His eyes shot back to me, and I could see the brief shimmer of darkness dancing in them.

No other words needed to be said. He was across the room before I could come up with anything else to tease him. His mouth slammed into mine, the kiss was strong and passionate like he was starving and the only thing that could satisfy his hunger was me.

The ale and fruit were still sweet on his lips, and the deep groan at the bottom of his throat sent chills down my spine. He lifted me off the ground. Instinctively, I wrapped my legs around his waist, needing to feel him pressed against my thighs. My body melted against his as he trailed his fingers through my hair, pulling on it gently to tilt my head so that his kiss could run deeper. His strong arms pulled me closer as he carried me over to the bed. He laid me down gently never breaking this fiery kiss.

The sheets felt smooth against my skin as Kole laid me on my back. He broke away from the kiss and I could see the darkness dancing in his eyes. If I looked closer, I could see the flames reflecting from mine. The hunger of his lust was pouring off him and feeding the desire in me.

"You're just so beautiful," he said softly. If he needed me anymore under his thumb I would have to shrink. He dropped down to his knees, his eyes never leaving mine as his mouth closed over the most sensitive parts of me, sending a shockwave through me.

My back arched in response as his tongue teased me, gliding over my center with purpose. He stopped momentarily, allowing me to regain myself before burying my head under the pleasure all over again. I made no attempt to quiet myself. The gods would just have to cover their ears. I would scream his name into the heavens if I had to.

Kole's tongue persisted, bringing me closer to losing myself. I reached out and grabbed his head pulling him in closer to me. He made no motion to move away from me, devouring everything in his path, flicking his tongue insistently over my center.

I knew he was smiling. Don't ask me how, but I just knew. I was so close to finishing, just needed him to never take that beautiful mouth off me. I laid my head back to ride out this feeling as he thrusted a finger inside of me, causing me to yelp in surprise. I gripped him tighter as he slid in another finger, completely sinking me into climax. My legs were shaking as I screamed his name.

"You taste amazing," he licked his lips and made his way up to me, because clearly he was not done with me.

"You might have mentioned that before," I put my hand on his chest and stopped him in his tracks. "Now, let me find out how you taste." I pushed him off me and dropped to my knees in front of him. I was always impressed with how big he was, but something about tonight made him seem like he was in amazing stature.

"Something piquing your interest?" he asked with a smirk, noticing how I admired him

"I would say it's more than peaking," I chuckled. I grab him before he could respond, and he struggled to hold his composure, but I know exactly what he wanted. I rubbed my tongue over the top of him and watched him shudder under my touch. "Don't run away from me now, my king," I smiled.

"I'm not running, I'd never run from you," he tried to force out the words in-between is deep moans. I wrapped my other hand around him and guided him into my mouth.

Whatever he was expecting this was even better. I maintained the rhythm of my hands as I whirled my tongue over him. I had no intention of stopping until he was finished, I wanted to taste him, all of him. His moans grew deeper, rumbling from his throat down to his feet as his toes curled.

He grabbed my hands to stop me, but I didn't want to stop ever. He was mine to please, mine to protect, all of him was mine. His eyes said the same as he pulled me up and claimed my mouth again, dancing to the same song that we have been since the first time he kissed me.

"You think there is any scenario where I don't end up inside you," he growled in my ear.

"I hope not," I responded as best I could, I was almost drunk with passion.

Kole lifted me up off the floor, laid me back onto the bed, and he spread my legs gently with his knees. The length of him kept me on the brink of anticipation as he slowly thrust into me, allowing me to feel all of him, every single inch.

I felt like I was going to explode. My husband, my king, my life… all of it was here in his eyes. I grabbed his hand to guide his palms to my breast, his strong hands gripped them firmly in response. His thumb grazed my hardened nipples, while his tongue swirled over the top of them, driving me crazy. He was sucking and teasing them, and I was struggling to keep my breath as he drove into me repeatedly. It was pleasure unlike anything that has ever hit me before.

"Don't stop!" I pleaded.

"I'll never stop," he smiled.

Grabbing my hips, his motion grew harder and faster. He locked eyes with me, the power was firing off in his eyes as he came closer to finding ecstasy. My nails dug into his hip, willing him to give me more and never deny me. His body responded to my wishes.

“Harder!” I cried as his purpose intensified.

The words shattered him in the way that I knew they would. I was obsessed with the way he looked at me. He cursed through his moans as he pulled me close to find his way to the finish. His body relaxed in my arms as he placed small, lovely kisses all over my skin. We held each other as our breathing began to calm.

It was the first night of our forever, and I didn’t want this to begin any other way. Kole laid down next to me and pulled me so close to him that there was no more room between us.

He pressed a kiss against my temple and interlocked his fingers with mine. I was starving but dinner would have to wait. I wanted to spend an eternity in his arms. My love, my king, my world.

When we managed to get out of the bed, Midselium as a destination was incredibly relaxing, the perfect spot for us to rest uninterrupted. Every room in this place would have to remember us because I honestly could not keep my hands off him. The bath, the beds, the dining room, and even the top of the pillars, just for the pure excitement of it. I’ve never had so much fun honestly.

In order to catch a break, Kole left me alone to enjoy this bath. Every time we tried to bathe together, it ended in us getting dirty again. I’ve never smiled so much in my entire life, and it was all I have been doing since I got here. But why did I feel guilty about it? Did I not deserve to finally be happy for once? I left a mess back at home and I think it was time for me to give myself a break, considering all we have been through.

"I didn't tell you to bathe alone so you could talk to yourself," Kole was leaning against the entrance.

"Sorry love, I was just..."

"In your head again," he interrupted. I nodded and stared at the water, knowing that there was no use in hiding the truth from him.

"Come eat. If we are going to keep this up, you're going to need energy," he winked.

"I'm not the one tapping out," I teased.

The dining room was laid out, as usual. Meat, bread, and plenty of wine and ale were placed all over the table, as it was every night. It never got old. We never had to cook or clean. This was literally the best life.

Kole was filling his plate and his cup before he caught me staring at him. It was one of the few instances where he caught me looking.

"Is there something on my face? You're staring kind of hard," he asked.

"No, just looking at your handsome face," I smiled.

"Is this going to turn into one of those compliment battles," he joked.

"What does that mean?"

“You know, I tell you you’re beautiful, then you say I’m handsome, then I say I don’t deserve you, then you say you were made for me, and so on and so forth.” I couldn’t help but laugh.

“Kole, I have zero intention on that ever being a thing. We both know that finding me was the best thing that has ever happened to you,” I shrugged.

“Yes, it was,” he raised his cup in celebration to us, and we toasted to the good life. Right as our cups came together, all the torches that were lit in the villa were extinguished with a strong wind gust, leaving us in complete darkness.

40 – Bitch Killed My Vibe - Kole

"What the hell was that?" I tried to hide how uneasy I was. No better way to ruin a honeymoon than being scared.

"I'm not sure, but nothing has happened here since the day we arrived, so this can't be a coincidence," Octavia said.

"Nothing is a coincidence," I recited Selene's words to myself.

The weather had remained the same the entire time we have been here, but all of a sudden the horizon took on more of a dark tone.

The energy felt disturbed, almost like an outside presence was infecting the natural order of things. Both of us got up from the table and ran out to the main hall, trying to figure out what caused all of this. The portal must have felt something, as well. When we arrived, the water was bright and calm. Now it moved with a dangerous caution, and it lost some of the colors it had previously.

"I don't understand what this means," Octavia's eyes were scanning the room all around us.

"Maybe the gods aren't too happy about all the action I've been getting in the villa," I joked.

"Seriously Kole, not the time at all," her face was tense, but she was fighting the urge to smile.

"I mean, that one time in the dining room is probably what did it," I continued the joke.

"Shut up!" She punched me in the arm.

The joking stopped when we heard something hit the ground so hard it almost shook the entire villa. It felt like it came from the Omega. Suddenly, the joke about the gods didn't seem so funny at all. Maybe we did go a little overboard.

"Come on, let's see what is going on," I grabbed Octavia and opened a portal that dropped us right outside of the omega. It was so dark now that I could barely make out my surroundings, but something was moving in that direction.

Whatever was moving, it was small in stature so it wasn't anything that would overpower us. But it was waiting for us to approach.

It looked like a little boy. His clothes were filthy and ripped to pieces, and his skin was dry and cracking. How the hell did he get in here? As far as we know, no one has been able to open that gate except for us. Octavia crept closer to the boy, maybe he got lost somehow. He didn't seem lost. He looked like he was smiling, laughing even. Nothing about this made sense.

"Octavia, slow down... something isn't right,"

"Kole, it's just a kid. We can't leave him here."

The boy had his back turned to us, his shoulders bouncing up and down muffling what sounded like a sadistic laugh. This was so creepy, something had to be wrong. I reached down for the darkness, willing the Odin sight to show me what my naked eye couldn't see. Something about all of this just felt wrong.

Everyone has a certain essence and the sight allowed me to see what someone's essence was made of. When I looked at Octavia, I could see the familiar Roman flame coursing through her, burning bright at the center. Even when I looked at Rollo streaks of lightning emanated off him.

The boy's essence was stifled all the way down to his feet, and shrouded at his center was the same mist from the arena. Fear snapped my vision back to normal.

"Octavia, get back now," she spun around responding to my panic. "It's Delphi, she's here, get back! I don't know how she got here, but she's here possessing that little boy."

"What the fuck?" she yelled in surprise.

I thought Midselium was supposed to be safe, but I should have guessed that didn't apply to ancient vengeful spirits. She could probably come and go as she pleases. Something that I never considered when I chose to come here.

The boy glanced over his shoulder, and I could see how distorted his face was. Delphi had done the worst to this boy. His eyes were offset, half of his nose was missing, and he was missing patches of his hair. It looked like it was ripped out.

The spirit made no attempt to hide her sinister laugh after realizing we discovered the truth.

"Very clever of you to figure it out, my boy. It took you long enough. I've been here for days watching you and your wife pretend like you have won," his voice still had the tone of a little boy, but there was something so dark behind it.

"Won what? All we want to do is live in peace. Is that so much to ask for after being your playthings for thousands of years?!" I yelled.

"And that deal to save the vampires? Was that for peace? Because what it felt like was a move to undermine me. You tried to make a fool out me!" the boy snarled.

"And my sister paid the price for it!" I could feel my anger quelling the power inside me, but I had no way to kill the spirit, she would just jump into another body.

"Nature has already set out to balance your little deal. I promise you it will not play out the way you intended but unfortunately that won't be enough for me," the boy skipped around the omega, the green mist leaking from his face and pulling it in the most unnatural position. Delphi's voice started to polarize from every direction.

"Some of the gods don't approve of the little stunt that Odin and Mars pulled. We Romans aren't very keen on working together, let alone with Norse. You two have been making enemies from the beginning."

"What choice did we have?" Octavia asked.

"There is always a choice, young one. You could have ignored the call and let things run their course. You could have stayed in your homeland, Kole, and lived happily ever after. You could have allowed the gods to continue to fight this war the way they see fit," she had to have some kind of endgame. Why else would she come here to do this instead of when we were still in Alexandria?

"So, I could have stayed locked in a box until I starved to death or those men decided to kill me?" Octavia asked.

"The world is cruel princess, is it not? And you Kole your father would still be alive had you ignored the call." The boy responded with an evil smile.

"Do you have a reason for being here Delphi or are you just going to talk us to death?" I was done with all the riddles.

"I'm here at the behest of some of the other gods. While my vendetta has been settled, I have no problem helping them thwart your pathetic plan for a new united world." This coming from this little boy was disturbing.

"What other gods?" Octavia asked.

"I know you two don't know much, but look at all the other symbols in this omega. Surely you realize there are plenty of other gods, and while their descendants might not be known to you, they do exist," Delphi stretched the boy's face once again.

"What the fuck do you want, Delphi? I didn't think it was possible, but you are turning my paradise into a nightmare. Yet again you exceed expectations."

"It's easy, my boy. Return home and undo what you have done. Return home to Najora and Octavia you return to Gracia, keeping the world separate. Do that and all will be forgotten," the boy stopped skipping and stood in front of us waiting for an answer, almost impatiently.

"Well, if that's all you want then that's easy, no!" Octavia said. There was no need for me to say anything, it was clear that my answer was the same.

“I had a feeling you would say that because without motivation why would you even consider it?” The boy paused for a moment.

“You’re right, I’m not motivated, just annoyed that you wasted your time coming here.” I felt the power thirsting to be set free. Delphi seemed completely unfazed by us, the boy started to laugh. It was a deep and evil laugh right before he raised his hands to the sky.

The clouds began to shift and barrel into each other, one behind the other. His laugh was unhinged, and you could hear the hoarseness in his voice as his throat began to give out. The dry cracked skin began to peel and rip apart as his smile stretched unnaturally across his face.

“Motivation is what you shall have, little king and queen. How about you spend some time in here to mull over your decision,” her tone was almost a command.

“Wait what?” The green mist shot out from the boy and straight to the villa faster than we could process. The boy’s body went completely limp, and we were left in silence. The sky returned to its normal state, but something was different. Like when she disappeared, she took something with her.

I opened a portal and brought us back to the entrance of the villa and all I could hear was the sinister laugh of the little boy replaying over and over in my head. Panic and dread slammed into me all at once as I looked into the portal that would allow us to leave, and it was nothing but a dried-up pit.

“Kole, what just happened?” Octavia’s voice trembled with fear. I did not want to say it because it would make it true, but there was nothing I could do to lighten this blow.

"Delphi destroyed the portal. We are stuck in Midselium."

What The Fuck Do We Do Now?

THE END